A Lunatic's Guide to Interplanetary Relationships

By R.L. Andrew

JaCol Publishing Inc.

Copyright 2017 by JaCol Publishing Inc.

FIRST PRINTING

August 2017

JaCol Publishing Inc.
2008 Hoquiam Ave NE
Renton, WA 98059
818-510-2898

ISBN: **978-1-946675-07-1**

E-book: 978-1-946675-05-7

JaCol Publishing

Table of Contents

Acknowledgements

I'd like to thank my husband--you're incredible and I love you beyond belief, my daughters and their partners, my special Trace–aka my awesome yet occasionally questionable best friend, gardener, crime channel narrator (by the way shut-your-face), my other kids, Leah and Nathaniel, my amazing in-laws, Mr & Mrs Alien Man, my friends/family: Deb, Jen, Su, Tash, Tami, Katie, my doctors, Writers World critique group in particular Eva and Ginette, Randall Andrews my editor, mentor, and publisher, along with all the other valuable critiques I received.

To the two artists Katie Ketchum, who did the painting, and Karen Brosinsky, who did all the lettering. To Maggie McGarvey, who did the format editing.

To all of you, words cannot express how much I value and appreciate your support. Without it I wouldn't be where I am right now. I am also thankful most of all for not being Annu or Shayne. And lastly thank you for the inspiration: Zecharia Sitchin, Erich Von Daniken, Gerald Clark and Michael Tellinger for their research regarding the Annunaki.

Chapter 1: Crazy Like a Falling Coconut
Ardrossan, Adelaide, South Australia, Australia, Earth

How did I, Shayne James, a Demi-Goddess and daughter of the Great God Ki, end up in a nut house? It's God damned ridiculous. Literally. I've got to get out of here. I can't do another night in this stupid place.

Shayne shook the gate; her fingers ached and rust embedded beneath her nails. "What kind of screwed up torture is this? Haven't I suffered enough?"

She surveyed the yard for Geoffrey from Ward 3, her one true fan, believer and stalker. Where he went, hospital staff followed. Yard all clear, Shayne counted on her fingers. "How many weeks have I spent in this shit hole?"

2 or 3? Fuck. I don't know.

The medication they'd thrust into her made time a slippery worm difficult to grasp. The morning's pills jiggled next to her phone in Shayne's pocket. She'd hide them with the others. The few missed days cleared her brain and the memories returned. The instant their effects wore off, Shayne realised the governmental nightmare with its hard beds, terrible food, and bad TV, interfered with her true destiny on another planet.

Shayne kicked the metal lock. Pain shot through her foot. "Shit. Crap."

She hopped in a circle and cursed dodgy hips connected to short legs. The bastards prevented her climb up the Wistingera hedge beside the gate without assistance, and she couldn't find anyone to hold her steady without grabbing her arse.

Can't get out the gate, can't break the fence, can't climb the hedge. I've tried all the doors. Which leaves what exactly?

Shayne breathed in crazy free air and ran through other options. "Oh fuck it. I can't think of any. What to do, what to do?"

Her shoulders drooped; Shayne's freedom remained as distant as Orion.

Even if I did escape, what then? How do I get home and back to Orion? Why can't a wormhole just appear right here? Huh?

Frustrated with her lack of control, Shayne grabbed the top fence rail and shook. Each rattle represented wasted minutes spent there and the time taken from her future with Annu. The striving for freedom pulsed through her; it interrupted her thoughts and shoved her out of bed each morning. All to face a day filled with half baked escape concepts and pleas to release her Godly self.

Shayne moved her anger down a rung. "That nobody fucking listens to."

Her arms ached; she relent her hold on the fence. Shayne shifted from the gate across to the hedge filling the fence and smushed into the middle of it. The faint scent of rosemary comforted her, a fresh wave of memories flooded Shayne's mind.

Shayne wriggled her middle finger, not a scar or mark indicated its former separation.

I can't believe I got a finger chopped off and it grew back, let alone all the other stuff.

Before being found on the pantry floor by her son and taken to the hospital, Annu held Shayne in his arms inside a stone room. Both Demi-Gods fresh from ascension, and filled with universal power. All they'd been through to get there seemed like a dream, and she'd fucked it up.

Shayne in the ultimate moment of stupidity mentioned Earth one too many times, and in a flash a wormhole ripped Shayne back to her home planet and away from love.

True fucking love and shit too.

Annu's shocked expression tormented her. "Damn you medication for making me forget it even for one second."

A branch stuck into her back, Shayne wriggled further onto the hospital's back lawn, a large pile of dried bird poop on her right fared better than her. "We did everything right and in return we weren't given time to soak in our success; the greatest moment of existence. Let alone kiss and enjoy things. No, not me. I got cosmically shafted. As usual."

Shayne yanked out a wad of grass and tossed it to the side. "I remember when, I remember, I remember when I lost my mind, there's something pleasant about that place, even your emotions had a gecko, and so much pace. Mmm. Does that make me crazyyyy? Does that make me–oh wait apparently it does."

Neighbourhood dogs howled; a flock of magpies a few metres ahead shot into the air.

Bastards don't appreciate a good voice. Oh what does it matter? My new life waits on the other side of the Galaxy, through the stupid wormhole–an hour and a half, several security guards, and several door alarms from here.

Shayne resigned herself to no Knight in shining armour arriving to rescue her from the current dilemma.

Rather, a retard in tin foil waited on this one planet, on the hospital lawn, deep in thought and determined. "It's not the first time I've saved myself. It's probably like the third. Surely I can do it again?"

I miss my chocolate hulk.

Shayne shook her head, Annu lingered in her mind. Her belly gurgled, doubt poked into her thoughts.

Is he still waiting for me? No, he probably gave up, and I can't blame him. He's probably relishing in glory–alone.

Shayne tried to twirl her jade ring, its absence on her naked finger shot another wave of panic through Shayne. She'd grown accustomed to the odd piece of jewellery despite its catalytic nature.

Where did it go? I must have lost it when I burst through the wall. It's got to be under the pantry shelf.

Shayne massaged a lump in her shoulder and sighed. "Another thing that doesn't matter because I'm not getting out right now, so fuck it and fuck them."

She scanned again for any sign of staff; all clear. Eyes squinted; she pulled out a smoke and lit it. Shayne inhaled to her lung's capacity, held the breath and fought coughing.

Hold it in, don't waste it. Any second now it will be worth it. You've got to cough to get off don't you?

The scratch in her lungs eased, a warm rush numbed her senses and removed life's edges. While it didn't remove the body pain, it made not caring about it easier.

Another toke and the sweet smoke filled her chest. The reason Shayne sat next to the gate drifted away with the breeze.

Three quarters of her mind mushed, the remaining quarter niggled at her.

Focus. Don't waste more time. Don't fall back into old habits. Oh yeah - escape plan, future leader, blah blah blah. Wait, focus on what? What else can I do? I've got no powers, no ring, no wormhole. A big fat nothing. Protesting gets me nowhere and all my other attempts are well–unrealistic.

Shayne blew smoke rings into the sky. "Where are you when I need you Ghost Dad? Huh?"

He hasn't answered to that name yet. Maybe I should call him Ki unless he tells me otherwise?

Eyes closed, mid puff–she attempted telepathy again.

'Ah Ki, can you help me, please? Or am I too far away for you to hear?'

A bird on the lawn squawked, no one else answered her. "Okay so that's a no then. Fine. Whatever."

Shayne pushed off the grass and levered up her legs to stand. She pulled the phone from her pocket and re-read Erin's last text message.

'I don't know if I'm coming for a visit tomorrow. It's hard for me to visit you in there, Mum.'

The words buried Shayne in guilt and mocked her efforts at becoming a better parent, let alone have kids proud of her. "Hah. Another epic fail dickhead."

Once they know the truth everything will change. I've got to make them believe me, show them somehow. Any ideas rolling around in my brain feel free to pop up.

Birds chirped, bees buzzed, and her mind remained empty.

None–really? Oh why is everything so fucking hard? All this thinking is stressing me the fuck out.

Shayne raised the smoke to her lips and killed all negative thoughts. Mid drag, the joint flew in one direction, the lighter in another. Her mouth dropped, Shayne's last piece of sanity disappeared. A flick on the arm drew her attention to reality and away from herbal oblivion.

Hand to her chest, Shayne faced the buzz-killer culprit.

Nurse Rye. Fuck, crap. Of all the people to catch me. Shit, shit, shit.

A thick plume of smoke exploded in the nurse's face, she coughed in response.

Shayne swished the smoke away. "Oh fu–u–er, flip. Nurse Rye–what a surprise. Damn woman, are you a ninja in your off time?"

Her bowel clenched, the nurse's presence scared the crap back up into her intestines. A number of excuses ran through Shayne's mind, all with better things to do than come out her mouth.

Geoffrey's head poked around Nurse Rye's middle and pointed at Shayne. "Found you, your highness. See, you can't escape me. Ha. I win."

Since arriving at the hospital Shayne followed a Forrest Gump's reasoning; if crazy is what crazy does, Geoffrey fell into the bat-shit category. "Geoffrey for the twentieth time it's goddess not highness. And I know–I can't escape a damned thing."

A deep growl erupted against Shayne's ear; she flinched. Geoffrey bolted from the nurse's side and out of sight.

The nurse's shadow blocked Shayne's sun. "Right this is the last time I deal with you. All you do is spout nonsense, smoke drugs and try to escape. If that wasn't bad enough, and worse still, you refuse to accept the help you desperately need. You make my job impossible. One way or another you will follow the rules."

The nurse's grip tightened; she glared at the lighter on the ground. Her crinkled face resembled a prune. "And, you have contraband. Where did you get it from?"

Quick, dick-head make something up.

"Off a visitor. I hid it in my sock."

I reiterate, dick head.

Nurse prune grunted, a vein pulsed in her forehead. "You're forbidden from the common room and confined to your bed aside from meal times. Now, I'm taking you straight to the doctor where I'll give her a full report. Move it."

Shayne shuffled at the nurse's side, the nurse's death grip prevented playing dead. Breasts considered unnatural wonders smushed against her cheeks, with the consistency of tennis balls in wet socks, they swung in hypnotic rhythm. Shayne stifled the urge to poke them to see if they acted like memory foam.

Headed toward the main building, the unlikely duo caught the immediate attention of both patients and medical staff. Crazy and sane eyes followed their path through the main doors and down the hall.

Great, an audience. Like I need another one of those.

Shayne mumbled into inflated flesh. "Couldn't you have taken me around the side way and maybe made less of a scene?" Her arm throbbed under the nurses grasp. "Ouch, when I've got my powers back you bitch, you're done for. This is totally unfair."

Heat burned the top of Shayne's head, the nurse's voice bored through her soul. "Oh, yes, that's right, your amazing magic powers. They haven't done you much good so far have they? And I bet they didn't remind you about your doctor's appointment this morning either?"

The small buzz from the half joint went stone-cold dead. Bam, a wet fish smacked Shayne in the face. "No and no. Crap."

Escape plan escalated to top priority, finding real chocolate can wait.

******

On a mission, Nurse Rye barged into the doctor's office. Doctor Unders poked her head above a sea of paperwork. Eyebrows thick enough to hide in covered the middle of her face.

Geez I wish you'd pluck those. Maybe she'll let me do it one day.

A pen fell from Doctor Unders mouth and landed with a plop on the table. "Nurse Rye, what the hell are you thinking? Remove your hands from this patient immediately."

The ground rumbled; Shayne suspected steam might erupt out the nurse's ears.

"If I let her go, she'll run off again. I caught her out the back alone and smoking drugs–again. She somehow manages to evade the staff and sneak off. How I do not know. And there's no doubt she's probably plotting another futile escape as we speak. I have a great deal of work already to do, and not enough people to spend time chasing around after her. She should be medicated adequately so she can't get out of bed and cause trouble."

Shayne imagined kicking the nurse's shin.

If it didn't get me put in solitary I'd relocate your nose for you.

To her credit, the Doctor didn't appear intimidated. "You'll leave the patient's diagnosis to me, thanks. Perhaps if you supervised your staff better, this wouldn't happen. How about you go investigate how Mr. Berris is able to swap his lithium for Viagra any time he likes and leave me to my job."

Saggy old balls dangled for a moment in Shayne's mind, a cold chill followed.

Nurse Rye released her grip on Shayne's arm and slapped her own thigh. "Fine. I expect you'll put her on report."

Shayne remained wedged between the nurse and the door frame without care. Even if she could move, she'd stay put and witness this show down. "Ding dong, the wicked witch is dead."

"Stop telling me what to do. If you don't leave my office now, you'll have staples to remove from your forehead in thirty seconds." The doctor grabbed the stapler. "Twenty."

The tension in the room intensified, Nurse Angry prune transformed into the Furious Tomato.

Despite the nurse's fury, Doctor Unders didn't waver. "Ten."

With a huff, Nurse Rye wedged backwards out of the room.

Once she'd reached a safe distance away, Shayne pushed off the doorframe, past shelves filled with physiology text books, towards the one un-cracked plastic chair. She sat adjacent to a deconstructed torso, and hung pictures drawn by patients.

The childlike art broke up nausea inducing yellow, but nothing hid the aged furniture and pea green stained carpet. Shayne recited by memory the names of each text book on each shelf and artist on the wall.

Dr. Unders used her motherly voice. "Shayne, you forgot your appointment and got caught smoking, again. What are we going to do about this?"

Several of Geoffrey's pieces took up the middle section. None of hers, she hated art. It ate into her TV watching time.

Maybe I could try being invisible. Eyes closed and focus.

"Shayne? Are you with me?"

Shit. She can still see me. Suck it up. "No, I'm not with you at all. I want to go home."

Doctor Unders' sigh ricocheted off the desk. "I get it, we all do. But the fact remains; you are still heavily influenced by your delusions. They haven't altered in strength one iota since your arrival."

"Well duh. Because it happened, it's all true and I'm not nuts. Simple."

"Do you understand we need actual evidence other than your say so about you being royalty and all? And there's your physical issues, which further complicate things. However, I'm sure we're close to discovering why you have such high levels of DMT in your blood. That's one thing at least."

Why don't people listen to me?

"For the hundredth time, I'm a goddess not royalty. Different kettle of fish."

Get it right, you morons.

Shayne picked at a strand on her pants. "Huh? DM what?"

"Aha. DMT is a chemical found in people immediately prior to the moment of death. You have a consistent high level in your blood, which I believe may be linked to this delusional behaviour."

Shayne tapped her head. It echoed. "You won't find anything wrong with my brain. What about the –"

Doctor Unders cut Shayne off with a raised hand. "Before you say it, we can't find any biological evidence of you being immortal or having magic powers, nor of your finger being chopped off and, ah, grown back."

Stupid narrow-minded people surrounded her. "For the tenth time, you aren't using the right equipment."

"Shayne, it's time you faced facts. This other planet–Orion–with all these people and fantastical events are a creation of your mind. None of it happened. It's illogical. Do yourself a favour and let it go. Concede you need help. In time, if you respond to treatment, you will be able to go home."

The strand came loose, Shayne selected another. "No, I won't change my mind. I can't, every part of it is real. The good, the bad, the ugly. Somehow, someway, I'll prove it to you."

A curl broke free from back of the doctor's head, it sprung into her face. "Are you still taking your medication?"

"Yes."

I'm still taking vitamins.

The Doctor raised an eyebrow. "If you don't take the meds, they don't work. Shayne, I've always had a lot of time for you. Yet, it's a struggle to balance this duality within you. I know there is a healthy person in there. They're just buried under a mountain of tragic events and bad judgment. When you're not talking about Orion, and the kitchen hasn't run out of anything chocolate flavoured, you appear mentally sound. With all this in mind, at this point in time in good medical consciousness, I can't release you."

Shayne's stomach climbed her abdomen, up her throat, and dropped onto the floor. She refused to cry, instead stabbing a pencil at the desk.

Can't someone cut me some slack?

"First of all, the chocolate flavoured shit's the only thing substituting for lack of actual chocolate because you consider the wrappers a choking hazard. Second, for fuck's sake. I AM NOT nuts. Yes, long ago I spent some time in a psych ward for a few weeks. This is different."

Doctor Unders' tone softened. "I didn't say nuts but you had nightmares, migraines, and hallucinations then too. Except for a much more elaborate delusion, how is this time unlike the other? This man Annu you've created, coincidentally, turned into the love of your life and a perfect match. And, his mother, Irica, is the mother you've longed for."

Shayne shoved Irica out of her mind, and shuddered. "Don't talk about Irica again."

"Alright, I'm sorry. I forgot."

She'd not let defeat claim her; Shayne grabbed inner strength. "Look it's not the same at all okay. Well, actually it's kind of a bit the same, but not. Back then, I saw and heard some strange things which didn't make sense. Myself, boosted by a few others, thought I'd lost it. Until I travelled to Orion recently, I realised those so called hallucinations were visions of my future, and I wasn't crazy at all. I did get pulled into a wormhole in my pantry and onto Orion. Me and Annu defeated an ancient God, Sham-man, I mean Shamesh, and a few others along the way. It wasn't easy. Plus I got kidnapped, froze people, got hurt and all sorts of shit–yet ended up back home, where again, no one believes me. And trust me, if I made up a dream world, do you really think there would be so much death and destruction in it? I'd design it so I walked in, got my powers, and life turned into butterflies and fucking rainbows. Not ended with me here powerless in a mental hospital with a chronic illness."

Shayne stuck her finger in the hole she'd created in her pants. "Which is caused from me being from Orion not Earth. My DNA isn't meant for here."

Doctor Unders glasses dropped on the desk beside the pen. "I thought you accepted you're sick from the autoimmune disease Psoriatic Arthritis. Shayne, your fantastical evidence can't be validated. Like the magical ring, which you don't have, wormholes no one else sees, and life on another planet. Which you claim to be a Demi-God of, and none of it can be proven. And yet it won't sink in that head of yours. Shayne, what about the effect this has on your kids? If it were true, wouldn't they believe you? Wouldn't someone have seen something?"

Bam, smacked on the other side of the face with another wet fish. "Leave Erin and Ryan out of it. They don't understand yet, but they will. As soon as I get out of here. I just need to get back home."

"Well I've got to tell you, it's going to be a while and you aren't getting out of this session. I've got 20 minutes left Shayne. Can we talk about your ex husband?"

Where were all these fish coming from?

"No. At least that son of a bitch is dead."

The doctor probed her face. "Each of these wrinkles is your fault." Another curl on the opposite side broke free; together the curls formed white horns around the doctor's face. "Fine. Let's start from when you moved into the other house."

Do I spend twenty minutes fighting the session, or play nice and use to the time to figure a way out of this crap hole?

"Shayne?"

Shayne spotted the Doc's handbag next to the desk, no easily accessible keys stuck out the top.

Damn, I better think of another idea.

Chapter 2: Welcome to the House of Strange
3 Bailor Street, Rendelshem, South Australia, Australia

Stuck in a metaphorical sardine tin with a hole in the bottom, Shayne sank into an ocean of crap. With no life jacket in sight, and no one to blame for the mess but herself. No longer surrounded by water, Shayne now lived by girt and shit. "I'm such a dumb arse."

The concrete step bit into the back of her legs, she scooted her butt forward. Sam's tail lights faded down the road, his absence hit her with a thud.

I'm all alone in this house from hell.

"Why didn't I beg Rosie and the kids to stay longer?"

Oh yeah, the kid part.

Shayne scanned the front yard for Bear, her half-blue heeler half-coffee table dog. "Bear, here boy. Bear."

Only the buzz of crickets answered. "Wait until you find out there's no beach buddy, then you'll be back."

For the last half hour, Shayne didn't look at the front of the house. Doing so allowed her to pretend the unit remained. Yet, fantasies don't change facts–she'd lost her home; failure and loss were cornerstones of her existence.

A sore rear-end begged for a new position. Shayne got one free sit on something hard each day; the rest cost her. One hand each side of the step, she levered herself to a hunch.

She shuffled her right foot 180 degrees, the left foot followed. Right. Shuffle. Left. Shuffle. Her new home in its glory punched her in the face.

Don't cry, keep it together. It's not so bad.

Pot plants placed on either side of the front door, a garden overhaul, and a fresh coat of paint might brighten the front façade. If someone donated a shitload of money for any of those. Shayne's tears puddled on the chest of her KISS T-shirt.

With despair on her back, desperation followed Shayne into the entry. Determined not to let both overwhelm her, Shayne's favourite comfort food flashed into her brain. Situations this dire always called for chocolate, the taste pushed her down the hall towards the kitchen.

Shayne stopped dead. "Crap. Fuck."

To obtain it meant entering the kitchen. Last she'd looked in there, NATO cordoned it off. "Do I pick misery or mess?"

Ha, like it's a competition.

Shayne's stomp/slip down the hallway bellowed across the wooden floor. She slid the last part to the kitchen, and froze in the doorway. Another room in the house needing renovation, or better, demolition. No point in a fire, she couldn't claim insurance for two years.

Love it or hate, it's where she lived. "Hate, hate, fucking hate."

The puddle on Shayne's chest grew, sobs racked her body. Pain scored her ribs; she clutched her stomach and tumbled to the floor. Pain and regret mixed with failure poured out. The tears eased the burden on her soul.

I need chocolate, but I don't want to move. Why can't it come to me?

Despite the linoleum floor being not clean enough to crawl across, Shayne did it with salvation in her sights. "Argh. I fucking hate my life."

She yanked the door open from the bottom and used it for support to climb up. A lone block of chocolate sparkled on the top shelf. "God bless you, Rosie."

Shayne reefed it towards her; the first row didn't touch the sides. Half a block down, gooey satisfaction melted in her tummy.

"Oh God, please don't take chocolate off me too. I couldn't bare it."

She tapped the wooden bench beside her, Shayne didn't tempt fate. If God existed, he and his bastard sense of humour hated her.

To her left, stacks of old newspapers covered the bench top, before her unopened boxes filled a third of the room. The size of the kitchen swallowed her four-person round dining table and left enough room to swing a couple of cats–if she didn't despise them.

On the opposite side to the cooking centre, stood a walk-in pantry. A room perfect for things like appliances and tinned food Bear didn't eat. "May as well check you out while I'm in here."

Shayne took short steps towards it, twice the distance, half the pain. Goosebumps covered her arms. "Huh? It's not cold in here."

The closer she got, the larger the bumps. At the doorway, Shayne shook off a cold chill.

An old wooden gate acted as a door, and a rusty latch and bolt as a handle. From the outside the pantry looked like an innocuous closed room. No apparent reason to get the creeps.

Shayne jiggled the bolt, and slid to the right, it stuck. "Shit."

A kick to the lock hurt her toe, not the door. "Mother Fu-."

Executive decision made–Appliances stayed in their respective boxes for now.

That left Shayne with unpacking stuff, trying the door again and more chocolate.

She slid across the floor back to the other side; her cackle erupted through the kitchen. The fridge door clunked and creaked open. "Oh no you don't. You hang in there. I can't afford another one."

With her back to the bench, the stack of papers on Shayne's right caught her attention. She dragged the pile along to her, the yellowed paper crinkled in her fingers. The dates started at 1955 until 1966. Each pile covered a decade with the headline:

'Local woman or man missing. Is it a curse on Bailor Street?'

"Oh fucking great." Another reason to hate this place. Shayne pushed them back against the wall, and tapped her fingers on the bench.

Afternoon sun beamed through the kitchen windows, she glanced at the clock.

Too early for bed, what the hell else can I do? Or should I say want to do.

With a combined shuffle and slide, Shayne returned to the pantry. Two handed she tried the lock again, 1, 2, 3, pull. The bolt freed. "Whoohoo."

Jiggle, jiggle, the door creaked open. Shayne pinched her nose closed against a dank dirt smell.

She patted hands along the wall, and fumbled for the light switch. "What the—? Oh duh." Two inches from her face hung a white cord. A quick tug illuminated the room; a set of wooden shelves the approximate age of the first newspaper stack ran down either side.

Shayne stepped into the room, someone walked over her grave. She smacked herself in the forehead.

"Of yeah, I watched The Boogeyman movie before sleep last night."

Hadn't he killed someone in a dark pantry?

With a box as a door stop, Shayne pushed the toaster, blender, and half a dozen shopping network best sellers onto the top shelf and lamented her late night decisions. How many times could you give those things as Christmas presents only to get them back the next year? Four.

Satisfied she'd accomplished one thing that day, aside from consumption of saturated fat, Shayne closed the door without latching it. "Mmm. Fat."

A step away from the doorway, something thudded in the pantry. "Fuck, they didn't stay on the shelf long. Please don't be broken."

One-handed Shayne tugged the door, it didn't move. "How is it even fucking possible?"

A punch in the middle of it hurt her hand and raised her blood pressure.

Arsehole thing. Think.

Shayne's cocoa levels dropped dangerously low, she headed to the fridge for the last bar in the block.

Shit, how am I going to get through the rest of the week?

Shayne grabbed her phone, smeared chocolate across the screen, and tapped out a message. 'Sam: can you come ver tomorrow and fx pantry dor? and bring chocolate and some inspiration?'

There's no need for me to worry. Sam fixes anything.

With no desire to do much else, Shayne texted and shuffled out the door towards the bedroom.

Thud. Thud. Thud.

"Grr." Hands raised to the ceiling, she bellowed. "God, why do you despise me, oh mighty smiter? Seriously?"

Bang. Thud. Crash.

Shayne revised the text to Sam: 'Can you bring another Toaster and two blocks of chocolate? Double strength. Stat. Dire emergency.'

Her shuffle slowed, the bedroom door loomed further away the closer she got. Her joints stiffened, her muscles ached, she'd give her last piece of chocolate for the ability to walk right again. "Don't be stupid, no I wouldn't."

*****

Shayne flopped onto the pillow. "Sleep deprivation sucks." Between restlessness, and falling asleep only for the floor to vibrate and wake her, she gave up. For the last two hours the pantry thudded, banged and drove her to desperation.

She pelted the pillow across the room. "Fuuuuuck."

In the early hours of morning, a truck snuck into the bedroom, backed over her a number of times, and disappeared.

Shayne feared death from mixing insomnia, stupid dreams, and stress. It clouded her mind, and she'd pick worms out of jelly easier than thoughts from her brain.

On her side, Shayne pulled her sweat soaked pajamas off.

Too wet to stay in bed, but I can't be fucked doing anything.

She considered her other option: a big fat joint followed by a couple of pain killers. "Mmm. Oh yeah. The breakfast of champions."

The thought got her upright; she stopped halfway and checked the contents of her tin on the bedside table. "Fuck it, empty. And I forgot to go to the chemist. There goes that idea."

Shayne threw the tin against the wall. It hit with a clunk and landed on the pillow. "Dick-head."

No need for other enemies, I manage to fuck myself up well enough on my own.

A glance at the time on her phone solidified Shayne's bad mood; another day to kill with no unpaid cable TV, and no wifi for her tablet. Sensible people used spare hours to unpack boxes, and turned shit holes into homes. They'd no longer kick the boxes each time they walked past and cursed.

Oh to be a sensible person, but that ship sailed long ago.

Shayne swung her legs off the bed, and stood, trying not to hurt herself.

Crack. Pain tore through her shin. "Ouch, fuck it. What idiot put a pile of books right there?" A bruise formed next to the day before's batch. "Oh yeah, this one."

She limped/shuffled to the toilet, a long and painful journey most took for granted. "Well, people don't think about not hurting themselves walking to the toilet, and to the kitchen to make a cup of tea. Lucky arseholes."

Shayne's slippers dragged across the carpet, her sole hit wood. "Don't fall apart yet."

The kitchen door opened inwards, her shoulders drooped. No sight of the cleaning fairies Shayne wished fixed the kitchen overnight; dismissed them as an explanation for the night's mayhem.

What the hell's making the stupid noises and keeping me awake then? With one hour sans life supporting substances and time to kill, Shayne headed to the pantry and re-tried the door.

Yank, yank, jiggle, jiggle; no movement.

Bastard thing.

"Fuck you then."

Shayne gave it the middle finger and returned to the fridge in hope of a chocolate miracle.

Aside from a puddle of green goop on the bottom shelf, it contained nothing. "Another fuck you."

Shayne tossed her phone on the bench beside her and banged the fridge door open and closed. "What the fuck do I do now?"

The phone buzzed. Shayne grasped at it before the device hit the floor. Smart phones lost their smarts after they'd collided with hard surfaces.

Which box are my damned glasses in? I should have unpacked them first.

She squinted to clear the words:

'Open up. At your front door with chocolate and inspiration.'

Tingles ran up her spine. "Oh Sam. You're awesome."

Chocolate, you're better than sex.

Shayne's taste buds tingled; she'd missed his knocks and the vehicle's diesel engine.

The front door shuffle took half the time as the toilet trip. Shayne fell into Sam's arms, and inhaled the scent of man. Two blocks of brown heaven and a bag of green on top appeared under her nose.

Sam's middle squished between her arms, Shayne patted his back. "Bless you Sam, thank God you're here. Can you please try to open the pantry and look around in there? The door's stuck and for some reason the room creeps me out. Oh, and all night banging noises came from the kitchen. I have a terrible feeling everything I put in there is on the floor broken."

Sam moved his bulk over the threshold. "So did you want me here for a weed and chocolate delivery or as a handyman? Every time you ask me to do something it's the worst case scenario with you woman."

"No it's not. It's not my fault this shit happens and the pantry's got weird vibes."

He shook the latch and slid the bolt. "How can a pantry give you the creeps? It's where you keep food. Food's amazing."

Shayne held onto his jacket. "I don't know, but when I go near it, it weird's me out. Plus I partly closed the door last night but didn't lock it, and now the fucking thing won't open."

Head tipped in her direction, the kitchen light beamed off Sam's naked skull. "That's hardly a reason not to like the pantry."

Sam scooped Shayne up, and cradled her to the kitchen. Once inside the room, he placed her on a kitchen chair. "You stay here out of the way."

She pealed the wrapper off a block, it crinkled, and all became right in the world.

Before Shayne licked chocolate from her fingers, he'd returned to the pantry and leaned the door against the wall. "Damn. You're so quick."

Sam poked his head inside the room, and flicked the light on. "Don't tell my next girlfriend that okay? He backed out and into the kitchen. "Here you go."

"Awesome, thank you. Can you get the toaster out for me please? I'll make us chocolate on toast for breakfast if you want?"

"Couldn't you have asked me a minute ago?"

Shayne plastered on a smile and gritted her teeth. "Ah sorry. I didn't think of it then."

"Yeah all right. Sounds good." Sam disappeared into the pantry, his voice boomed into the kitchen. "Bad news. There's no toaster in here, but your blender and half a dozen tins are on the floor."

Shayne bolted upright and hit her knee on the table, pain shot through her leg. "Ouch. What? Are you kidding me? I put the toaster in there before the door jammed. No one else has been here but me."

She regretted the stomp instead of slide to Sam's side. "Ow, ow, ow, ow."

Sam positioned closer to her and offered her the crook of his arm. "Here, lean on me and have a look for yourself."

A thorough search of a room void of a toaster tested her patience. Not the floor, nor shelf. Dust from her stomping feet flew into her mouth. "What the fuck? Where did it go? Now I can't have toast and I can't afford another toaster. Fuck. Why does the universe hate me?"

Sam's frame shrunk the doorway. "Can you take your elbow out of my rib?"

Shayne eased off him, and rested on the wall. "Oh sorry."

"You probably didn't unpack it."

Shayne jabbed a finger at the shelves. "Yes I did. It's not like I thought I unpacked it but didn't. I had it in my hands and pushed it onto the top shelf right next to the blender, right before I shut the door."

"Well it's not here now."

"Oh, this is bullshit. My life is such a joke. Nothing ever goes right."

"I know things seem shit right now, but they will get better. Shayne, at least you have somewhere to live. One of your relatives died for you to get a house, instead of you sleeping on my couch. And, you've got friends like me who left early to get you chocolate for breakfast."

Hello guilt. Who needs a heater–not me.

"Yes I know. I am thankful." Her left hip nibbled its sharp teeth on bone. Shayne shifted her weight to the other side. "How long until you can put a new door on?"

Sam's chest heaved beside her ear. "A day or two. Is there anything else you want to say to me while I'm here?"

Huh?

"Didn't I thank you for the chocolate and inspiration? Oh, and the door."

"No you didn't. Anything else?"

Shayne searched Sam for something important she'd missed; she found crow's feet, a grey ring of stubby hair, and a pimple. No hint of his expectations to calm her elevated anxiety.

Shit, wing it. Flap, flap.

"Of course, I'm saving it until later. Thank you for everything. You're a life saver."

Sam's shoulders lifted, a broad smile filled his face.

Anymore winging it and I'd make a great bird.

He wrapped an arm around her shoulder. "I knew you hadn't forgotten. Well, I'm off; I've got a job to finish before lunch. I'll talk to you later on."

Panic bubbled, Shayne grabbed his arm. "Really? Can't you stay a bit longer? Can you check why the house is noisy and the floor vibrates first?"

The smile and shoulders reversed. "It's probably just you getting used to a different place and the house shifting. It's old, they do those things. When you moved into the unit, you convinced me possums were in the roof. Then you decided someone hid up there waiting for the right moment to kill you. It gave you nightmares and me a massive headache. It ended up being what, oh, yeah, a branch scraping on the window."

Shayne's thermostat blew. "There was something in the roof, you just didn't find it. Don't dismiss my ideas so easily, there's always news stories about weirdos who sneak onto people's roofs, only to butcher them while they sleep. The newspapers on the bench over there are full of reports of missing people who lived in this house. There's something going on, and it's not my imagination. Can you please check and make sure? When I'm dead you'll feel so bad."

"No I don't have time. Stop watching so much drama, crime shows, and horror movies and lighten up."

"Fuck you. None of it explains why the floor vibrated most of the damned night and the missing toaster. You can't deny the reports in the newspaper. Take a look yourself if you don't believe me."

Sam turned the other way, glanced at the papers and sighed. "A dream perhaps? You said yourself you've had weird ones since you moved in, which as I said, I put down to crap TV. As to the newspapers, people go missing all the time. The person who lived here before you, your uncle, he didn't go missing, yet collected newspapers about others who did. Or, maybe he killed them all and is still in the roof space, waiting."

Shayne smacked him across the arm, her hand reverberated off muscle. "You're a shit face and a smart arse. I still love you though."

She reached on her tiptoes and checked the back the top shelf herself, disappointment pushed her down.

Sam's head rested on Shayne's, the mystery perplexed her. "It wasn't a dream."

Maybe.

"How do you explain missing appliances?"

"You know, it's only missing if you actually put it in there to start with."

Shayne needed less sarcastic friends. "Oh, my God. I put it in there. Thanks so much for coming and giving me the shits."

Sam wriggled eyebrows formed a long a black caterpillar. "Yes, well I'm sure you will make the insults up to me tomorrow, right?"

Shit, think. He's not getting married? No. New girlfriend? Crap.

"Yeah I'm sure I will."

"I've no doubt Rosie is in on it too."

Mental note: call Rosie as soon as Sam leaves.

"Of course."

She closed the door behind Sam, retrieved her tin from the bedroom floor, and rolled a big fat joint. "Later."

Chapter 3: Boredom, Booze & Boobs
Yebu Township, Enki, Orion
1300 Light years from Earth

Flying orbs overhead reminded Annu of swarming buzzard flies. Annu averted his attention and relished his place at ground level.

With his horse Jonny tethered a long walk short of his desired stop point, Annu slung his bag over a shoulder and power walked the rest of the way. No matter how he adjusted it, the sack clunked into his ribs with each step forward.

This close to town, Annu's anxiety levels rose and the wind pummelled him from each direction. Throngs of people spilt through the stone gates into the streets, their focus elsewhere. His personal space shrank.

Take a deep breath, I'm not like them. I'll do what I need to and get the flark out of here.

Light caught the gold locket around Annu's neck and seared a reminder of Jaid into his corneas. He fought against glare and widened his eyes. If he closed them, visions of Jaid with her swollen belly, followed by the moments before she died, tortured him. The memories ripped away the scab barely healed on his heart.

It's been so long. Hundreds of years–do I grieve forever? Will it always be so hard? Probably because no one compares to you.

Annu rearranged his shirt over the locket and inhaled fresh air.

Push it aside; think about something else in the here and now.

The night before's argument with Irica replaced Jaid. The answers about Annu's past moved further away, her weeping destroyed his focus at the time.

All she'd said replayed in his mind.

'I can't tell you right now. Please trust me a little longer.'

"Why should I? Don't I have the right to know the truth now?"

Annu's wrist vibrated, despite a hand flicked at the irritation, it continued to annoy him. An examination of his arm revealed no bug, only the communicator sparked to life.

He tapped at the device; his fingers spread across the screen. "Flarking work you stupid piece of junk."

Annu swiped over the accept call icon, Irica appeared, the morning light emphasised her strong features. "You only have to tap it lightly, not pound it with your huge bear-sized fingers."

Five ships belted past overhead, exasperation niggled at him. "Good morning Irica."

Irica's puffy eyes showed lack of sleep. "Good morning."

At least I'm not the only one.

Frustration tempted him to throw the communicator, Annu shoved destructive actions aside. "Damn it. Is that all you've got to say to me?"

"No. Are you wearing your band? Are you staying out of trouble? I've got a bad feeling."

Annu fiddled with the piece of gold on his wrist, he often forgot it existed. "You're talking about the one my mother gave me, for reasons you refuse to explain."

"Annu, we've been over this."

"Why Irica? Why can't you at least tell me who they were, why I'm older than everyone else on Orion? Haven't I waited long enough?"

"I, I don't. I'm sorry, I can't. Please let it go for a few more days. Believe me, if you push things, it will only bring you trouble and danger."

Keep calm, there's a life sentence for murder, and she's all I've got.

"Fine, what choice do I have?"

Irica squinted and surveyed the area behind him. "Why do you still insist on riding your stubborn horse around? All you have to do is replace the crystal in your PFD, and you'd have been to town and home already."

"So we're changing the subject are we?"

"Yes."

His frustration rose, Annu held a deep breath. "I hate those things, I'd rather be kicked in the head. Man isn't meant to fly. It's not natural. And why the hell do they abbreviate the name? It's not like it's hard to call it a Personal Flying Device."

"Oh for goodness sake." They sighed in unison, neither relented. "You're the most stubborn son I've ever raised, you never heed my warnings."

"Aren't I the only son you've raised?"

Irica's smile drooped; she opened her mouth to speak and paused.

Hairs prickled at the base of Annu's neck. "Seriously, what the flark's going on? Why did you pause?"

"It doesn't matter right now. Trust my feeling."

His thermostat soared. "The problem with your bad feelings, Irica, is they allegedly come from the Gods and I'm yet to see proof they exist."

"Of course they exist, you of all people should…."

To rely on faith in make believe Gods made as much sense to Annu as licking toe jam. "No thanks, you keep your beliefs and lies, for now. There's no fate, no destiny, no crap. Only me doing what I do, alone."

Irica aged a decade each minute they talked. "One day son, you'll discover there's more important things than you, and there's someone else out there for you who'll love you more than you imagined. Your life is only beginning."

His head thudded, Annu rubbed the base of his skull. "Yeah right. Listen Irica, it's hot, what's the point to your call?"

Contrition flashed across Irica's face, her tone smoothed. "Well, I do want some things from town and I knew you'd go." Her eyes widened and dipped to Annu's feet. "That's your gem bag, which means you're going to the black market. Now the bad feeling makes sense. Good Gods, how many times have you narrowly avoided capture? I swear it's like the words forbidden and illegal flip a switch in your brain. You can't help yourself."

The bottle of rum in the saddle bag called to him.

Drink me, I'll shut her up and make you feel good.

"I'll do what I please. Besides one of the sites I go to might hold the key to my past."

"Annu, this isn't the way. You must trust me, I beg of you. Town's full of Peace Officers looking to arrest someone. Didn't you hear that Grand Counsellor Sh - ah Griffin has denied disaster aid to Enlil and cut funding to medical centres? Protestors were shot and killed on their way to Yebu under his direction and in a separate report around half a dozen men similar looking to you are missing."

The thud against his brain increased, Annu regretted saving the communicator from the kitchen bin earlier. "No. I avoid the news, it's biased. I haven't been caught yet, and I am not aiming to. Unless you open up, stay out of my business."

"Umph. What's the point of me saying anything? You won't listen to me, you never do."

A groan erupted deep within his belly, matricidal urges close behind. "Finally, something we agree on."

"Will you look at me while I'm talking to you?"

Annu shook his hand and swayed side to side, Irica's features wobbled. "Oh no. I'm–I'm losing you–gggggoooo–."

He shoved the communicator into his pocket, the headache eased. "God damned woman, she's the lock and key to my problems."

Irica's voice bellowed through his pants. "I'm still here idiot, you didn't end the call."

Brain pain returned at full charge, Annu jabbed at his leg. "Flarking hell."

******

Holographic billboards projected from tight knit buildings and assaulted his eyes. Annu turned off the main street into the industrial area. The glare faded. He ducked across loading zones and lay lines avoiding cargo ships.

Down a side street, two peace officers turned a corner ahead of him. Annu's heart leapt into his throat. He slipped into a fish shop, clasped his nose against the stench and took the back door into a laneway.

A left, two rights, and another left; market stalls appeared down each side of the street. Two thirds the way down, he entered the only antique cell phone shop in Orion.

The old man slouched across the counter, his eyes glazed. He delved into a tobacco pouch and pulled out a rolled smoke.

Annu waved and paused adjacent to the counter. "Afternoon Macci. How's business?"

A lighter flicked, Macci inhaled, the smell of tobacco filled the shop. "Shit thanks smart arse."

"Good to hear. What's new?"

Macci flicked ash onto the floor. "There's been a shit tonne of PO's around town of late taking random DNA tests. Apparently it's some old by-law which allows them to do it. Like I've said for years, that damned Griffin and his Council are behind some weird, sneaky, evil stuff. They'll have something to do with it for sure."

Goosebumps scattered across his arms, a shiver ran up Annu's spine. "Oh, not you too. For Flark's sake. Why would Griffin and the Council want DNA tests?"

"Hell if I know, but whatever it is won't be good. Don't shoot the messenger."

"Yeah well I don't plan of being anywhere near either him or the council anyway. If only I could live my life in peace."

"It doesn't pay to be ignorant about what's going on around you. Look, my advice to everyone who walks through my doors is be careful. If you've got any ah - unchartered digs coming up, I'd cancel them."

Annu's guts churned and his butt hole constricted. "Thanks for the warning. Which reminds me; did the genealogy search finally come back? It's taken what–months?"

Macci cocked an eyebrow. "If you answered your communicator more often you might have heard something about it."

"Oh, so you heard something?"

Ash dropped onto the counter, Macci used a hand to wipe it off. "No, but that's not the point. Let me tell you, it's the darnedest thing. I've never had a report take so long and come against such problems accessing information."

Annu's shoulders dropped, his heart sank.

I convinced myself you'd have answers.

"Damn, can you try again?"

"Sure thing, it's your money. Hey maybe you're the Grand Counsellor's long lost son and they're looking for you?"

Annu crossed his arms. "You're hilarious old man."

Macci coughed between cackles. "You heading out back?"

"Yep."

"Head on down, I'll let you through."

Annu strolled to the rear of the shop and waited in front of a dust covered shelves. With a crack, the shelf shuddered across and revealed the bustle of clandestine markets. Annu walked a memorised path.

Perched in his usual corner position on a stool his girth asked too much of, Tayl wiped his hands on worn pants. "I expected you two days ago."

Tayl pointed to Annu's gem bag.

Annu dumped the sack on a glass counter. "Yeah, well, shit happens. I'll leave this with you and be back for my coins later. Have you seen Kan?"

Tayl remained seated and dripped sweat onto the counter top. "No, he should have been here for his shift two hours ago."

Little shit.

"Damn, well if you see him, tell the flarker I'm looking for him."

Annu ignored the man's mumbled reply, pushed off the counter and headed in the opposite direction. He aimed for the closet rum stall and scanned the faces of people exiting a shop a few feet ahead.

In the middle of a group, recognition surged his anger. Annu bellowed over the crowd's noise. "Kan, you little shit. I've been looking for you."

Kan in his sights, Annu weaved through the crowd. "Wait right there kid. Do not move."

The boy froze; his skinny limbs parodied a grasshopper's. The girl holding his hand released it and stepped to the left.

A smile hardened a pitted face. Kan slicked a hand through his hair. "Oh, An, hi. Hey, ah, how did the gold site work out?"

A step closer, Annu jabbed a finger in the kid's face. "It's Annu to you, kid. You flarking heard how the site went, and I spent an hour in emergency getting lasered up. Unless you give me back my coins right now, I'll use you to drill post holes."

Kan's eyes darted side to side; Annu envisaged the kid ran through his short list of escape options.

Trembling, Kan licked his lips and checked the contents of his pockets. "Geez, calm down. You're not normally so angry."

"That's what a few hours of hell and getting messed around does to me."

Kan scratched his chin. "Look, I don't have your coins on me, but I have an old map. The guy who sold it to me said it's some secret place and full of jade. Which is the gem you really like right?"

A piece of yellowed paper shook in Kan's hands, interest replaced Annu's desire to kill.

When Annu focused on the paper, the noise around them drifted away, and he dismissed tearing the boy to pieces. "You have my attention."

An inch forward at a time, Kan handed Annu the paper. A single touch sent shivers up his spine, the hairs on the back of his neck rose. Unfurled, it revealed a map of Orion.

The continents appeared different to Annu's recollection. "Have you shown this to anyone else?"

"No, not yet. I kept it in case I saw you."

Dust wiped from the map onto his shirt sharpened its details. "Sure you did."

When he traced a finger over Yebu, Annu's gold band pulsated. If he removed his finger from the map it stopped. The same thing happened each time he touched the paper. Kan appeared oblivious to the map's effects on him.

Holy shit, it's too much of a coincidence. It must be associated with my parents, and my past. Finally, I might have a clue. Flark yeah.

Faded red lay-lines crisscrossed the map, highlighted energy and magnetic fields only discovered in the last 200 years. Further, no one used paper for at least 1000 years. "Where's the strike meant to be?"

Leant over the map, Kan' pointed to an almost indistinguishable shape.

Annu focused on the paper's edges. "It looks like half a map and I'm not sure yet. Give me a minute." At the top of the page, scribbles formed words. "Enki Isle. Flark it's an island about 3 hours flight away."

I'd have to fly there to find anything out.

Annu's bowel churned, anxiety fought with curiosity.

Over his shoulder, Kan's breath overwhelmed him. "You can read it?"

Annu took short breaths and fixated on the island. "Yes. Why?"

"No one else can read it. Hey, maybe it's meant for you, and I ended up doing you a favour. Are we square?"

Maybe I can get someone to fly me? No, then whatever I find, they'll want. Which leaves flying myself. Flark, flark, flark. I'll have to buy another crystal and re-register the PFD. Won't Irica love that?

Annu glanced at the time and fidgeted. The parts stall closed an hour ago, which left one option. "Damn, I'll have to call Zex. Unless there's another way."

Fingers clicked in Annu's face, he re-traced around the island.

Kan waved his arms up and down. "Hello? Are we even now?"

"Mm, we'll see." Annu shrugged off his daze and grasped Kan's shoulders. "Do not tell anyone you had this, or you gave it to me. Got it?"

Kan wriggled, Annu tightened his grip.

The smell of fear collided with body odor. "Yeah, of course. Take it easy."

Annu slipped the rolled map into his jacket pocket; his mind raced a million miles a second. Oblivious to his surroundings, he danced through the crowd, home his focus.

Chapter 4: Valium & Comas
3 Bailor Street, Rendelshem, South Australia, Australia
Earth

Shayne wanted a valium for each level of stress she suffered. Like no amount of worry changed her financial status, all she rubbed and probed didn't iron out wrinkled skin. Another sleepless night turned her nerves into guitar strings. With a slight twang on a chord, she'd slaughter someone.

To add further misery, a lumber jack split wood in Shayne's head and piled it across her skull.

Her fingers propped up crow's feet and stretched her forehead smooth. "Fuck you gravity, and you stupid house. I need a vat of anti-wrinkle cream. Argh."

Shayne stuck her tongue out to hall mirror and followed the hall's turns into the kitchen.

Halfway down, Shayne reached an epiphany; her sanity depended on ending the house's madness. "Time to sort this shit out."

At the precipice of the kitchen, Shayne glared at the fallen door and its cracked frame. At 4 a.m., repeated slams and kicks to it seemed reasonable. "Another thing I fucked, but Sam can fix. If he bothered to answer me."

Shayne slid to the table, plonked on a chair, and checked her phone for the fifth time in two minutes. "It's been days, Sam, why haven't you messaged me yet? I need you."

Of all the times for him to ignore her, Sam picked the shittiest. Shayne racked her mind for an hour figuring out why, the chocolate bar on her left provided breakfast.

Morning light cracked through the window and highlighted a trail of dust along the window sill, which matched the overall decor of her home. Shayne's household skills remained at necessary, like when actual visitors, not friends, arrived. Unless a giant dust bunny threatened to strangle her, dirt and mess stayed put.

Pain jabbed into Shayne's hip joint, and reminded her of its existence. She eased the weight off, and dismissed a round of pain killers. What little brain cells remained in her head after the amount she'd smoked the night before didn't require further hampering.

Shayne stumbled over possible causes of the house's problems and how to fix them. She flipped open the Yellow Pages with one hand, and licked remnants of chocolate off the packet in the other. Pages upon pages of builder's advertisements dulled her vision.

Sam's point about the house moving prompted her to find a logical solution first, despite actual strange events niggling at her.

In little more than a week, without a trace she'd lost a toaster, blender, and half a dozen tins along with her mind. "How is it possible? Is it a ghost who wants to blend stuff or make toast? If so where's my fucking share?"

Shayne cracked off another chunk of chocolate, and sucked it down.

From its position in the corner, the pantry taunted her with a creepy aura and empty shelves. "Alright, time to adult. I'll try a builder first, and if he finds nothing, maybe I'll get a Priest. I bet they work free."

The phone vibrated on the table and broke her daze. She pulled it closer and selected the speaker. "Hi Rosie. How are you?"

Children screams echoed through the phone; their shrills pierced her ears. A chill shot up her back, her stomach gurgled.

Thank God my kids are adults.

A sharpness to Rosie's tone put Shayne on edge. "Hey Shay. I've only got a minute so I'll make this short, but it won't be sweet. You forgot Sam's birthday the other day, again."

The chocolate curdled in her gut.

Fuck.

"Fuck shit, fuck shit." She jumped from the chair, and kicked the table leg. "Ow. Crap, which is why he acted so weird."

Shayne smacked herself in the forehead.

I meant to call Rosie days ago.

"Three years in a row, Shay, a hat trick. Which I can't understand because I reminded you constantly for a month before it. I know you've got lots going on, but, you need to think about people other than yourself sometimes. Sick or not, step outside your bubble. If you don't you'll lose more friends."

Shame stung her cheeks.

Yeah that's me, good old, Shayne Self-Orientated James.

"Does that mean you too? Why do you have to sound like you're my mother."

"No not me, and honey someone's got talk to you straight without beating around the bush. As such, I'm talking to you as your best and currently only friend, get it together. Sam will come around eventually, but you're going to have to put in effort. I'm talking real effort required, more than just a text message apologizing, which is not really your forte."

The walls closed in, Shayne wriggled uncomfortable in her skin. "Ouch. Okay I get it. I'm a shitty friend and human being. I suck at relationships with anyone other than my dog, whom I haven't seen since we moved in. So maybe I suck at those too."

"Oh for God's sake Shay, stop. It's not all about you. Sam busted his butt for the last month to help you pack up the unit, get it ready for sale, and move you into the new place. All of which, as you recall, came from your own doing. Regardless, he did help you without asking for anything in return except your friendship. And what do you do? You forgot his birthday. Then, instead of doing something about it you feel sorry for yourself."

She plonked back onto the chair, tears wet her lap. Plop. Plop. Plop.

There goes the rest of my self esteem.

"Shay–are you there?"

The moisture in her mouth evaporated, Shayne's voice crackled. "I don't know what to say."

"I know, it sucks, I hate being the one to tell you this stuff but I don't want to see you end up alone for a stupid reason, especially one you can do something about. So, please think about what I said. Are you feeling okay? Sam mentioned you heard some sort of noises in the house and you were confused about stuff you'd unpacked. Are you taking your antidepressants?"

Like I'd fucking tell you. Great here comes a different lecture anyway.

"I haven't slept much since I moved in, but I am not confused. On the first day a couple of hours after you left, I unpacked the toaster and a few other things in the pantry. Then after a lot of noise and shaking each night, they disappeared one by one. Sam thinks I didn't unpack them to begin with. I did unpack them. They disappeared afterwards."

"I admit it does sound weird, but come on, you've got an overactive imagination. This isn't the first time. Remember the–"

The urge to kill returned, Shayne pushed it aside. *A dead friend, or no friend?* "Don't say it, and forget I said anything about weird stuff. It's probably possums or a hole in the wall Sam couldn't see. Anyway, I'm going to get a builder to look at the house and see what's going on."

Rosie placed a velvet tip on her sledge hammer. "How are you going to pay for the builder? I hate to ask but I need some of the money back I leant you last month. The triplets have a kindergarten trip, and we're short for the payment until Dave get's paid Saturday."

Shit.Crap. I'd forgotten about the loan too.

"Um, yeah sure. No problem."

Liar, liar.

"Is fifty bucks on Thursday okay?"

Where the hell can I get fifty dollars from?

"Yes, fifty would be great, thank you." A squeal interrupted the conversation. "Crap, got to go. Mace, Mace put the cat down."

The ended call engulfed Shayne in silence, desperation lumped a cold wet blanket onto her back.

What the hell can I do? Not a bank on earth would lend me money, I wouldn't lend me money.

Shayne called her one possible option; it rang twice before Ryan answered. "Hi Mum. What's wrong? Are you okay?"

Guilt smacked her with a thud.

How low can I go?

"Hey son. I'm okay other than the usual tired and sore. I, I hate to ask you, but I really need to borrow some money."

His sigh stabbed her heart, his tone twisted the knife. "Again? How much this time?"

Shayne sunk into the chair, a slug on the seat. "Fifty dollars."

Another male mumbled in the background. "Is your mum on the phone already? Jesus. I've got to work soon and I didn't get in until late."

Ryan's voice drifted away from the phone. "Ssh, go back to sleep. I'll take care of it."

A pound of regret added to her guilt, Shayne banged her head on the table. "Sorry, did I wake Joey?"

Ryan clicked his tongue. "You know you did. You heard him, it's six in the morning, Mum, and he didn't finish his shift until three a.m."

She'd succeeded in selfish and rude before most people got out of bed.

Great.

"I'm sorry. I'll call you back later."

"Okay–" yawn, "Actually, I'm calling in this afternoon around five for a visit, I'll give you the money then."

"Sounds wonderful, son, now go back to sleep. Please tell Joey I'm sorry. I love you, Ryan. Both of you."

"I love you too, mum, even if you are a massive pain the arse."

Shayne flooded with relief, despite all her faults Ryan loved and accepted her. The same couldn't be said for other people in her life.

Hopefully he won't tell Erin about the latest loan.

Shayne reflected on the mess she'd gotten herself into. Only God himself could save her sorry arse, and he hadn't answered her last requests.

She rolled her shoulders back and forth, and re-scanned the builder's ads for hints of cheap fees. "If I flashed my tits these days to get out of paying something they'd charge me extra for their subsequent psychiatric help."

******

A deep dark crack between two pale mounds captivated Shayne, her eyes glued to the sight. If complimented by glorious landscapes and abundant valleys, she'd understand her fascination. Yet, the view derived from a builder's arse jammed in a size too small footie shorts.

Given the other option of his hairy back, her eyes and stomach chose arse.

He scratched his head and pushed off the ladder. "Sorry lady. I can't see any reason the house makes the noises you say it does. Aside from a few stumps and a support beam needing replacement, the house is structurally sound. Surprising given its age. Of course, my advice only covers the cursory inspection I've done. If you want me to check under the house and roof, it's a full inspection for an hour costing three hundred bucks."

Curse you small slightly saggy boobs.

Slumped against the wall, poverty dripped from her pores. "I can't afford three hundred dollars. Can you check the kitchen again real quick? The noises sound like they come from there. "

"Which is the reason I looked all through it with you next to me four times. I can't find any problems in there either, and I can't waste any more time. I've got paying jobs to get to."

"Well do you have an idea of what else could be going on? How do appliances disappear? Why would the floor vibrate? Anything?"

He bent down and dropped a tape measure into his tool bag; his butt tested the boundaries of the short's fabric. "It's possible when you've got the washing machine on it vibrates and shakes through the floor. The wooden boards echo the sound."

"If I did more than one load of washing a week, I'd buy into your explanation. So it's not that. And what about my missing appliances, can I blame the washing machine for those too?"

"Look, maybe you didn't unpack them, you just thought you did. Shit doesn't go missing without a reason." A sniff of the air gave him in a swine like appearance. "Smells a bit like mould in here."

Shayne conducted her own survey, the results deflated her.

Yep, definitely mouldy, another problem. Never mind, add it to the list along with condescending males.

"Oh my God. I did unpack them, I'm not an idiot. Well, not all the time. What is with you men? What about the other noises?"

"Hell if I know, maybe a possum got in the washing machine or the roof space. Either way I can't help you."

Shayne clutched the ladder, and imagined hitting him with it. "Is there anyone you can recommend who might have a better idea of what the problems are?"

"Not if you're only paying them the same amount as you did me. Fifteen bucks doesn't get you far these days, it barely covered my petrol here."

Shayne tightened her grip. "Yeah, don't I know it. Thanks for coming anyway. Ah, I don't have any cash on me. Can I do a bank transfer or drop the money off later in the week?"

Which I won't do until I get some money, a lift to the bank and care enough to do it.

"Bank transfer is best."

Shayne shuffled one foot forward down the hall, the other took its time to follow. "Alright done. I'll walk you out."

The plumber strode through the doorway and paused. "Thanks. Have a nice -."

Shayne closed the door and leaned against it. "What a huge waste of time."

The house wobbled, Shayne clutched the door frame, her legs turned to jelly. "This is fucking ridiculous. God help me."

Shayne closed her eyes, and counted, *1, 2, 3, 4. Maybe God will listen to me this time.*

Ripples vibrated across the floor, Shayne slipped to the ground, hands over her head. The roof cracked, the house groaned. Thuds, bangs, and crashes erupted from the kitchen.

"Okay God, I see you still hate me."

1, 2, 3–done.

"How much more of this shit can I take? Actually no, don't answer me."

After a whole minute of calm, Shayne rose from the floor. Phone in hand, she stumbled to the kitchen. "I'll figure this shit out somehow myself. I'm not completely useless."

Again don't answer that.

Shayne stomped through the doorway into a green and orange haze. "What the fuck."

Several exploded eggs from a carton on the counter, dripped over the side onto the floor. A kaleidoscope of coloured lights flickered out the pantry doorway.

Shayne's heart fluttered, the clock ticked louder each second. Sweat dripped down her back, goose bumps covered her arms. Her heart in her throat, Shayne slipped across the floor to the pantry.

Head poked around the doorway, bright lights pierced Shayne's eyes. "Holy fucking shit."

No ratty possum, thief, or psycho killer lurked in the pantry.

Along the rear wall, swirls of light collided, a funnel formed projected forward. Tendrils crept from its edges, and invaded the white space. Shayne's lungs screamed for air, fear muddied her thoughts.

How much will it cost me to fix the Twilight Zone?

The phone slipped between her fingers and clunked onto the floor.

A tremor resonated through the house. Shayne hunched over, and clutched the door frame too late. Her legs crumbled, her butt kissed the floor with passion.

Hot thrusts of agony winded her, waves of torment shuddered across the ground and resounded up her spine. "Fuck. Fuck. Fuck."

Breathe, don't let the pain control me. I control the pain.

The chaos around her stopped once again, Shayne's chest heaved. Her body recovered from shock, and screamed blue murder. Agony searched for a place to settle, finding plenty of them.

Fuck, stop controlling me.

A hot metal rod stabbed her hips and back, the pantry faded into oblivion. Breath shallow, Shayne's ability to think outside the pain shut down.

The front door slammed, footsteps pounded in her direction. "Mum? Mum? Where are you?"

Chapter 5: The Glory of Jaid
Yebu, Orion

On the doorstep of his house, Annu's heart remained homeless; room after empty room, Jaid's absence slapped across his face, the sting of loneliness clung in the air. Annu's pulse raced. After Jaid died, the house transformed from a home to being somewhere to sleep.

Annu considered a move somewhere else for the hundredth time; but like the other times, he refused to leave her memory behind. The constant state of tired and lonely wore him down; yet, he'd suffer in silence as long he deemed necessary.

The map hummed in his pocket and shifted thoughts of his dead wife aside. Annu stomped through the entry into the kitchen, laid out the map on a bench and anchored the corners with a couple of glasses.

A stroke across its surface tickled up his spine; this time with no alcohol or sex required.

With both hands on the paper, the gold band tightened and pulled against Annu's skin. "What is your part in all this?"

Not for the first time in his life, Annu tried removing it. He grabbed precious metal snips from a drawer, slipped the band between it, and squeezed.

The tool bounced off the gold and flung across the bench. "Flarking hell."

An examination of the band revealed it unmarked. Annu tried a metal saw; upon touching gold, the saw repelled like opposite poles on a magnet.

He dismissed hurting himself with laser tools and attempted to lift up either side. The gap between it and his wrist, not wide enough to examine the underneath. "Flark it, onto to the next piece of the puzzle then."

Annu dragged the GPS dragged across the counter and typed in the island's longitude and latitude. The search garnished no results. Not even a mention of an island named Enki came up.

Annu scratched his head, zoomed into Boogle-Orion and searched its approximate location.

Nothing, nada, zilch. "Of course it's difficult, nothing's ever easy."

A message appeared on the communicator, Annu swiped it open.

'By mandate of Grand Councillor Griffin, you're required to appear at Yebu medical centre tomorrow for random DNA testing under subsection 33 of the Orion Council By Laws Ed 5,500,001. Note your attendance is mandatory. The GC Offices, Yebu.'

"Ah no. As if. Even if you guys told me where I'm from, it's not worth getting tied up with you."

What is this Griffin guys deal? Surely, he can't be involved in everything he's accused of? What does it matter? I don't care.

Macci and Irica's declarations about the council moved to the back of his mind.

Tap, tap, tap, Annu drummed his fingers on the bench top and dismissed searching pages about Griffin or the Council. Instead, Annu filtered through an assortment of Orion's maps from the start of recorded history until present day.

Again, obtaining information about the island eluded him. "You've got to be there somewhere. Unless this is another of Kan's scams? Nah, he's not clever enough and it doesn't account for the weird shit."

The paper vibrated under his hand and removed any doubts. "How else can I find out information without flying to an island which might not exist?"

Annu kicked the kitchen cupboard, the answers he needed came from the person who wouldn't divulge them. If anything, she'd further complicate the situation and give him a bigger headache. "There's no other way. I'm going to go there. Flark it. Crap."

His heart thudded, Annu tapped Zex's number into the wrist communicator.

Zex's expression suggested a storm brewed on his horizon. "Annu, what the flark do you want?"

He plastered a smile across his face and sweetened his tone. "Hello Zex. How are you?"

"Get flarked, I'm not in the mood for you."

"So, you're still pissed off at me?"

"You stood up my sister after I kept up my end of the bargain, again."

Isla's face flashed into his mind, his dick shrivelled, a testicle leapt into his stomach. "Yeah, well I have issues dating women with more facial hair than I do."

"Flark you, Annu. It's not her fault; she's got a hormonal disorder. What do you want?"

Ugly isn't a hormone disorder.

"Ah, I need to borrow a Personal Flying Device, ASAP."

"You, Annu, want to borrow a ship? Ha, like I'd lend you anything right now anyway. And for flark's sake it's a PFD."

Annu leant over the bench, the map before him.

Damn you. Why are you so intriguing and mysterious?

"I can't believe it myself. Look, I'm onto something and it's the only way I can get there."

"Coming from you, 'something' either means arse, or gems. Both of which, always get you into trouble, and I never get my money back. Besides, you can't fly and I don't want my ship flarked."

"I see your point, but this will be the last time I ask you for help. I swear you'll get your money back; this is different."

Zex poked his head side to side and searched the area around Annu. "Where are you flying to? Have you told Irica about this?"

"Why would I? I'm going local, not far at all. Trust me. Nothing's going to happen to the ship."

As long as I don't crash and die.

"Fine. You flarking owe me big, and I mean huge. I'll send a ship over in the morning, but you make a date with Isla this week— no excuses. I'm calling her in a couple of days to make sure you have."

Horror dampened his mood. Annu shoved the behemoth's face out of his mind to prevent it rooting there. "Great. Thanks, buddy. You won't regret it."

"Oh and stay out of trouble."

Annu ended the call before Zex questioned him further; today's events tumbled through his mind.

I'm close to finding out something out about my past for the first time. Is my family from the island? What could have happened there to wipe it from history? Why is Irica hiding it from me? What if it doesn't exist anymore and this is a waste of time?

Silence echoed around him. "I've got nothing to lose."

Buzz, buzz, buzz, buzz.

The communicator flashed on the wall, and vied for his attention. Annu ignored it and made a list of things to pack, as well as a last will and testament in case he didn't make it back.

Vibrations erupted across the floor and shimmied the bench. Apples rolled, his drink toppled over along with the two glasses holding the map in place.

Annu grasped the half map before it fell, the floor steadied. "Huh?"

The wall communicator buzzed and assaulted his ears; the ground danced unbalancing him.

Hand over hand, Annu edged along the bench and reached the communicator's base; both annoyances ceased. "Flarking fish balls."

Annu turned around, buzz, buzz, buzz, buzz.

A jab at the screen, and frustration poured from his mouth. "What is so damn important you kept calling until I answered?"

Irica flinched and raised her eyebrows. "Well, hello to you too."

"This isn't a good time. A quake a few seconds ago knocked a heap of shit off the bench, and I'm busy."

Concern cast a shadow across her face. "What quake? We don't get seismic tremors this side of Orion."

"Well, we flarking did tonight. Probably one of those energy companies drilling around of the canyons."

"Still, it's a little strange. How did things go in town?"

Lie, keep her out of it.

"Ah no, the heat got to me so I headed home instead. I wanted an early night."

Irica's deadpan expression filled him with dread. "Annu, there's something different about you, what are you hiding from me?"

Annu bit the inside of his lip. "Ha, that's rich coming from you. I'm not hiding anything."

"I don't believe you, what are you up to Annu? Oh Gods, I hope you haven't done anything stupid after we last spoke."

Guilt stabbed him; Annu removed the communicator from the wall, wobbled side-to-side and dropped it to the floor. "Oh no, another tremor, it knocked the–."

Penance pierced pain to his temples; coloured lights flashed behind closed eyes. He found no escape into darkness. The smell of wet stone and old earth wafted past him, muddled images fought his sanity.

He stumbled from the house into cool night air, sucked in oxygen and exhaled projectile vomit. Annu tumbled to his knees; bile burnt the back of his throat.

With his head thrust between his legs, the pain reduced in his brain. Second by second, the pictures faded and subsided to a dull roar. He rolled onto his back and shared a view of the twinkling stars next to his lost dinner.

Annu's mind wobbled, he wiped vomit around his mouth. "What the flarking hell is going on?"

Chapter 6: A Wormhole Pantry Incident
3 Bailor Street, Rendelshem, South Australia, Australia

Pain deafened her with a symphony of hammers on a tin roof. Shayne writhed on the floor. Waves of agony unrelenting washed over her, each ebb left a bitter taste. Its intimacy alarmed her; its touch, closer than a lover.

When did I submit to this tortured relationship?

Seconds dragged; exhaustion only a tide away.

Hurry up Ryan.

"Mum? Mum? Where are you?"

Shayne used the little energy left in her body. "Ryan, I'm in the kitchen."

The thud of footsteps settled beside her. "Christ Mum, what the hell are you doing on the floor?"

I *can't cope, I'm not strong enough. It's too much. Please someone take it away.*

Ryan appeared beside her. "Mum?"

Focus.

"I fell. The floor—it–"

Strong arms slid beneath Shayne's back and lifted her off the floor. Ryan cradled her like a child and deposited her on a chair.

With the change in movement, a fresh torture commenced. She gripped the sides of the seat. "Oh God no, please stop."

Worry tainted Ryan's voice, he stroked her hair. "Mum, do you want me to take you to the hospital?"

Shayne's chest heaved, she slowed her breathing. "God, no. They're butchers. Can you get me a couple of the white pain killers from my top drawer?"

Inhale, hold it. 1, 2, 3, 4, 5, Exhale the pain. 1, 2, 3, 4. Come on fucker, God damn you. Stop.

Ryan ran from the room, returning with two magic pills and a glass of water. He shoved them under her nose.

Shayne threw them back; the pills dragged down her throat. She emptied the glass and swallowed until the pills shifted. "I've got 15 minutes before I'm a blubbering mess. I have to tell you something."

"Mum, you need to go to bed and sleep. You look like hell. Whatever it is can wait."

Shayne's energy faded quicker than a winter sunset. She grabbed his arm. "No, not yet. Listen, something weird happened in the pantry."

"What are you talking about? Have you slept at all lately?"

"No but it's not about that. A portal opened up on the back wall of the pantry. An explosion of lights and colours everywhere."

Breath. Ouch. Ouch. Ouch.

"Fuck! Wait a few minutes, it might happen again."

Ryan bent over, checking her over for bumps and bruises. He found several of both and scooped Shayne back into his arms, their roles reversed.

As a toddler, he'd refused to leave her side; as an adult, Shayne missed him. "Mum, you're yawning every second word. You're exhausted; you've had a fall because you're clearly not taking care of you. It's got to stop before you really get hurt."

The shifted position redistributed pain across her rear end. "No, no, no. I swear it happened. Take me over there, I'll show you. Please, I beg you."

"Alright if it will make you happy."

Ryan's sighs accompanied their long agonising journey to the pantry.

He poked his head through the doorway. "There's nothing in here except a few tins on the floor alongside an old piece of paper and a green ring. I'll put them on the shelf before I leave. Sorry but the back wall looks like a back wall. Now, will you go to bed?"

"What ring and a piece of paper. Where did those come from?"

"Don't worry about it. You can look at it when you feel better, but there's still nothing strange going in there."

Maybe with the house shaking it came loose from somewhere.

"Wait a little longer, at this time of night it's especially active."

Disbelief soaked Ryan's words and sunk her heart. "Oh. You've seen this portal thing before?"

Shayne's determination wavered, she clung to his sleeve. "Not the wormhole, but a lot of thudding and things disappearing from the pantry. Earthquakes and shit, it's all driving me crazy. Neither Sam nor a builder found a cause, and I now understand why. Because it's not the house, it's other worldly."

Ryan's shoulders dropped and lowered her position. "Mum, now you're telling me you think there's a worm hole in your pantry? Good Lord. How do you even know what a wormhole is?"

I sound nuts to myself. Maybe I've lost it. No, it happened. Focus a little longer.

"I watched a month of alien shows on cable before it got shut off. They explained it all."

His chest expanded and pushed Shayne further into the room; not a sparkle of activity appeared to save her. "Well, there's your first problem. What else?"

"I told you–banging and shaking. Plus most of what I put in here, toaster, blender, TV show crap, disappeared."

"Did Sam bring a fresh batch of his weed over? You always see weird stuff when you take pain killers and smoke that shit. I've told you a dozen times, it's a terrible combination. I bet you didn't even unpack the stuff you say is missing."

Did they train males to be inconsiderate before birth?

"Bullshit, Ryan. Are you men in a league? Do you swap sarcastic remarks before leaving the house? It's got nothing to do with smoking, and for God's sake, I didn't take pain killers until you gave them to me. It happened, why won't you believe me?"

Ryan backed out of the room, his posture stiffened. "Because everything with you is dramatic, and earth shattering. Why can't you be a normal mother and knit socks for the grandchildren I can't give you? Watch old *Murder She Wrote* episodes, or maybe bake a damn cake? Speaking of which, there's 80 dollars on the side table in the hall. Use some of it to get food and eat it–NOT just chocolate and weed. For fuck's sake, I get here, you're on the kitchen floor, which is bad enough, but then you start babbling to me about wormholes in the pantry. I can't keep up. It's exhausting being your kid."

The hairs on the back of her neck bristled. Shayne flushed, the pit of her stomach gurgled. "Thanks, Son, for the money and overwhelming support. I greatly appreciate it. Put me down."

Ryan tightened his hold and glared down at her. "I'm not putting you down because you've got the shits with me. You still need help getting to bed. Please, promise me you'll see your doctor tomorrow and eat properly?"

When did I lose parental power? Hell did I ever have it?

"Fine, I will. Take me to bed."

His tone softened, he closed his eyes. "Mum, it's not like I don't want to believe you, but come on, what you're saying is pretty out there. Your wild imagination is fuelled by too much time on your hands."

Pain killers, take me away from here.

"Ancient aliens isn't crap, and it's got me through some long nights. Take me to bed, please."

Her elbow found his ribs.

Jab, jab.

Shayne gave another couple for good measure.

Jab, jab.

"Ouch. Alright. Jesus, you can be brutal. Have you heard from Erin?"

Fuzziness wriggled into her brain and softened life's edges. "No. You?"

"Yeah. She's busy at work tying things up before Nathaniel and she go away this weekend."

A troupe of pain killer soldiers broke through the first line of defence; they fired weapons at the enemy. Pow, zap, zing. "Why–"

yawn

"Doesn't she call ever me?"

"Probably because you hardly ever call back, anyway, let's not get into it now. Joey's okay by the way. Thanks for asking."

Shayne's fingers and toes tingled; a warm blanket fell upon her shoulders. "You know what I meant, sorry. I'm glad he's okay. Do you want me to sing you to sleep?'

"God no, and you're the one going to sleep."

"Ryan, I've tried to be a good Mum."

His feet slid across the floor; the trip to the bedroom passed in a blur.

Ryan placed her in the middle of the bed, leant over her and kissed her forehead. "I know. Mum, it's just hard being your kid sometimes. Aside from the other stuff, Erin doesn't understand how you lost the unit or the whole financial mess you're in and why you keep lending money off me. I kind of agree with her, but it's done now."

Shayne liquefied into the mattress, any moment she'd welcome oblivion. "You told her I borrowed more money off you? Shit she's going to be pissed —"

Ryan's voice grew distant, almost disembodied. "Good night, mum. I'll check on you tomorrow."

"Mmm morrow."

Shayne drifted along a tranquil sea of fluffy pillows and soft blankets, pain and consciousness waned. Mountain peaks appeared in the distance. Lightning cracked between dark clouds, forests and gullies occupied the skyline. A man called for someone called Ashera.

Chapter 7: Safe Landings & Clenched Butt Holes
Enki Isle, Orion

The ship landed in an open field, Annu's intestines wedged in his oesophagus. He unclenched fingers from the armrests, wiped sweat and tears from his cheeks, and swallowed his arsehole.

Annu exited the ship; his equilibrium wobbled and nerves swayed in time with his legs.

He kissed solid ground, the grass moistened his lips. "Okay, I'm alive, and the island exists. Two problems solved, but where do I go from here?"

Abandonment coveted the island, loss and obliteration probed the dense atmosphere. The gold band glowed; Annu pulled the map from his pocket and shook off the creeps.

Its strange behaviour amplified under his touch, and it hummed a low tune. "Impressive, what else are you good for?"

A dense forest to the left, mountain ranges to his right, valleys in between. He turned in a circle with the map; and faced each direction; it quieted until he faced north.

The map's tune intensified, dulling the sounds of wildlife and unsettling his nerves. "Okay, now we're getting somewhere."

Annu fitted a backpack from the cargo hold with climbing gear and headed off in the direction of the mountains. The map's merriment of song led the way. The clearing ended several metres ahead and opened up for a ravine resplendent with flora and fauna.

His blood rushed, adrenaline combined with the map and compelled him over the rocks and face first into a mass of moss-covered stone statues; refugees of a long forgotten time, patience in wait for discovery, their second chance at importance. Annu brushed shrubbery off the face of the first statue with a definitive female shape and revealed features too deteriorated by age to define.

Her stone skin released a rush of endorphins with his touch. He hunted the surroundings for information but found more destruction. The next several statues missed heads and limbs; some shattered into small pieces as if the ruin purposeful.

Annu followed a line of effigies, each more obscured than the next, leading to tombs, elaborate in their construction, in degrees of disarray. Fresh-dug piles of dirt sat beside the entrances. Scattered broken pottery pieces, and tainted jewellery heavy with gems, the likes not seen by his eyes, spilled from a box on the ground.

Wariness tickled Annu and heightened his senses, settling at the base of his neck. He fumbled for answers. "Grave robbers don't leave valuables behind. Who else knows about this place and wants information?"

Aware of unusual sounds, he walked closer to the tombs; unrecognisable symbols marked the entries of all but one of the six. The middle monument different in structure to the others. Its symbols gouged out of the stone, and its images destroyed.

Annu poked his head through the doorway. He pinched his nose against the stench of decay.

The tomb's contents were strewn throughout the stone room, coffins toppled over and skeletons deposed. "What the hell happened here?"

He egress, his boots crunched, Annu jumped back and examined beneath his feet.

A familiar shaped bone rested in pieces on the ground, a part lodged in his boot. Annu's stomach wrenched, he used a stick as a lever and pried bone from his sole.

Annu searched the ground; skeletons scattered the undergrowth, several with weapons pried in long dead fingers, skulls with gaping holes, and smashed faces leered.

A nausea inducing thought struck him, bile leapt up his throat, Annu swallowed vomit. "Please don't be any of my family I stood on."

He stumbled away from the bones and tipped over with his head between his legs.

Keep going, stay on task.

Annu's mind cleared. With no satisfactory answers found among the dead, and the map vibrating against his hip, he propelled off the ground. "Alright. I'm moving."

He weaved between structures; oblong shaped mounds poked their heads up from their bushy surroundings on either side. "Hello? Is anybody there?"

Aside from the more recent destruction, each section showed no signs of active human habitation. Frustration and anticipation blended–one leg in front of the other, Annu pushed ahead.

I need to find answers or a shit tonne of here. I won't go home without them.

A mountain appeared ahead, the statues lessened in numbers, shrubbery sparse, the air chilled.

Annu passed the last thicket of bushes, and entered thick grass lands; two stone statues a foot taller than their predecessors guarded the mountain's base. The map's song reverberated; it slipped out of his pocket into the air before him. Annu grasped at it, the band brightened its glow; his heart palpitated.

An overwhelming force thrust him to a female figure on the left; almost identical to the one he'd first encountered. Perfect emeralds as eyes, a gold band on one wrist, an imprint on the other where another once rested.

Her arm pointed to a path of gold, scattered with gems, up the cliff face leading to a stone structure.

Moisture evaporated from his mouth, he smoothed over the stone woman's forehead and soaked in her essence. "Holy shit. Oh my Gods, crap. I think she's my mother."

Tears welled in his eyes, overwhelmed with emotion; Annu rested her face in his hands. "Where are you? Help me find you, please."

He examined every inch of her and searched for anything to tell him more, a hint or clue; the lack of results deflated him. The male statute adjacent to her, with his expression peaceful, pointed to the same gold path, an indentation on his finger where perhaps a ring once encircled.

Annu prepared his climbing gear, the path between them the logical choice. He set a tether, tying a harness around his waist. His pulse raced, heart thudded in his chest, adrenaline pumped in his veins. Nausea derived from anticipation swept over his body in waves.

He rolled his shoulders back and forth, one foot on the earth, the other against the cliff; Annu heaved his way up, heart in his throat, his possible past waited at the top.

Chapter 8: The Room of Doom
3 Bailor Street, Rendelshem, South Australia, Australia

The night before consisted of messed-up dreams starring the piece of paper Ryan found in the pantry which spoke in an unknown language about people and places. To top it all off, endless noise consumed the house. At her wit's end, Shayne stood before the room from hell.

A pain-killer hangover dragged down Shayne's mind–whispers of madness and danced along corners of her mind, pushing her to question everything. She picked up the ring and the paper from the bottom shelf.

Shayne held the paper to her face; a half old hand-drawn map, nothing mystical stood out. "What's your story? Can you take me away from here and fix all my problems? Or are you a sign of my impending insanity?"

Faith and hope; dreams she couldn't afford.

The stress and sleep deprivation theory dissolved when Shayne re-considered the facts. She'd not turned the washing machine on in a week, yet the floor shook all night.

Did it really happen?

Shayne's over active imagination taunted her reasoning, uncertainty wriggled into her thoughts.

Am I looking for an easy way to explain my stupid decisions and escape this shitty place? Probably, but what can it hurt?

Vibrations rippled along the floor, bells tolled and echoed through the house, plates rattled. The tins on the middle shelf fell into the dirt.

Shayne clutched the door frame. "Well there's no denying this shit.

The tremors calmed.

Shayne's blood chilled, goosebumps covered her arms. "Enough is enough."

A tug on the light cord scattered the darkness. Dust filled her nose, a cockroach scrambled for safety. "Hello anyone there?"

Idiot.

Shayne levered up the bottom shelf and investigated the top. "Still no toaster. Bastards."

She plunked back down, shifted across to the rear wall and knocked on it.

Rap, rap, rap.

Chunks of paint chipped off. Shayne poked her finger at it; the concrete didn't give. "Ouch."

What's your next idea stupid?

Shayne examined the piece of paper. Strange markings for land masses; the longer she stared, word's formed. "It looks like a map, well half a map. Where the fuck is Enki? How would I know, I suck at geography. Why's it in here?"

She held the half map where the light last appeared and turned it left and right. No matter what she tried nothing happened. "I'm a moron."

Shayne slipped the paper back into her pocket.

Give it time, something is bound to happen.

She wiped dirt from the ring, the jade shone. "What's your story? How do you fit in?"

She slipped it onto her finger. Shayne's body hummed, her skin buzzed, the pain diminished.

"Holy shitballs."

Shayne removed the ring, the pain returned and the buzz stopped. "Well, fuck me."

Ring goes on, stuff happens. Ring goes off, it stops. Cool. Ring goes on.

A pinpoint of light broke through the pantry doorway, bells rang, her heart fluttered.

Okay I'm not so sure it's cool anymore. Don't walk; run. Don't stop and pack, or get dressed. Bolt out the front door and pretend none of this happened. It's all a figment of my imagination. I'll sleep on Rosie's couch.

As if nailed to the floor, Shayne stared at the wall.

Why am I still standing here? Why haven't I left?

Shayne's head buzzed, her tongue stuck to the roof of her mouth. A lump in her throat proved impossible to swallow, adrenaline coursed through her veins and went nowhere helpful.

The light on the wall increased each second, shock disrupted her thoughts. "Crap, shit, fuck, hell, poo. Please stop."

Shayne willed her feet to move, and her arms to grab the shelves; Shayne's limbs ignored her, devoted to the site as willing participants to the anomaly.

Explosions of vitality from the light's core rippled across the room, ebbed under surfaces, and transformed solid into liquid. The central beam consumed the rear wall, a rainbow of colours illuminated Shayne; its beauty equally transfixed and terrified.

The ring vibrated on her finger, warmth spread around her body, her skin shimmied. "What the fuck?"

The light's surface rippled, pink orbs shot from the centre in different directions, flittered around the pantry and investigated the space.

Thousands of crickets buzzed in her ears, a cacophony of bells drilled into her brain. Shayne's ears screamed for relief, she blocked the noise with her hands.

Fear poured in sheets down her back. The radiant crux of the pool twisted, turned, and manipulated itself into a funnel.

Concentric circles rotated the 3D circle, and collected speed with the revolutions.

Her feet moved of their own volition and propelled her closer. Unable to stop herself, Shayne's synapses misfired, her thoughts blasted together. "Oh God, help me."

Millimetres from the surface, panic consumed Shayne, her screams bounced across the room, and echoed through her ears. She stepped into the liquid, no longer in the pantry, the world she knew disappeared.

Someone, please help me....

An explosion of radiance absorbed her and broke her into molecules; Shayne lost awareness of her physical self and propelled down a dark tunnel surrounded by scattered clouds. She slid along, whooshing through twists and turns without control.

Distorted sounds confused her sense of direction and washed away reality. A bombardment of images screamed past; shapes too fast to define, faces in segments, followed by a familiar object.

My blender. What if the same thing happens to me; I can't get back and I'm stuck pulled apart tumbling around this place?

Terror gripped Shayne in cold dead fingers and squeezed the truth from her soul, emptying the barrow of lies she'd constructed her life with. Her mortality in question, Shayne's pitiful existence replayed through her mind; the wasted time, money, and complete disregard for others smashed her, forcing Shayne to confront her deepest self.

Shame, regret, and self-hatred accompanied realisations.

Please, whoever sent me here, I beg you, take me home. I'm only a pot smoking chocolate addict with occasional homicidal tendencies, but I never really mean what I say. I'm sorry I stole plants, and swore at the gas man. I'm a total fuck up, not an astronaut or paranormal investigator. If you send me home, I promise I'll be a better person.

A barrage of orbs responded, crisscrossing the tunnel, circled her and reappearing further ahead. Streams of stars detonated and bordered the tunnel; waves of light ebbed and pulled her into a rip of pulsing energy, towards a blazing portal.

No fuck given, with the passion of a debt collector, she careened towards it.

A metre from the gateway, Shayne's movement paused. Radiated by light, the sound of bells tolling bored into her ears and invaded her mind. Shayne attempted to scramble her wits into one place; they scattered in different directions.

Noise ceased; a disembodied voice echoed around her, and carried the possibility of freedom with it. "Ashera."

The lack of visible source filled Shayne with fear.

Disjointed, disassembled, and desperate, she grasped at the human contact. "Hello? Who's there? Please–"

"Ashera, it's time for you to come home."

It's the voice from my dreams last night. Please be good and don't hurt me further.

"Who are you? I'm sorry, but I'm not Ashera. You've got the wrong person. Please, I–"

Bone-deep cold diverted her focus, the portal widened; pulsating light surged from the core, and crept towards her.

She drifted in its direction and willed herself to stop. Shayne plead to all things holy and unholy; she no longer cared who listened and answered her prayers.

Shayne bellowed above the roar emitting from the porthole, clinging to a speck of hope, and a second chance to live. "Please–help me."

"Have faith, it's time for you–"

"Please, don't go. Don't leave me alone here, send me home."

Conversation over; Shayne propelled into the encroaching brilliance, ready to envelope her with abandon. The light swallowed her whole, sweeping Shayne away from anything tangible, and her only possible assistance.

No. No. No. Not again.

Obliterated into particles, Shayne's being flung forward, and zipped through rainbows of energy. The last colour, or lack of colour–black–replaced all light, and seeped into her thoughts, while insanity danced at the edges of her mind.

A dank stench infiltrated the air, a wall of stone formed in the dark, a whirling tunnel in the middle. Shayne regained awareness of her physical body, and belted towards it.

Shayne fumbled in midair, her arms and legs flailed.

Chapter 9: Nothing and Something
Enki Island, Orion

Annu re-searched each corner of the last stone room, his enthusiasm waned. "Nothing but a flarking stone altar in here. No information and a big sign saying I'm from here–go there for answers. And nothing to bring back and confront Irica with. Shit on a brick."

In the hallway, Annu attempted to glean information from tablets covering the place and ran his hands over them. Edged in gold, fitted with symbols and pictures, Annu wracked his brain to understand them. The tablets lacked light or energy, and whatever excited them into life.

Annu had wasted hours wandering the tunnel with no end, and explored rooms with more questions, and no answers. Infuriated, his blood simmered; hope got further away each turn.

The torch light wavered, frustration pooled into a hot river, Annu stumbled back into the tunnel. "Come on. This can't be all that's here."

The map's song hadn't diminished at all, it chirped with the knowledge of something he didn't and kept it to itself. "Flark you stupid thing."

Annu rolled the paper; it bent the opposite way and rendered it impossible to fold. He shoved it under his waist band; it tingled across his belly and tormented him. "You've shown me nothing much at all. I'm not listening to you anymore."

Back the way he entered, Annu cast the light through the rooms one more time. The gold, emeralds, and rubies in the walls shimmered; his aggravation soared yet dollar signs flashed behind his eyes.

It's clearly a sacred place of some sort but not for a long time. No one's going to come and stop me. Who's going to miss a few gems here and there?

Guilt niggled at him. Annu shoved it aside and replaced it with practicality.

I've got to have some compensation for this damned trip. I won't be coming back here anytime soon.

Annu followed torch light to the entrance where he'd left the back pack and collected it. He pulled out precious gem hammers and chisels onto the ground beside him.

His pants trembled, and sent another surge of adrenaline. A male voice boomed up his leg.

Why do people call me at the worst times? Why do they call me at all?

Zex's voice ran across his thigh. "An, are you there? What the flark is going on? The Oceanic Peace Office called me demanding to know why my PFD flew off the continent without registering the trip and receiving permission. You told me you were going local. Flark it, Annu, get back to me." Beep. "It's Zex."

Beep.

Flark.

"Which is why I didn't tell you." His mind raced, twice in an as many days someone mentioned the Peace Officers, never a good sign. "Shit. How did they see me?"

The ground rumbled; chunks of the stone roof broke free, bells tolled. The noise intensified, tremors erupted around him.

Annu dropped the torch, and fell onto one knee. "Can't anything go my way?"

The ground shook; he stumbled across the ground and probed for the torch. Annu touched metal, clasped his fingers around the base, and pulled it to him.

Disorientated, Annu swung the torch to find the way out. Light hit the carved, gold edged tablets on the walls. They emitted their own faint glow and increased intensity with the bell's tolls.

One by one the tablets shimmered. Radiated energy and demanded attention. The markings cleared in his mind, words and pictures formed, and streamed information into Annu's brain.

The ground rumbled and broke his concentration. Annu focused on stability and leant against the wall's base. He waited for it to steady; the desire to leave weaker than his need for information.

Bright light blasted down the tunnel from the end stone room and blinded him. Annu shielded his eyes; the tablets hummed against his head and flipped their centre pieces.

What's going on in there?

An almighty crack bellowed; the light increased to unbearable, and Annu struggled keeping his eyes open. His breath shallow; he stumbled down the tunnel in the light's direction. Shrills invaded his ears and ricocheted around him. Annu leapt over rocks and avoided fallen chunks of stone.

Crack, crack, crack.

Annu entered the room and turned to a whirlpool of light piercing the middle of the far wall. It encapsulated the room; he froze too amazed to move. A bolt of lightning crackled from the light's core and gave birth to a shape.

His heart pounded against his chest as a person-like form emerged screaming. Its terror billowed around the room before it landed at his feet. A bunch of strange objects tumbled out after her and broke into pieces on impact. Annu's mind blew and he stepped back.

The tremors, noises, and lights all stopped–silence resumed. "Well, shit."

It's a small person, maybe a child? What the hell did it go through? How? Why?

The moisture zapped from his mouth. Annu stepped closer, his hands trembled. "Hey, are you alright?"

******

Fuck meets Flark

Enki Island, Orion

Annu's sense of reality shattered and blew into tiny pieces. He stared at the figure on the ground, a calamity of thoughts jumbled. His overall concern increased as minutes passed; despite continuous prompts, the body hadn't moved since the eruption.

A visual examination of the strangely clad figure revealed nothing to suggest where it originated from, which confused him further. The size of a ten-year-old child who wore a fluffy coat imprinted with strange characters, along with one socked foot, a slip-on shoe on the other. He'd never seen clothing like it.

This whole mess is beyond fathomable. Unless a rock hit me on the head and I'm passed out in the tunnel tripping off my gourd.

Annu pinched himself on the arm and stuck his head out the doorway. Convinced he didn't lay dead in the tunnel, Annu returned to the kid's side.

"Hey are you alright?"

Annu nudged the child with his foot; no response.

Please don't be dead. I don't do dead.

"Kid? Wake up. I'm not giving you mouth to mouth."

The kid grunted, moaned, and spat out a wad of dirt.

Thank Gods.

"There you go. Cough it up. You'll be okay."

Face down, it mumbled to the dirt. "Argh. Oh God. Am I dead? Where am I?"

Relieved, Annu knelt down and softened his tone. "No you're alive and safe. Are you hurt?"

68

The kid turned a panic stricken face in his direction; its eyes snapped open.

Shit. It's a girl child. Pale as snow, almost white. Poor kid must be sick or something.

She scrambled backwards on her hands and touched one of the strange objects beside her; dust filled the air. "What the fuck is my toaster, blender and shit doing here? Who the fuck are you? Where the fuck am I? Please don't kill me."

His pulse quickened, offence singed the back of his neck. "It's okay. Relax. I'm not going to hurt you, I'm trying to help you. My name's Annu."

The girl scanned the room, her gaze went between him and the wall she came from. Her screams pierced his ear drums, Annu covered his ears.

Can this day get anymore strange?

"Hey. Stop freaking out. I won't hurt you."

The kid scrambled away, her screeches louder if he moved closer.

"Flark this shit. Gods damn it. Calm down. I'm trying to help you."

What the flark am I meant to do? Irrational females might be the death of me.

The girl shook her head and moved closer to the doorway.

Annu's thermostat climbed; he jumped to his feet. "I'm not a monster."

She bolted upright and took off in a limp-waddle in the direction of the tunnel behind him.

Annu followed, in short steps, and caught up with her. "Hey be careful. Wait up. It's not safe out there."

The girl turned, screamed, and ran, smacked into a wall, and crumpled to the floor.

"This is ridiculous." Annu clenched his fists at the roof. "What the flark is going on?"

Exhaustion overwhelmed him, Annu trudged a line back to the girl in a heap. "Flarking Irica's got some explaining to do when I get home. It just became the right time."

Annu swept her into his arms and almost threw her into the air; she weighed less than a bag of grain. She hung limp; her head lolled from side to side.

In an adjusted position, Annu poked her side. "Hello, are you still breathing?"

A check over revealed a line of drool down her chin, a huge lump on her forehead, and her chest moved up and down. "Looks like it."

The climb over rocks with a child in his arms proved challenging, Annu paused every hundred metres and caught his breath.

At the cave's entrance, Annu's thighs pumped, his heart pounded, and sweat replaced the water down his back.

The empty gem bag rested against a wall; he dismissed stopping to get it.

Out into the night with the cliff side before him, Annu slung her over his right shoulder and carried her to the edge. "At least the rain's stopped."

Annu laid the girl on the ground beside the harness. He fastened the harness around his waist and tightened the ropes. Once secure Annu triple checked the guideline and tied the girl to his front.

His heart thudded, Annu released his grip and dropped several feet through the air.

A metre down his descent, he glimpsed the back end of a PO control ship, Annu's arsehole returned to his throat. "Flark, flark, flark, flark."

Search lights scanned both sides of the ship, his hands burned, his guts gurgled, the ground approached. "What the hell are they doing here?"

Solidity under his feet, Annu un-hitched them both from the climbing gear, threw the girl over his shoulder and ran for cover behind his mother's statue.

A tinny sound boomed through the forest, he dropped with the girl and scattered grass over them.

Annu jabbed her ribs "Please wake up. I need your help."

She snored and snuggled into his side.

Great, just great.

"Sector G is all clear. Report to control."

This must be the worst, and most dramatic day of my life.

"Roger. Control confirms repeat sweeps until otherwise notified."

Annu's lungs screamed for air, his testicles leapt into his stomach and wriggled their way up to join his rectum. The rear of the ship passed over. With the girl tucked under his side, Annu bolted for the gorge ahead.

Along the way, he hid behind statues and structures. "Are they looking for me or something else?

Each rustle and crack in the bushes scared the shit out of him and enticed a burp from his uninvited guest.

On alert, Annu stumbled amongst the last break of trees, the girl bounced in his arms.

Zex's PFD appeared as obvious as Jonny's balls. "Flarking hell."

Annu carried the girl into the ship and through the cockpit. He slipped her into the passenger seat and slid into the pilot's seat. Annu punched buttons until the system booted. The thrust fired, his fingers slotted into the arm rests earlier imprints, and the ship lurched.

Calm down, I can do this, I have to do this. What I didn't need is someone to take care of.

The ship rose to the height of the trees, levelled and waited for coordinates. The information tumbled around his brain, smashed into each other, and disintegrated.

Fingers crossed, Annu tapped a couple of buttons. The machine shunted forward, his face smacked into the console. "Flarking son of a bitch, bastard, cocksucker."

The girl flung into the console, and woke upon impact. Screams erupted from her mouth, billowed around the cabin, and re-pierced Annu's ears.

I don't need this.

He lacked spare hands to cover his ears. "What can I do to get you to stop screaming?"

A voice of doom crackled through his ship's PA system. "Attention PFD HUX99. You are in a restricted area. Freeze under order of the Orion Peace Department."

She assaulted his ears via high decibels.

Shit, shit, shit.

Annu smashed a few buttons, the ship shunted forward, the lump on her head connected with the console.

A hand flew to her forehead, she rubbed the bumps. "Ouch. That really fucking hurts. What the hell?"

Annu gut's churned. "Oh. Ah, sorry, accident." His butthole slipped out of his mouth and onto the floor, his heart palpitated. "Where did they come from?"

She blinked and massaged her temples. "Bullshit. You did it on purpose to shut me up. I think you bruised my brain."

Fingers fumbled across buttons, smack, beep, beep, beep. "Please work."

The girl faced him. "Where are we? Why did we leave the cave? Who are you?"

The ship shuddered forward a few feet. "In short, in a ship, it wasn't safe to leave you in the cave, and I'm Annu."

"You–HUX99–stop right there. You are ordered to freeze."

Annu pushed another sequence, in jagged movements, the ship jerked and ceased. "FLARK."

She rose off the seat and wrapped the jacket around her. "Why are people chasing you? Where are you taking me? I have to get home."

Annu jabbed at a red button, the PFD hurtled forward. The island disappeared behind him replaced by miles and miles of ocean. "We just left Enki island, which I'm never going back to, I have no idea why they're chasing me. I planned on waiting until you woke up to find out where you lived and drop you off but circumstances changed. Unless you live in the cave I found you in."

She paled, her skin translucent. "Oh God, the wormhole thing. Enki is the place mentioned on the paper I found. Am I in Africa?" The girl paced before the seat. "Please don't kill or rape me."

She has a map too?

Annu grasped at the control console. "Listen kid. I'm not like that so relax."

"I'm not a kid, I'm a grown woman. My name's Shayne."

His hands planted in the middle, a carousal of buttons lit up. "You're pretty small and white for a grown woman from these parts. Well, Shayne, I suggest you sit back down before shit hits the fan, and I'll get you home as soon as things are under control."

Which might be next week or next month at this rate.

"Next to a seven-foot-tall bowl of Coco Pop's I would look pale. How can I be sure you aren't a rapist, psycho killer who so happens to be ridiculously attractive. Like Ted Bundy."

She thinks I'm good looking?

"Well for starters, you're neither dead nor, ah, raped."

She wiped dirt from her face and brushed her hair out of the way. Underneath an attractive woman around his age appeared. "You might be saving it for —."

The ship dipped to the left, everything on the floor hit the roof. The woman smashed into the passenger side window and fell into the seat.

Annu flung over the side of the chair and gripped the arm rest, his legs dangled in mid air. "Ahhhhhhh."

It righted itself and flung him the other way. Legs over butt, somersaulting through air, Annu thudded against the controls. The woman clutched the sides of the passenger chair with her feet against the wall.

Pain pummelled his ribs, breathing laboured, he stumbled into the chair. "Mother flarkers."

The PO's authoritative tone terrified Annu. "I repeat, under order of the Council, you are demanded to stop. Enable docking, step away from the controls, place your hands behind your head and lean back in the chair. Officers are in the process of boarding the vessel to arrest you. I repeat you are to remain still and enable docking."

The woman shivered, hugged her legs, and rocked back on the seat. "This can't be real. It's got to be a fucked-up dream. I'm tripping for sure."

Annu drew a circle in the air with his finger. He dropped it onto a flashing green button. "I wish that's what happened."

Metal crunched, the intone of catastrophe exploded through the radio, the ship flung forward. "Thank you."

Zex's gravel mumbled from the communicator wedged under the seat. "Annu, are you there? It's been four hours."

Flark. "Ah can't talk right now."

"Under the Order of the Council, you have to the count of five to halt and comply or we shoot. One–"

The woman's eyes widened, she slid closer to the window away from him "What the fuck did you do? I am right and you're full of shit. Oh God, a chocolate hulk kidnapped me. How many people have you done this too?"

I can't deal with this right now. How can I go faster?

"Actually this time, nothing. I went looking for, oh it doesn't matter right now."

Annu pressed a sequence of orange, green, and blue buttons.

No, that changed nothing.

"Two, halt, freeze. We're in pursuit."

Her voice raised an octave per word. "You must have done something for them to want to shoot you. I can't die like this. What the fuck?"

Blue, green, red, red, red. Whoosh.

Okay that's faster, much faster. Don't look out the window or at my stomach on the floor.

The rear turbine exploded, black smoke leaked into the compartment, their death loomed. "I hope Irica changes my underwear before they bury me."

Ting. Ting. Thunk. Chunks of black metal flew past the front windows.

The woman screeched. "Shit, shit, shit. Do something."

"Hey, maybe dying won't be so bad, I'll see people I miss."

Like Jaid and Junior. No longer have a lonely, miserable life.

Bright white light erupted through the clouds and consumed the sky. Sound ceased, things from the floor floated to the roof, Annu and the woman drifted from their seats.

The woman covered her eyes and trembled. "Oh no, not again. Please no."

Annu's head hit the ceiling, ambient noise ceased. "I agree."

The PFD floated; a puppet on a string towards the light beam. Fear teemed down his back, his heart palpitated, Annu grabbed the back of the seat and pulled.

This is it–the end.

The woman drifted into the cargo hold, a funnel of coloured lights opened ahead, each colour rotated at increased speed; exploding from the core. Annu rethought his decision to start the day with only one bottle of rum.

Eyes squeezed shut, he held his palms to his chest and grasped at straws.

"If there is a God or gods up there, please, please help me. I don't really want to die. I swear, I'll be a better man. I'll drink and curse a lot less."

The ship flew into the tunnel's core, light enveloped the PFD. "Flark.

Chapter 10: A Distinction without a Difference
Somewhere, where?

The ship exited through the end of the tunnel like the one Shayne tumbled through, She patted herself down and checked for damage. Her fully clothed status provided relief.

Her head thumped. "Okay, I'm either asleep or I'm tripping out big time."

Shayne considered she'd scattered her marbles somewhere in space, with Annu a result of insanity. No other explanation made sense.

I should have watched the Twilight Zone more.

The craft approached a farm area; a short distance down an open road, they lowered to land a few yards from a large building. Shayne's heart fluttered and skipped a beat.

The similarity in structure to homes on Earth eased her anxiety. "Is this your place? Why are we here? If you're not kidnapping me take me home."

The chocolate hulk opened his eyes and glanced out the window. "Holy shit. Yes it is. I, ah, didn't expect to end up here."

You don't look psycho but how can I be sure?

"Either way, please you take me home?"

Annu's sigh fogged the pilot's window. "I'd prefer to have a few stiff drinks first and make sure it's safe first, but yes, I'll take you home. Where do you live?"

He reminds me of a bowl of coco-pops, only crunchy.

Relief dropped her shoulders from around her ears. "16 Bailor Street, Rendelshem, South Australia. If we're in Africa I'm screwed, because I don't have a passport. I'll need the Australian Embassy thing."

Annu tapped the computer screen and frowned at its beeping response. "I've never heard of those places, and the GPS can't seem to locate them either. Which side of Orion is it on? Urdu or Marduk continent? Long range GPS's struggles with co-ordinates around there. Thanks to our illustrious leader, not much infrastructure is available outside the city. But, you know that. Annu slipped off the pilot's seat and at the console. "Sorry but I'll have to try the inside unit."

He walked past her seat and disappeared into another room, Shayne ran after him.

I should have paid much more attention in geography instead of smoking and kissing stupid boys. How far way did I go? And I'm in my fucking pyjamas next to a totally hot guy.

Shayne tugged his sleeve. "Alright, fine. As long as you don't take too long. I need to use the toilet anyway. Those places you mentioned, I've never heard of any of them." Something he said niggled her brain. "Wait, where's Orion? How many sides does Earth have?"

How many classes did I miss?

In front of an opening, he faced her and cocked his head. "What? Earth? You should get those bumps checked. Here, where we are right now is Orion. The Planet we live on."

Annu took the steps outside the door two at a time, stood on the ground and held his hand out.

Shayne waited inside, her blood pressure rose, the pickle jar exploded, fragments of glass imbedded in her skull. "Say what? You mean Earth, right?"

Don't panic, there's a simple explanation. Like a brain aneurysm.

She gasped for her and gulped in oxygen, stars twinkled behind her eyes.

Annu re-climbed the stairs and stood one down from the exit. "Are you alright? I didn't think it possible but you're even paler."

Shayne slumped onto the metal floor. Bile burned the back of her throat, she dry heaved. "Oh God. Oh God. Oh God. Oh God. It can't be. How is it possible?"

Concern marked his expression, he waved in her face. "Kid–lady, where are you from?"

"I said my name's Shayne."

Oh God, oh God, oh God. "Earth. I'm from Earth?"

Annu squinted and scrunched up his nose. "I've never heard of it. Where the hell's this Earth?"

I have to get home, this makes no sense. Unless I've completely lost my mind.

"It's the planet I'm from, not Orion. And I don't know how far away it is from here or how to get back there."

Annu blinked repeatedly. "Another planet but not this one? Seriously?"

"Yes that's what I'm saying." Wracked by sobs, her ribs ached. "I want to go home. Oh, fuck me."

He scooped her off the floor and onto her feet. "I've got no idea what the flarks going on here, but I might know someone who can help."

Tears pooled on his chest. "You do?"

Annu carried her down the steps. "Maybe. Even though this sort of thing doesn't happen here, I bet she knows something."

At the bottom Shayne slipped from her arms, and wiped snot from her face. "There's no space travel here? Then how can this person help me?"

What if she can't get me home and I'm stuck here? Crap. I don't have any weed or chocolate to get me through. Oh fuck, shit, fuck, shit.

Wind belted through her pyjamas, cold settled in her lower half.

Shayne's blood pressure dropped, she held her breath.

Don't think about it now. Put it aside for a later freak out.

An old woman emerged from the front of the house, arms waving.

She looks nuts. I hope it's not her.

The crazy woman ran towards them, hair whipped around her face, a six foot plus tall Witchypoo from HR Puffnstuff.

Annu thrust out his chest, and motioned to the woman. "Well that saves me a call."

She glanced at Shayne and fixed on Annu, her voice deeper than Shayne's preferred level. "Oh, thank the Gods, you were gone so long, I worried they'd found you. We have to get out of here as soon as possible." The woman pointed to the ship they'd exited. "Why did you fly? What happened to the ship and where did you go?

Oh fuck. She better be talking about taking me home. "I'm Shayne, Annu said you'd help me."

The wind showed Shayne an equal amount of attention as her companions.

Annu's tempered tone boomed beside her. "Whose they?"

"Peace Officers were at my place looking for you over an hour ago, we've got to leave before they come here."

"Hey? Shit. How did they find me so fast?"

Irica clicked her tongue. "Where did you go, Annu? What did you do to incur the attention?"

Annu removed his half of the map. "I got this which led me to Enki Island, and I went looking for information about my past you weren't willing to tell me. She's got the other half. Anyway, I went there and all I found were a lot of ruined statues including my mother, then this woman fell out of wall in front of me, and the Peace Officers showed up. While evading them, bam, the ship gets sucked into a thing in the sky and we end up here. You know what's going on, so spill it."

Tears streaked Shayne's face, a hot salty river of torment and misplacement. "I don't care about any of that. I want to go home."

Irica jabbed a finger in her direction; while not Annu's height, she towered over Shayne. "You've both got half the map, where did you get it from? It's been missing for centuries."

Annu cracked his neck. "I doesn't really matter how, but we did."

Irica squinted at Shayne. "This is the being who fell?"

Annu's sigh drifted in the breeze. "Yes, this is the woman who dropped through the wall. Now tell me what's going on and how to get her back home to Earth."

Am I fucking invisible?

Irica and Annu flung around to Shayne. Speaking at once, Annu motioned to Irica to speak first. "Earth, the planet Earth? How?"

Crap I wasn't prepared for them to actually pay attention to me.

"Long story short, yes, I'm from Earth. After days of weird shit, I found a ring and the other half map in my pantry." Shayne presented the ring on her finger and waved the paper. "I put on the stupid ring and a wormhole thing brought me, well, here. This is all a horrible mistake and I want to go home."

Irica grabbed at Shayne's shoulder. "My Gods, the only way you'd travel with the ring on is–did you arrive in the altar room on the mountain?"

Don't think about how far away I am.

"I don't know and I don't remember much."

Annu's poker face revealed nothing. "Arrive makes it sound pleasant. I'd say land and yes, which is why I bought her back to you."

Irica stepped back, her expression filled Shayne with dread. "Yes. There's been two signs, and she, she must be the other Demi-

God. The last sign doesn't occur until right before the ascension. Wow. Better late than never. The process begins, even though I resigned myself to tell you anyway, it's truly time. Which means you're in even more danger. It's imperative we go immediately, it's safe at my place. My other place. It's a several hours from here and it's protected." Irica tugged Annu's sleeve. "Now. We can't waste time."

Shayne clutched her chest. "Wait so can you take me home or not? I don't understand what this has to do with me? These Police people trying to get Annu not me."

Annu stomped his foot, dust filled the space around them. "First you won't talk, and now not only won't you shut up, you're spouting nonsense. What the hell are you talking about? What other place? What signs? What Demi-Gods? Have you lost your mind? What about sending her home, and yes, why are they after me?"

Irica rocked on her heels. "It's complicated, I'm sorry. You haven't done anything wrong as such, but please, I'll explain everything on the way, I swear to you. Both of you."

Panic bearhugged Shayne's neck and suffocated her. "In case you didn't hear me, I can't go anywhere else. I - need - to - go - back - home. To Earth."

Red flushed Annu's chocolate coloured skin. "Look I'm sorry but it doesn't appear this will be as easy as I hoped." He jabbed at Irica. "Dammit Irica. This better not be a ploy and you better not be messing me around. Given recent events, I'm inclined to trust you. For now." He nodded at Shayne and strode two feet ahead. "The toilet's inside, follow me. I'll show you the way. I'll grab a few things together and we'll leave, I'm flying."

Shayne's brain imploded and dropped to her knees, the ground gave nothing; Annu shrugged and disappeared inside the house.

Arms across her chest; Irica stood beside Shayne.

Shayne's brain wobbled, nausea waved through her; she dry heaved on the ground, the contents of her stomach curdled. "No I can't go somewhere else, I need to go back to the island. Why did this happen to me?"

Irica whispered in her ear, "Take deep breaths, it's going to be okay. There's a celestial divine event occurring which you and Annu are linked to. It will all make sense soon." Shayne's head thudded, her skull tightened.

Shayne slumped onto her butt, head between her knees; Irica stroked her back. "I don't want to hear soon, tell me, why can't I go now?"

"I don't have time to explain at the moment. You'll have to trust me."

Shayne's hope train sped past all stations, and derailed at the last stop in violent fashion; no passengers survived.

Her self importance disintegrated. "You don't understand, people will look for me. They'll think I'm dead or missing and shit."

Irica raised an eyebrow. "I'm sorry. You'll have to wait. Get up and clean yourself up quickly. "

Shayne gulped in air, fanned the cold across her face and blinked away burgeoning panic. She held onto the chance of going home, alive. "I, ah, but I don't understand."

Stay focused; I'm not alone here, I'm in the only place to get help, so they say. Maybe they won't hurt me, and I'll be taken care of. I got through a wormhole alive once, I can go through again to get home. I'm sure it won't take long. The negatives are too traumatising to dwell on, push them aside. I'll never get through this if I keep freaking out.

Her head cleared, the fuzziness lessened, she pushed onto her feet; Irica supported her.

Shayne expected pain to shoot through her legs and hips after sitting so long. It didn't arrive; reconsidering the ride over, she'd experienced panic not pain.

I bet it's going to hit me all at once.

Irica led Shayne to the house, with an arm around her shoulder. "You will, just not right now, and I need you to move before we run out of time."

Shayne dragged her feet. "I don't want to go anywhere except home."

Irica pushed instead of led. "You don't have a choice, you can't go home yet. I already explained it to you."

Each step towards the house solidified acceptance of her position, Shayne dug her heels in. "Why is it complicated? I've only got your word on this. Why should I believe you?"

Irica's clipped words irritated Shayne, frayed her nerves, and added annoyance to her list of problems. "Because it is. I can't go into it now, so at the moment you're going to have to listen to me, toughen up and get with the program."

'Toughen up,' and 'get used to it,' were unwelcome concepts which forced Shayne to accept her current dilemma. "This morning at home I thought my life sucked. Now I'm on an alien planet and can't get home yet, give me a break."

"Ah, that explains your attitude. By the way you're the alien here."

Oh fuck me, this is messed up. Someone tell me what the hell's going on or send me home now. Please. I'll be nice, even courteous to people. Alright—maybe not courteous, but maybe I'll stop swearing at them. Is it a deal? Hello? Aw fuck it.

Chapter 11: Past Disclosures
Yebu Mountains, Enki Continent, Orion

In the pilot's seat of Irica's PFD, Annu wriggled into the chair. The engines purred, the ship raised and shuddered. He directed it down the long lane and towards the gates at the start of his property.

Irica trembled from the co-pilots seat; the moment of disclosure hung like overripe fruit. If not picked in time, each piece fell and rotted. Both parties waited, anxious for the other to speak; an invisible wall built with bricks of deceit separated them. The bond between foster mother and son had altered in recent days, its continued success reliant upon Irica's coming revelations.

Shayne perched on a container between the two seats and hugged herself. Her presence added more complications to Annu's problems. Needy, insistent, demanding, and complaining; the longer he spent with her, the more she tested his patience.

Irica shifted in the chair, tension built; she licked her lips; his heart skipped a beat.

Physical exhaustion transformed into drunk tired, Annu lost the strength for defiance.

I'm too old and there's no point flying off the handle.

"Alright, we're here. Cut the shit and make it simple. What the flark's going on, why haven't you told me before, and how long have you had another place I don't know about?"

Irica smoothed her hair in anxious waves. "Well, first of all, once I tell you who you really are, your enemy also becomes aware of you. It's like when you're told a cosmic light goes on he sees. He won't know your exact location but enough when combined with the technology we have on Orion and his connections to figure out where to look. Hence the danger and time it took to tell you. Some years ago myself and some others, who I'll get to later, discovered a place near the mountains where the magnetics affect your enemies' abilities. I hoped we'd reach the other place property he and his cohorts find out. Only a handful of people know where it is. The other property is also part of the story."

Annu tossed up getting Irica medically assessed and listening to the story.

Somewhere in it there's the truth I hope. "And how to send Shayne home fits into that?"

"Yes, it's not me who can send Shayne home, it's both of you, but not–"

Shayne yawned, her arms protected her chest. "Hang on. Can I get a jacket or a blanket? It's freezing in here."

The hairs on the nape of Annu's neck stood. "Now? Come on. You could have asked before she got started."

"Duh, I wasn't cold then, and I didn't realise she'd take so long."

Annu's eye twitched.

Don't stick her in the corner, it's not right.

"I'm positive there's nothing I'll require her help for so tell me how we send her home, and I'll do it right now. No waiting necessary."

Irica pulled a hand woven blanket from the back of her seat and handed it to Shayne. "Here you go, now can I keep going or I can't guarantee what will happen to you next?"

Shayne wrapped the blanket around her shoulders and buried herself in colour. "I'll shut up if you get right to the part I go home."

"I can't start from there. Look, please trust me."

Shayne scowled, stomped her foot and mumbled. "Fine, whatever. It's not like my problems are important and I'm stuck on another planet or anything. By all means go ahead."

Annu's skin crawled; a Shayne induced migraine loomed. "Please Irica, continue."

Irica's hand returned to her hair. "I had this whole speech prepared with details and explanations but now with Shayne here, I've got less time. Hence I'm cutting it short. Which makes it hard to know where to start."

Annu perched on the chair's edge and veered from the property into a back lane. "Well, might I suggest, telling me how to get rid of her or anything really?"

The gates at the start of his property appeared in the distance.

Irica drummed her fingers on the control console, her eyes fixed on him. "Okay, you aren't regular people. You two are the Demi-Gods I mentioned earlier. Annu, your mother's the Goddess Ann. Shayne, unless you know already, I can't confirm who you're mother or father is just yet. Regardless of your unknown parentage, as I said, you're also a Demi-God. The island is the place the Gods resided many eons ago. What you both need and what your enemy wants is on the island. The same one you found Shayne on Annu. The tunnel in the sky you went through, and how Shayne got here, are via wormholes. Which are the signs that something called ascension is approaching. It only comes around every one thousand years and you've both got a huge role in it."

Shayne's clap reminded him of her presence. "It was a fucking wormhole. I knew it. You're nuts about the Demi-God stuff. It explains nothing. For the tenth time, how do I get home?"

The alcohol's anaesthetic effect disappeared. "No flarking way."

What? I can see how I resemble a God but Shayne? Unless Irica's finally flipped her lid.

Irica's statements registered in chunks. "If this other place is so safe why didn't we go there straight away or days ago?"

"He'd have had more time to find you, and you'd be unprepared when he did."

Annu's mind boggled. "So you're saying my mother is Ann? As in, Ann and Ki, your Gods? Ann, the one I'm named after?"

"Yes, she's your mother."

My mother's a Goddess? I'm a Demi-God?

Torn between shock and incredulity, Annu combined both. "Why didn't my mother raise me instead of you? Where's my father? Where are they now?"

Pink flushed Irica's face, guilt threatened his determination. "She wasn't able to, and because of past failures we altered our methods, and we decided you weren't to be told until your chance for ascension arrived. However, without Shayne you would have faced this alone. As for your father I've never known who he was, sorry."

Shayne thrust out her chest. "Ha, sucked in. Home, Irica–remember?"

Annu's mind tumbled in a spin cycle of information. "Wait, I'm confused. If I'm a Demi-God, how can I, we, be in danger? How far away is this ascension thing? What is it?"

"Because you're enemy, Shamesh, is a former God and more than capable of killing you both and others to get what he wants." Her shoulders drooped. Irica's voice maintained a hypnotic rhythm. "In ancient times you're mother, others, and one named Shamesh, belonged to a group of Gods called the Annunaki. The Creator charged them with the spiritual and humanitarian welfare of the inhabited galaxies. Part of their role was to teach human kind farming, art, music, healing, technology, innovation, planetary power, using nature, and even weaponry–"

Shayne smacked her lips and twiddled her thumbs. "Oh, my God. I didn't realise this would be an epic tale the likes of War and Peace before you told me anything I gave a shit about."

Irica gritted her teeth and faced the window. "Will you let me finish. You need to understand this–oh no."

Annu drifted along an almost empty lane towards the main ship lay-line and settled on a steady pace. "Oh no what?"

Shayne pounced off the container. "What's wrong now? Did you forget where you're up to? Fabulous. Please tell me you don't have to start again?"

Irica pointed to her left and jumped off her seat. "There's a Peace Officer's ship behind those trees."

Annu's blood ran cold; the day continued its doomed path. "Oh shit."

The ship flew by them, and turned around. A blue light flashed, a siren sounded. It zipped into the lane and hovered behind them.

"This is the Yebu Peace Department. Veer left out of the lane and land in the emergency bay. Now!"

Irica ushered Annu from the pilot's seat. "Both of you go and hide."

Shayne remained in place, her mouth agape. "Huh?"

Annu's arse stuck to the chair, his butt hole constricted.

Crap, crap, crap.

Irica smacked Shayne on the shoulder and Annu on the head. "Move now."

Shayne jumped off the container. "Why does this keep happening? I haven't done anything wrong. You even said so. I don't understand. Peace Officer's sound like Police on Earth and they're generally good. They might be able to help me faster."

Annu slid off the seat, his pulse soared.

I hoped we had more time.

Irica pinched Shayne's earlobe, pulled her to stand and out of the cockpit. "Trust me. You don't want or need them seeing you either. You're someone I can't explain."

Annu's ear recalled Irica's signature move from his youth, he massaged the lobe.

Thankfully you didn't stay stretched.

He stumbled around the seat and into the cargo hold.

Shayne froze in the middle of the bay.

Annu grabbed her arm and lead her towards a container. "Are you always this much hard work?"

Shayne whipped around and snarled. "Fuck you. I'm starting to realise you guys might be full of shit about–"

Annu swept her up, deposited her in the container and shut the lid.

He ducked into a nearby cupboard and closed the door.

Please don't find us, please, please, please.

Irica followed the Peace Officer's directions, and veered out of the lane; the ship landed.

Feet crunched on sticks and rocks outside, someone knocked on the outer door. "This is the Peace Office. We're boarding your craft. Open up, and stand against the wall with your hands in the air."

Annu swallowed a lump in his throat and waited for his testicles to descend.

Are the two connected?

The cupboard dulled Irica's voice. "I'm coming, just a minute. It takes me a while to get around these days."

The click of her cane on the metal floor rattled his nerves.

When did she become such a good liar? How many secrets does she have?

Chapter 12: A Wormhole Wake-up Call
Yebu Mountains, Orion

Shayne's spool of sanity unraveled and slipped through her fingers. Plastic grooves on the container dug into her back, she shuffled over and wedged herself in the corner.

This is fucking crazy. I'm probably not even on another planet, I'm somewhere on Earth found by some whacko cult. I better remember not to drink the kool-lade if anyone offers me any.

Shayne tilted her head and peeked through a lock hole, her heart skipped.

Irica clicked past Shayne's container, hunched her back and opened the rear door. The cane trembled. "Officers, how can I help you?"

A man who equalled Annu's size and colour entered the ship with his weapon aimed at Irica. "I'm Sergeant Winkle from the Yebu City Peace Department. Step aside ma'am, and put your hands in the air."

Am I in the land of chocolate giants or what?

Irica hobbled the few steps to the wall and leaned against it. "Okay but I can't let go of the cane, I need the support."

Since fucking when? This is not right.

Winkle jabbed Irica in the ribs with the gun barrel. "Put both hands in the air ma'am. I will not ask you again."

Irica dropped the cane and raised her arms in slow, staggered movements. "Why are you bothering an old woman? I demand you tell me what this is all about."

Lady you'd kill it in Hollywood. Damn. She's so convincing the rest of what she said are probably lies? Shit. Shit. Shit.

Shayne's mind raced, her pulse rocketed. The ring on her finger warmed and tightened, her skin hummed.

Okay, I can't deny the ring and the wormhole but so - does that mean she's right about the God stuff? Fuck. I don't know what to believe or think.

Winkle patted Irica down from head to feet. "Do you know the whereabouts of Annu from Yebu?"

Why do these guys care about Annu so much? Irica didn't get to that part yet.

Irica slumped her shoulders. "Who? I have no idea who you're talking about."

Winkle's frown sent a shiver down Shayne's spine. "Ma'am you're aware of the penalties for providing false information to the Peace Department and aiding a wanted suspect?"

"Of course, but I don't know what you're talking about."

Shayne's knees ached; the hard surfaces offered no comfort.

Fucking hell, but no mention of a cult yet and what the fuck is a Yebu? What am I going to do?

Winkle stepped back. "Ma'am, after being spotted on a restricted island and requested to land, Annu fled Peace Officers in a dramatic chase which ended when officers lost him in a strange weather system. Subsequent to this, it's on record Officer's Reli and Smit attended your premises at which time you advised you didn't know such a person, or their whereabouts. However straight after said visit, you immediately flew to the suspect's premises, and here we are."

Irica grimaced. "Oh, oh that Annu. Sorry, old age muddles my brain."

Of course I end up somewhere in the middle of trouble. Except this time, I didn't cause it. Maybe.

The officer motioned behind him. "Officer Del, restrain the suspect. You're coming with us until we clear this issue up."

A younger officer stepped into the cargo hold, stood in front of the container and blocked Shayne's view.

Fuck. Crazy or not, either way, if they take Irica I'm stuck with the chocolate hulk and neither of us have much idea of what's going on. I need help and this shit needs to get sorted.

Panic flooded Shayne; she pushed the lid open and sprung up.

Her mouth worked before her brain. "Wait, stop. She's the only one who knows how to get me home. Possibly. As for Annu, I'm not a hundred percent sure where he is but, he's around somewhere, I think. Actually I can't say for sure because I didn't see him hide. They said we didn't do anything wrong. Why do you want him? Is he a liar?"

Winkle and Del turned in Shayne's direction, stunned expressions plastered their faces.

Irica lunged at Shayne, Del restrained her. "Shayne, what are you doing? Stop. You don't understand. You're making a huge mistake."

Winkle stumbled sideways and pointed. "What, who, it's a small white humanoid thing. It can't be from here." He shook himself and straightened his back. "What's going on?"

Irica licked her lips and flipped her attention between Shayne and Winkle. "I, ah, she's, she's a sick child with a rare disorder. I'm taking her back to her parents?"

"Oh for fuck's sake when will the lies stop?"

Pot calling kettle black, nimrod. Oh do shut up.

Shayne climbed out of the box and onto the metal floor. "I'm not a child and I'm not sick. Well, I am but not here. Anyway, I'm from Earth and she's going to tell me how I can go back home. Unless you know how to get there? If not I'm screwed without them."

Winkle frowned and faced Irica. "What the hell's going on here? You've got a sick kid shut in a container and you're hiding a wanted suspect. Tell me where he is and it will reduce your prison sentence."

The cupboard behind Shayne burst open, shock froze her in place.

The chocolate hulk beelined for Winkle, collected him around the middle, and slammed the officer against the opposite wall.

Winkles' gun flew into the air, and landed towards the cockpit.

Del let go of Irica's wrists, and went for Annu.

Annu stretched his upper half, and punched Del in the side of the throat. Del stumbled towards the outer door; Annu shoved the man out of the ship.

Shayne's levels of guilt and panic mashed together. "Shit, Annu watch out."

Annu spun on his heel, and raised his fists.

With a set of black cuffs in one hand, Winkle jumped Annu from the side, and grabbed Annu's wrist.

Oh crap. This escalated quickly.

Winkle pulled Annu's arm towards Annu's back. Annu resisted, his bicep bulged, Annu dragged his wrist and Winkle in front of him.

Annu raised his knee and connected with Winkle's groin. Winkle released his grip on Annu and grabbed his crotch.

Irica rubbed her wrists and crept along the wall towards the container beside Shayne.

Venom tainted her former kind tone. She opened the lid and removed a black device. "You've got no idea what you've just done and how much trouble you've gotten us into." Irica glanced at the thing and quivered. "I'd give you the stun gun to help, but I can't trust you with this."

Hunched over, Winkle stumbled at Annu.

Annu side-stepped, put his foot behind Winkle's and swept it across. Winkle hit the metal floor, his head bounced.

Guilt buried her; a tinge of regret tickled the back of Shayne's neck but not enough to admit it.

Irica approached Winkle's rear, put the device to his neck and depressed the trigger. Winkle seized, his arms dropped to his side. Irica zapped him again. Winkle flopped around, his arms flailed.

After a final twitch, Winkle stop seizing and rested inert on the floor.

Annu dragged the officer under the shoulders to the open door. On the precipice he swung Winkles' legs over the side and pushed him out.

Door closed, Annu wobbled on his feet. "Irica, why didn't you use a real gun? Once he wakes up he'll report us."

Irica stuck the stun gun into her jacket pocket. "You know I can't kill anyone or anything. Dead or alive, once they didn't answer home base, they'd send patrols out looking for them, and they'd find their bodies. Either way we're in a bind."

It's possible I might need to start thinking before acting, and speaking.

Annu bee-lined over to Shayne. "Yeah, but it would have bought us more time. Though it's irrelevant thanks to Miss Jack-Arse in a box."

He directed her towards the cockpit.

Oh great, I'm screwed.

Irica followed him a step behind, her expression chilled the air.

Shayne's self dignity laid in jeopardy. "Oh, come on. I can walk on my own."

Annu's lower tone added another layer of fear. "What were you thinking?"

It appears I've fucked up. Though results are pending.

"For fuck's sake. If they took her, I'm stuck with you, plus so far there's no evidence other than the wormhole and ring backing up Irica's story, you two are criminals wanted by Police, and you just tossed them out of the ship. How do I know you're not going to do the same to me, or sacrifice me to some God or something?"

Annu released Shayne's arm and growled. "If I were, I'd have done it by now. At the moment I really, really, and I do mean really want to put you back in the container, but I haven't yet. So don't push it. I saved you and brought you with me, got help from the one person who could, and in return you tried getting us arrested or killed. In my book that makes you the crazy one."

Oh ouch. Good points.

"You're angry with me aren't you?"

His sigh sealed her dignity's dismal fate. "No, I'm not angry, I'm disappointed."

That sucks. I'd prefer angry. I hate how he feels like that. Why?

Shayne smoothed down her pyjama top and slunk along the wall. "Good to know. I think we're all clear now. Right-o, what's the plan then? Irica tells us the rest of the, uh, story along the way to this magical place of hers?"

Mental note: don't piss off the chocolate Hulk. Unless I find another super hero to back me up. And somehow send myself back home.

Irica followed a step behind Annu. "It's not a story, Shayne, and it's going to have to wait a while thanks to you. We need another ship, and it's going to take time we didn't have. You've just put yourself in more danger, and they know we've got a woman who says she's from another planet with us now."

Annu groaned and pushed her into the cockpit. "And we'll have to leave the main lay lines and fly manually."

I did not think this through. Maybe I should find someone else to be in charge of my thoughts. Shayne dragged her heels. "I have no idea what you're talking about."

Annu grabbed the container she'd sat on and moved it against the cockpit wall. "I mentioned earlier there's no infrastructure for anywhere 70 kilometres outside of Yebu. Which means less than desirable people live out here; hence it's called The Bad Lands. Okay?"

Shayne relented, and allowed Annu to sit her down.

Now isn't the time to ask too many questions.

She gave her best dazzling smile and battered her eye lashes. "I did us a favour then. I didn't totally fuck up."

Annu loomed, a big, dark, disappointed cloud ready to storm. "No, because we'll have criminals, real ones, to deal with and no Peace Officers around. Are you happy?"

Shayne slunk against the wall, and twirled the ring on her finger. "Ah, that remains to be seen. Minor error in judgment. Give me some time, I haven't gotten started yet."

God please protect me instead of fucking me over, or at least stop me from doing it to myself.

Chapter 13: Holy Mother of Gods
Yebu Mountains, Enki Continent, Orion

Kilometres from the main flight lay lanes, Annu directed the ship one handed, and emptied the bottle of rum with the other. Ever present of threats, adrenaline buzzed through him. Paranoia turned each light in the sky into a PO ship, and each craft which passed recognised them.

The rum warmed his guts, and offered a fake calm. At this juncture, any calm helped. He stretched and dropped the empty beside the pilot's chair.

Irica glared, ended the call and crossed her legs. "It's not a good idea to drink and fly Annu."

He held his breath and imagined the million places he'd rather be.

Hell for starters.

"Trust me when I say it's for everyone's own good. So what did Zex have to say? Flarking son of a bitch. How could he not tell me about his involvement? I suppose it explains his extra pissy attitude when I spoke to him on the island. Well, there's no way I'm going out with his sister or paying for the damage to his ship now. He can get flarked."

"I understand why you're angry but we had no choice since we wanted you to survive."

Annu rifled around beside him for another bottle, and clasped his fingers around one. "So what did he say?"

Cuddled up on the container against the wall, and away from him, Shayne's sigh scraped along Annu's facade. "I want to move closer. I said I'm sorry. It's too cold back here and I can't hear what's going on."

The peace he sought evaded him. "If you can compose yourself and be rational, you can move." One crack and the open bottle touched his lips. "Irica - what did Zex say?"

Irica followed the movement from his hand to his mouth. "He's going to meet us outside a small town–Remi in about an hour. He'll drop off a new ship and some weapons. Going this way will take longer, but like you said we won't see any Peace Officers. Oh, I wish we had more choices."

Tension gripped Annu's shoulders, being on constant alert exhausted him. "Hell, this turned into a shit fight real quick."

Shayne popped up between the chairs. "You got that right. At least you're still on your home planet."

Annu flinched, half the bottle of rum spilt onto him and the floor. "Flarking hell. Will you stop doing that? We need to put a bell around your neck."

She does have a point I should consider.

Irica leaned on the arm rest. "Oh, relax. Less won't hurt you. Going back to Shayne being the second Demi-God - it all makes perfect sense, it's brilliant really."

Annu wiped rum from his pants. "Twat waffle. Who does it make sense to, exactly?"

Irica threw an 'I'll whack you in the back of the head' glare. "Look, no one thought to look on Earth, and other planets for the other Demi-God since they're shut off. We couldn't know about her, so neither did Shamesh. We're a step ahead for the first time."

Shayne's clap rang through his head. "It explains why I haven't had any pain since I've been here and why I've always felt different."

This is nuts.

Annu bypassed a glass, and drank from the bottle neck. "I'm guessing that's not why you felt different. You don't know what real pain is. Stubbing your toe doesn't count."

"No, idiot. On Earth, I'm sick. I have an immune disease which riddles my body with pain and eats my joints. It's disappeared while I've been here. Now, I know why."

Surprise slapped him; Annu reconsidered his opinion of her.

Perhaps I judged her too quickly. Maybe her illness and the trip over caused her unbearableness.

"Oh, I'm sorry. I didn't know."

Shayne shrugged. "How would you? I'm sorry I got you guys into more trouble." She faced Irica. "This ascension thing you were talking about is that how I get home? When can we do it?"

A sucker for apologies, Irica's expression softened. "Alright, thank you. You've said sorry enough. I mentioned the Annunaki and how they taught mankind on all planets. Peace reigned through the planets, and people prospered, but as time went on, some of the Annunaki lead by Shamesh, also grew to detest humans. These Gods wanted the power and knowledge to themselves, and worshipped by all. This lead to the enslavement of mankind. Ann and Ki confronted Shamesh and objected which lead to a war against the dark Gods. Shamesh overpowered and imprisoned them within Enki Island.

"After Enki discovered what Shamesh had done, he punished the Gods, stripped their powers and sent them away. Except for Shamesh, who remains imprisoned on Orion amongst the beings he enslaved, until he's able to get his powers back."

Irica paused, her breath laboured.

Shayne perched on the container's edge. "Okay, but I don't get what this has to do with us now?"

Annu's irritation burst from his mouth and sliced the words off his tongue. "Will you please let her finish?"

I've never met anyone so irritating.

Shayne's cheek's flushed. "Okay, Jesus, sorry."

Irica slumped forward onto her elbows. "Seven days from today, the Annunaki power is available to Gods and Demi Gods, through a process - ascension. It involves an incantation in the altar room - the one Shayne appeared in on a specific day when the planets align. The incantation is contained on a scroll which is now protected in three pieces in special mounds on the island. Either two Demi Gods ascend together - you two, or a single God - Shamesh. Thereafter, the power is used in accordance with the will of the ascended ones, and they'd control the galaxies for the next thousand years. We're yet to succeed."

Annu emptied the second bottle in one gulp. "Why do I get the feeling you're not telling us something or somethings?"

Irica's grimace sent shivers up his spine. "Another wormhole won't open until then to send Shayne home."

His chest tightened, his brain pounded. "Hang on; a week from today another wormhole will open."

Irica held her hand up. "Yes. There's another thing and it's big. Sha–"

Shayne dropped the blanket and grabbed Irica's arm rest. "A fucking week. Are you kidding me? Are you telling me I can't get home for a week? Oh my God, oh my God."

Annu bounced off the seat and banged his knee. "Are you saying we're stuck with her for a week?"

Irica sucked her bottom lip. "Yes, and yes. I'm sorry, it's the only way, and in the meantime, you need to train before it's time to get the scrolls, and Shamesh is also looking for them, and enter the ascension room in time to ascend. And–"

Annu blinked repeatedly. "And? And, and. How many ands are there? It can't get worse."

Shayne paled, and stared behind him. "Huh? No. You're crazy."

Irica pushed back against the window. "Yes it can get worse, and no I'm not crazy. Shamesh is ah - integrally linked to the Peace department. Which is why being in trouble with them is so much worse than normal."

Some things made sense; others ran in the opposite direction. "Holy crap. That's why they're doing DNA tests and nosing around on the island?"

Irica sighed, and pursed her lips. "Yes, he's refined his search techniques over the centuries."

The empty bottles rolled under his seat and clanked against the wall. "Why you? How do you fit into all of this?"

"After it all happened as your mother's apprentice I became responsible for the care and preparation of their children. You're the first ward I've considered a son, and grown to love. In so many ways you're my boy, and I won't lose you."

Annu's reserve softened. "How many before me–us?"

"You're the fifteenth, and the only one to survive this long."

The pit in his stomach churned, his heart quickened. "The fifteenth?"

"I've pinned all my hopes on you both this time."

Shayne paced behind the seats. "You crazy fool. What kind of messed up place am I in?"

The room shrank; pieces of puzzle scattered in Annu's brain, and waited to fall into place. "Us, stop a God? I've fought a couple of people max, but they weren't gods. Now, all of a sudden, I'm a faced with this huge responsibility lumped on my shoulders. How am I meant to deal with all this?"

Shayne paused behind Irica's seat. "I prefer it when I thought you were crazy. This is a total nightmare. I and we cannot do this."

"A group–called the Protectors–will help ah, protect you from outside forces as best they can. They'll arrive at the other place to teach you to defend yourself. Instead of months to prepare you have days. But, you're both still alive. You'll also obtain three powers each which will assist you in obtaining the scrolls and ascending."

Annu plonked onto his seat, a chill settled around his kidneys. "Oh a whole three powers. We'll piss it in then. Did either you or my mother stop and think this might be too much information at once?"

Irica leaned forward. "I know it's a lot to take in, but this is Shamesh's last chance, if he fails, he's sent to the lowest hell. He won't wait until ascension to get you, and the scrolls. We had to do whatever it took to get this far."

Shayne slapped the back of Irica's chair. "Hold the phone–powers–as in magic type powers? That changes everything. I hope one of mine is making people do what I want them to. And making chocolate appear out of thin air."

Irica's voice cracked. "Magic suggests the power comes from nowhere, but that's not the case. You're DNA enables you to channel, as in use the power from the planets, and universe that exists around all of us."

Shayne bounced on her heels and rattled the seats. "Does this mean once I've got my powers I automatically know how to do martial arts and fight like in the movies?"

Annu faced the other way and rolled his eyes.

Ignore it, she doesn't know better. There's bigger things to focus on. Like dying and not dying.

Irica looked between Shayne and Annu. "I, ah, don't know what movies are, but unless you already know how, you'll have to learn to fight."

Shayne slumped, her arms dropped. "Oh boo, but it's still worth singing about. Because I'm happy, clap along if you feel like a room without a roof. Because I'm happy–"

Annu's blood ran cold, anxiety fought disbelief. "Oh Gods. Whatever that noise is stop right now."

Shayne's mouth dropped open. "Huh? I'm singing arsehole."

Annu's ear's ached. "Well stop." He turned back to Irica. "And if by some miracle we succeed?"

Irica cocked her head. "Ah I thought it would be obvious - you two get the power and an evil God doesn't. And you rule the galaxy."

This is what I am meant for? Everything before this moment leads up to a spectacular death.

"Being a Demi-God sucks so far. What possible advantages do we have?" His heart raced, puzzle pieces clunked into place, he gripped the steering shaft. "This is crazy. What kind of Gods would make a situation like this? Seriously? Talk about odds not in our favour."

Shayne stopped between the seats. "If it's the same God who fucks with me all the time, I'm not at all surprised. He's got an ironic and cruel sense of humour. He'd be laughing his arse off right now."

The walls closed in on Annu. "Even with an army of protectors, and a pain in the arse from Earth, he's killed fifteen others before me, most of those in pairs. We've got no hope, it's lunacy."

Irica reached towards him. "His physical age will have lessened his abilities somewhat, and he doesn't know where you are yet. I aim to get there before he does. As I've said, only a handful of Protectors, and myself know the location of my other place. I also managed to keep it off the town charters, and you'll be safe until it's time to get the scrolls and ascend. Hopefully, Gods willing."

Shayne resumed pacing, and flung her arms. "Oh fuck. Oh shit. Crap."

I've got to be smarter, and quicker than the past ones.

"Why don't I, we, get to him first? Do you know where this Shamesh is, and how to find him?"

Irica mumbled into her fist, and examined a tear in the arm rest. "Here's the other part you're going to hate, and will probably think you're being punished but, Shamesh is Griffin."

Shayne poked around Irica's chair. "Sham-man's a who?"

The contents of his guts curdled, the moisture evaporated from Annu's mouth.

Incredible information overload fried his brain and disrupted his thoughts. "Wh, wh, who did you say?"

Irica squirmed, and squeezed her eyes shut. The words tumbled from her mouth. "Annu, Shamesh is Griffin."

The warmth zapped from his body, his ribs jabbed into his lungs. "Griffin?"

Sound inside the ship disappeared, Annu's pulse jiggled. "Did you say Griffin. Griffin, Griffin. The Grand Councillor of Orion, Griffin. The one you're constantly going on about who runs the planet, and makes people disappear on a whim? That one? Griffin is Shamesh, the guy I have to kill, destroy or stop, whose main mission right now is to kill me?"

Irica huffed, and laid her head on her heads. "Yes."

The console blurred, his hand on the gear stick wobbled. "Are you sure? One hundred percent sure? How's this possible? He'd be what 18,000 years old?"

Irica sounded a million miles away, on another planet, one he won't die on. "At least that old. I'm positive, there's no doubt it's him. He used to be capable of changing his looks to reduce his aged appearance, but I don't know if he's got any other powers anymore. Most Orionion's only live a maximum of two hundred years. By the time anyone notices, they're too old, or disappear."

I'm dead. We're dead, the whole planets dead.

His body trembled, and legs wobbled.

Annu's blood pressured plummeted, his heart rate soared. "We're so flarked."

"No. I don't believe so, I've got faith in you, and the Gods. You're capable of doing this, I know you are. This is a completely different approach, he won't see it coming."

Shayne dragged the container back between the chairs and plonked on it. "Faith isn't going to help us succeed or get me home. If I've learnt anything it's faith is useless." She slapped her knees. "Well we're dead. It's been nice meeting you both. Sort of. At least my obituary will be interesting, and I won't have to pay those bills anymore. Bear might miss me though."

The rum soured in his gut, his sense of self shattered. "Well, I guess I've got nothing to lose aside from me, which doesn't seem to bother anyone."

I'm going to die, and I'm not sure even I care anymore.

Chapter 14: Alien Ant Farm
Yebu Mountains, Enki continent, Orion

In mere hours, Shayne travelled through a worm hole, landed on another planet, discovered her true identity, and gotten in trouble with the local police. Not since an acid trip at University had she waded in such deep shit.

Now I'm an intergalactic fuck up. That's real talent.

In a clearing between trees in buck-fuck somewhere, Shayne rested her back against a tree trunk and twirled the ring on her finger. It slipped off onto the dirt; she retrieved it and pulled the map from her pocket. Moonlight gave it a mystical appearance in contrast to their current location.

Shadows of trees grew arms and reached out to grab her; unseen wildlife shrieked and screeched, moving closer to where Shayne sat. At irregular times a black shape flashed through, around, and above the trees before it disappeared.

I don't even want to imagine what's making those noises or what that is. Think about something else.

Shayne shook off the creeps and smoothed over the map, tingles ran up her arm. "Maybe I'll wake up and this is all a crazy dream. If it is, I suck at making stuff up. I really gave myself a hard time and I could have picked a much better leading man than fuckface. One who actually liked me, and I didn't disappoint."

There it goes that thing again, up, down, and sideways. It better not come here.

"Hey what's the black thing in the trees over there?"

Annu unpacked crates from Irica's ship and stacked them behind him. Sweat beaded across his forehead, his muscles bulged. "What thing?"

A tickle rippled down her back and across her groin. *Fuck off hormones. I don't need you back in my life.*

Shayne pointed in the thing's direction. "Behind you in the trees, it flies between them and stuff."

Annu inhaled and followed her line of sight.

A flock of black birds exploded from the tree tops and invaded the air.

Annu returned to packing.

Dumb arse. "Oh. Ah, okay. But it looked different to that."

Irica rifled through the crates and put what she took out into a duffle bag. Her hard work and efforts tired Shayne.

Moving on.

Shayne crossed her legs. "So Irica, the ring and Annu's band have to stay on until after ascension right? How long do we actually have before we have to get the scrolls and ascensdio? Can we get them earlier and wait? Oh and you didn't say what the map's are for."

Irica brushed hair off her face and dirt from her hands. "It's ascension and really? Now? You have the worst timing Shayne."

Map in hand, Shayne pushed off the trunk, and jogged over to Irica. "Well it's another cross you can put against my name. I might forget to ask another time."

Annu stopped, and in a few steps joined them. "I admit I'd like know too. With everything else going on and what might happen next, I don't want to waste an opportunity"

Irica's tired demeanour rubbed off, Shayne stifled a yawn.

Irica leaned against the stack of containers. "Alright, now's as good a time as any." She stared into space. "The wormholes opening were the first signs the process has begun, a pre-warning the ascension arrives in seven days. And, after that time, before the scrolls become available, a parade of comets fills the sky. You then have an hour to obtain the scrolls, half an hour to make it to the ascension room, and chant the incantation before the opportunity disappears for another thousand years."

Shayne stomped her foot, dirt covered her pant leg. "Oh, my God. I'm sorry I asked. Why is it all so fucking complicated? That's not long. What about the map? Do we have to do a special fucking dance to make that work too?"

Irica held her breath. "For all the reasons I've mentioned, it can't be easy. The map shows you where the scroll mounds are located on the island. Shayne, hold your half up, Annu, take out your half and hold it next to Shayne's."

Annu removed it from his pocket, and placed is beside Shayne's piece. Gold light started at the top where they met and sealed a line down the middle.

The whole map shone and hummed, pins and needles ran down Shayne's arm. "Oh wow."

Annu reefed it from her hands, and folded it in half. "I better hold onto it. You can't even keep your ring on."

Shayne stuck out her tongue.

No one thinks I'm capable of doing any-fucking-thing. One day I'm going to show them. Maybe. But not today.

"Whatever. Fine you look after it. That way if you lose it, it's your fault not mine."

His shrug intensified the atmosphere; Annu slipped the map back in his pocket. "Done."

Shayne crossed and uncrossed her arms–and mind. "While we're going, I've been thinking and as I'm part of this, a big part, and blah, blah, blah. I've got a suggestion about the whole Shamman situation."

Irica rubbed her eyes. "Oh alright. What can it hurt? Let's hear it."

Annu raised an eyebrow; a smirk broached the corner of his mouth. "I wondered why you looked constipated over there."

Arsehole, but at least it's some progress. Maybe the rest of my time here won't suck as much.

"Well it's been a really long time since the last ascension thing, has anyone considered actually talking to this Sham-man person? Instead of just attacking him, perhaps we go and speak to him about it. You don't know, maybe after all this time he's gotten over it, and he doesn't want to kill and maim anymore. You did say he's as old as fuck."

Annu stumbled into the container's side, and shook his head. "Ah, it's Shamesh. Interesting suggestion. Perhaps ah, Irica can knit him a blanket? We'll send it over with a cake. If we ice it, he might kill us quicker or give us afternoon tea. Seriously, leave the important stuff to me; you go back to the tree trunk, please."

Shayne stuck her middle finger up. "Ah, how's 'get fucked' sound Mr. King Dingaling wannabe."

A vein on his forehead bulged, Annu's left eye twitched, his fingers wrapped around a nearby branch. "You speak the same language as me, and yet I can't understand even half of what you say. Now go away until you've got something worth listening to."

Shayne's bladder tingled.

Remember how I wasn't going to piss off and disappoint the chocolate hulk? I blew that out of the water.

"Okay, fine, I'm going back to the tree."

She chose a grassed spot and shuffled back against the trunk.

The black thing weaved between trees, paused, and flashed a light around.

Birds don't have lights on Earth- maybe they do here?

Shayne raised onto her knees, and pointed. "Hey Annu, Irica, what's–."

Annu's stern expression with his hand gripped onto a branch glued her mouth shut, and dumped her butt on the ground.

I've changed my mind, being here's still going to suck. I can't wait to fucking get home and never see those two again. When I get some powers then they'll know whose boss. Aresholes. Thank God they need me; I don't know what would happen to me other.

The crunch of branches behind the tree froze Shayne's train of thought, and skipped her heart.

Body odour and the stench of testosterone preceded two men at least seven plus feet tall into the clearing. Both resembled inbred killer men from a number of horror movies; the one on the left missed his front teeth and an eye, the fat other lacked an ear, and a scar trailed from his brow to his chin.

Shayne scrambled onto her feet and away from the tree.

Oh shit.

The man with one eye crept towards her. "I've never seen one of you before but you'll fetch a good price."

The other–the fat fuck–cracked his neck. "What is it, Jude?"

One eyed Jude lunged at Shayne's shoulder. "Looks like a little white version of us to me, Mel."

Pee trickled down her leg and rewet her pyjama pants. "Don't touch me." Her voice cracked. "Help. Annu."

What if he hates me too much to help me? Fuck. Fuck. Fuck.

Annu frowned and glanced in her direction. "What –"

At sight of the two men, Annu dropped the contents of his arms.

Irica backed up against the containers, and fumbled in her pocket.

Annu jogged over towards them, his hands shook. "Jude, let her go."

One-eyed Jude pulled Shayne onto her feet by the shoulder.

Don't touch me you creep.

He tightened his grip, her skin pinched between his fingers. "Annu, it's been a long time since I've seen you in these parts. I thought you'd given up this kind of life." One-Eyed Jude shook Shayne, her shoulder tore. "Does this belong to you then?"

A combination of fear and anger unglued her mouth; she struggled against his hold on her. "I'm not a this. Let me go."

Annu's feral expression terrified even her. "Now's not the time for feisty, Shayne. Yes Jude, Unfortunately she is with me."

The hand on Shayne's shoulder drifted down her back, nausea bubbled in her guts.

Please don't let them take me.

One Eye tranced a finger along her waist. "I believe you still owe me for the job we helped you with a few years ago."

Annu stepped closer to One Eye, Fat Fuck Mel blocked his way.

Shayne's heart fluttered, her chest heaved.

Oh crap. It's two against one.

A gleam in Annu's eye offered hope. "I paid what you were owed you greedy bastard."

Jude maintained one-eye contact with Shayne. "Not for losing my eye you didn't."

Shayne shrunk into herself, and wrapped her arms across her chest. She swallowed a sixty forty spew burp and blinked away tears.

Fat Fuck Mel jabbed Annu in the gut. "What's it worth to you?

One Eye pulled Shayne around and held her to his front. "From the look on your face, I think it's worth a lot." He grabbed a chunk of her hair and yanked.

Pain rippled through her skull, Shayne rubbed the sore spot, and kicked him in the leg. "You fucking arsehole."

One-Eye flicked her off, and yanked harder. "Maybe I should take the woman over there too and we'd be about square. What do you say?"

Sweat teemed down Shayne's chest, fear cloaked her mind.

The black thing whizzed across the open area, and around the ships. No one appeared to notice it aside from her.

Now isn't the time to bring it up.

Annu growled; the air thickened. "I say this is your last warning, or you'll find out exactly what they are worth to me. And nobody likes it when I'm angry, which you're probably too stupid to recall is why you lost the eye to start with."

Images of disconnected eyeballs tangled around thoughts of her impending death.

If I wasn't such a selfish cow - Annu might have stopped them by now.

One Eye removed a knife from his side and rested the tip against Shayne's throat. She held her breath. "Ah–"

The blade shone in the moonlight, a trickle of blood ran down its length.

Annu lunged at One Eye; Fat Fuck stopped him with a weapon aimed Annu's face. "Uha. This time it's on our terms."

I'm sorry for all the mean things I've said about you God, and I realise this is a last minute dash for salvation but please fucking save me–us.

Chapter 15: Crap on a Cracker
Yebu Mountains, Enki Continent, Orion

The fear in Shayne's eyes tore him apart, the gun at Annu's head provided clarity but no solutions. "You know, since we've met, my life's taken some shitty turns."

Shayne quivered; her fragility never more evident than now. "Well don't blame me. The feeling's mutual."

I must protect her, make her safe. She's not capable of getting through this on her own.

Jude's arm tightened around Shayne's chest; Annu's heart pounded. Testosterone clouded his judgment, tension gripped him.

I didn't even hear them coming. Who knows what they'll do to her. Okay. I need an idea or plan—something–anything quick. Flarking hell. Try talking our way out of it first.

Annu raised his hands with Shayne in sight. "Take it easy, Jude, and don't be foolish. Don't lose your head. Think about this, it's idiotic."

Jude dragged the knife down Shayne's cheek; her shriek elevated Annu's pulse.

Next plan, there's only a few inches between me and Mel. If I lunge for the gun it might go off by accident. But if I knock it out of the way first and shove him into Jude, I should get to Shayne.

The patch over Jude's missing eye shifted, and revealed a deep black hole, Annu's gut churned.

Jude sneered and replaced the patch. "On the contrary my friend, I think this is the smartest thing I've ever done."

Irica came around from behind Annu and aimed a gun at Mel's head. "Let her go." The grip trembled, her words unsteady. "Put down your weapons now or I'll shoot you."

Jude and Mel glanced in Irica's direction, refocused on Annu, and dismissed Irica's threat.

Fury roared through him; Jude's subsequent scoff infuriated Annu.

Do it, don't wait.

Annu kicked Mel in the shins; Mel bent over and grabbed his sore leg.

A slap across the wrist from Annu ejected the gun from Mel's hand.

He grabbed Mel around the middle, used him as a battering ram and pushed him into Jude.

The sudden movement of Jude's arms caused the knife to slice the side of Shayne's throat. Instead of screaming, she winced and shoved her elbow into Jude's ribs.

Maybe there's more to you than first appeared.

Jude steadied himself and clipped Shayne up the back of the head.

Shayne stumbled backwards away from Jude, her eyes glazed, blood trickled down her arm.

Annu held his breath.

Hang in there, Shayne. I'll fix this somehow.

Cortisol pumped through his veins, Annu ran at Jude, and slammed his shoulder into the man's guts.

I'm going to flarking kill you.

Annu slammed Jude's back into a tree trunk and raised his fist.

A fist came from nowhere directed at Annu's head, he ducked. Mel punched the tree and wailed.

Irica continued to wave the gun in all directions. "I, ah, Annu stop moving."

Annu hooked a finger in the side of Mel's mouth and pulled. "Bit flarking hard." He turned Mel in a circle, and struck his elbow into the man's neck.

Jude lumped on Annu's back.

The air whooshed out of Annu's lungs. *What the?* He pushed him off; Jude fell back first onto the dirt and probed for the knife.

Annu's heart pounded, his chest ached, he lunged at Jude and kissed the ground. Annu flipped around onto his butt. "Flark it."

A sneer hardened Jude's features; the knife glimmered in Jude's hand. Jude jabbed it at Annu.

Annu pushed off the dirt, slapped Jude across the face and another at the hand holding the knife. It flew in the opposite direction and disappeared in shrubs.

Jude swayed side to side; Annu kneed the man in the nose—blood splattered Annu's pants.

In Annu's periphery, Mel hobbled towards him.

Will you just flarking go away?

Annu spun around, strode a few steps and collided with Mel halfway. Bad breath whooshed from Mel's lungs into Annu's face.

Zip, zip.

Annu and Mel froze mid fray, zip, zip.

Laser beams skimmed Annu's back, and hit the tree behind. "Flarking hell, Irica. Watch it."

Irica shrugged, the gun wavered. "Sorry. I aimed for them."

Mel utilised the distraction, and walloped Annu in the ribs with a thick branch. Annu landed flat on his back, with Mel on top of him.

Annu shoved Mel off his chest, and raised his knee into Mel's groin. One push and Mel tumbled sideways.

Now where's flarking Jude?

With a hand on her throat, Shayne hobbled beside Irica and took the gun from her.

Jude appeared and swung wild punches at Annu.

Two handed, Shayne swept the gun side to side "You fucking arseholes, leave him alone" and fired.

Zing. Zing.

The blast grazed the back of Annu head, the stench of burnt hair forced him to jolt forward. He head butted Jude, the crunch of broken teeth and bone rang through his ears. Pain bored from the top of his skull, down and along his jaw.

Annu's teeth rattled, he spat blood on the dirt.

This is going to flarking end now.

He whirled around with three fingers aimed at Jude's good eye. Jab, jab; Annu stopped short of repeating the same move as last time.

Jude's scream sent shivers up Annu's spine. Jude dropped onto his knees, a hand over his eye.

Zing, zing.

Heat and pain tore through Annu's bicep; a laser sized hole ran straight through.

Shayne dropped the gun, and threw her hands in the air. "I'm so fucking sorry. Please don't kill me."

Annu clutched the wound, his blood pressure lowered. "Are you kidding me?"

Mel hooked Annu around the throat with his arm.

Annu's breath caught in his chest, his Adam's apple became a razor and dragged down his larynx.

He forgot about the laser shot, held his throat and fought the urge to fall. Annu's legs went from under him, he stumbled forward, Mel wobbled on his left.

Irica's warning arrived too late. "Watch out. Oh."

Annu shoved aside the pain, turned on his heel and punched Jude. "You flarking cock sucking, donkey flarking twatt."

Annu's internal temperature soared, sweat beaded across his forehead. A hot rush ran from the top of his head and down his body.

He grabbed Mel's sleeve, pulled the man closer, and punched him in the ear.

Mel stumbled over his feet and tripped forward.

One handed and half eyed, Jude caught him before he fell to the ground and tugged on Mel's sleeve. "Come on, let's get out of here."

Mel dribbled spit and blood. "No flarking way. Let me go."

Jude whispered in Mel's ear.

Mel's demeanour flipped from angry to panicked, his eyes scanned the treed area behind them.

Annu's head thudded in time with his heart beat. "What's going on?"

"You'll find out soon enough." Blood and goop wept from Jude's good eye. "This isn't over. Next time we see each other you're done for."

Jude and Mel skulked away, and disappeared into the woods.

Stunned, Annu's lungs burned, he gulped in air. "Yeah you better get the flark out of here."

Someone tapped Annu on the shoulder, fists raised, he whirled around. "I thought you–"

Zex jumped back, a smirk on his face. "Take it easy it's me. I see you're still making friends everywhere you go."

Annu dropped his arms, and rested against a tree trunk. He wiped blood of his cheek. "Yeah, well smart arse I showed them."

Shayne and Irica rushed to Annu's side.

Shayne folded her hands in front. "I'm so fucking sorry I shot you."

Irica twisted her shirt. "I'm sorry she shot you too. Are you alright? Who were those men?"

Zex cocked his head and stared at Shayne. "Who did what? Oh you're the, ah, Earthling Irica's talking about. The second Demi-God. I'm Zex. Sounds like you could all do with some lessons."

Shayne extended her hand out; it disappeared inside Zex's. "I'm Shayne. I'll try not to shoot you too."

Zex focused on something, he paused mid-handshake. He leaned forward and paled. "Ah, Annu, you didn't happen to notice the PO Probe in the trees over there while you were messing around?"

Any adrenaline and energy left from the fight disappeared. "The flarking what?"

Annu peered around the tree trunk, the probe flashed along the closest tree line; its blue light scanned the area.

Panic propelled Annu off the trunk, he froze mid stride.

Shayne followed his line of sight and pointed at the drone. "Oh that's the thing I kept seeing earlier that you two weren't interested in hearing about."

His heart palpitated, his butt hole constricted.

It might pay to start listening to her from time to time.

"We've got to go right now and in the new ship."

Irica's thrust a hand over her mouth. "Oh dear."

Annu scooped up Shayne and put her over-his shoulder. Zex followed close to his heels.

She wriggled and bounced in his arms. "What are you doing? Put me down."

He tightened his hold and stopped her bouncing. "No can do. Have to be quick. Irica stay close to me."

Irica clutched her chest and dawdled. "Yes, of course. This hasn't gone well so far has it?"

Shayne hit his back. "Why are we rushing now?"

Annu readjusted her position. "There's a PO drone here which has been recording us and reporting back to Head Quarters the entire time we've been here. Any time now they'll find us. Shit flark. I look forward to them not being a problem."

Shayne kicked her legs and his ribs ached. "That's not a reason to carry me. Put me down."

Annu stopped in the middle of the open area and placed Shayne on her feet.

He turned to Zex, daylight diminished. "Where's your ship?"

Zex pointed. "Over there. I'll take Irica's and it might distract or divert them for a while."

The whirr of a PFD in the distance shot fresh fear into Annu. "Yeah right. I don't like our chances but good idea."

A siren wailed and quickened Annu's pace.

Shayne and Irica jogged beside him towards Zex's ship.

Annu reached the ramp; his wounds had almost healed, yet nerves formed a noose around his neck. The sirens grew louder, closer, and insistent. The rope tightened, his chest ached.

They want us bad to come out here. Unless we think of something spectacular - this might all end before it's began.

Shayne stepped onto the ramp, smoothed over her ring finger, and stopped. "Oh shit."

She turned around and hurried back down the ramp.

Annu's pulse raced, disbelief coveted him. "What are you doing?"

Shayne sucked on her bottom lip. "I've lost the ring. I'm sorry; I've got to get it back. It must be where we all were."

Chapter 16: Not in Kansas
Yebu Mountains, Enki continent, Orion

Search lights broke through the outer forest, a siren deafened the ambient sounds. Shayne's heart skipped, for the twentieth time, she sifted through the dirt.

Please, please, please be here.

Annu crawled on his hands and knees, sweeping in the opposite direction. "Have you found it yet?"

Irritation crept up her back, and settled on her nape. "Have I said I've found it?"

His clipped tone distracted her. "I might have missed it. Flark, I can't believe you flarked us over again. You're irresponsible."

Yeah, yeah. Like I haven't heard that before.

The ship hovered beside them; the craft's lights aided their search.

Another light from behind caught the corner of the ship and swept across the area.

Annu dropped onto the dirt, Shayne slipped next to him.

Behind the ship's pilot side window, Irica waved her arms in the air and mouthed something unintelligible.

On her stomach, Shayne combed in circles faster.

Come on, where are you?

Annu crawled over and grabbed her arm. "That's it. If we don't leave now we're done for."

Rock, dirt, another rock and more dirt. No ring. Fuck.

Panic trickled down her back; her stomach churned. "I can't leave it here, you heard Irica. What if it was your bracelet or the locket around your neck?"

Annu stroked the locket, urgency dripped from his words. "I know what you're saying, but if we get caught there's no point having the ring or the band."

Tears stung Shayne's eyes and ran down her cheeks. "Damn-it. Just one more try. Please?"

How it is possible I fuck up everything? I'm going to die here and it will be my fault.

Annu clicked his tongue, and dug around. "Argh. Alright."

Okay, please God help me out here.

Shayne held her breath, turned to the left and raked the dirt towards her. Almost to her knee, she hooked something solid around her finger tip. Shayne blew the dirt off her hand, slipped the ring on and held it in place. "Got it."

Annu bounced off the ground. "Thank flark. As soon as I can, I'll glue it to your damned finger."

Shayne dismissed a kick to his shins. "That's a little –"

The entire ship lit up from behind, light invaded the area.

Shayne's blood ran cold, her stomach churned. "Oh shit."

The sirens intensified, and increased in pitch the closer they got.

Shayne shuffled left and right, her brain in a tizz. "Crap, shit. What do we do?"

Annu shook himself and cupped her elbow. "Move. Let's get the flark out of here."

He guided Shayne around the side, up the ramp and into the ship.

Every crazy event since she'd arrived on Orion replayed in her mind.

It's too bat shit nuts even for a midday movie.

The dried blood on her neck and healed knife wound solidified Irica's Demi-God declarations in Shayne's mind.

The door whooshed closed; Annu disappeared through a door at the end of the cargo hold.

Shayne stood beside the back windows and clutched her chest. Adrenaline coursed along her veins, too much energy, and nowhere to go.

Her skin crawled, her mouth watered.

I can't remember the last time I dealt with any sort of trauma not stoned. Possibly primary school. Which before this were like when I'd run out of chocolate or my hip hurt. I would kill for a fucking smoke right now. Or my couch, or even a fuckstick debt collector.

A massive ship blazoned with Peace Office insignia and an array of weapons positioned from front to rear burst through a clearing several metres behind.

The PO's search lights illuminated the entire forest and barrelled Shayne with fear. "Oh this won't be good."

Their ship shunted forward and took off at high speed.

Shayne lost her feet and banged into a cupboard, pain shot across her hip. A sharp edge ripped the bottom of her pyjama top. "Fuck it."

The top half of a hazy man appeared before Shayne; her pulse soared. "What the fucking hell? Do I see ghosts now?"

The man's mouth moved but no sound came out. He pointed at her. A computerised voice injected fear into Shayne and demanded attention.

"This is the Yebu Peace Department. You're ordered to land immediately and prepare for boarding. If you do not comply we are authorised to fire."

Their ship flew faster; the figure disappeared.

Shayne steadied herself and walked with her hands on the wall towards the cockpit. "Oh fuck. Oh fuck. Everything about this situation is fucked."

"Stop and land immediately. This is your last warning. I repeat, this is your last warning."

Can someone remind me firstly why I got out of bed this morning, and second, why I thought I should find out why my house went mental?

Her foot slipped on something, Shayne slid to a stop. "That day when I found the map and the ring, I should have torn it to pieces and burnt both. Then gotten smashed as an avocado in guacamole and spread over the couch. All this would have gone on without me, and I'd be none the wiser. Literally."

The hazy figure reappeared and waved. "Ashera–"

The weapons on the roof of the PO Ship lowered and aimed at the ship. "We're in pursuit and will fire at will."

The ghost man frowned, his gestures urgent. "Please —"

"Now's not really a good time. Come back later. Like much later." Shayne exited the cargo hold and followed the wall along a partly lit hallway. "When the ship goes down you better be ready, when the ship goes down you're gonna be fucked."

Crack, crunch, snap. Something scraped along the roof outside.

The ship rocked side to side and slammed Shayne into the opposite wall. "For fuck's sake."

Shayne fell to her knees and crawled the rest of the way into the cockpit. A seat waited behind Annu if Shayne could reach it.

Boom. Boom.

The steering stick wobbled, Annu struggled maintaining his grip. "Flark. Irica turn all the lights off."

Irica's voice cracked. "Is that a good idea? They'll see us with their lights anyway."

The voice of doom returned. "Land or we'll fire again."

Annu licked his lips. "Trust me, they mean it. If I get away from them somehow and find a place to hide it's a shot I'm going to take."

The cockpit darkened, Shayne covered her head, and the ship rattled and shook.

Boom, boom, boom.

Smoke and the smell of burnt metal wafted from the cargo hold into the cockpit.

That's at will. Good to know.

The engine ground instead of whirred. It dipped, and the ship slowed.

Shayne grabbed the back of the seat and pulled herself onto it. "How far away is your other place Irica? Are we going to make it?"

"I'm praying so." Irica sorted around in a box next to her seat and pulled out two green items. She thrust one at Shayne. "It's two hours flight or a day's walk. Here take this in case you need it."

Shayne clasped her fingers around the grip and hovered over the trigger. "Ah it's a gun. What am I meant to shoot? No way I'm shooting at them and making it worse."

Annu glanced over and removed the weapon from Shayne's hand. "I agree especially after you shot me instead of the bad guys."

Shayne rolled her eyes. "I said sorry, and I didn't mean it. Besides it healed."

Sweat poured down his cheeks, the shaft vibrated. "Not–the–point."

The rear of the ship exploded, parts, metal, and debris blasted down the hallway and into the cockpit.

An object hit Shayne from behind, flung her into the cockpit and against the console. Her ribs crunched, a band of agony wrapped around her torso.

Red lights flashed, alarms screeched, oxygen masks fell from the ceiling.

Annu wrestled with the shaft, the ship's nose dipped.

He released his grip, and held onto Shayne.

With Shayne in his grasp, Annu rose from the seat and motioned to an emergency hatch in the middle of the floor. "It's going to be better if we jump before we crash. More chance of survival."

A full-fledged panic attack arrived, the room shrank, Shayne's mind frazzled. "Better for whom? What about Irica she won't heal?"

"I'll protect her."

And I'm back looking after myself again. Fuck.

Chapter 17: Defend Thyself
Enki Township, Enki Continent, Orion

Aside from minor incidents I've avoided the Peace Office for five-hundred odd years and in twenty-four hours, they've nearly killed me three times.

Annu's guts flipped between nauseous and ulcerated, fear's noose hoisted him high and kicked the chair away.

Irica trembled and gripped the back of Annu's shirt; Shayne hooked her arm under his.

Annu wedged the map deep in his pocket and cracked open the emergency hatch. Hazardous objects below flashed by, his heart fluttered. "This isn't going to be an easy trip. We've got to wait until the ship drifts closer to the ground and it's not so far down."

Shayne tugged his sleeve; stress reversed her age and became more child-like. "Then let's not do it. Isn't there parachutes or something?"

Annu's brain fuzzed, he slowed his breaths. "I know what you're talking about for once, but there's too many trees and it's not far enough distance down for it to open."

Shayne squirmed and edged back from the hatch, tears glistened in her eyes. "Great, so we're going to die or get totally fucked up. I don't like this Demi-God shit at all."

Irica patted Shayne's shoulder. "I don't blame you but there's no choice."

They're both right and I've got to take charge.

The longer they waited–Annu's brain hurt, his skull tightened. "Shayne, when we get to the right spot, I'll lower you down as far as I can first, Irica you hang onto me and we'll drop down after."

A blast of cold air swallowed the women's replies and blew the three of them away from the hatch.

Irica head butted his shoulder blade, the impact flung sideways. Annu grasped and missed, she slammed into the back of the seat.

Shayne's shriek diverted Annu's attention behind him.

Shayne tripped over her feet, thrust forward and fell face first into the open hole. "Fuck–"

Annu grabbed a leg, her top half disappeared, she dangled in between–only he stopped her probable death. "Shit, flark, shit. Try not to move."

Her scream sent shivers up his spine, he pulled towards him. Shayne's pants dragged down and revealed her butt, his cheeks flushed.

Not bad considering.

Annu pushed them up and re-covered her rear end; Shayne dropped another inch, his hand slipped to beneath her knee.

Pay attention dickhead.

Annu shook, and refocused. "Shit."

The wind whipped Shayne–a human pendulum back and forth. Annu's fear caught in his throat.

Irica appeared at his side, dropped to the floor and caught Shayne's other leg. "Hang on, we've got you."

Fear steeped Shayne's words. "There's—nothing–to fucking–hang on to. Even if you really hate me please don't—let—me–go."

Annu swallowed bile, nodded at Irica and pulled towards them.

The wind created resistance, and turned a hundred pound woman into a stone monument. Each centimetre they succeeded, the wind dragged her back down.

Shayne kicks in self preservation loosened his grip. "I don't–want to die."

Panic burned a line up his throat.

Who'd have thought at the start of the day I'd be saving her arse and not killing it.

"I don't want–I mean need you to die either."

Zing. Zing. Zing.

Lasers blew holes into the pilot's side wall, air and smoke filled the cockpit, the ambient temperature plummeted.

Irica lost her grip on Shayne and fell onto her butt. "Oh–gods help me."

Annu's hold wavered, Shayne dropped, his hand slipped down her leg and stopped at the ankle. Her slip on shoes fell onto the ground before him and slapped him with fear.

He pushed them aside, tightened his fingers around her foot and yanked. "Come on."

Irica scrambled towards the hole at Shayne, and failed to make and maintain contact. "I can't reach her."

Zing, zing, boom.

The ship shuddered and flung him sideways into the wall. Irica flew into the cockpit and smashed into the console.

Shayne plummeted into darkness, her screams followed her descent.

Annu's guts roiled. "Shayne –flark. No."

It's my fault I couldn't keep hold of her. Given her size there's every chance the fall killed her.

He crawled to the hatch's edge and peered over.

I should have pulled her in faster, held her tighter. Without her we've lost our chance. I'm sorry Shayne.

Crack, crack, crack.

An explosion blasted the section behind the cockpit, the ship wobbled, saliva pooled in his mouth.

If I don't get Irica and I out of here, we're dead too.

Annu crawled backwards and into the cockpit.

Irica slumped across the passenger seat, blood smeared across her face. He used the seat for leverage and pulled her to him, her head lolled.

With Irica under his arm Annu dragged them both to the hatch.

The cockpit separated from the rest of the ship, dipped and hurtled towards the ground.

Annu crashed into the wall, Irica groaned. He steadied himself and lifted Irica back under his arm. Annu placed her on the ground and sat. Their legs dangled through the hatch into the unknown below.

Unable to reconcile recent events, Annu's mind fractured. "On the upside it's the perfect time to jump."

Annu filled his lungs and held the breath, Irica's head moved with his chest.

He bear hugged Irica to his front, slipped over the edge and into the night. The ship hurtled by above them, objects from inside and wreckage showered Annu's fall. The odd, unseen thing, scratched, scraped or walloped into him.

After the first metre bushes, branches, sticks and shrubbery assaulted them from every direction. A large branch snagged the corner of Annu's jacket; they stopped falling, and rocked side to side.

The ground loomed an unknown distance below, Annu dangled at its mercy, expectant–ready for it to break and end their misery.

Irica roused and struggled. "What, what happened? Where are we?"

The branch creaked; a small crack behind him tightened his chest. "Oh, well not much. Remember, we got shot down, lost Shayne and had to jump from the ship before it crashed."

Irica clung to his jacket. "Oh Gods. Shayne," A higher branch broke and fell past them, she followed its path and wrapped her legs around his, "Are we, are we stuck in a tree?"

Crack, they dropped, Annu grabbed a thicker branch nearby. "Yep. Bet you didn't see that coming when you had that bad feeling the other day."

Irica clicked her tongue. "Smart aleck. We've got to find Shayne."

The branch holding them broke and spun them around to face the tree trunk.

Annu jumped onto a lower branch and balanced Irica beside him. "I think we've got more immediate problems than finding her."

Creak, creak, creak.

A gust of wind pushed them, the jacket tore and freed from the tree. Irica slipped between his arms, Annu plummeted towards the ground.

Chapter 18: Painful Regret
Yebu Mountains, Enki Continent, Orion

On the way down Shayne realised death may not be the worst thing to happen a person. Sometimes it's the best thing, a relief of sorts. Like her current problem–plummeting towards unseen danger, terrible things do occur without you dying.

What if I live and I break every bone in my body? Or worse, I damage my brain?

Several rounds of vomit preceded Shayne; her throat hurt from screaming, her bladder frozen with fear. All manner of shrubbery combined and stuck in Shayne's hair; cuts and scratches covered available flesh. When one healed, something else battered her and left its mark.

I can't believe those mother fucker's dropped me. They really dropped me. Bastards probably meant it. Oh no, Annu won't lose the map, he just fucking loses me instead. Thanks to them, I'm going to fucking die. When I see them next they're fucked.

Wind ripped Shayne's dressing gown off and exposed more bare skin. "Please someone, anyone, I don't want to die like this. Well any way of dying won't be good. Even though I'm totally unworthy please save me. Again."

Thank God Annu's got the map. Not that it will do him much good without me. Arseholes. My life fucking sucks. Maybe it's a good thing it's about to end?

A hazy figure's upper half appeared right way up at Shayne's side and reached for her. "You're –Ash I'm fath…"

The figure followed, without sound. Whack, a canopy of flowers disguised thick underbrush; it shredded her arms and chest.

A bug flew up her nose; she spat it out. "Where were you on that one? This isn't the time. You've got the wrong person. Get help."

An explosion erupted in the approximate location Zex's ship headed and deafened other noise.

Shayne suppressed a crazed laugh in favour of denial. A combination of grief and disbelief muddied her thoughts. "Oh fuck. There goes my ride."

Shock waves rippled the air and turned her sideways. Shayne spun, her guts dropped, the figure disappeared. She grabbed at passing branches ripping the flesh from her hands and nothing more. Shayne flapped her arms and attempted to gain some control.

The rocky ground below approached. Shayne placed a hand on her chest. "Oh Gods and ghost guy please fucking help me. If I'm meant to be here and do this shit prove it and save me."

Moonlight glimmered across the ring and diverted her attention. A stick jammed between it and her finger prevented it coming off. Shayne stroked the surface; the ring warmed, a buzz overtook fear, her skin tingled. She stopped spinning and her fall slowed.

A couple of metres lower, and above the rocks, Shayne halted and hovered. "Oh thank you ring, God, and ghost guy."

Shayne uncurled her legs and expected to drift to ground level, but didn't go any further down. "What the fuck?" She jumped and stayed in the same spot. "Maybe they don't want me to hurt myself on the rocks? Okay good idea."

Shayne picked sticks from her hair, smoothed down the bird's nests and air walked above the rocks to a flat area between woods.

I remember we flew over one like this; maybe, it looks like all the others.

Dawn broke over the landscape and removed the eerie aspects of the woods. Shayne squatted, stepped, leapt, and somersaulted–no matter what, she stayed put.

The stick under the ring likewise refused to budge. "Of course my first power is a pain in the arse and not helpful at all. Jesus fucking Christ. And yes, God, I said it, but don't smite me for it. I take it this is another of your ironic tests?"

Stuck, helpless and exhausted Shayne plonked her butt onto the invisible line. "With no sense of direction whatsoever plus no idea where I am, what the hell am I meant to do?"

Three quarters of ghost guy re-formed beside her, this time sharp enough to define features similar to her own.

He gasped, frustration emphasised each arm movement. "I'm trying–to tell you–you're true name is Ashera and I'm your father Ki."

I'm such a fucking idiot.

Shayne slapped her cheeks and perched on her knees. "Oh shit. Dude, I mean dad? I'm so sorry."

Emotion overwhelmed her; she tried to hugged him and went right through.

His voice reminded her of warm chocolate, his skin salted caramel. "It's alright child. Until, I'm not strong enough to fully for–"

Ki flickered, his bottom half disappeared.

Tears stung her eyes, Shayne's heart swelled. "No don't go yet. Please. Everything is all messed up. Annu and Irica might be dead, we're the worst choice for this sort of thing, and I don't know where they are if they are alive or where I am or where I'm meant to go."

Half-Ghost Dad's face blew away with the wind. "Head in the crash's direction and –"

A panic avalanche rumbled. "And what? Don't stop. How do I get down?"

Ki's words drifted. "Have faith and concentrate."

Shayne rubbed grit from her eyes, when she reopened them, he'd gone. "Easier said than done."

She poked the space he'd left. "Of all the screwy times, I finally met my father."

A snake large enough to swallow her and twenty other people whole slithered underneath Shayne. Its hiss shivered her spine, it skimmed her butt, and she held her breath and curled her legs. Each centimetre it slid by tortured Shayne, she froze and waited for the snake to pass.

A freakout sped past the panic and tested her sanity.

Alright, if life's shown me anything it's that losing my shit changes nothing. This time, I'm going to be logical and calm, see where that gets me. Which is easy to think now that mother fucker's gone. Argh.

Eyes closed, Shayne stroked the ring and imagined being on the ground. She lowered a centimetre at a time until her feet touched dirt. "So far so good. Maybe this experience can change lifelong habits."

The black smoke in the sky reminded her of what she lacked. "God damned I want a joint."

Shayne sucked on her lip and followed the smoke through the trees. Leaves and sticks crunched under her feet, she stepped over clumps of something indefinable and smelly. With her leg raised a small creature scampered in front of her and ran into nearby bushes.

Shayne leapt out of the way, her screams echoed around the woods. A bunch of bats burst from the tree tops and screeched their way in the opposite direction. Her heart skipped, her chest ached, and a trickle of pee ran down her leg.

The buzz returned and calmed her, Shayne raised up and down in succession from the ground.

Whatever, at least it saves my legs and feet walking. Okay now to move forwards.

Shayne visualized the path she'd walk, and after a jolt, levitated along it. Shrieks terrified her; she blocked her ears and refused to imagine what made the noises.

Please don't eat me.

A light broke through trees ahead and lit up the area. The familiar sound of a PFD engine palpitated her heart, the buzz dissipated.

Shayne ducked down, hid behind a tree and peeked around the trunk. "Whoever's in the badlands forest at this time of the morning cannot be good."

Ah, like me, Annu and Irica? Yeah but look where that got us.

A banged up ship landed in a small clearing, the ramp clunked down. Shayne sucked on her lip and slowed her breath. Tubby fucker Mel and One eye Jude exited the door and carried a large container.

Oh, no fucking way. I didn't fall far enough away from where they were.

Jude's voice sliced through her. "Chances are it was Annu that crashed over there. Serve the bastard right."

Mel picked his nose and flicked it. "Shame about that little white woman with him though. We're running low on our quota."

Oh that's so gross, and I don't fucking think so.

With her last run in with them scorched in her mind, Shayne crept low around the tree and opted for a different route.

Something dropped onto her head and dug its claws in. Fear rippled along her spine, she bit her tongue and suppressed a scream. It climbed down the back of her head and clung to her neck. She pulled at it; it clawed and hissed biting at her hand.

Shayne swung around and hit it against the tree trunk, it dropped onto her back and out of sight. "Fuck, fuck, fuck, fuck."

It scrambled down to her hip and onto her stomach. A black, grey matted thing with red eyes growled and bared its teeth.

Only a thin piece of pyjama top material protected her skin. "Calm down creepy thing. Don't eat me."

It went for her face; Shayne grabbed it on the back and pulled. It and the bottom half of her pyjama top detached. She flung both away, turned and banged into Mel.

Shayne's wrapped her arms around her midriff and stepped back.

It can't all end like this.

"Hello pretty. Look who we've got here Jude." Fat Fuck Mel glanced behind her. "And it looks like you're all alone this time."

How many near death experiences can one person have in twenty four hours? Three, definitely three.

Chapter 19: Sticks & Stones Will Break Your Bones
Yebu Mountains, Enki Continent, Orion

Thanks to Annu's back, Irica suffered only minor injuries, while every inch of him hurt. His rear side bore the brunt of the fall and screamed with pain. Warm liquid trickled down his back, his spine swelled, some of his vertebrae protruded through the skin and rubbed against his shirt. Cuts savaged his arms and legs, lumps covered most of Annu's skull.

Irica groaned and pushed off his chest. She wiped her mouth, and examined her wounds. "Are you alright?"

Annu's head thudded, he tasted copper, his breath laboured. "Not at all."

A search light, emitted from the PO Ship, investigated the crash site and headed in their direction, the whir of the PO's ship followed.

Any chance at respite and hope of escape fled, his internal thermostat soared.

Irica slid to the side and onto the ground. "Oh no. What do we do?"

Annu gritted his teeth and sat up, agony threatened his sanity. "I'm really starting to hate it when you say oh no. Our two choices are die or hide, whichever comes first. Right now dying sounds wonderful."

Something sharp inside Annu prodded his lung, he chewed his lip and levered off the ground. Movement amplified the agony, Annu's breath caught; pins and needles consumed his arms.

Saliva pooled in his mouth, the bottles of rum he'd drunk earlier promised a hangover of epic proportion in the future.

When will this nightmare end? I need another flarking drink.

Halfway to upright his brain went one way, his skull the other. Annu's legs wobbled, he swayed and dropped onto the dirt. *Maybe not.*

Irica rushed to his side, and helped him up with an arm around his waist. "Lean on me. I know it's no consolation but this will heal."

She slumped under his weight.

Annu eased off her and stumbled towards a bunch of bushes a couple of metres ahead. "You're right, it is no consolation. But as long as you're alright it's so worth it."

Irica squeezed his middle. "I'll ignore the sarcasm because I'm alive thanks to you."

The search light brushed the back of their legs and beside them, his heart skipped.

I won't be surprised if I get a flarking stomach ulcer from this shit.

Annu fastened his shuffle, and pulled Irica along. "Flark. Don't thank me until this is over and we're still standing."

Light illuminated the trees to their left; at the front of the bushes Annu shoved Irica in the middle. "Sorry."

A mass of shrubbery muffled her reply. The light hit the trees next to them; he clutched his abdomen and dove in beside Irica.

Irica grabbed some of the broken sticks and filled in the hole they'd made, her hands trembled.

Annu pulled her back and took over. "Leave it, I'll do it."

The search light turned from white to blue and re-scanned the ship.

Irica froze—her panic evident. "What are they doing?"

Air invaded the open wounds on his face; a fresh layer of pain walloped him.

I want to lay down and feel sorry for myself. I wish I'd never tried to find out where I came from.

Annu took shallow breaths, each one torture. "Scanning for signs of life. Once their done with the ship, they'll check the surrounding area. We need to stay out of their way, which won't be easy because they can take hours before they're satisfied. Flarking hell this is a total mess."

Concern consumed her expression; she scraped dried blood from a scratch on her cheek and shivered. "Which means it's going to take even longer to find Shayne and somehow get to my place. Time's ticking by." Tears rolled down her cheeks, her face flushed. "Despite risking everything and almost alienating you to keep you alive, I've still messed up. The God's won't forgive me. How can they when I've failed in my duty so many times?"

Guilt slapped Annu, he patted her shoulder. "Look it's not your fault all this extra shit happened and ruined your plan. I brought this on myself, no one else did it. Because of you I am still alive and able to be killed any moment, and it shouldn't take long to find Shayne because we didn't get too far from where we where before getting shot down. I have no doubt she's okay and cursing us somewhere while she waits. She's tough. Okay—maybe not tough but too stubborn to die. Okay."

And what if she's not okay? What then? I guess I find and kill Shamesh on my own. As annoying as she is, she's kind of interesting. As a friend—she's not calm and placid like Jaid—

The light drifted towards their hiding spot and circled the trees around them. Annu grabbed Irica's wrist and guided her out the back of the bushes.

Alright Gods, Mother, I'm going to try praying. Help us out here please.

The band on his wrist warmed and tightened, his body buzzed, the pain lessened. Annu's vertebra clicked back into place, the ones poked through the skin slipped back inside. The jab in his lungs and displaced ribs reversed themselves.

Under the moonlight the wounds on his arms healed, only dried blood and dirt remained. "Holy shit."

Annu straightened, a rush of energy flowed through him, and tingles tickled his back.

Irica ran a finger over a former cut, her pace slowed them down. "I told you that would happen. Didn't you believe me?"

Yes. No. Yes and no. Alright I guess no but now I do. "Of course I did."

The PO Ship left the crash site and extended its air search towards them.

The sound of its engine frayed his nerves, and forced him into action; Annu scooped Irica under his arm, ran to the bushes.

Annu dove in; Irica lowered onto her knees and crawled in beside him. Her joints cracked and creaked, her descent slowed.

Moonlight emphasized the lines on her face, for the first time in his life Irica's age became obvious.

His heart ached, a life without her unimaginable to him.

How did I not notice you got old? When did I start taking you being around for granted? Sometimes I can be a selfish arsehole.

The PO Ship turned around and backtracked the way they'd come.

Please don't send out ground scouts, please.

Sweat ran down Irica's cheeks, her chest heaved; a rattle in her chest alarmed him. "I can't keep doing this Annu. I'm not much help anymore am I? Once upon a time I used to train the Demi-Gods myself. Now I can't evade a few Peace Officers. I think my time has come my son."

You're not going anywhere for a long time.

Despite the cold of dawn, heat flushed through him, another unwanted distraction.

Annu loosened his collar and clutched her shoulder. "Stop talking like that. It's rubbish. I'll carry you from now on so you don't have to worry about walking. You rest as often as you–"

The search light headed straight for them, Annu lifted Irica off the ground and bolted. He weaved around trees, crash debris and thick shrubs.

They reached a collection of rocks with a ledge underneath. Annu lowered, heat ran from the top of his head to his toes, small flames trickled down his arms and caught on Irica's skirt.

Irica squirmed and lifted her rear end. "Annu–"

Burnt fabric invaded the air; Annu dropped Irica onto her butt and patted the flames. "What's going–?" He ripped out the map and handed it to Irica. "Take this before it burns."

The PO ship landed near the crash site, officers marched down the ramp, the flames on his arms increased, Annu vomited in his mouth.

This really isn't my flarking day.

Chapter 20: Creature Feature
Yebu Mountains, Enki Continent, Orion

In a cage in the cockpit of Fat fuck Mel and One eyed Jude's ship, Shayne curled up in the corner, and hugged her legs. From the forest they'd delved further into the woods. For the second time Shayne headed in the opposite direction than needed.

Neither Ghost Dad nor Annu arrived to save Shayne. Left to her own devices she'd broken off the edges but the stick remained under the ring–aside from permanency and occasional levitation–likewise it offered no help.

Between peeing herself and crying, Shayne lacked bodily fluid, a paste formed on her tongue.

Should be called the fucked up lands in my opinion. Why is this happening to me? What kind of Gods are they? Why am I meant to suffer so much? Actually who fucking cares. Not me. I don't care about any of this, I want to go home.

Exhaustion dragged Shayne down, fear propped her back up. Stuck in the middle, she drifted off to sleep only to wake up seconds later. Minutes, hours and days melded into an incompressible blob.

I hate this fucking planet. Nothing like this would happen at my place.

One eye scared Shayne the most, something about the way he looked at her like a juicy steak.

Oh Gods what if they rape me?

Panic washed over her, the last trickle of pee warmed her crotch.

His voice matched a face not even a mother would love. "Check on our passenger."

Shayne's heart skipped a beat, a cage bar dug into her back, she sympathised with zoo animals.

God if you get me out of here I'll start a petition. Even a fund raiser, anything, please.

Fat fuck leaned over the co-pilot's arm rest and poked her with a stick.

I'm not going to show you I'm scared anymore. I'll make you suffer as much as I do.

She grabbed the end and yanked it from his hands. Shayne broke it over her knee and threw the pieces at him. "Stop fucking doing that you son of a bitch."

Fat fuck thrust his chin. "How did you know my mother's a bitch? Flark you really are magic?"

Maybe it's not a good idea to piss off these guys? Unlike Annu they've got no attachment to me. Nah screw it–fake it until I make it.

"So you're stupid as well as fat. Not a great combo for a criminal."

Fat fuck blinked, his expression dropped. "For someone so small you are really mean."

And while I'm on a roll.

"I guess you two can't get dates like normal men and that's why you kidnap women."

Fat fuck sucked in his bottom lip and turned around. "Geez you're a bitch."

One eye reached over and slapped FF's arm. "She's right you know. How many times do I have to tell you not to talk to her? She's trying to flark with your head, which isn't hard. If you weren't my cousin I would have killed you by now."

One-Eye tapped a button on the side of the Pilot's chair.

Zap, the cage electrified, shocks surged through her, and she seized and banged against the bars. Shayne's brain wobbled, her sense of reality displaced, the electricity stopped. She slumped against the corner and caught her breath.

Shayne kicked the cage, the hinges rattled. "Let me out you mother fucking pieces of shit. You won't get away with this. You've got no idea who I am. I'm–"

Zap, zap, zap. Shayne flopped around, her muscles spasmed, her mind froze. She bit her tongue, saliva pooled in her mouth and dribbled down her chin.

One eye cackled. "That shut you up."

Fat fuck's voice drifted around the cockpit. "How long do we have to keep her for?"

Awareness prodded Shayne, it hurt to breath, her muscles burned.

Listen. It's important.

One eye's levity broke through her fog. "Bilbo's meeting us at our place in a couple of hours. He's excited. This is the payoff we've waited for friend."

Fuck, fuck, fuck. God knows what they'll do to me during next couple of hours. This other person is probably ten times worse than them. What am I going to do? There's no way out and I'm not strong enough to kill myself before they do.

Shayne choked on a sob and blinked back tears. A last ditch at reason poured from her tongue. "It's not too late to stop this and drop me off somewhere. I won't tell anyone who you are or what you did, I swear. Please, let me go. I'm a person like you just from somewhere else."

One eye's tone turned ominous. "And that's the exact reason we won't let you go."

Shayne's guts dropped, fear threw a wet blanket on her back.

I'm going to die in this cage without anyone knowing where I am.

"How much further do we have to go?"

One eye's growl sent a shiver up her spine. "Never you mind now shut up."

Shayne's chest heaved; she checked the cage's hinges–all secure, none loose. The electronic lock vibrated each time she went near it, Shayne wriggled it anyway.

One eye held his finger of the button. "Get away from there or I'll zap you again."

The ship slowed, lowered and shuddered to land, the entire craft rattled. The door cracked open, a hatch on the floor released the ramp, and cold air invaded the ship. Shayne alternated rubbing her arms, and blowing warm air into her hands.

One eye left his seat, Fat fuck followed a step behind until they stood either side of the cage. Unwashed man and some unidentified stench wafted up her nose.

Shayne pegged it closed, and breathed through her mouth. "Fucking hell, you guys stink. You might want to think about having a shower before you see anyone else."

They lifted the cage and stepped onto the ramp, half dead trees and brown grass surrounded the ship, a rundown cabin sloped to one side metres ahead.

"Oh well now I see you're place it all makes sense. It's a fucking dump. Hey, were you guys extras in the movie Deliverance?"

Fat fuck's mouth dropped open. "How, how dare you?"

If I get them fighting with each other hopefully they'll leave me alone.

Shayne faced Fat fuck. "Hey maybe the money you get for me you could spend getting a new ship or a new place. They're both fucked. No wonder you're single. You two don't still live with your mothers, right?"

Fat fuck stumbled and almost dropped the cage. "No we don't. There's nothing wrong with where we live."

It's working, not sure where to go from here, but it's a start.

"Yes you do and yes there is. If he cared about you he'd provide a decent place for you to live. You mentioned you were cousins, I bet you're kissing cousins aren't you?"

Fat fuck flipped his gaze between her and One Eye. "What? What the hell are you saying?"

One eye reached over the cage and punched Fat fuck in the arm, Fat fuck dropped his side of the cage.

Shayne smacked her head on the roof. "Ow you mother fuckers. And I do mean that literally."

One-Eye righted the cage, pinched Shayne in the shoulder and glared at Fat Fuck. "For flark's sake, you moron. Keep going too, and I'll forget we're related, and you'll fill the empty spot in the garden. Got it?"

Shayne rubbed her arm and shuffled away from him.

Maybe if the cage drops the lock will open?

"Yeah dipshit."

Chagrined, Fat fuck's shoulders slumped. "Yeah alright, but how do you expect me to not comment when she says shit like that?"

One eye side stepped down the ramp. "Ignore her and practice some restraint. Just once I'd like to not worry about you, and you do your job without problems."

They hit the ground and headed towards the cabin, images of fleas, animal shit and dirty dishes filled her mind.

Have I ever been immunised against Ebola and shit?

"You two heard of disinfectant and soap? I'm sure it's cheap here too."

One eye's sneer closed her mouth. "Bitch you've forgotten you're alone with us for the next while and if you don't shut your mouth, I'll put something in your mouth that will."

My plan is not working, I repeat not working. Abort, abort, abort. Try not to freak out. Actually it's the perfect time to freak out.

Chapter 21: Mama Said Knock You Out
Yebu Mountains, Enki Continent, Orion

Whether or not Annu patted, cajoled, and pled, the flames travelled from his hands up his arms, pulsed down his spine and engulfed his upper torso. The breeze increased their size and veracity, the grass beneath his feet smouldered.

Officers entered the woods in teams of two and headed in different directions, ensuring they covered most of the forest.

Wedged under the ledge, Irica paled. "Of all the times for your first power to arrive this is the worst. Try calming down, it won't be long before they look here."

Annu became a flame beacon screaming 'here I am, come shoot me.' "Yeah I know. How am I meant to calm down given the situation? Are you kidding me? Oh yeah, it's perfectly normal to be on fire but not burn. Flark Irica. It's all I can do not to explode right now."

He twirled his hands, the flames danced along his skin; despite time constraints its beauty captivated him.

Irica clapped a hand to her mouth. "Get down, there's two officers coming this way."

Annu dropped onto his knees, and crawled under the ledge away from Irica, the flames dwindled and disappeared. "Thank the Gods. Or not?"

Irica shielded her face from the smoke, and sighed. "I also had all these lessons for you on how to control your powers. If we make it–there won't be time for it now. And so many other things."

Oh thank flark.

"What a shame. It sounded fascinating."

Her demeanour lightened. "In that case I'm sure we could squeeze it in somewhere."

Dickhead.

"Let's just see how we go if we survive this, alright?"

Two officers reached a thicket of bushes metres from the ledge, and mumbled to each other. One shone a life scanner in random movements around the woods.

The light hit the trees above the ledge, and beeped, Annu held his breath.

You can't see us, you can't see us, you can't see us. Please don't see us.

The officer, an older man on the left, pointed at a higher branch; leaves rustled. "What are you new? It's a possum Dimi. You've got it aimed too high and you're not paying attention. Give it to me."

Annu sucked in his gut and wriggled further back, his soles hit the rear wall.

The officer with the scanner, a middle aged man, shrugged and held it away from the other officer. "No, I'll do it."

The beam swept inches from the entrance; Annu's heart skipped–the light hovered.

The middle aged officer tapped a button on the side of the scanner, and turned the beam off. "How much longer do we have to search? The ship's scanner didn't show up anything, and I hate being out here. It gives me the creeps."

Think calm, peaceful thoughts. Ignore the fact there's a good two dozen armed men looking for us with orders to shoot to kill. What do we have on our side? An old lady with gout and a seven foot fire ignition switch who has never killed anyone. It doesn't matter, because all I can flarking do is I pray they don't force me into action. These bastards don't deserve to die just for following orders–they don't know better.

The older officer rolled his eyes. "You hate being anywhere but the City. You know the orders are to search for the bodies if there's no sign of life. And it came from the Grand Council and you know what that means."

The middle aged officer turned the scanner back on, spun on his heels, and flashed across the area behind them. His high pitched voice grated on Annu's nerves. "Yeah more wasted hours in this place looking for criminals who are probably dead or soon will be, and dodgy paperwork because of Griffin."

Irica shuffled beside him, she grasped his arm, her heart beat audible.

A fart rumbled from his lower gut and down his bowel; Annu clenched his butt hole and held it in alongside his breath. His lungs and arsehole burned.

Hurry up and flark off already. Not that it matters more will come any second. Damnit. I need a way out of here for us–if I can carry Irica. Flark, shit, flark. And I've got no alcohol.

"Hey careful, you don't know whose listening around here. You know what happens if you question–"

The officers dawdled towards the next set of trees, Annu exhaled and gulped in air.

'Annu.'

He gritted his teeth and pressed a finger to his lips. "Shh, they could still hear us."

Irica cocked her head, her whisper echoed off the rock. "What? I didn't say anything."

'Annu.'

Annu's brain tingled; a foreign presence probed his mind. "There it is again." He shook himself and considered alcohol withdrawal. "Nah, surely not enough to hear voices."

Irica's expression suggested she doubted his sanity. Concern tainted her words. "What again? Are you feeling alright?" She pressed her palm to his forehead. "You're a little warm but that's probably from the fire power. Poke out your tongue–do you feel nauseous? Are you going to vomit?"

Don't get angry, you'll ignite again.

Annu swiped her hand away. "No stop it. I'm fine."

Maybe, I'm not totally sure.

Tingle, tingle, probe, probe.

'Annu. It's your mother, Ann.'

He bolted up, thump, and banged his head on rock, pain belted across his skull. "Ouch. Where are you? I can't see you."

Calm, a forgotten sensation of late, rippled within him. Clarity twinkled in the distance.

'I can communicate with you telepathically this close to the ascension, though it's an unreliable connection.'

Disbelief and long held satisfaction wavered, Annu's thoughts collided. "Oh, oh. I, I, I don't know what to say."

Irica bit her lip and held her cheek. "Who are you talking to?"

Annu massaged the lump forming on his head. "Oh, ah not you–my mother?"

Irica clutched her chest. "My goodness–your mother? Right now? What is she saying?"

Wriggle, tickle.

'I've missed you my son, I wish I could be at your side, I trust Irica explained the reasons why it isn't possible.'

The two conversations and realities scrambled into batter in his mind. "Yes sort of but—wait–I'll tell you in a minute. Shit."

Irica added more eggs to the mixture. "I'm confused, are you talking to me or her?"

'You must find Shayne and get to the mountains. It's imperative.'

Lingered rejection smacked him, and muddied his thoughts. "I know but ah–I'm kind of stuck here at the moment trying not to get caught and shot."

'Ascension approaches and we must succeed.'

What is it with women and pressure? Why must everything be done immediately? Maybe if they planned things better to start off with and didn't wait until the last damned minute, they wouldn't need to rush. "Look I'm doing my very best so maybe you can help me out here?"

Tears welled in Irica's eyes. "Okay, I'm guessing you're talking to her–Ann. Tell Ann I'm sorry, I thought I'd done my best. Please ask her to forgive me. I'll make this right somehow."

Annu slapped himself in the forehead. "Not right now. Flark. It's gone from neither of you telling me anything, to both of you at me at once. Give me a minute, okay?"

A shocked Officer's face popped under the ledge in front of Annu, a gun appeared between Annu's eyes.

The officer's yell bored through his brain. "Hey, over here they're still alive."

Irica gasped, her hands trembled.

Anger and frustration consumed him. "Oh great. Just what we needed. Here goes nothing."

Annu erupted in flames, lunged at the officer and shoved him. A dozen more ran in their direction, their guns raised, their yells drowned by the roar of fire.

Chapter 22: Levitate Me Baby
Yebu Mountains, Enki Continent, Orion

Incarceration conflicted with Shayne's personal space yet provided an illusion of safety from her captors. Each minute in the iron cage gave her time to think and reflect, neither of which Shayne enjoyed. Instead, she surmised her limited, aka no options, and struggled to find an escape plan. Any scenario Shayne's imagination devised, reality destroyed.

Aside from a dull headache, remnants from multiple electric shocks didn't deter Shayne's brain from trying. "Isn't anyone going to come and save me? And by anyone I mean fucking Annu. He better be dead or maimed right now. Selfish conceited arsehole."

Shayne jiggled the lock in case it unlocked in the last few seconds.

Nope. Still locked. Fuckhead doesn't want to look for me. He probably breathed a sigh of relief and went on his merry fuckhead way. Surely Irica will convince him they need me, they do need me right? She said she did. Where are my fucking powers? Fucking hell. This is bull shit. Thanks for nothing Ghost Dad.

Fat fuck and One eye sat around a kitchen table; a half bottle of brown liquid between them.

One eye refilled both glasses and slid one to Fat Fuck. One eye sipped the drink, massaged his temples and cracked his neck.

Fat Fuck checked the clock for the hundredth time, downed his drink and pushed the glass back to Jude. "How long until Bilbo comes? It's been hours."

A vein bulged across One Eye's forehead, another at the side of his neck. "Not flarking soon enough. Next time we come across something like her, we're running the other way."

You took me so you fuckers are going to suffer along with me.

"Hey dip shit, I want a drink of water and something to eat."

One Eye grumbled to the table top. "You ate half an hour ago and you've still got water."

"Well I'm still hungry and thirsty."

One Eye scraped the chair across the floor and banged the table. "Maybe if you didn't talk so much you wouldn't get so flarking thirsty. Now shut up or so help me I'll wring your damned neck. I don't care if I get less for you being dead. Scientists will still want your body so don't push me."

Shayne sat on her knees and levitated off the cage's bottom.

I hope this is actually useful at some point other than a cool party trick.

"I have that effect on people here but nonetheless I'm hungry and I need to pee. Oh, and a blanket or something. It's cold in here. Can't you losers afford heating?"

Fat Fuck steeled his shoulders and glared at Shayne. "Can you shock her again? Please?"

One Eye's bulging veins grew. "It doesn't make much difference and I've fried the battery trying."

"Maybe we should give her back to Annu. We can drop her off somewhere and message him the details."

Hope tickled Shayne. "Oh yeah, do that. Great idea."

One Eye dipped his head. "No, if he's alive, I'm not giving that bastard the satisfaction, although I cannot figure out how or why he put up with her."

Fuck, almost. Damn you Annu. You better not be dead, or think I am.

Shayne inhaled, raised her chin and rattled her cage. "I need a hero, I'm holding on for a hero at the end of this night—or this song, and he's gotta be strong, and he's got to come soon, and he's got to win a fight."

At some point maybe I should learn the actual words to the songs I sing.

"I need a fucking hero, come on hero before the end of this night."

Fat Fuck grimaced and covered his ears. "Oh gods what the hell? Please stop."

Shayne raised her voice an octave and increased the tempo. "I need a hero. Someone get me a hero and I don't know more than the chorus so I'm going to make it up. I need a hero, yeah, yeah, yeah. I need a–"

One Eye turned on the chair, his expression horrified. "What is that terrible noise?"

Shayne stopped, and cocked her head. "Huh? What noise? I can't hear anything."

One Eye rose, and tipped the chair backwards. "The horrible one coming out your mouth. I can't believe it but it's worse than listening to you speak."

Shock smacked Shayne across the face, her cheeks flushed. "There's nothing wrong with how I speak, and are you talking shit about my singing? How fucking rude and insulting are you? My son and lots of other people says I'm a good singer."

By lots I mean three, and one includes me, myself and I. He doesn't need to know that.

Fat Fuck gasped, his expression fell. "You're a parent? You've got children? You mean there are more like you? Flark, are they around here?"

Shayne crossed her arms, and thrust out her chest. "You guys are arseholes. Yes I'm a parent to two wonderful adult kids, who aren't on Orion so relax. Don't bust a nut. And I sing like an angel. Even I admit I'm good. Wait a second I'll sing a different one. Maybe you didn't hear me properly over the sound of your shack screaming for help."

Quick think of a good one. Oh got one, and it's perfect. "I stay up too late, got nothing in my brain. That's what people say, mmm. That's what people say. I eat too many dates, I can't make them pray, that's what people say mmm. Shake it —."

One-Eye paced around the table, and wriggled a finger in his ear. "I don't know what that is and I don't want to. It might fly wherever you're from but not here. My ears are bleeding. I beg you, don't do it again, it's torture."

Shayne pouted, and swiped a tear away. "Arsehole. No one's ever said that to me before. You're so mean."

One Eye marched towards the cage and loomed. "Oh, that you get offended at. What kind of messed up thing are you?

My mouth is going to be the death of me one day, and yet—

Shayne shuffled against the back side. "I'm Shayne, and I'm a Demi-God. Have you forgotten? Did you forget your 'I'm stupid' sign today?"

The vein on One-Eye's forehead palpitated, his eye twitched. "If I didn't need the money so bad I'd flarking tear you to pieces. You've got two choices before I completely lose my shit. We either put you outside or I think of other things we can do to you. None of which you're going to enjoy."

Oops, and that day is coming sooner than expected. Freeze to death or other imaginable things.

"Ah, outside sounds great."

One Eye nodded, the vein jiggled, his sneer chilled her. "Thought so. Mel get over here and grab the other side."

Fat Fuck dragged his feet. "As long as she doesn't sing again."

Shayne rolled her eyes at him. "I said I wouldn't. So get over it."

Fat Fuck grabbed one side of the cage, One-Eye the other. They lifted it off the ground, she slipped towards Fat Fuck.

Shayne held onto the middle, and raised a hand. "Actually before you take me out, I still need to pee."

One eye's cheek forehead twitched, and travelled down his cheek, Fat Fuck lowered his side.

One Eye glared at Fat Fuck and shook his head, Mel picked up the cage, the front door of the shack whooshed open, cold air steeped into her marrow.

Dick head, this is all your fault. How am I going to get out of this?

Chapter 23: Anger Management
Yebu Mountains, Enki Continent, Orion

Irica shrieked and scrambled further under the ledge. Annu threw the man at the officers behind and created a short distance between Annu and the others

The first officer rolled on the ground and diminished the flames. Once out, he huffed, puffed, and collapsed.

If only the rest of them were so easy.

Annu raised his flaming hands. "You men don't understand what's really going on here. I don't want to hurt you, but if I have to I will. So don't make me."

A senior PO stepped towards Annu and turned his head to the officers behind. "Hold your fire." He returned his focus to Annu, his gun hand lowered. "We've got our orders, and you're under arrest for a number of serious crimes—but—how are you able to do that with the fire? Is it some kind of magic trick? I've never seen anything like it."

The other officers stared with their mouths agape and their weapons aimed.

Fire trickled up and down his arms, power surged through Annu. Part of him wanted to burn them all and leave nothing but ash.

The other part fought harder. "It's no trick and it's a long story we don't have time for. The short version is your orders come from an evil man with his own agenda, and if he succeeds in what he wants, we all die. But if you walk away now, I can do what I'm meant to and fix things on this planet."

The senior PO's frown offered hope. "What the hell are you talking about? You mean Grand Counsellor Griffin? And you're a political prisoner who can somehow manipulate fire?"

The delay ate into his time to find Shayne and wore Annu's patience. "Yes him, and not exactly but sort of. It's obvious I can annihilate you all right now but I haven't. Surely that has to prove in part what I'm saying and that we're not criminals."

The Senior PO lowered his weapon a fraction further, Annu held his breath.

Come on, please make this easier. Don't be stupid.

"Mother you around? I need your help here?"

The senior officer raised his gun and aimed at Annu's chest. "As intriguing and fanciful as your story is, either way you have to be taken into custody until your claims can be verified. If we believed all suspects claiming to be innocent for whatever crazy reason the planet would be in chaos. Aside from the fire thing what makes you any different to them?"

I guess not and I'm winging it.

Annu's frustration soared, fire spread over the rest of him.

Annu's clothes crumbled into ash and revealed a naked body.

Not my finest fighting moment.

"Look, I understand you've got orders and protocols but sometimes things happen outside the normal, like now, and I don't have time for this shit. Either you let me go or–" He flicked flames onto the ground and rolled his neck. "I'll have no choice but to go through you all."

"No can do." The senior man raised his gun to Annu's head. "You're both under arrest. With an added charge of threatening Peace officers, which is a federal offence, and means either a death sentence or life in prison. You, Annu, put the flames out, your hands in the air and take a step back or we'll shoot to kill."

Irica stood a metre from his side, she shielded her face, either from the heat or his nakedness, Annu didn't know. "Please listen to him. If there's a shred of decency in you, or hope for a better world for everyone, you'll let us go."

The others behind the senior officer snapped out of their daze and followed suit. A couple of dozen weapons clicked, red lasers appeared on Annu's and Irica's chests.

Irica's sigh matched Annu's and bounced around the trees.

If you're alive Shayne, hang in there. We'll get there at some flarking point.

Annu mumbled out the side of his mouth. "Irica, get behind the rocks and don't come out until I come get you."

The panic in her voice apparent. "Are you sure?"

Power and energy rippled down his back; he rose a few centimetres from the ground in a red aura. "Get behind the rocks now."

Irica shivered and hobbled out of the way. "Oh dear God's please keep Annu safe–"

"Pray for them not me." The ground beneath the aura smouldered, the ambient temperature rose. "You've left me no choice. I warned you."

Annu drifted towards them, the fire and aura increased.

The senior shook and stumbled backwards. "What the–fire when ready. I repeat fire when ready."

A preponderance of laser beams illuminated the area around Annu, skimmed his aura and bounced off.

I don't want to do this. I have to do this. Someone give me another choice and I'll take it. Please?

No one and nothing arrived to save the officers and prove Annu's actions wrong. "Oh hell. Here we go."

Annu drew power from within into a fire ball between his hands, in one thrust it projected outside the aura. He created another; the first blasted a row of officers. They burst into flames and melted into mush on the ground.

Shock and a modicum of guilt froze him mid-blast.

Flarking hell. That's extreme.

Annu's aura and power dwindled; a chill ran over his naked groin.

Laser shots whizzed through his aura, skimmed his arm, and forced him to attention. "Flark. Shit. Idiot."

Annu focused his rage, and the protection, the fire intensified. Radiant heat seared any flora in the vicinity, he pushed it out further. The officer's available skin seared and bubbled. A collective dropped weapons and protected their faces.

You should have listened to me; this is your own fault.

Annu rose above their heads and streamed fire at them. Piles of ash and the stench of cooked humans remained.

His anger sated, Annu searched the area for other officers, finding none Annu lowered onto the ground and slowed his breath. His aura diminished, the flames dwindled to nothing. The cold morning made its way up his legs and spine.

Annu rubbed his arms and covered his bits. Leaves crunched behind him, he whipped around and reignited.

Irica back-pedalled, her demeanour expressed fear. "Wait, stop, it's me Irica."

Relief shut his powers down, Annu's hand returned to his crotch. "I ah, well. Flark."

Her eyes flicked to his lower half, Irica's cheeks flushed. "We need to find you some clothes for now and some fire retardant ones as soon as possible. You're not getting the map back until then."

Annu concentrated on a patch of fried grass at his feet. "Ah, yeah. I better look for other officers before we do anything else."

Irica removed her jacket and handed it to him. "I already checked and snuck into their ship while you were busy. All of them were out here."

"Well I guess we've got a ship to find Shayne in and get to the mountains. And we won't get pulled over in the time it takes to do both."

Irica tapped her chin. "One more thing which needs attention before we leave."

Annu slumped his shoulders. "What?"

She pointed to his left. "We have to put out the small forest fire you've started."

Fire trickled from the dead officers along the ground and caught on anything dried. "Oh for fuck's sake. Is nothing ever easy?"

Chapter 24: Oh Crap
Yebu Mountains, Enki Continent, Orion

Shayne's nipples became fripples, any harder they'd cut glass—but not metal. Blue lips numbed, hands and feet ached; the rest of her lived in denial in order to save sanity. Dawn broke through the trees and illuminated the area around the cage. The temperature fell further; dew glistened on the grass and froze on the bars.

Shayne huddled into a ball and hugged her legs. "I want to go home. This isn't right. I don't deserve to die of hypothermia. I fucking hate the cold."

Frozen snot stuck under her nose, Shayne picked off chunks and flicked them.

Or do I? I'm kind of an arsehole but at least I feel bad about it after. Sometimes.

Alright, occasionally and I'm working on it.

An unseen creature in the woods behind the cage howled; something in the tree above wailed and jiggled branches. Leaves and sticks dropped onto Shayne's head. She brushed them off and shuffled to the other side of the cage.

Thank God they can't get in here. Yeah and nor can I get out. I'm useless. I can't save myself. How the fuck would I do that?

A half-cat half dog-like thing jumped behind the cage onto the tree trunk and climbed into its depths. Her heart fluttered, Shayne's shriek scraped across her dry throat, her bladder tingled. Terror provided a hot rush and a temporary respite from the cold.

1, 2, 3 and it's gone. I'm going to die out here and no one fucking cares. I should care. I, I, I, I do care and it makes no difference.

The ring vibrated, the tips of Shayne's fingers turned pale blue and buzzed. The colour intensified and covered the rest of her. The cold abated, warmth spread over Shayne.

Just my luck it's probably a hot flush from menopause.

Shayne's skin hummed. "Shit, that cannot be good."

Desperation overtook Shayne, hidden reserves of self preservation scrambled for attention.

Hang on; do I really want to die without trying to save myself? For once in my life, no. What's wrong with me being strong and smart enough to get out of this? Apart from the smart? Nothing. I always give up and don't do anything, waiting for someone else to fix things.

Eyes closed, Shayne touched the ring and flicked her other hand at the cage. "Alright, open the lock now."

The tree shook. From the noise above, Shayne surmised the howling creature caught the screeching one; its wails filled the air.

A dark liquid dribbled down the tree trunk, Shayne swallowed vomit.

Thank God that's not from me.

Eyes back open, she glared at the lock. "Ala vegemite sandwiches–open lock."

It remained unaffected; the creature clawed its way down the trunk with its dead quarry in tow. "Oh shit."

Shayne held her breath and waited for it to pass.

You can't see me. Don't make me sing to you. I'm not fucking here.

Once safe, Shayne wriggled her nose and blinked. Nothing happened. "Fucking hell. It worked on those TV shows."

Shayne levitated off the ground and bumped her head on the top of the cage. "Really? God damnit. Actually don't that's what got me into this mess."

Back on the bottom, Shayne held her hands to her chest. "Open sesame. No wait - open lock." She swirled a hand around. "Peanut butter sandwiches."

The lock glimmered in the dawn sun's light and taunted Shayne. "What else can I try? I'm running out of ideas. Ghost Dad, are you around?"

A succession of birds erupted from the trees into the sky.

Shayne gave them a half frozen finger. "Okay, no then?" She grabbed the bars aside the lock. "By the power vested in me from the Gods blah, blah, blah, I hereby order you to unlock you cock sucker, dick head, fuck face, shit licker, bastard thing."

Icicles appeared on her visible flesh and in seconds covered her. A river of ice flowed down her arms and onto the cage bars. The bars lock and Shayne's thoughts froze.

Shayne removed her hands and stroked the icicles on her hands. If she pushed them down, they bounced back. "Ah, I, I, well. That's something and I'm not cold anymore. So fucking cool." Her cackle verged on crazy. "Well, duh."

A door slammed inside the shack and snapped her back to reality. Shayne pushed herself into the cage's corner and grabbed the bars behind for leverage, they froze from her touch.

Crap, that's a huge problem when I need to pee. Oh well, I'll worry about it later.

One kick and the cage's side shattered, shock plastered her to the corner. "Holy shit. It fucking worked."

Shayne crawled out and stretched out numerous muscle kinks.

Alright I'm out.

The cabin stood to her right, Fat Fuck and One Eye shuffled around inside. The more Shayne thought about them, the higher her anger rose.

I should just leave and find a way to Irica's but there's no fucking way those two are getting away with this. I've never killed anyone but there's always a first time for everything.

A couple of metres from the front door, a PFD whirred in the distance and almost stopped her. Fear poked Shayne's newfound bravado.

No, these guys get it first.

Shayne kicked it in the guts and strode to the door. "You're after this fucker."

The door creaked open, Fat Fuck and One Eye jumped from their seats.

One Eye smoothed down his shirt. "About flarking time, Bilbo," and turned around, "This is the last time—"

Shayne plastered a smile on her face and twirled her frozen hands. "Good morning arseholes. I bet you didn't expect to see me this morning did you?"

Fat Fuck fell back towards the chair, missed the seat, and landed on the floor.

One Eye did a double take and ran towards Shayne. She pushed aside her usual flee instinct and channeled rage instead.

He grabbed at her arm. Shayne sidestepped out of One Eye's grasp and brushed his hand. One Eye's entire arm froze; he yelped and held it to him.

The arm cracked in half, shattered, and fell in pieces to the floor.

"Now I can call you One Arm, One Eye. Or One-One. Ha." Shayne stomped on the chunks closest to her and pointed at Fat Fuck. "I fucking told you two I'm special and shit. Now it's time you mother fuckers respected my authority."

One-One's expression mixed disbelief and ire. He whipped around and side swiped Shayne around the middle.

Shayne hit the ground with him on his feet beside her. She froze his ankle and foot, One-One fell. "Look out, you got a new name.

Shayne climbed onto her feet and jumped over One-One, with Fat Fuck in her sights.

Fat Fuck backed up until he hit wall and threw his hands in the air. "No, please, don't hurt me."

Less than a metre from him, Shayne paused. "I haven't made up my mind about you yet, but for starters if you both don't want to become icicles, swear right now you'll leave me and Annu alone—forever–and won't ever do this to another person or thing again."

One-One sat on his knees and gathered the body-part-ice into a pile. "My arm, my foot, their, their frozen. It can't be."

That's so fucking gross. Oh well.

Shayne crossed her arms, a blue aura formed around her. "Unless you both swear to me right now I'm freezing your dick and balls next. Got it?"

Fat Fuck nodded, his hands protected his crotch. "I swear."

With a short slide Shayne loomed over One-One. "And you fucker? Are you swearing too or do I finish the job?"

He sorted through the pieces before him. "Maybe they can put them on again, or replace them."

Shayne poked his shoulder. "Oy, you. Swear or the pile gets bigger. I'm not fucking around here."

One-one's pathetic expression almost guilted her. "Yes, I swear. You won't ever see —"

The front door clattered open; a skinny old guy flicked his eyes around the room, backed up and closed the door behind him.

"You just saved yourself, buddy." Shayne headed for the kitchen. "Before I go what's left to eat? Oh, and I need some warm clothes."

Chapter 25: Leadership
Yebu Mountains, Enki Continent, Orion

In addition to morning suns, search lights shone in every direction and left no where un-searched.

Calm for once, the map rested in Annu's pocket. He turned the ship and repeated a loop around the area Shayne fell. "This is the last rotation we can do."

Irica wrapped her fingers around the arm rest. "Why isn't she here? Unless she's being chased by something, but I can't see her running. Could we have missed her? Maybe she's hiding? We are in a Peace Office ship. Gods don't let her be dead."

A PO's spare shirt crept up his back, Annu pulled it down. "There's no blood or body, and there's no place to hide we haven't looked. Where's left?"

They reached the edge of the woods where it crossed with old lay lines; no Shayne appeared to ruin their day.

Where is she?

Irica rose off the chair and leaned against the side window. "She has to be somewhere. She can't just disappear."

Come on Shayne; give us a hint or something.

"Are you sure? Could it be one of her powers?"

Irica's shoulders slumped. "I don't know. I don't know anything anymore."

Annu slapped the console before him. "Now don't you start giving up hope or we're definitely fucked. I mean flarked."

Damn you Shayne.

The console radio crackled to life, Annu heart skipped a beat:

'Ship 355, this is Lieutenant Meni of Head Quarters, report your status. Have the suspects been found?'

Irica sank into the co-pilots chair. "Oh shit. You can't answer them, what will we do?"

Annu hovered over the button. "You never swear."

Irica shrugged. "It's been a strange kind of day–well night. Oh you know what I mean."

'Ship 355. Respond immediately–do you require further patrols for assistance?'

The pit of Annu's stomach gurgled. "If I don't answer them they'll send more out anyway and find us."

Irica slid off the seat. "Are you —"

Annu pressed a finger to his lips. "Ssh." He cleared his throat and tapped the button. "This is Ship 355. Ah–sorry didn't respond. We were ah–"

Think idiot.

"Everyone else but me is dead. I'm wounded and heading back to Yebu. But the suspects are also dead. I confirm the suspects are dead. No need to send assistance."

The back of his brain tickled. *'Annu–it's your mother.'*

Annu slapped his forehead. "Not right now."

'Ship 335, what not right now? What's your name and rank? I'll send a ship to meet you along the way. They'll debrief you on route.'

'Annu. Shayne is with–.'

Annu removed his finger from the button. "Mother can you please wait a second?"

'You can think what you want to say rather than speak them son.'

Annu's patience frayed, another chunk of sanity broke off. "Yeah well I'm not good at multitasking. Flark it, let me get one thing sorted. Where is she?"

The Lieutenants voice scraped across Annu's nerves and compounded his problems. 'Ship 335 respond. We've activated the GPS on the ship. Patrols will arrive in approximately an hour to your location.'

Annu's left eye twitched. "Fucking brilliant."

'She's with the two men you encountered earlier in the night.'

A chill settled across his kidneys. "You mean Mel and Jude? Flark no. Is she alright?"

The brain tickle dwindled to nothing. '*Yes she's with them....*'

Annu kicked the bottom of the console and jiggled the steering shaft. "Mother fucking, cock sucking, twatt waffle."

Irica slid against the window and away from him. "Are you alright? What's going on? Oh, is it your mother."

Annu's jaw ached from gritted teeth; fear for Shayne muddied his thoughts. "No I'm not right at all. Give me a minute to think."

We've got an hour before they come here and about an hour and a half in this ship to the mountains. But they'll track it. Right after we rescue Shayne, we need another ship. Again.

The radio button depressed under his finger, Annu held a deep breath. "Sorry for the delay lieutenant. crackle, crackle, crackle. The radio's breaking up and I'm having ship trouble. I'm looking for help. Over. Crackle, crackle.'

Annu ripped the cables from underneath the console, the radio switched off. "Alright. That's going to give us a little while and the PO's think we're dead. As long as we get out of here before they show up again, we're safe to travel to your mountain place. And don't contact anyone there or anywhere else because our calls will be monitored and they'll know we aren't dead."

This is getting crazier by the minute.

"By the way I know where Shayne is."

Irica wriggled into the middle of the seat. "Where is she? Did your mother tell you?"

Bile soured his mouth, Annu considered the multitude of ways they'd hurt her before they got there. "Jude and Mel have her."

"Oh no."

Annu guided the ship through the woods, over the lay lines and towards Mel and Jude's ramshackle shack. "Please don't say that anymore."

His heart thudded, his hands shook, and alcohol withdrawal complicated the issue.

I need a flarking drink or six.

Irica's gasp cemented Annu's fear. "Annu, what will they do to her? If they kill her it's all over."

Concern surprised him; he stacked it next to guilt in the too hard basket. "Not completely. I can still um kill Griffin/Shamesh."

Her voice crackled. "It takes two of you Annu. One's not enough, believe me. Fly faster."

A dull thud rippled across his skull. "Oh super. Of course we do. We better get her back then."

Trees, trees and more trees. If I never see another damned tree again it's too soon.

They sped through the last forest before Jude's place and into a clearing. A familiar PDF turned into the area from Jude and Mel's drive way, Annu's chest tightened.

He gripped the steering shaft. "Bilbo."

Irica broke his daze. "Who?"

Panic lumped along Annu's shoulders. "A dirty rotten black market dealer. Shit, no guesses as to why he went to their place."

At site of the PO craft, the PFD stopped mid-turn in the centre of the lane.

Annu drifted the craft and landed beside Bilbo's ship. He waved at Bilbo and slid the pilot's window open.

Bilbo frowned, two massive eyebrows merged into one. "Annu, what are you doing in a PO Ship?"

Annu tapped buttons on the console, a laser cannon projected from the ship's front and aimed at Bilbo's craft. "Never mind. You've got one chance to answer me, have you got the woman or do they?"

Bilbo's chest heaved, he paled. "Oh. I, I, I don't have her, I didn't want her and I don't think you want her either. Too much trouble. A strange looking thing with weird powers. She froze Jude's foot and hand off. I got out of there before she turned on me."

Annu's chuckle surprised him.

That's our Shayne, Thank Gods she's alive, and seems full of surprises.

He lifted the cannon to Jude's head. "You sure? I'm coming to check your ship before I take it, just in case you're full of shit."

Bilbo nodded, a thatch of white hair fell across his eyes. "Yes, yes, yes. But I swear she's not on here. Why do you need my ship, you've already ah got one."

Annu stroked his chin. "Yeah, well, it's no working for me anymore so I need yours. Don't worry; I'll give you directions where you can drop it off for me."

Bilbo licked his lips. "Huh? I can't do that. They'll arrest me or worse kill me."

Annu dispatched the second cannon and zoomed it a metre from Bilbo's head. "What's that?"

Bilbo shook and flung his hands in the air. "I'll adjust the seat for you."

Annu turned from the window and faced Irica. "When I've checked the ship can you please you come over and keep an eye on Bilbo while I get back with Shayne. However, if Shayne appears, run out and get her. Okay?"

Irica's clap drilled into his brain. "Of course. Thank the Gods. It's all working out after all."

Annu slid out of the seat, relief lightened his step. "Don't bust your gut getting too excited yet. You've forgotten it's me and her against Shamesh and so far we haven't matched well."

At the entrance to the cargo hold Irica screeched. "Oh there she is, she's running down the drive way. It's Shayne. Annu, it's Shayne."

He exhaled, and strode through the cargo hold. "Awesome. About time something went right."

A weight dropped from his back.

Thank you Gods, if you're responsible. Maybe things aren't so flarked after all. We've got safe travel to the mountain place and with no one but a few people knowing where it is, we're safe until we do this ascension thing. It's been a rough ride but everything going to change now. A hell of a test, but we passed it.

Chapter 26: Stranger Danger
Yebu Mountains, Enki Continent, Orion

After several years of absence, and her liking it, the sudden return of Shayne's sex drive unsettled her.

Of all the fucking times and places you picked this one.

A seven foot plus chocolate God drove them to pursue a last ditch attempt for sex. The way the PO's clothes hugged Annu's body and emphasised his muscles gave Shayne butterflies. The fact Annu treated her like a child in return, didn't change a fucked-up thing.

Shayne replaced thoughts of Annu's naked body with the huge pizza she'd eat once back home; one topped with crispy salami, melted cheese, and enough calories her arse jiggled for days. The taste tingled on her tongue, imaginary oil dripped from Shayne's chin onto her shirt.

Oh yeah, that's much better. And I'll wash it down with a big huge joint followed by a man sized Kit-Kat. Mmm. Man size, like Annu. Oh shit. That went to hell quick. Try again, pizza, pizza, pizza.

The ship shuddered and returned Shayne's attention to the present. They drifted over a huge barn style home with several outbuildings scattered across the property, and abutted mountains upon mountains. Shayne shivered and rubbed her shoulders. Annu landed in an adjacent paddock behind the house.

We're finally here and safe. Except for the fact I can't get home yet, and the whole ascendino thing, I saved myself and I'm okay.

Irica bounced off her seat, the joy in her demeanour a solo endeavour. "We're here. I can't believe it, we're actually here."

Annu's sigh matched Shayne's; one massive problem behind them, more and bigger ones were on their way.

Irica hobbled past Shayne's seat and disappeared into the cargo hold.

Half a dozen people, the same size and colour as Annu and Irica ran from the house. They collected weapons from a container on the porch and headed for their ship.

Oh crap. Are they going to shoot us? Shit.

Shayne smoothed her top down and fixed a few misplaced buttons.

I didn't think about other people seeing me. I'm in shitty ripped pyjamas, my hairs a fucking rat's nest, and I stink like arse and dirty socks.

Annu cracked his neck, rolled his shoulders and pushed off the arm rest. Her hormones flip flopped, her ovaries yearned.

I want your sex, da di da di, I want your love. Da, di, da, di, da. I want your–

"Hello Shayne?"

Sex, sex, sex. Shit. He's talking to me. Focus you idiot.

Annu pressed a succession of buttons on a console and stood beside her seat. "Did you hear me?"

Shayne held in the masculine aroma. "Huh, no sorry. I was ah, thinking."

He cocked an eyebrow. "You can't sit there all day." Annu adjusted the locket around his neck.

I wonder if you taste like chocolate topping?

"Why do you wear that?"

Annu looked the way and covered it with his shirt. "Are you coming or not?"

Interesting. Must have hit a nerve.

"Do I have a choice?"

"No."

Shayne wriggled to the end of the seat and slid onto the floor. "Fine."

A long step behind Annu, she followed him through the cargo hold. On a rack beside the door Shayne grabbed a ratty jacket and slung it over her shoulders, the hem brushed against the dirt.

Outside, the cold air fought with the warmth in her lungs. Shayne gasped and tightened the jacket around her. A group of six; all armed, two women and four men including Zex, encircled Irica. At sight of Annu and Shayne, Irica and the group rushed over to them. Zex's familiar presence comforted her.

Both women, one a redhead, the other a blonde matched the men in height and resembled Amazonian goddesses. Even if Shayne spent a month in a tanning bed, she'd never attain the caramel of their skin glistening in the sun.

Great, fucking competition for Annu I'm no match for.

Irica pushed her way to the front of the group, and stood between Shayne and Annu.

She puffed her chest like a proud grandmother, and grabbed an arm from each of them. "This is Annu, his mother is the Great Goddess Ann, and this is Shayne, her father's Ki. Oh and they have a complete map of the Island." Irica extended a pointed to Zex. "Annu, Shayne you know Zex of course. Annu knows Bu." Irica dipped her head close to Shayne's ear. "The blonde is Bu. She'll be training you along with Zex and Rand."

A shorter compact version of Annu, with more muscles than not, nodded at them. The shaved-headed muscled man waved. His serious demeanour and obvious love of exercise terrified Shayne. "The one on Rand's right is Hyl, he's a protector. Others will arrive in the next few hours once the word is out–the old fashioned way."

Annu tipped his chin at Zex. "I knew you'd be fine."

Shayne stood on her tiptoes. "Good to see you made it okay."

I might have survived being kidnapped but training is going to fucking kill me.

Zex placed a hand on his chest. "It wasn't easy, but it's a story for some other time. Thank the Gods you both made it too."

The blonde bitch, Bu, waved manicured fingers and winked. "It's been a long time Annu. You look good."

Listen woman I'll scale those long legs and strangle you with my chewed finger-nailed hands.

Annu's expression alternated between relief at Zex, and adoration of Bu's perky tits. Another inch closer to Bu, and they'd take his eye out. He stared like a deer caught in nipple lights.

Idiot. What's with men and their fascination with boobs? Maybe I'd know if I'd been graced with any.

Shayne whispered to her left breast. "Don't feel bad. It's not your fault we missed puberty."

Irica motioned to a white haired man. "And last but not least, are Jonn, the head of the protectors, and the red headed bomb shell is Banna, his daughter. Banna's also second in charge."

The enthusiasm in Jonn's step bellied his age. "You're here. I can't believe it. Though you're a little more worldly or shall I say otherworldly than I expected. We also believed Shamesh obtained the map some time ago. That's another win for us."

Banna tapped Jonn's shoulder. "Father, calm down." She examined Shayne and Annu up and down. "I agree, you're both not what we expected, but it's great news you're not dead and made it here."

Something about Banna's tone and stance crept doubt into Shayne's relief at being there. Everyone else in the group appeared legitimately ecstatic about their survival and subsequent arrival, but Banna's smile and soft tone didn't convince Shayne. An expert at fake, she spotted one a mile away.

Don't be stupid. I'm only suspicious of her because she's got long legs and tits. Why do I always have to put a negative spin on everything? Time to make a change. Take each person as they come. Don't over dramatise.

Irica's smile widened, she hugged Shayne and Annu to her. "It's finally happening."

Shayne strained her neck at Irica. "Whatever happy pills you took before can I have some please?"

Irica frowned and glanced between Shayne and Annu. "Pardon?"

Shayne's muscles ached, exhaustion fogged her brain. "Never mind. Now we're all introduced can I please have a shower, clean clothes and something to eat?"

Irica released her hold on Shayne and Annu. "Oh yes of course. Silly me, I got caught up. After all you've both been through over the last twenty-four hours you deserve a rest."

Irica led Shayne and Annu by the shoulders towards the rear of the house.

Her legs miles long, Bu ran ahead and opened the back door. "It's still a little dusty but it's pretty clean. We've got food and supplies arriving with the rest of the protectors in an hour or so."

The idea of a long shower followed by sleeping off a food coma kept Shayne on her feet. "Sounds good to me. Show me where the bathroom is and I'll see you when the food arrives."

Annu brushed past her, a tickle ran over her groin.

I still want your sex, di, di, da, da, di. But probably not your love.

The stick dropped out from under the ring and took the ring with it."Crap. Not now."

Annu sighed and retrieved it. "I'll put it on a chain for you. Then this won't keep happening."

Maybe he does like me. He might want my sex.

"Oh that would be lovely thank you."

Chapter 27: Lead Feet
Yebu Mountains, Enki Continent, Orion

Annu bypassed the main area filled with a few dozen protectors and strode towards a set of trees in the rear yard, grateful to dodge Shayne for a moment.

Halfway there, he stopped Banna, a female version of her strong featured father. "Everything's under control. I'm going to get some time to myself. I've got my communicator on."

The late afternoon showed the beginning of crow's feet, Banna raised an eyebrow. "No problem. Take it easy. If you want any company let me know."

Nah, your father and Irica would wring my neck. Besides I don't need to have slept with two of the women who are meant to protect me.

Banna's toned legs and pert arse almost changed his mind. "Ah no thanks. I'm ah--no. Not a good idea. Maybe some other time."

Am I sure? No, yes, no. Dead cats, dead birds, nuns and Irica naked. Okay, yes, I am sure.

The sky alight, Annu jogged into the night and the East woods. He picked dried Grenberry from beneath the bush and crumbled it into a smoke. With his back against a trunk, Annu slid onto the grass, and stargazed.

Annu inhaled his lung's capacity and held it, his body relaxed limb by limb. "I never thought in a million years any of this would happen. I'm important and I've got a purpose. Who'd have thunk it?"

A finger traced constellations, comets zipped by. Owl's hooted; animals of the night eyed him with curiosity and went on their way. The needed time to gather his thoughts at hand, Annu liquefied into the trunk.

Branches crunched, leaves rustled, wariness replaced calm.

Please don't be Banna, please Gods. I'm not sure I can or want to refuse another offer.

Shayne pushed through a bush and strolled towards him, hugging herself. Annu welcomed relief with a hint of sexual frustration.

Her delicate features swallowed by one of the protector's children's clothes. "There you are; I've been looking for you." Shayne held out the chain. "Thank you so much for this. I really appreciate it. Ah what are you doing out here by yourself?"

Tranquility interrupted, tree bark dug into his back. "The being by myself part."

Annu inhaled the smoke; the breeze wafted the aroma in Shayne's direction.

Her eyes widened, her mouth dropped open. She lunged at him. "Oh my fucking God. Is that what I think it is? You shit head, you've been holding out on me."

Annu held it mid puff. "Huh?"

Shayne crouched down in front of him and shook his knees. "The stuff you're smoking idiot, it's weed, ganja, the whacky tobacky–right? It get's you smashed, makes you relaxed and get the munchies? Great pain killer, makes life less sucky–that stuff?"

Annu shrugged and readjusted his position. "Oh well, then yes, but it's called Grenberry. Grows everywhere."

Shayne plonked back against the trunk beside him. "Oh, my fucking God, you're kidding me? At any point since I've been here I could have been smashed out of my gourd?"

The buzz dwindled; Annu's happy place became invaded by oestrogen and uncommon sense. "No to the first question and what the flark to the second."

Shayne wriggled her butt closer. "If you tell me there's a chocolate version of it, I might have to jump you. Please, please, please, can I have a drag?"

Annu flushed, and avoided eye contact.

What's with women tonight? Have I become irresistible? Maybe they detect my Godliness.

"I'll roll you a whole smoke if you don't jump me."

Shayne's clap sealed the deal on his no-longer-alone fate. "Done deal. Can you please make it a big fat one after today? Why isn't everyone high all the time?"

Annu placed his smoke on the ground next to him, and rolled another for Shayne. "What's the point of that, you'd never get anything done."

She looked at him like he'd grown a dick on his forehead. "Yeah, so?"

He passed her a smoke and a lighter. "I've got to warn you, it's strong stuff, and you're only little."

Shayne held it to her lips and dragged. "Oh please, I can handle my shit. I'm a seasoned professional."

She coughed, looked at the smoke, at him, "Geez things are a little blurry," and repeated the process.

Annu re-lit his and kept her in the periphery. "You get that. How do you feel now we're here and safe?"

"About as good I can after several near death experiences and the whole freezing people shit. It certainly made me feel, ah, alive. Though I did have to save myself."

The memory perturbed him, but not enough to care why.

All she's got going for her is she's easy on the eye, for a pale, little person.

"Why is it wrong to save yourself? You got out before I got there and it's all over. So get over it."

Shayne clicked her tongue and licked her lips. "Alrighty then grumpy. I'll keep that in mind for the next time. I sure hope you don't need me to rescue you one day."

Frustration stampeded what remained of his happy place. "As f–"

Be patient. She's young. Don't start an argument and totally ruin my night. And the next couple of days with her. Change the subject to something light and fluffy.

"What's Earth like?"

Shayne smoked like she talked, nonstop. "Oh, so now you're a chatty Cathy. It's the same but different I guess. It's hard to say given I've only seen your place, a shit load of trees, One-one's place and the cave we met in. I've noticed everything's bigger, including the people, brighter and more advanced here. Though Earth has its own amazing unique wonders. Although I haven't seen any of them. Maybe one day you'll see it and decide for yourself. If we make it through this."

Mental note: don't ask who One-one is.

"Yeah maybe."

Puff, puff, puff, blow and repeat. "I could return the favour."

She's not so bad. Being stuck with her might not suck as much as I thought.

"What do you do with your time there? Do you work?"

Shayne turned away from him and spoke to the opposite tree. "Ah, what I'm doing right now pretty much sums it up. Like I said, on Earth my body is sick. So I had to give up working, but then again, I never really worked consistently and there wasn't much to stop doing."

Empathy urged Annu to understand. "But not here? Are you bedridden? Is there anything doctors can do to help?"

Shayne wriggled her toes. "No. Not so far, but in both regards, my options are limited. There's probably lots of things I can still do, but until I came here, I didn't consider them. I, ah, had a few issues."

Why did I dismiss her so quickly?

"What about your kids or husband? Do they live with you? Who's looking after them while you're here?"

Shayne drifted into his side and slumped against his shoulder. Her puffs got further apart. "My kids are adults so they look after themselves, and often me too, thankfully. I kind of suck at parenting, but that's all going to change when I go home, believe me. I no longer have a husband. We divorced and he died. Well, killed by a manure truck."

Annu remembered why he'd kept her at a distance on an emotional level.

Yeah, these kind of things.

"You should never take your children for granted. Nor should you wait for an epiphany to change into a good parent. You must make up for it. And I assume divorce means you ended the marriage on purpose. Why would you marry someone and then break up? It's a huge commitment."

"Oh Grumpy's back. Yeah, I know all of that, so don't you give me a hard time about it. I don't see a wife and kids running to your side, buddy. Where are they, huh? Who exactly is in the locket?"

Shayne reached towards it, Annu slapped her hand onto his chest. "My life and family is none of your business."

Shayne retracted her hand. "Oooh, touchy, touchy. Don't get your knickers in a twist."

Annu moved the back of her head from his ribs. "What are knickers? You know we talk the same language but I don't understand half of what you say."

Her words grew teeth and bit. "Look I'll sum things up for you. I'm not perfect and my life story is a fucking downer. For fuck's sake, I don't need to explain anything to you. Just roll me another one okay?"

Annu worked the smoke between his fingers, mastered it one-handed and gave it to her lit. Her revelations niggled at him and refused to leave him be.

I don't know why I care, but I do.

"So on Earth you can get married and break up if it doesn't work out? That's ridiculous. Marriage isn't something you should take lightly or make frivolous decisions about. I hope you don't plan on doing either parenting or marriage again. So you're not a good parent, and purposely did this divorce to your late husband."

Shayne drew on the smoke and exhaled another two times. A cloud of smoke mushroomed from the ground around them. "You know jack shit about it. Considering you aren't married, you aren't in a position to be fucking judgmental. I'm not getting into this with you. It's none of your —" Shayne jumped and pointed into the woods. "Holy shit. Did you see the size of that fucking unicorn?"

Annu cut off the piece of his mind on the tip of his tongue and followed her line of sight, ready to pounce. "What did you see?"

Shayne plonked onto the grass, her hands on her knees and rocked back and forth. "A fucking unicorn. It took off after the purple koala and they both looked furious. I'm not a hundred percent sure but I think the koala had a block of chocolate."

Annu placed a hand on her forehead, her temperature didn't feel hot. "Are you okay?"

Shayne swayed, her eyes drooped. "I blan't teel my pegs, bland my tips ningle."

"I warned you."

She slumped forward face first onto the ground, thud, and snored.

Leave her or take her to bed?

His conscious made up his mind. "Flarking hell."

Annu picked Shayne up into his arms and carried her back to her room.

Chapter 28: I Want Your Sex
Yebu Mountains, Enki Continent, Orion

Mellow from a recent holy shit weed session, Shayne crossed her legs under her butt and rolled her neck side to side. No more worry about kidnappers and police afforded some peace of mind. The Shamman situation drifted to the back of Shayne's mind, far away next to debt collectors and chocolate withdrawal. Not even all the training they did, nor the suns behind the clouds, deterred a nice buzz and tingles down her back.

Shadow dulled Irica's dark features and gave her a magical appearance. "Now you've received some of your powers, mental development and state of mind, particularly learning control–" she glared disappointment, "are equally as paramount as the physical parts. After a few more sessions, you'll begin navigating the traps located around the mountains here. Unlike the real ones, the fake ones won't kill you if you get it wrong, but they do bite. Each mistake will cost you, so don't muck up."

Annu shuffled beside Shayne and shifted between arse cheeks. "So what's the point of this shit? Surely there's better things we should be doing?"

I wonder what you taste like. Chocolate topping or hot chocolate?

Irica aimed a wooden cane at him. "Do you know how to use your powers yet?"

Annu protected his face and wriggled back. "No. But––"

The cane emphasised each of Irica's words. "Do you know how to fight, and protect yourself yet?"

Annu lifted his chin. "Well, sort of. I'm getting there. It's not like it came with a manual."

Or Chocolate ice cream with crushed nuts?

Irica jabbed the cane in her direction. "Shayne? How about you?"

I don't get stuck on the roof anymore, and I haven't frozen my bed for hours. "Ah, yeah, kind of."

Irica waved it side-to-side. "Oh, well you're all prepared then to face Shamesh aren't you?"

Shayne fingered the chain around her neck, her legs tucked under. "No, I didn't exactly say that."

The cane swung before them. "Then both of you shut up and listen. And don't forget Shayne, the only reason you've still got your ring at all is because Annu put it on a chain for you."

Shayne flounced her arms; Irica shaved off a layer of peace. "Geez, I know. There's no need to bring it up again. Talk about a buzz kill."

Irica stopped mid rant. "Suck it up princess, or shut up and nut up. You know, I've always wanted to say that."

Shayne uncrossed her legs and suppressed giving Irica the finger.

Calm blue ocean, calm blue ocean.

The buzz tickled the back of her neck.

Ah, there you are.

The cane remained at her side. "Aside from staying alive of course, the most important part out of everything is the incantation. When the three scrolls are re-joined, they form the words, but you must pronounce them correctly. Fortunate for us, long ago I obtained a copy of it. I've written it down for each of you to practice with."

Irica passed Shayne a faded piece of paper of indecipherable words no matter which angle she tried. "It looks like you threw up the alphabet on here."

Irica passed one of the same to Annu, who vocalised her thoughts. "Are you kidding me?"

"Don't be overwhelmed by how difficult it seems. I've written it phonetically as well to help pronunciation. The first word, Eheieh, is the divine name, you say it three times. Yaweh Eloah Va Daath, means bring down the light from above. You say that after Eheieh, five times. Please practice it every chance you get, the order must be right."

Blades of grass jabbed the back of Shayne's legs. "Well, we're fucked if it comes down to this. I can't even speak English properly."

Annu held the paper at the tip of his nose. "I agree. Do you have any idea what happens if we do manage this? What if we step on the circles and get blown to smithereens?"

"I doubt after putting you through the arduous process, the Gods would then blow you to pieces. It kind of defeats the purpose dumb arse."

Ouch. Ha. For once it's not aimed at me.

Irica droned on and on. "Other than obtaining all the power, I don't know. History from here is unwritten; it's up to the two of you to make it." Irica tapped her hand on her hip.

Annu scoffed; his arms across his chest. "I can see the history book's title now, 'the adventures of balloon girl and flame man'."

Shayne drifted up from the ground. "You're just jealous because I've got two powers and you've still only got one."

Annu placed a hand on her head, bobbing her up and down. "Yeah, whatever."

Irica slammed the cane on the ground. "Enough. Leave each other alone and practice meditation or the incantation. Something not related to annoying the other. You've got to take each aspect seriously. The protectors have dedicated their lives for you and this opportunity, treat it with the gravity it deserves."

"Oh yeah, I guess it explains why they are so uptight."

Irica combed a hand through her hair. "If by uptight you mean, they are completely dedicated to the Gods and want us to succeed on their behalf, then yes you are right. Now shut up and meditate."

Annu tensed; his shoulders stiffened. "God's dammit woman. Fine, but if someone sees us, you're both dead to me."

Shayne rested her hands onto her knees. "It's sort of fun and I always wanted to learn how."

Mostly for when I ran out of weed and valium.

Annu plucked tufts of grass and flicked them. "Let's get this over with before I want to wear a skirt or something."

Irica tapped her cane against his left leg.

Her condescending tone tested Shayne's patience. "Oh, for goodness sake, relax, drop your shoulders and lift your heads up. Work on clearing your mind."

Annu's smirk highlighted his dimples. "That won't take Shayne long."

If I wasn't so baked and still lusting after you, I'd punch you right now.

Smack, Irica struck him on the leg, Annu grabbed at the cane; she whipped it out of reach. "Too slow. Shut up and be calm for Gods' sake."

Shayne closed her eyes and imagined the beach–her toes squished in the sand, the wave's edge lapped her feet. Her muscles relaxed, the few thoughts in her head ebbed away with the tide.

Okay, this isn't too hard.

Whack, whack.

Annu boomed near her ear. "Ouch. Stop doing that."

The imaginary scene faltered, sea gulls squawked, tourists laid their towels along her beaches.

Oh for fuck's sake. Try again. People all gone, it's only me. Beautiful day, calm sea. Mmmm, that's it.

Whack, whack. "Annu, stop twirling your thumbs."

Shayne's last nerve snapped. "Oh, for fuck's sake. You're killing my buzz."

Annu grasped the cane, broke it over his knee, and threw it into a nearby tree branch.

Irica's face fell; she watched its path. "Hey that's 2000 years old."

"If I didn't throw it, you'd be wearing it."

Irica squinted, her teeth gritted. "Alright well, start again." She stiffened, her expression darkened. "Oh, no."

Shayne followed Irica's line of sight, sobriety smacked her across the face.

One of Rand's security men, Lauc, bounded in their direction, the man's shirt ripped, his face dirty. "Excuse me Annu, Shayne, Irica."

Shayne's guts dropped, her chest constricted. "What's going on?"

It can't be anything bad. We're here. It's all meant to be rainbows and fucking unicorns now.

Lauc's Adam's apple jiggled. "Sorry to interrupt."

The concern in Annu's voice raised her panic level. He pushed off the ground onto his feet. "No better time, what's going on? What happened?"

Stormy seas with rogue waves crash onto the shore. Bastards.

Sweat poured from Lauc's forehead. "We caught some men in the woods not far from here. All but one got away, and we've got him restrained. Rand's questioning him now."

Panic froze Shayne's movement; she painted on a brave facade. "What's he said so far?"

Agitation permeated from Lauc, he finger combed his hair. "Ah. Nothing helpful–"

Annu grabbed his shirt front. "Spit it out."

"He says they were camping in the woods nearby and had no idea anyone lived here."

Shayne's panic lessened, she perched on her knees "There you go. It must be a coincidence then. No need to flip out."

Annu released Lauc and ignited in flames. "I don't believe in coincidences. Take me to him now."

Annu's paranoia invaded Shayne's calm. A chill ran down her spine. She raised her own aura and levitated beside Annu.

No, it can't be. He's just being his usual macho self. Right? Ghost Dad you there?

Chapter 29: Erectile Dysfunction
Yebu Mountains, Enki Continent, Orion

With hours of endless training, dealing with Shayne's proclivity for being smashed, alcohol withdrawal, sexual frustration and the intruder, Annu struggled not to explode. Tension crackled in the air, his skin hummed.

Annu held the intruder by the jacket and an inch off the ground.

Bu, Rand, and Zex stood a metre back from the intruder, in states of disbelief.

Shayne hovered at one of his sides, Irica the other.

A group of protectors watched from across the yard, yet despite all the people around them only Annu and the man existed.

Annu's temperature soared; he grabbed the man around the neck and raised him higher. "Who sent you here? How many of you are there? Tell me."

The man's innocent expression and tone only irritated Annu further. "No one sent me, you maniac. I don't know what you're talking about. My friends and I were camping in the woods. It's a good place for elk. We do it every year at this time."

Irica used her stern mother voice. "Calm down. He might be telling the truth. Don't hurt him when you don't have to. You need to be in control not let it control you."

He'll pay for stealing the modicum of safety I felt.

Annu shook him, the man's jaw rattled. "Of all the places in Orion you chose near here to hunt. Bullshit it's an accident. You've got one more chance to tell the truth or I turn you into a pile of ash."

Shayne tapped his shoulder, her hand icy. "Look, after an hour of you scaring the shit out of him and us–he's sticking to his story. There's obviously nothing to worry about. Besides you creating an issue of course. He'll go back to his friends and they'll tell everyone about us now."

Despite no actual evidence, a glimmer of hatred in the man's eye warned Annu otherwise.

Annu shrugged Shayne off and lowered the man onto his feet. "Back up. I'm not taking any chances and he's not going anywhere."

Shayne flung her arms in the air. "Will you at least listen to one of us before you screw things up?"

Flames enveloped his body, everybody jumped several metres back. "No one's going to flark this up when we're so close. I won't allow it."

Blood thick in his veins, rage bubbled through him. Annu allowed the heat to consume, burn, fuel and excite his ire. Patches of dead grass caught fire, embers drifted into the air. The man's shirt and skin burned, Annu dropped him, and he landed with a thud.

Rand and a few protectors rushed to the man, and diminished the burning clothes and flesh.

The fearful faces in the vicinity didn't concern him, Annu rose an inch from the ground, the clothes crackled and peeled from his body.

Annu ignored Irica cries and Shayne's pleas. Power pulsated through him, absolute, undeniable.

How dare they treat me like a common mortal? Shamesh and his men must know how powerful we are. Let him live in fear.

'Son. Don't give into it.'

'It's incredible, amazing. I'm a God, nothing can touch me.'

Icy water blasted him from three angles, the fire doused. Annu dropped to the ground, his former glory shrivelled.

Balls in the dirt, his godly disintegration abrupt. "What the flark?"

Rand loomed, hose in hand, drops of water plonked onto his leg. "You over yourself now, friend? I thought we'd lost you there for a bit."

Frustration splashed with humiliation propelled him from the ground. "Get that thing away from me."

So much for fire retardant clothes.

Rand threw the hose aside. "Hey, where are you going?"

Annu stomped towards the house, and ignored all pleas, a bare arse his only reply.

Great, I made an idiot of myself in front of people who are meant to respect and admire me.

Two feet from the backyard, a firm hand on the shoulder stopped him. He flung around. "What do you want?"

Bu's frown incongruent with her beauty; she stroked his arm, goosebumps formed. "What's going on? That wasn't like you at all? You seemed out of it." Her eyes drifted over his lower half. "None of you is yourself right now."

Past the worry of dignity, Annu slumped against a nearby tree. "There's so much going on. All this responsibility on my shoulders, it's overwhelming. And I have this power I can't control, we keep messing up training and we're yet to even see the practice traps. Plus time is short running out. I'm the only one who thinks that man's trouble. Maybe I'm losing my shit and the powers going to my head."

Bu leant against his chest. "Possibly a little, but it's understandable given the circumstances. Hey the training you've been doing is paying off."

Annu nodded, the pain in his head escalated. "Really?"

"Oh yeah. Look at you. Damn, I've never seen you this ripped, toned or as in control. You've got your shit together. Don't lose faith in yourself now."

Her skin shone—her legs endless. If he lost himself between them, he'd plough away vexation.

Damn, I've earned it.

Bu traced a line down his bare chest, a shiver rippled through his groin. "Well I see you've managed to lighten up a little."

Annu pulled her close and kissed her. He'd forgotten how good she tasted; her insistent tongue drove him crazy. Annu kissed along her neck and nuzzled into her shoulder, inhaling the coconut fragrance. Annu delved further, and froze. A flash of blue bolted through the trees, Shayne ran towards the front porch.

He released Bu. "Flark it."

Bu tugged his arm and grabbed his balls.

Annu suppressed a purr.

That feels so flarking good. But I can't–it's not right. Shit.

He stiffened, his erection drooped.

Bu paused massaging his balls one handed. "What's wrong?"

His heart thumped an uneven rhythm, guilt flushed him.

Annu shifted her hand. "Shayne, she saw us."

Bu stiffened and stepped aside. "So. What does that matter whether she did or not?"

He imagined what Shayne might think; it took too long. "Nothing, I guess."

Bu uncreased her top and pulled her skirt down. "You like her don't you?"

Annu's face burned. "No. Don't be ridiculous. She's a complete mess, from another planet and totally wrong for me."

"He," She pointed down, "Suggests otherwise. When you make up your mind either way, you know where to find me. No strings attached, including those on my underwear."

The moisture evaporated from his mouth, Bu disappeared into the bushes. "Damn woman. You don't play fair."

I hope Shayne's okay. Shit. I messed up again.

Annu banged his head against the tree. "Flark, what the hell is wrong with me?"

The unwelcome answer hit him with as much force as the iced water. "Oh crap."

I'm not just attracted to her, I fucking like her. How did that happen? What the hell do I do now? Nothing, it would only flark things up. Shit. Apparently without alcohol I make terrible decisions.

Talk about terrible timing. Hell, she's nothing like Jaid. She's the exact opposite, it's not practical. I've got to keep this under control.

A cold breeze swept between his legs, Annu pushed off the tree and headed to the house in search of clothes and rum.

Chapter 30: Dirty Rotten Bastard
Yebu Mountains, Enki Continent, Orion

Amped up by the ire of a scorned woman, Shayne obliterated the boxing bag Rand held. Bang, bang, bang, she pounded, her pulse raced.

Blood and sweat from her knuckles dripped to the ground, and Shayne loved every minute of it. The realisation she enjoyed exercise no longer bothered her.

Rand tightened his grip on the pads and held them aside. "If I'd known pasting Annu's face to this pad worked this well, I'd have done it ages ago. The last few rounds actually hurt my hands. Well done, Shorty."

The image of Annu and Bu locked in their embrace tormented her; the jealousy streak grew with the day. "Thank you. The god damn, sonnofabitch, fuck face, nimrod, dick nose." She dropped her arms and wiped her nose. "Can I take a smoke break for a minute?"

"Another one? It takes you another twenty minutes before you're focused again. I need you on your toes."

Shayne's irritation level increased. "Yes, I want another one. The last one wore off. Don't test me today, man."

Maybe I am smoking too much. That's the fifth person to say something today alone. Surely it doesn't matter? I'm a fucking grownup and Demi-God after all.

Concern softened Rand's features. "Look, even though they kissed, it doesn't mean anything. They haven't been an item for a long time, and even then it was barely anything worth mentioning. Basically just sex. Look, maybe he needed to let off steam. I wouldn't worry about it if I were you. Unless he takes that locket off, you've got a chance."

Interesting and fucked. Great, Just sex. Like that makes it easier to not care.

Shayne tugged a smoke out of her pocket and lit it.

Wait what did he say?

A warm blanket fell upon her shoulders, but didn't diminish her shock. "Oh my fucking God. I can't believe this shit. How do you know what happened?"

Rand shrugged, a smile broadened. "Everyone knows. Word gets around here fast. There's not much to do besides talking on our rare time off."

Shayne smacked herself in the forehead, her body hummed. "This place is worse than a small town, nothing's secret."

Smoke it away. Puff puff goodbye.

Rand wiggled his eyebrows.

Now what?

"Why are you doing that? Oh shit. You think I like him." Her blood ran cold, embarrassment flushed her face. "It's not just you is it? Who else thinks so?"

Rand glanced at Lauc on his left. "Most of us, I guess. It's pretty obvious."

Shayne spat out a fly. "Argh, disgusting. Well, I don't like him, alright. I'm just miffed because he finds time for a love life while I'm busting my arse out here."

I don't do I? Oh shit.

Rand opened his mouth to speak and closed it again.

She jabbed a finger at him, the bitter taste of insect on her tongue. "Don't shut up now for God's sake."

Shayne wiped her tongue on her sleeve and took another drag. Her annoyance drifted away, she forgot why she glared at them.

Rand and Lauc's attention shifted behind her, their expressions transformed from jovial to worried. Shayne turned; heart in her throat, a group of protectors raced past them with their weapons drawn. The smoke fell from her mouth onto the ground.

A laser gun replaced Rand's punching bags, the levity in his stance gone.

Shayne searched for a weapon of her own, spotting several laser sticks against a tree, she lunged at them. She misjudged the distance and grabbed a chunk of tree bark instead. Shayne shook herself.

Idiot. You stupid woman.

A stick in each hand, Shayne caught up with Rand. Her brain wobbled, the buzz in her body slowed her. Shayne legs waded through cement, she fought to sober up.

Annu, Zex, and Bu barrelled towards them, guns drawn. Annu paused and her grabbed Shayne's arm. His hand hot on Shayne's skin, Zex and Bu continued ahead.

Shayne swallowed fear close to eruption. "What the hell's going on?"

Annu's unreadable expression injected panic and weighed her dulled senses. "I hate saying it but I'm right. That guy's one of Shamesh's men. We're under attack. Stay close to Rand. I don't think we should be together, then they can't get us both at the same time. At least this way, maybe--" Annu directed his attention to Rand; they walked and talked in the direction of the outer yards. "Keep an eye on her no matter what. Give me your word?"

Rand slowed his pace to match hers. "Of course. Flark. How bad is it?"

Annu ignited and took the gun off safety. Sweat seared across his forehead. "Bad."

Shayne's thoughts tumbled, her body on automatic pilot. "Shit, shit, shit. I'm not ready yet. I so wanted to believe him."

Annu swung back to her; a shiver ran up her spine. "You'll be alright, remember our training and be safe." He pulled her towards him and squinted. "Flark. Are you off your face?"

Shayne shrugged him off. Her guts churned, anxiety increased each step. "No, of course not. I'm fine."

Fuck, fuck, fuck. This time my lies might kill me. I don't want another reason to disappoint him.

"You wouldn't be stupid enough to jeopardise all our safety now, right?"

Yes, yes I would.

Shayne stared ahead. "I said no. So fucking leave it."

Annu's expression hardened, a cold wall built from her lies, and his hope went up between them. "Fine. I'll take your word for it."

They ducked through bushes, around trees, and over stumps. The end of the woods marked the commencement of mayhem and the end to her sanity.

A chill settled at the base of her neck, a cacophony of screams echoed through the open paddocks. The smell of burnt flesh infiltrated the air. Blood painted rocks, the ground, and its benefactors.

Shayne broached; the sound of her heart loud in her ears. She lost sight of Rand, Zex, and Annu. A tidal wave of war swept over the landscape, Shayne stood alone amongst a sea of strangers all intent on her death. She whipped the sticks in rotation; people attacked her in a blur.

A man lunged, his hands raised. Crack, crack, her reactions slowed, she struck him. The sticks vibrated off his chest, he shrugged, reefed the sticks out of her hands, and threw her aside.

Shayne flung into the front of a male protector.

He dragged her behind him. "Get out of the way. Go and hide somewhere. I'll cover you."

Shayne searched for familiar faces. "No. I'm staying to fight."

The noise of battle buried her response; Shayne struggled to focus, push aside the gory scenes around her and play her part.

Three men stormed at her, shots from a laser gun behind them zipped past her head, forcing her to act; she dove out of the way.

Shayne regained her footing, stumbled over legs and feet and landed on her knee. She took the opportunity and scrambled across the ground for a safe place.

Smack, pain erupted across her back, a force stomped on her ankle, and twisting it left. She kissed the dirt, agony swept through her. Shayne rolled between oncoming legs, toward a laser gun in the hand of a dead man over to her right.

Feet surrounded her; she dodged a parade of boots ahead. Knees grazed, Shayne reached the outstretched arm and released the fingers around the gun.

Shayne blasted rounds into the air, the immediate area around her cleared. Shayne jumped up, swung the gun side to side and shot in a circle. A foot connected with her hand, sending the gun into the air, and her sideways.

A man twice the size of Annu grabbed her by the shoulder and thudded her into a tree trunk. The air whooshed from her lungs; a boot snapped her left arm in half. Shayne screamed and clutched the pieces to her. Eyes closed, she missed an incoming punch to the face. Two more followed the first, her brain exploded in light.

Shayne dropped to the ground; trampled by random feet, agony tore through her. She bit down on her tongue and wriggled toward a group of herb bushes. Blood streamed down her face into her mouth, the cold hand of death tickled her neck.

She reached the edge and leant against thick shrub; her head lolled; ahead, dodging a slew of bodies, Zex and Annu slashed through several men.

Weapons raised, two men came up behind them. Her screams intensified the pain; she clutched her stomach and clawed at the dirt. "Annu, look out."

Annu erupted in flames and incinerated those around him; protectors filled the empty space of dead enemy.

An attacker raised a laser sword at Zex's head; the attacker swept his arm down and split the man in half. A sight not fit for human eyes, each side slipped to the ground, something in her mind snapped.

Rand appeared from a set of rocks and fired his gun at the man who'd killed Zex. He failed to see two men behind him; one shot Rand, his head exploded.

Her sword raised; Bu dragged a leg towards a group of men; a large gash down one side of her cheek oozed. A woman came up behind her and sliced Bu around the middle, Bu crumbled to the ground.

A dry raspy croak came out instead of a scream.

Lightning cracked overhead, storm clouds filled the sky. Big fat rain drops plopped onto, terror blinded Shayne's vision.

Feet stomped her outstretched broken arm, another kicked her in the ribs.

Shayne fell backwards into the bush. "Annu--"

Pain crippled her mind, unconsciousness offered salvation. Shayne succumbed; Ki appeared in white light in the distance. 'Hold on, child."

The light around her grew, soft music filled her mind; the pain subsided. "I'm so tired, and it hurts too much."

******

Occupied by the fray and confident in his decision to separate them, Shayne slipped his mind. With the enemy fallen or perished and no sign of her, Annu searched the line of people going past. Guilt leadened his step.

Adrenaline overtook pain; he trudged through the battle area. "Shayne?"

Zex's, Bu and Rand's death replayed in his mind, nausea bubbled in his gut.

I can't believe he's gone. Oh gods, if Shayne's—no don't think about it. If I didn't care about her, this wouldn't be so fucking hard.

Clothes tattered; hands held over a deep wound to her thigh, Apri, a younger protector approached him. "I'm sorry, we haven't found her yet."

Annu's bowels churned.

Please, please be okay.

"Keep looking. Once she's found, you get yourself fixed up."

Her gaze downcast, she winced. "At least we won, this time."

Annu turned away, tears burned his eyes. "Did we?"

He walked off and pushed past protectors who gathered injured enemy, in the direction of the furthest yard. It took all his strength not to stop and tear them apart, make every one of them pay.

His throat constricted, the gash on his arm bled a trail on the dirt.

'Mother are you there? Please, please let her be alive. Keep her safe until I find her.'

'Mother?'

Of all times for her not to answer him, she picked the worst. Scenarios of Shayne's death played through his mind and removed his rationality.

The crew cleared the bodies from the adjacent section an hour ago, not yet reaching this field.

Be here.

"Shayne, where the flark are you?"

Wind pushed him towards the shrubs. He fought wind belting him towards the shrubs, and examined the area a foot at a time.

From one side of the paddock to the other, he stepped over bodies and checked faces. Hope soared and faded with each wrong person, nature replicated his emotions.

Annu had no luck within the grass area and returned to the tree break beside the shrubs. Leant against a bush, a tingle ran up his spine.

'In the middle, quick—'

Annu delved in; a flash of red revealed his worst fears. "Oh Gods, no."

He lowered and pulled an inert arm towards him. Her pallid skin and bloody sleeve stopped his heart.

Annu swallowed vomit and dragged Shayne from her entangled prison. "No, no, no, no."

She crumbled into his arms, bones broken, limbs twisted. A lifeless parody of the woman she'd been. He wiped the dirt from her face and picked leaves from her hair.

Tears mingled with the rain and spilt across blue lips. "I'm so sorry. This shouldn't have happened."

Annu wiped his thumb across her mouth and kissed her.

She spluttered; mud projected from her lips onto his face. Shayne heaved in air.

He flipped her onto the side and patted her on the back.

Muck spewed out her mouth, she trembled in his arms. "Am I dead?"

Annu wrapped his jacket around her. "No, not if I can help it."

Heart in his throat, he power walked to the medical tents, in a careful embrace.

Annu pushed backwards through the doors and launched at the first doctor in sight. "Help her, please."

Staff surrounded him; a woman removed Shayne from his arms and nodded. "I'm Doctor Andrew. She's in good hands; we'll take it from here. Open up Exam 3, fluids and damage control stat. I want the IC Unit in here now."

The doctor rushed into a nearby examination room, Annu stood outside the glass doors. She slid Shayne onto an examination table like a child's toy. Several staff flooded into the room, dragged over beeping machines and plugged her in. She fought their attempts to insert an IV and passed out.

Annu grabbed the arm of a nurse exiting the room. "Will she be okay?"

"If we can get her body to take over the healing of the major injuries, she'll be fine in a couple of hours. Being small, fragile, and badly hurt, I don't know, it doesn't look good. We'll do everything we can."

The smell of jasmine swept past him, the kind in Jaid's garden. He realised he'd not thought about her until now, when death arrived. A fresh tonne of guilt smacked him; two hundred years and he'd forgotten her.

Surrounded by people, loneliness consumed him. Annu hungered to share, experience, feel, love.

Yet thoughts of Shayne confused him and muddled his focus.

I can't do this now; it will get us both killed. I've got to stay distant.

From now on, he'd keep her safe by his side, but whatever flarked up things he felt for her, ended now.

Chapter 31: Day of the Dead, A Grieving Empire
Yebu Mountains, Enki Continent, Orion

With his arm around Irica's waist, Annu absorbed her strength. Tears and emotions buried, he'd grieve alone later. A flick of a protector's wrist levered Zex, Bu, Rand, and thirty odd Protectors into their respective graves, his confidence in success went down with them.

The horns mournful tune set the tone for the day. The attack cast a shadow over the camp; dampened spirits and destroyed faith. Diminished contact with Annu's mother increased his burgeoning unease.

Grateful for the respite in rain, Annu kissed Irica's head and pulled her closer.

Irica trembled; his shirt stifled her sobs and soaked her grief.

Annu bit the inside of his mouth and steadied himself, the last funeral forever scarred upon his soul.

Shayne's absence at his side left a hole, unexpected, and unwelcome.

Well I've got myself to blame for not telling her so.

Annu, the night before, questioned the Gods' benevolence and lack of intervention; an answer eluded him. Were they chess pieces on a giant board, manipulated and played with when suited?

His wounds itched; he embraced the discomfort as a reminder of their situation.

Like I need another one.

The funeral process completed, Annu turned to the diminished group behind him.

Their eyes belied shock, fear and hopelessness; not an unmarked body between them. "As difficult as it is, we are staying here for now. I want to pack up and leave, but, it's pointless going to the island yet. We're all deeply affected and the losses we suffered were enormous. Despite this, stick by us and see this through to the end. No matter what it brings."

A long pause filled him with dread, Jonn spoke for the group. "If you both remain in control, there'll be no issues."

Relief chipped a chunk of worry off his mind. "I won't let you regret it."

I hope.

"Lauc remains in a coma, medical aren't sure he'll make it. If you don't already pray, now would be a great time to start." Breakfast lumped at the back of his throat. "Training recommences in an hour. Meet back here." His head thumped, the pain in his ribs vibrated through his chest. "Get some rest, food; clean up, whatever, it's your last chance. Be safe, I'll see you all later."

The prior morning they'd bounded off with enthusiasm, this day, they left with the weight of the world upon their shoulders.

Buried in his own thoughts, at some point he'd missed Irica leaving his side. Annu strode towards the house, a quarter of the way out of the field; his legs buzzed, vibrated and tingled.

Annu shook them and stretched his calves, the sensation intensified. His hands and temperature cool, Annu pinched the flesh on his thigh. It responded to pain as usual, yet the strangeness remained, no indication of its intentions.

Annu walked four steps ahead, his feet drifted from the ground.

His mind boggled, he jumped, hopped, skipped, and spun in the air. No matter what, Annu stayed put. "Of all the flarking times. Surely I don't levitate too, it doesn't make sense?"

He closed his eyes. "Alright, clear mind."

Knee first, Annu thudded to the ground. "Shit."

He brushed off dirt, his attention drifted to the medical rooms at the other end of the grounds.

Annu's heart fluttered, he'd left it too late to visit. As much as he wanted to hold and comfort Shayne, her proximity ensured a torrent of emotions.

Before he'd realised, Annu walked halfway to medical. He turned back to the house, the leg buzz returned; stronger, insistent and strange, as if his limbs detached from his brain.

With no regard to gravity, he burst from the ground into the sky.

Annu soared out of control, above the trees, through cloud layers, higher, and higher. The air thinned, his lungs burned, his heart palpitated. The sky turned from blue to grey, his ascent ceased. Panic consumed him; Annu flailed his arms in desperation.

As quick as he rose, Annu plummeted feet first back to Orion. His screams heard only by the flocks of birds who watched him fall.

The tree tops in sight, his journey slowed, Annu's pulse lowered. He maintained a hover at roof height, the ground unattainable.

Beside a black ring burnt into the dirt where he'd taken off, Irica and the Protectors gawked. Irica yelled something indecipherable.

Annu concentrated and staggered down in short, sharp, stages. He dropped the last quarter distance and somersaulted along the dirt to a stop.

He rolled onto his back and patted beneath him. He and the sky back where they belonged. "Thank flark."

Irica wore a tired smile. "Well I didn't expect to see that today. This power might take more practice than the others. Are you okay?"

An epiphany struck amongst his minds confusion and bodies shock. "I think I've worked out how we get through the first trap."

Chapter 32: Empty Vase
Yebu Mountains, Enki Continent, Orion

The vase of wilted flowers on the side table shared Shayne's emotional state, peaked, and circling death. She held her breath and willed away another panic attack. Shayne dared not close her eyes, if she did the battle replayed in her mind.
Cold settled into Shayne's marrow, self hatred and grief filled her veins, bitterness flawed her thoughts.

How did they find us? We're meant to be safe. This isn't fair. It's so fucked up and I'm so fucking stupid. My lack of self control nearly killed me, but it did kill others. It's my fault.

She'd never experienced such physical and emotional torment. Her self-identity remained in the field she'd almost died in.

Doctor Ruc, a shorter, round man, probed the faint scar on her left arm, despite his gentle touch, Shayne cringed. Only the memory of bone stuck through her flesh, shattered ribs, and twisted spine remained.

No. Don't think about it.

The faded bruises left tactile yet intangible evidence of her ability to survive.

The doctor examined close to the bone. "Stretch it out as far as you can. Easy, nice, and slow."

Shayne moved it back and forth, the stiffness gone and muscle healed. Ruc repeated the process with the other arm. When finished, he released the limb and reached to her side.

Shayne flinched and shifted away from his grasp.

Doctor Ruc adjusted his glasses. "I have to check those injuries too."

Shayne protected her torso with an arm; faint boot marks dirtied her skin, her body a war zone. "Don't worry about it, it's fine."

The doctor scooted across the floor on his chair to the desk and slumped his head onto his elbows. "It's understandable to feel this way. You were in a bad way when you came in here, but you got through it. Please, I need to check for myself. I'll be gentle and re-warm my hands."

Shayne focused on the puffs of white hair out his ear hole. Her arm stayed, she wriggled back on the examination table. "No."

The long white eyebrow in the middle of his face wriggled as he spoke. ""Alright, I'll take your word for it, this time. Though I can't say this about your stomach, you've healed remarkably well, physically, in a short time. Of course, the emotional damage takes longer to repair, and you don't have any."

"So, suck it up and keep going?"

Doctor Ruc tapped the desk. "Aha. I can't legitimately keep you here any longer, not when we've got people who may not recover from the attack at all."

Her moral sank lower, Shayne's natural selfish instinct rose again. "Please don't make me go. I can't go back out there yet."

"I'm sorry, Shayne, short of pushing you out the door, we need you out there, not in here."

She willed tears away. "Every time I close my eyes, I relive it all and can't breathe. The air in the room thickens. My chest gets tight and I see stars."

His warm honeyed voice offered little comfort. "Well in fairness to you, it only happened yesterday. In normal circumstances, I'd recommend a lot of therapy and rest. Is everything after you went under the bush still a blur?"

Shayne dispersed a sigh and slipped off the bed. "Yes. Hey doc, who brought me here?"

"I'm not sure that's a bad thing Shayne. I don't know who brought you in; I wasn't on duty at the time. You can check with the nurse on your way out, she'll probably know."

Not FuckFace, because he didn't care enough to visit let alone anything else. He's going to blame me for this. He knows I was smashed as fuck. I'm a stupid cow and I've screwed it all up.

Shayne swallowed regret and self pity. "Okay, thanks."

He flicked off the digital monitors. "Anyway, sorry, we're done here."

She pushed away from the bed and past him. "Alright, I've put it off long enough. I'll grab my shit and go."

"Shayne?"

Half way out the door, she stopped but didn't turn around to look. "Yes."

"I don't want to see you back in here."

"Ditto."

Shayne headed to the recovery room and gathered her few things–a pile of tattered, boot marked blood soaked clothes, alongside a mushed up sandwich she'd stashed the day before. The incongruent mess, surged panic, the stench of death invaded her senses.

The room shrank, her throat constricted, gunfire replaced the hospital noise. Burned flesh, raw bone, open skin, infiltrated the antiseptic aroma.

Shayne slumped onto the mattress, sucked in air, her thoughts scattered, invaded by anxiety. Shayne swallowed bile, her head fuzzy.

Thud, she dropped into a pair of arms, and not onto the floor.

The room swam; unable to focus on her rescuer, Shayne blinked at the three faces. "Oh God. What's happening to me?"

Annu wavered through her stupor; he swept the clothes from the bed onto the floor, and lifted her onto the mattress. "I think the technical term is freaking out. You'll be alright, lay back on the bed. I'll get the doctor."

Shayne clutched at his arm. "No. Don't go. I don't need him."

"Are you sure? You don't look good."

He came. He does care?

"Yes. Why are you here? You're a bit late to see if I'm okay." She raised off the mattress, her brain wobbled. Shayne lay back down. "I'm okay."

Annu's shuffled his feet. "Don't be like that. I, I, I'm not good at this and you're not right."

Shayne's blood pressure plummeted, her lips buzzed. "At checking on someone who's mortally wounded? You're right, you suck."

"I shouldn't have come. I thought I'd—I wanted to tell you—ah —-"

She rolled to her side, the bodily mayhem subsided. Second by second, her pulse lowered, her mind calmed. Shayne waited for him to finish. Tick, tick, tick.

Patience had never been her virtue. "Oh for God's sake. What?"

Annu flinched and thrust his hands in his pockets. "We're training in an half an hour."

Shayne's resolve dissolved. "Is that really what you came to say?"

"I—no—yes."

"Well, thank Gods you did jack arse. You do realise it's too fucking soon. I'm not ready yet. None of us are."

Annu stiffened and pursed his lips. "We don't have the luxury of waiting until we are. We have to do this. I nee—"

An iota of hope poked its way in, Shayne tipped her ear closer. "You what?"

His demeanour stiffened. "I—Ah, forget it, just be at the west field in half an hour. Don't smoke beforehand. That's probably—"

Shame slapped her across the cheeks, Shayne stared at the ceiling. "Don't fucking say it alright? I knew you didn't believe me."

Why should he? I'm full of shit. Why am I still lying to him about it? Why do I fuck myself over all the time?

His stomps ricocheted throughout the room and down the hall. Each plod of his foot represented rejection.

Her heart ached; regret and unrequited love sucked monkey's balls. "I need a fucking smoke. It's been—"

Right before the attack when I trained with Rand.

The harsh truth smacked her, she'd nearly died along with several others, pissed off the man she cared about, and her first thought above all related to getting high. "What the fuck's wrong with me? When did I get like this?"

Shayne lay still until her stomach settled and slid off the bed, her legs wobbled. She struggled to recall at time her life didn't revolve around weed or chocolate.

One hand on the bed rail, she regained her equilibrium. "I've got a fucking problem, don't I? What sort of messed up Demi-God am I? Thank God Ghost Dad isn't around to see his daughter all fucked up."

I have to stop using weed as an emotional bandaid. If I can't stand myself sober, I need to do something about it. Go cold turkey. Me being the turkey. I was already partly there a few days ago. I can do this. I have to do this. Before I get myself and everyone else killed.

The moment of truth arrived; even if she stayed here and hid, they were probably fucked. No way to change the situation, but what she did about it remained hers.

Sit and wait to die or get up and give it everything I've got.

"Nah, fuck it. I got myself into this shit fight, I'll damn well get myself out. Or die trying."

She released the hand rail and staggered towards the door. "Gonna make myself do rehab baby, and no one's gonna know, know, know."

Chapter 33: Orion Shattering Disasters
Yebu Mountains, Enki Continent, Orion

His shoulders up around his neck, Annu paced the East perimeter and checked each trip laser. The lights from the camp grounds dulled in the distance, the glow from his torch the only illumination.

Every other stop Annu kicked something; this time, a peach bush copped his wraith. "How the flark did seven Protectors disappear from the property without anyone noticing? And why am I only finding out about it now?"

Everything's going to hell. We're doomed, flarked and screwed.

Hyl followed him step for step; alternately, calibrated the warning system to a hand-held device and dodged Annu's rage. "Without Rand and the other chunk of security we lost, we've had to do more, with less people. I hate to say it, but there's always a chance they weren't taken, but left voluntarily."

Annu whipped around, the torch light flicked around the woods. Something about Hyl unsettled him; he put it down to an increased distrust of everyone. "What the hell do you mean?"

Hyl flung his arms and fumbled to regain hold of the device. "I, I, I'm not saying they did, just–it's possible. Maybe even preferable to the other option."

His temperature soared, the torch melted in his hand. He dropped it, the light died on contact.

Annu stomped out the flames; the stench of burnt plastic ruined the air. "Shit. Give me your torch."

Hyl unclipped it from his belt and paused halfway, before he handed it over. He glanced at the mess to Annu's left and retracted his arm. "Maybe I'll keep hold of it."

Annu exhaled in a gush and cracked his knuckles.

How much longer can I keep all this wound up inside me?

"Yeah, good idea. Has. Has anyone mentioned they wanted to leave? Flark, I don't need to worry about this shit too."

By torchlight, Hyl's face appeared grotesque, the deep lines across his face, now caverns. "Not that I've heard, but things are pretty crazy around here."

Annu turned back to the trip laser and flicked his leg across it. "Why isn't that one lighting up now? Are you sure you guys put it in right?"

"I swear to you it worked when we checked it before."

"I should have been here to do it myself."

"You were talking to Shayne and can't be everywhere at once."

What's she doing now? Does she ever think about me? Shayne probably thinks I'm a massive arsehole right when she's getting interesting.

He found her new strength and determination magnetic. It messed with his head and conflicted with the emotion free barrier.

She added another layer of suppressed frustration to the list. "What the fuck's going on around here?"

"Fuck, Sir?"

Shit. Get out of my head woman.

Annu slapped his cheeks. "I meant flark." He wriggled the trip guide and loosened it from the base. It came off in his hand. "Well there's the problem. It's not in there properly. You've still got spares right?"

Hyl rifled through his jacket pocket and pulled another piece out. Annu replaced the part, Hyl tapped at the device.

Three beeps later, the trip switch came back online. "Great, onto the next one."

Someone ran through the woods towards them, a flock of birds scattered from the tree tops and filled the air with screeches. Annu ignited, and prepared to fight.

An older Protector, Wynter, burst through the trees. The bun in her hair, unravelled around her face. "Sir."

Annu dropped his hands, his heart followed. "What's wrong? Are Shayne and Irica okay?"

Each nod unravel more white hair. "Yes, they're fine. It's not about them. Elijah and Apri haven't been seen since dinner. Have either of you seen them?"

He twisted the bottom of his shirt into a knot. "No I've been out here all night. Hyl you?"

"No, me either."

Annu's blood bulged in his veins; his pulse thudded in time with his head. "Oh my Gods. Are you kidding me?" He reefed the trip pole from the ground and threw it into the trees. "Alright, no one is allowed to go missing or get taken from now on. This is ridiculous."

Hyl flipped between Annu, and Wynter. "Ah, sir?"

His chest tightened. "Oh you know what I meant. Wynter, gather everyone together in the main tent. Hyl, send me a list of missing people, replace the trip and head over there too."

"Sure."

Wynter bounded off back the way she came, Annu left Hyl and bounded into the trees.

Sexual frustration, unreasonable attraction, death, life, stress, pressure, responsibility, destiny, fate, wisdom, leadership, control; it piled onto each other. A snowball of misery tumbled down a hill in his mind; all built into a major avalanche.

Bubble, bubble, toil and trouble.

The lump in Annu's gut doubled in size and soured his last meal.

Keep it all in. Be the man. Be in control.

Annu combed fingers through his hair, his thoughts also tangled. Panic only a millisecond away, he grasped at any remaining sanity.

He shot from the ground and flew to the main tent, landing near the entrance. People streamed past him, eyeing him with curiosity and concern.

Annu leant against a post, and mentally prepared what he'd say.

Okay everyone, I've gathered you hear to tell you we're flarked. Anyone got—

Shayne strode towards him accompanied by two middle aged female protectors. He'd yet to learn their names. He nicknamed the one on the left wobbles, her splayed shovel hips jiggled independently. The other, a giant with big arms, bubbles. Both gave him the creeps, but protected Shayne in his stead.

All three conducted a visual scrutinisation of him, their stances suggested the interruption unwelcome.

Shayne gazed past him to the tent. "What's going on?"

Annu observed the women's reactions either side of her for any hint of collaboration. "A heap of protectors are missing, all in the last hour or so."

Shayne's strong veneer cracked. "Jesus. How? Why?"

"I've got no idea. Clearly we aren't safe at all. Hyl suggested some may have left of their own accord, but I don't believe all twelve did."

Vulnerability cloaked her words, Annu wanted to hold her, to make it alright again. "Twelve. Fucking hell. What's the plan?"

The moonlight emphasised her pale skin, and gave a translucent quality. His heart fluttered, he dug a nail into his palm as a distraction. "A new security system. When you and I are together, all of us stick together. If we have to split up, the group splits in two. When we're in the traps tomorrow they stay outside, we stay inside."

"Sounds reasonable. We've got to find out how they—"

Irica hurried around to the front of the tent and burst between he and Shayne. "Has anyone seen Barri? She left with Apri hours ago to pick mushrooms."

Shayne shrugged and screwed up her face. "No, but I avoid her like the plague."

Annu checked the list of names Hyl provided, the lump in his guts somersaulted. "Flarking great. So we're up to thirteen, for now. We better get inside before we're all that's left."

Chapter 34: Chilli Chocolate
Yebu Mountains, Enki Continent, Orion

Whoever said familiarity bred contempt lied. It achieved one thing; increasing Shayne's feelings for Annu to a frustrating degree. Over the final cavern in the first trap, Shayne levitated to the end of the opening. A foot from the edge, she jumped onto the other side. Annu, waited, his arms crossed.

When her drug haze subsided, the emotions she'd tried to bury rose to the surface. Between mixed signals of sly smiles, a touch or kind comment, and being mad at her; Shayne waded in confusion. Despite their circumstances it reached the point of implosion within her.

Shayne bounded to him, a calm exterior belied cacophony of emotions. "Let's do this."

Their feet crunched on the shattered stone floor toward the fake altar, tension in the air exemplified. The exhaustion she'd dragged around all morning, now replaced by a surge of adrenaline.

Shayne plonked her hand on top of Annu's over the trap release; a shiver ran across her neck. She resisted the urge to tighten her fingers around his and prolong contact.

Damn you. I wish I still hated you.

They pushed the button as one, clunk. An escape hatch opened behind the altar, and relief flooded through her.

Hope glimmered, the first in the series of failures up against them. "Oh thank God–Gods. Finally. Yes. It's almost better than chocolate."

Don't get too carried away.

Annu's hand remained under hers; he grabbed them both and shook. "Yip—flarking–yay."

He scooped her into his arms and hugged the life out of her. The attraction niggled at Shayne. She squeezed his middle; his smell threw her hormones into a frenzy. She ran her hand up his shirt over his bare skin and curled her fingers through his chest hair.

A growl erupted from within him; he grabbed her arm and slotted his fingers through hers. Annu bent down, her heart flip flopped; she leant up and kissed him.

The moment her lips touched his, he rebuked her advances. "What are you doing? This isn't right."

Shayne crunched over the shattered pieces of her self esteem. "I thought, I, we, were having a, ah, moment."

He looked like she'd grown another head. "Yes, no, no. It's a terrible idea."

Her cheeks stung from the slap of rejection. "Oh, oh. I–"

Annu pushed her an arms-length back, and stroked the locket "No. Big mistake. Huge."

Shayne dropped her arms, dazed and confused.

I can't compete with a dead woman.

"I agree it wasn't great timing, but a mistake? That's fucking harsh. I thought you wanted it too."

An invisible barrier surrounded him, the closeness between them evaporated. "Because I'm nice to you, doesn't mean I'm flirting. Look, we don't have time for this. We've got to get out of here and to the next trap. We're running late."

Shayne backed away from him. "Oh right. We're doing that routine are we? Fucking fine."

Annu walked around the altar towards the trap door as if nothing unusual happened, his ability to compartmentalise both astounded and infuriated her.

Boy did I misjudge that whole scenario. Moron. Idiot. It's possible, my radar's pretty fucking rusty. Ahhh, I want a fucking smoke. No, I'm not doing that either.

Shayne edged her way out after him and blinked at the invasion of light. "Wait a minute, can we talk about this? I don't want things to be weird, well, weirder between us."

Annu ignored her, his dismissive attitude flipped her switch from embarrassed to angry.

Shayne trailed behind him around the temple corner. "This discussion isn't over fuck face."

They turned into the troupe of protectors, their expressions and stances relaxed.

Jonn rushed at them, and clapped his hands. "Excellent. One successfully down."

Their obvious enthusiasm dampened her frustration with Annu, Shayne recalled their objectives.

Idiot. It's still all about me.

Annu stood beside her, silent and teeth clenched; his mood unreadable.

Do I have to do everything around here?

"Yep, everything's under control with us. Right Annu?" She jabbed an elbow into his ribs.

Annu shook himself and nodded. "Yes, it's all fine. Did anyone go missing while we were gone?"

Jonn's continued claps dragged across her nerves. "No, sir."

The second trap mound loomed in the distance to the West, Shayne mustered her strength. "Okay well let's move onto the next one and try it again. For the hundredth fucking time."

In silence, Shayne trudged beside Annu down the hillside, through the valley, and past the forest. Unable to levitate along an incline at the base of the temple hill, Annu flew to the top and tethered an anchor for her.

Shayne clipped the carabineer to her harness and chicken winged it up the side to the top. Two feet from the cliff's edge she reached the ancient structure. A choice of four entrance, carved letters above each. It lost none of its oppressiveness with familiarity.

Annu looked from entry to entry. "Let's do the opposite of what we did last time. You take the left and I'll take the right."

Shayne strode to the last opening and into a dank hallway. She flicked on the torch; her temperature rose, her anger at Annu wavered.

He does make a good boogeyman shield.

"I hate this shit."

Three quarters of the way down Shayne hit a pit of hell to end all pits at her feet; a labyrinth of rooms on the other side. Shayne wore a coat of despair. She slumped against the rear wall, tired, sore, and annoyed.

A tension headache split her brain in two and thudded across her skull. Shayne massaged her temples.

Please Ki, Ann give us a break.

Annu popped up behind her. "There's one of those in here too? Flark. I hoped you'd had more luck."

Shayne wanted to maim, punch, and pummel him. "Maybe we misread the symbols. What the hell does 'give up something precious to you, blah, blah, blah,' mean anyway? Irica never mentioned it, plus we've been wrong before." Her temperature plummeted, icicles formed down her arms.

"Irica probably didn't know about it. She can't spoon feed us all the time, or hold our hands. We've got to figure some stuff out ourselves."

Furore consumed her thoughts and tongue. "I realised that, fuck face. I've absolutely had it with your snide condescending remarks. You act like my father sometimes, and we can't have a proper conversation with me about feelings and shit, but you've got no problem dishing out nasty remarks. What the fuck?"

The heat of his breath stung Shayne's cheeks, spittle hit her face. "Oh, it all comes back to you, how you feel and what you want. None of what we've been through has made you any less selfish. From being a bad parent to irresponsibility and putting others lives at risk, why would I ever get involved with you?"

The truth stung, self righteous anger pushed it aside. "How dare you. You fucking arsehole. I knew you couldn't let that shit go and didn't believe me. You're such a hypocrite. You've got no right to judge me or anyone else. I might not have cared about anyone when I first came here, but I sure as hell do now. I've felt each loss as deeply as anyone, and I'm not the one fucking around with one of our trainers while in the midst of a galactic destroying event." The cold drawn sensation flowed down her back.

Great, you're back. Where were you before, at the fire traps when I lost my eyebrows–again?

"I thought I cared about you too, but boy did I fuck up there. I'd put it down to post interstellar travel and rampant hormones. A good dose of your true self stamped that out."

Annu removed the distance between them. "Just because you liked me, doesn't mean anything in a zillion years would ever happen between us. I'd never like, let alone love, someone as shallow and malicious as you. You're the exact opposite of someone I'd even say hello to, let alone kiss. Even if I was rolling drunk I wouldn't touch you. I wouldn't use a friend of a friend's dick to touch you with. When this is all over, you take care of Earth, I'll take care of here and I never want to see you again."

A blue aura encapsulated Shayne. "At least I haven't acted like a complete fool and exposed my naked self to all and sundry. You aren't even married and don't have kids. You've got no fucking idea about how hard it is. That locket's so precious because it's probably from your last girlfriend–in school."

Flames erupted around his head and flowed down his body. "I was married, the locket came from my wife, you little bitch. No one will ever be worthy enough for me to take it off."

Vague rumours heard around camp jumbled around the back of Shayne's mind, far too late to reach her tongue. "Oh, well no wonder she left, you're an arrogant prick."

Steam spouted out his ears, the heat between them amplified. "She died as did our son, and you pale in comparison to her. You'll never, ever, and I do mean ever, come close to being anything like her. Don't you dare even talk about her. Get out of my face before I pole drive you through that wall."

Shayne threw a fraction of guilt out the window, stomped on it and set it alight. Her upper body exploded in light blue flames of ice, wherever she touched froze. "Go right ahead, I fucking dare you."

Annu's chest heaved against to her face. "Don't make me angry. You won't like it, and neither will I."

The cold from her and the heat from him repelled. A thin barrier formed, blue on one side, red on the other.

In her mind, Shayne shoved Annu. "Yeah, well don't fuck with me either."

In reality, he thrust backwards and hit the outer wall with a smack. Rubble fell in a circle around him.

The bottom of her gut churned, Shayne's hands flew to her mouth, shocked flooded her. Annu stood amongst the debris, amazement plastered his face. She opened her mouth to apologise; before the words formed, he came at her with volcanic hatred.

The force of a cement truck pummelled her through three rooms; she landed with a thud on the floor of the fourth. Annu hovered a few feet away, his eyes pitch black.

Power and fury pulsed through her; Shayne sucked it in and pushed at Annu through her hands. The thrust of energy sent a shockwave along the lower structure, walls crumbled, roofs and floors imploded. Thousands of years of ancient craftsmanship destroyed in seconds.

Shayne's arms protected her from rocks and stone dust. Her heart flipped, she searched for Annu over boulders and around corners.

Holy shit, this is crazy. We've got to stop this. What the hell are we doing?

Annu tore through the centre of a ruined room, seven foot of rage aimed in her direction. Shayne rolled across the ground and ducked his fire balls.

Clearly, he didn't get the same memo as I did. Fucker.

Burnt hair invaded her nose, a clump of her pony tail dropped to the ground.

Shayne threw ice bombs in return; they discharged the fire before it hit her. For several moments they flung their respective powers at each other.

She misjudged his next shot and copped it across the chin. Shayne stumbled backwards, all sense of rationality; gone. "I don't fucking think so."

Overcome with decades of male oppression, Shayne drew it all together into one thrust at Annu. He flew past; it ricocheted off the rear wall, and back to her.

Shayne burst from the ground, the room disintegrated around her; sparks and icicles drifted through the air.

Debris muffled Annu's boom. "Flark. Shayne?"

Rocks and stone rained, Shayne flipped over and fell, face first into a hole. She plummeted into the depths below, arms flailed, her screams echoed.

Shayne's journey stopped mid air, her feet warmed. Blood rushed to her head, Annu dragged her several feet up onto a solid surface.

Annu lowered her down and bulleted through the ceilings into daylight.

Shayne plonked against a pile of rubble, bumps and bruises formed, and healed.

What the fuck is wrong with us?

******

Butt numb from the stone, Shayne levered off the ground, and climbed over wreckage towards the alveolate hole above. Raw emotions and a shit ton of guilt accompanied her journey.

Dirt crammed into Shayne's nails, cuts and scratches covered her arms and face. By the time she'd made it out of the mound, she resembled a plane crash survivor.

At the top, Shayne glanced behind her. They'd well and truly fucked it for anyone in the future.

Shayne ignored the protectors' questions and headed to the climbing gear. A hot shower and several drams of scotch in her immediate future.

Jonn, blocked her departure down the mountain.

She sighed, and stepped around him. He stood in front of her. "Oh come on. Get out of the way. Please."

His white eyebrows drew together. "You've ruined the trap mound. This is unacceptable behaviour."

Shayne shuffled around his left side. "It's not your problem. Your job is to protect us while we get this shit done."

Jonn stuck his leg in front of her. "While this is true, our ultimate loyalty is to the Gods, and galaxy, not you. It's time we took control of this situation."

How dare they?

Betrayal coveted her thoughts. "You can't do that. We're in charge here."

Jonn placed a hand on her shoulder. "If you fail, we all die. Beside the trap, and lack of unity, between the two of you there's alcohol and drug issues. We've lost several people and yet you fail to put your own motives aside."

The moisture in Shayne's mouth evaporated. "But, well, this one kind of fell apart. It's not our fault."

Liar, liar, liar. What will it take for me to tell the truth?

Jonn tightened his grip on her shoulder. "Perhaps. At Irica's encouragement, I'll give you both another chance. However, time is of the essence."

Shayne scrambled to understand, her bowel cramped. "Oh Irica won't support you taking over."

Jonn became the voice of doom. "While it filled her heart with sadness, she is behind us if it comes to it."

Nausea bubbled around Shayne's stomach, her heart tore. "I don't believe you. She knows we're trying our best."

"Our kind never lie."

I can't deal with this shit anymore, what the fuck is going on?

"I'm not saying your lying, I know you're not. I, ah, it's just. Damn it." Shayne shoved pride aside and faced the group. "I promise from here on out, ascension is the total focus. I swear. Please--"

The collective worry in their eyes didn't diminish with her assurances. Words meant nothing to these people unless backed up by actions. No fooling them with wit and enthusiasm. "We're nearly there. I beg you."

Jonn gave an imperceptible nod and shifted out of her way. "Alright, I see you mean it. Though I require Annu's assurance too?"

Shayne bit her tongue and tasted blood. "He ducked out for some fresh air. He'll be back soon. I've got to meet him at the next trap."

Apparently, today isn't the day I tell the truth.

Jonn bored through her head. "We'll be right behind you, watching closely."

Shayne strapped on the harness, positioned herself on the cliff side and took a deep breath. "Great, fucking great."

Shayne abseiled down the mountain amongst a sea of worried faces, sideways glances, and mumbled remarks.

I never considered inter-office politics as one of our problems. What kind of fucked up situation is this?

At the base, she unstrapped herself, dropped the harness on the ground and ran towards the main house. At end of the woods, gun fire chilled her blood.

Shayne bolted into an open field, three security men met her half way. "What the hell's going on? Is it another attack? Is anyone hurt?"

The tallest, Benni grabbed her shoulders, his hands trembled. "A group got into the camp. They took their guys back, but no one got hurt. I can't understand why, it doesn't make any sense."

I want a fucking smoke and a drink. Fuck cold turkey, fuck rehab. Maybe I'll mainline the shit instead.

"No it doesn't. Thank the Gods no one got hurt. Is everyone accounted for?"

He released her, his expression uncertain. "As far as I know. Not everyone's checked in yet."

Where the fuck's Annu? God I hope he didn't get taken. Do I really care? Fuck it, I do.

"You go ensure everyone's around camp, I'll double check the house and make sure Irica's okay."

And give her a piece of my mind, why didn't she come and talk to me? Or us? Why did it get this far?

Shayne ran to the house and through the back door full of justification and treachery, into an empty kitchen. Her pulse raced. "Irica?"

The sink full of dishes, the tumbled over chair and the drawers pulled open curdled her stomach contents.

Shayne doubled over, blood spots marked the floor. An arm across her stomach and sense of dread, she checked every room in the house, a dozen times. She screamed Irica's name over and over, her throat raw.

Terror needled her, Shayne searched the grounds, desperate for any place un-inspected; the garden, under the big oak tree, she'd turn up somewhere.

No, this can't be happening. She'd fight them off, and get help. Right?

"Oh God. Oh God. Oh God. No. It should have been me, not you."

Annu's potential reaction to the news frightened her. "Fuck."

Shayne stood under the night sky, hands before her chest. "Please God, Ghost Dad, Ann, whoever, let her be safe somewhere."

There's still time, we'll find her and get her back, before we leave here.

The upper half of Ki hovered beside Shayne, he pointed to the sky.

Irica's mentioned second and last sign–a parade of comets belted across, followed by dozens more.

It's time we left to get the scrolls. We don't have long before the end and I'm alone.

"Shit, shit, shitty, shit, shit. That's not the answer I wanted."

Chapter 35: Stone Cold Son of a Bitch
Yebu Mountains, Enki Continent, Orion

Annu rested on the cliff's edge and attempted to pin point the moment he'd become a total arsehole. The fight struck several nerves, sliced and scarred his conscious mind. He'd physically hurt Shayne, which twisted his soul, tore him to pieces and stripped him bare.

He replayed every angry word, his blasts at her, the truth in her verbal jabs. Shame coveted each memory.

'We bring out the most in each other, is this your intention mother? Are these selfish, ugly people are our true selves?'

Annu shifted his butt cheeks side to side and relieved discomfort the thought derived. An empty void replaced his numb sense of self.

Who is this person I've become? I'm not capable of doing what I have to do. I crack under pressure. They're better off without me. I don't know what the right thing is, I keep flarking it up thinking I do.

Where he'd messed up and how to fix it confounded him. The situation impossible to rationalise from any angle without more alcohol. The empty bottle rolled away from him, and fell over the edge.

Annu's laugh echoed off the cliff face. He deserved loneliness, not love, not happiness. When Ann next appeared, he'd end his part and tell her to create another child, a worthy one.

From his vantage point, the night sky sparkled free of encumbrances. The lights around Irica's in the gorge beneath, cast an eerie shadow across the landscape. Annu's heart beat loud in his ears, he suspected, as a symptom of guilt. Cold circled the bottom of his shirt and settled around his kidneys.

Annu sunk lower into despair, dragged into a riptide of shit and pulled far from the safety of shore.

The dark emptiness below beckoned and welcomed oblivion. "Maybe the world would be a better without me. I destroy everything I touch and bring only misery."

It's at least 1000 feet down. What if Shayne or Irica found my body? Does it even matter?

A hand squeezed his shoulder, Annu turned to the upper half of a woman, the image of the island's statue.

Annu rose off the ground and stood opposite her, his heart fluttered. *"Mother--"*

Ann sparkled in the moonlight.

"My son, I'm sorry. I'd be with you always if I could. Please, don't do anything foolish. More than the world suffers if you do so."

Shame flushed Annu's cheeks. *"You heard me?"*

"Yes. Please--step away from the edge."

Annu remained only an inch away. *"I've messed everything up. I hurt--"*

"Yes, you've made mistakes, both of you have. But there's time to change and finish this. I won't give up on you. Now, please move closer to me. "

Annu stared at his boots, the black of his thoughts an equal colour. *"Your faith is misplaced mother. It's too late. I'll fail you all."*

Ann drifted towards him and placed a finger on his lips. *"Shh. Not unless you give up. I can't force you Annu, the choice must be yours."*

She stroked Annu's back, smoothed his hair and whispered platitudes. He'd sleep for a thousand years, when no one he cared about existed. The air still, he stumbled away from the edge and leant against a stone monument.

Ann smiled; the unconditional love of a mother enveloped him. *"It's time for you to stop hiding behind your grief and alcohol. It's safe and important for you to feel, care and love. To save you from yourself. Don't wait too long and miss all the good things in this life."*

Tears flooded his cheeks. *"I'm not ready to let them go yet. I might forget them, they might disappear."*

Annu poured out his pain with freedom.

When he'd stopped, Ann held his hand. *"Never, Son. Let me show you something."*

His life up to this point streamed through his mind; the joys, sorrow, pain, the loss, and loves. Annu re-watched Shayne appear out of the wall onto the stone ground in a plume of dust, the catalyst to their cosmic mayhem. The insane events thereafter tumbled one after the other, until this moment.

Ann swiped her thumb over his palm; it tingled in response, the pictures in his mind changed. His future, both with and without Shayne, played out in his mind in detail. He'd forgotten all the lonely times, the loss of his past and the giant weight of loss he'd carried around.

The show in his head finished, Ann pointed a comet blazed across the sky towards Enki Island. A cavalcade of shooting stars exploded after it; a kaleidoscope of colours lit the ground.

Annu's chest tightened, his idiot status solidified in minutes. *"I'm so sorry. I've been foolish. Shit."*

Ann's image flickered, she faded into the night. Annu flew back to camp. Time to set things right and finish this.

Chapter 36: Tough Titties
Yebu Mountains, Enki Continent, Orion

The ultimate fake-it-until-Shayne-made-it arrived before, beside, and behind her. Protectors and security people barrelled questions at her. In a turn of events, Jonn, Banna backed her up.

A midget among giants, Shayne suffocated under her infiltrated personal space. "Everyone back up and calm the fuck down. I don't like this either, but I've got no choice."

A brunette woman with uneven breasts shrilled at her. "We're really going without them?"

Shayne's temperature dropped.

Fucking bitch.

She erupted in a blue glow, icicles formed across her skin. People cleared out of the way. "You wanted fucking control, I'm giving it to you. For the last time, shut the fuck up and listen. We leave in an hour. I'm splitting you into three groups. Each is responsible for the care of everyone in their group and any equipment. The following people are in group one and travel in the first PFD with me." Shayne pointed to the closet twenty. "The next group, you, you, and the eighteen behind are in the second PFD. Those who remain are in Group 3. Jonn, they are under your direction."

Look what it takes for me to organise people. I'm excelling at this shit.

A Yosemite Sam doppelgänger raised his hand. "We're really stuck with you aren't we? We've lost our chance and he's not coming back."

Do I be nice or punch him in the face?

"Each group carries weapons caches. Group 1 also carries, food, and medical supplies. Group 3; the camp and latrine equipment."

The brunette continued to annoy her. "When are we getting Irica back?"

One more interruption and she'd serve her head on a plate. "You're personally in charge of shit duty. Now shut up."

Breath, you can do this.

"Meet back here, ready to leave in one hour. Any one not here gets left behind. Have I made myself clear?"

The crowd grumbled but dispersed in their assigned directions. The sky's light spectacular shifted her anxiety from low range noise pollution into a heavy metal concert. Each comet acted as time bomb's fuse, burnt down close to the wick.

Please let Irica be okay. Damn you Annu. I can't do this by myself. If you don't come back soon we'll get slaughtered. Probably by the people protecting us. Shit, fuck, shit, fuck. Ghost, I mean Dad? Are you there? Still no? Someone, anyone help me out here.

Shayne shuffled through each tent and work station in a daze, checked and confirmed each process, the weapons selections and their current numbers. On the surface, she pooled inner resources and drove away panic. Underneath lie a wasteland bordered by denial and constructed by fear.

Shayne ran to first of the stationed PFD's, where two young men stacked ammunition into a crate. Sweat teamed down their backs. "How's it going here? Is everything in order and nearly done?"

They nodded in succession, the left one grumbled without turning in her direction. "Yes ma'am."

A large meteor exploded above the camp and illuminated the area around them. Shayne's heart raced; the lid about to blow off the pressure cooker.

Fuck, shit, fucking hell. What if I run away too? Leave them all with it.

Her controlled tone almost fooled herself. "Thank you, that's great. If you get done earlier, please help the next ship along."

Shayne inspected the other two ships for a third time, which left one place for her to check, the one she'd avoided at all costs.

On the precipice of the kitchen, Shayne's chest ached; bile burnt the back of her throat, stars danced behind her eyes. The noise of people on the other side spurred her forward; Shayne poised her fingers above the door button.

If she didn't see Irica's absence for herself, perhaps it hadn't happened. Shayne ran through her time with Irica, the good, bad, and obscure. The support and maternal presence she'd shown Shayne gave her a glimpse of something she never realised lacked in her life.

Shayne dared not open her mouth, in fear her heart leapt out of her chest and onto the ground.

Someone tapped her on the shoulder. "Shayne?"

Shayne flung back to reality. "Oh, Jonn. Is everything alright?"

He scratched his beard and nodded. "Yes. Everything's not far from being done."

She stepped away from the doorway. "Good."

Jonn frowned and lowered his voice. "We're leaving soon then?"

Shayne licked her lips, her mouth pasty. "Yes. I don't have a choice. Have you seen A—never mind."

"I'm sure he'll come to his senses as you did. Are you sure this is the right thing to do?"

No, no, no, no, no, no.

"Yes. I don't have a choice." Shayne nodded at the back door. "Can you confirm all the food supplies are taken care of?"

Jonn's gaze drifted to the kitchen door. "Of course." A brief smile, blessed his face. "I've known Irica for centuries. The one thing I know is she can take care of herself. She's a tough lady."

Please Gods, keep her safe.

"Yeah, I'm sure you're right."

Annu boomed across the back porch. "What the hell's going on around here? Why is everyone packed up already?"

Shayne's heart trampolined off her stomach. Her tongue froze, her lips moved, no sound came out.

Oh, fuck.

Annu blocked the suns. "Great, you're still pissed at me then? Shayne, we've got to sort things out." He walked around Shayne towards the back door. "Irica? You in there?"

Before Annu reached the button, Shayne blocked his way.

His chest expanded, he pursed his lips. "What are you doing? Can you please be mature and get out of my way. I don't need more aggravation."

Shayne gripped his fingers. "Annu, wait. There's something I've got to tell you."

Annu's eyes darted side to side. "Well, tell me."

"I, I–"

The colour drained from his face, he grabbed her shoulders. "Is it Irica?"

Pee trickled down Shayne leg.

I really should do some pelvic floor exercises if I ever get time.

"I'm sorry. It happened when we were–well you know."

"Flark. No. It can't be. Wait, that's why you packed up? To go get her back?" Annu searched her eyes for confirmation, his grip tightened. "I don't understand. Why aren't you going after her?"

He's going to fucking hate my guts.

The contents of her stomach turned to concrete. "You've seen the sign there's no time to chase after her."

Annu's demeanour hardened, he released her. Hatred replaced the confusion in his eyes. "No. I don't believe even you would leave her with him."

A cold sweat broke out across her back, Shayne swallowed vomit.

Stay strong.

"I've gone over it a hundred different ways. Even if we got the scrolls without being attacked or prevented, there's no extra time."

Spit edged Annu's words, heat steamed from him. "After all she's done for you, for all of us. You know what he'll do to her."

Shayne's head pounded, resignation dumped a wet blanket on her thoughts. "You know I'm right, but I need you with me on this."

Loud booms from above pushed her to the brink of insanity. Shayne grasped at the edges of reason, confident at any moment the walls of her mind would cave in.

Chapter 37: Matricide
Yebu Mountains, Enki Continent, Orion

Annu's inner turmoil bubbled, simmered, and spoiled. He hurled onto the lawn and wiped his mouth. Despair seeped into his bones, gnawing at his marrow. Annu pulled his jacket around him, the roar of regret loud in his ears. Desolation nipped at Annu's heels, bad thoughts filled his mind.

Only reality plastered his feet to the ground. "I'm. Going. To. Make. The. mother flarker. Suffer. Before. I. kill. Him."

Flark, Irica, I'm sorry. I'm so flarking sorry I let you down again.

Shayne's puffy eyes and panicked expression didn't dissuade his hatred of her and himself. "I'm with you there."

'Mother, how could you not warn me?'

Annu stumbled back from the pile of vomit; the sour stench burnt his nostrils. He re-tasted dinner, a stark contrast to its earlier palatableness.

What am I doing? No. It's our fault, my fault. I lost my shit because I can't deal with this. What the hell can I deal with?

Hunched, he tipped his head to Shayne's level, his eyes stung. "This is on me, I shouldn't have taken off."

Dark rings circled her eyes; she rubbed the bridge of her nose. "It wouldn't have changed anything. Well, not that anyway. We would have been in one of the traps. Don't blame yourself, I fucked up too."

People prepared the final details for their journey around them, in and out of the kitchen, arms laden with crates. Unaware of the catastrophe he buried inside, they avoided eye contact with Shayne and him and instead cast side glances as they passed.

In Annu's absence a shift in the protectors' demeanour occurred; the respect and awe they'd shown hours before, now replaced with hesitation, and perhaps, disappointment.

Hope, the last vestige for the faithful and disillusioned, dissolved within him, as useful as a pile of hot shit. "How long has she been gone?"

Shayne leant against a porch beam, and sucked her bottom lip. "A few hours."

Annu levered up to stand, hands up his legs until he stood upright. His skull went one way, his brain the other. "Did anyone else get attacked or taken?"

Shayne stared at the ground, shoulders drooped. "No, only her."

A middle aged woman bolted up to Shayne and shoved a screen communicator under her nose. Shayne nodded, tapped the screen and returned her attention to him.

A twinge of awe surprised him; her absolute state of control offered him a small comfort. The attraction he'd buried six feet down, scratched its way towards freedom, Annu threw another tonne of dirt over it. "He's using fear tactics to wear us down, make us vulnerable. I have the worst feeling he'll use Irica as collateral so we get the scrolls for him."

Shayne dragged fingers through her hair. "Fuck, you're right. I didn't think of that." She pushed off the beam and paced across the porch. "If we get those fuckers first, we can use them to lure Sham-man, ah, Shamesh to us. Then we get Irica, finish him and this saga."

She stopped halfway, her eyes lingered over him, his heart fluttered. "I'm so sorry this happened, Annu. She'll be okay until we get here back, I'm sure of it. She's even more stubborn than me and that's saying a lot."

Porch light illuminated Shayne from behind; the delicacy of her beauty captivated him. He reached to tuck a chunk of hair in front of her face behind her ear, Annu stopped himself.

In short steps Shayne placed a hand on his chest. She slipped her hand under his shirt, the skin beneath burned, and chilled. "I'm sorry for the all things I said. I feel terrible about it, and I don't want things to be awkward between us. I didn't mean any of it. I do–" She licked her lips, Annu held his breath. "You must know I don't hate you. I do like you. I–"

Annu lowered his head to hers, his pulse pounced, his hand moved towards hers. Irica popped in his head and reality with her.

Flark Man. Wake up. You fool, this isn't the time. Don't over complicate the situation.

Non resolution of their earlier fight and Irica's disappearance provided Annu with an opportunity, to maintain his distance and control without further explanation.

He brushed away her hand and stepped back. An emotionless response pained him; Annu nodded in the direction of the PFDs. "Is everyone packed ready to go?"

Shayne crossed her arms and turned away from him, the space between them magnified.

The hurt in her voice stung his soul. "Right. Of course. I, I, I, I think so, I'll go make sure. Ah, thanks for flying in the PFDs with us and not on your own."

Shayne stormed towards the loading zone, the three groups stood at the ends of each ship. An arm wriggled up from the emotional grave. Annu jumped, stomped, pushed them back into the ground and cemented over the top.

That will fix you fuckers.

A fresh burst of meteor showers boomed overhead, and intensified the tension in the air. Annu inhaled and shot over to the PFDs, his heart in his throat. "I need a fucking drink."

Torn between alcohol, duty, and Shayne, Annu ran towards the loading zone.

242

Chapter 38: A Door Shuts, a Window Opens and Breaks Your
Fingers
Yebu Mountains, Enki Continent, Orion

Once everyone loaded into their respective ships, Shayne sat in the Co-pilot's seat, with Hyl in the pilot's. She second, third, and fourth guessed her decision not to get as high as the International Space Station before departure.

What the fuck? I'm actually making logical choices, holy shit. When did I turn into responsible? Wait until Irica sees–

Shayne jiggled the ring on the chain, and relived Annu's latest rejection, her face burned. The first time in fifteen years, give or take another decade, she'd put herself out there, and each time he'd treated her like a Typhoid Mary.

Shayne sniffed under her arms and blew on her hand. A little on the hinky side, but not run-away-and-hide material.

If I only I had time to brush my teeth and shower first. Under real hot water. Mmmm.

Thoughts of home interrupted and muddied her focus. The place she'd longed, cried, and begged for late at night. Her crap house with Bear, and well, nothing else.

I haven't even thought about Rosie and the kids for days. Jesus. I'm fucked up. They'll worry about me. Wait until they hear.

Shayne thrust a hand to her mouth, a realisation shocked her. She wasn't eager to get back to her former life on Earth and herself.

Will I return to my old ways? Surely not after all this.

Her pulse raced, for a second Irica sat at the end of the table, unwanted advice poured from her lips. "If whining made gold, you'd be rich," and Shayne's personal favourite, "When the universe offers you a chance, take it. Don't be a dumb arse."

Shayne wouldn't allow her personal Yoda to die; not the woman responsible for her marked personality change and will to live. Shayne buried a sob; her chest ached, unprepared for the flow of memories which appeared.

How ironic the place I truly lived, loved and will probably die, is on another planet. It took off of this to make me realise how lucky I am. God I'm stupid sometimes.

The whir of an engine turbine snapped her back to the here and now.

Shayne smacked herself in the forehead, once, twice, three times. "What the hell's wrong with me? I'm a big girl, why can't I take a hint and get the fuck over it. Ahhhh."

Strapped in, Shayne took mental stock. *Shit, fuck, shit, fuck, shit, fuck.*

The engines whirred to life, lights blinked across the console, recycled air circulated through vents above her head.

With a few taps of her finger, Shayne connected the communication system to the other ships. Her twelve-year-old prepubescent voice crackled through the cockpit. "Okay everyone, this is it. The time is here. Keep your eyes open and weapons close all the time. Stay in constant contact with each other, we are about to become sitting ducks. Please confirm all doors and windows are secured and covered by armed personnel? Over."

Her heart skipped at Annu's response. "Group two, confirm. Over."

Jonn echoed through the cockpit. "Group three, confirm. Over."

Shayne cleared her throat, her balls dropped. "After we land on the island, Group 2, set up the first mobile base of operations. Each position is close to a scroll trap, and be ready to move at a moment's notice. Annu will advise the first set of coordinates when we get close to landing. Until then, please keep the airways open, and no extra chatter."

Is this actually me talking right now? Damn, I sound like I know what I am doing.

"That's it for now. Over."

Satisfied she leant back in the chair and glanced at Hyl. A man of few words, he nodded and tapped the launch sequence into the console.

Shayne bolted forward and reconnected the communicator with one finger. "Oh, and be safe. Group one, over."

The ship lifted from the ground, panic peaked around the corners of her mind.

Oh God, oh God, oh God. We're really doing this; we're about to fucking die. All these people are looking to me and Annu.

Annu sounded like gravel dipped in honey. "Okay. Over."

I'm sure he felt something too. I can't be totally wrong can I? Ah, yes I can and it's too late now anyway. No matter what planet I'm on I make sucky choices with men.

Jonn broke her thoughts. "Group three confirm orders. Over."

Shayne played with her seat belt. "Good." She replaced the hand piece. "I'm going down in a blaze of glory; I'm going down blah, blah, blah."

Hyl raised his voice. "Ah. Can you please not do that?"

Shayne shrank into the cushion and mumbled to the window. "Fine. Whatever."

Nobody loves me, everybody hates me; I think I'll go eat some worms.

The ships drifted into the night sky, an eerie stillness enveloped their journey. The meteors paved a starry path, bright and brilliant. Incongruent with what waited on the other side.

Dear Gods, Creator, whoever wants to listen. Please bless and protect us. Keep Irica safe until we can get her back. Please help us succeed. Oh, and do I really sing that badly?

Chapter 39: An Unholy Mess
Above the Continental Ocean, Orion

The ship ascended, his guts dropped, Annu imbedded his fingers into the arm rests. The pilot levelled off above the tree line and followed Shayne's PFD.

The last time I went to Enki everything changed. I got what I wanted and plenty I didn't. This time, one way or another, nothing will be the same again. I've got to keep it together.

Annu released his grip and grabbed a hand held communicator. Within seconds, longitudes and latitudes on the screen blurred his vision. He rubbed his eyes and plotted the first three bases, each with an alternate within running distance. His attention switched between the screen and the radar.

When are those bastards going to pop up and flark everything up?

The middle of Annu's brain thudded, he reached critical levels of frustration and inaction. Each noise strained his patience; chatter from the adjoined cabin drove him to the brink of implosion.

Tick, tick, tick, tick. The pressure built along with a desire to purge the anger and pain. Annu checked the coordinates a hundredth time, forcing himself to remain seated.

The heat from Annu's hands melted the device; he dropped it onto his lap, and blew his finger tips.

Come on, dickhead.

With his shirt as protection, he expanded the screen on an area further away from the hills behind the tombs. "It's got protection and cover. Makes a good alternative; now to find at least two more."

Annu swiped across and closed in on a wooded area several kilometres to the west of the last mound.

Banna burst into the cockpit, her footsteps vibrated across the floor, Annu bounced forward.

Thud, his knee smacked into the bottom of the console. The Communicator slid between the cushion and the arm rest.

Annu grabbed it before it hit the floor and rubbed his knee until the ache subsided. "Shit woman. You scared me. What's wrong?"

Boom, boom, boom. She leant over his chair and pointed out the window. "Sir, there are three ships port side. Not quite visible to the naked eye. Group 3 have them in weapons range. What do you want them to do?"

His blood pressure and thermostat sky rocketed; the stench of burnt plastic invaded the cockpit. Annu threw the communicator on the floor. "Already? How did they know which way we were going?"

The com system crackled throughout the ship. "Shayne, Annu, this is Group 3 reporting. The enemy's locked on our radar and we await your orders. Do we fire or track them?"

Shayne sent shivers up his spine. "Annu, I suggest we track them for now. We don't want extra attention, yet. What do you think?"

I should tell her how I feel. No I shouldn't.

Annu perched on the seat's edge, pounce ready. "Yeah, track for now. Don't shoot until we confirm Irica is not on board."

The pilot swivelled in his chair. "And how are we going to do that, sir?"

A valid question he'd not considered the answer to. "I'll work on it. Thanks Banna, return to your post."

She nodded and stomped her way out of the cabin.

Clear of the seat, lava replaced Annu's blood. "I'll be back."

He avoided the protectors and stomped through the ship's sections to the side door, his heart pounded against his ribs. Annu swiped the button; a blast of wind forced him against the door frame. He erupted out the door in ball of flames, the enemy ship in his sights.

Annu blasted a hole in the side of the first PFD and jumped through. People scattered for weapons.

A young man ran in the other direction, Annu grabbed him by the arm and squeezed. "Where's Irica?"

The kid spit in his face. "I won't tell you."

Annu shook him, his teeth rattled. "Where the flark is she?"

He pursed his lips and squirmed under Annu's grasp.

"One more chance, tell me."

The kid kicked and gouged at Annu's arms.

Annu tightened his grip and threw him out the open hole.

Annu clutched a woman's shoulder, his hands burnt through clothes and flesh. "Same happens to you unless you tell me."

She screamed, scratching at his face. The smell of cooked meat infiltrated the ship. "Never."

He smacked her cheek, her jaw cracked. "You sure?"

"Flark you."

His fingers melted into her, he touched bone, and she stopped moving. Annu removed his hands, she crumpled to the floor. "Guess you are."

Someone grabbed him from behind and pulled him back.

Annu flipped, launched at the man and burnt him alive. He thrust the remains at three men, guns raised, headed at him. Laser shots buzzed past his head, he projected energy bursts. Their screams ricocheted through the hull.

No one provided answers, all prepared to die for their cause; not unlike him. Power surged, the ability to vet a lifetime of ire—the ultimate aphrodisiac.

Annu flew out the ship's front window into the night sky. A short distance away, he fired, destroying the PFD into fragments. Satisfaction remained out of his grasp. Debris knocked him off axis, he somersaulted in air.

Thwack, thwack, thwack. Lasers from the other two ships fired at him. Annu increased his protective bubble, righted himself and delved into the closest one. He burnt a line through people, desperate for someone in charge.

A man leapt into the night, women struck him with laser staffs.

Annu blasted them into the next compartment.

He followed their passage. "Where's Irica, the old woman?"

Those in range fired, the shots bounced off and hit behind him.

Annu blazed past them, explored each compartment and tore apart cupboards. Each person he obliterated didn't bring Irica to him.

He ripped open the last ship like a tin can. Unlike their predecessors, the people Annu grabbed remained silent before his touch combusted them. Their flesh blackened—muscles and sinew charcoaled.

Annu expanded his power and imploded the last ship around him, his heart deafened ambient sounds.

Shock waves rippled the atmosphere. He poured his frustration into the sky, his throat raw. "You're next Shamesh. I'll tear you to pieces."

The protector's ships headed in his direction, their appearance returned his clarity. With no hint of regret, Annu flew back to his ship. He shook himself at the door, brushed debris from his clothes and strolled through the ship into the cockpit.

Shayne shrilled from the comm system. "Annu, what the fuck?"

Chapter 40: High Treason
Over the Continental Ocean, Orion Yebu Mountains

The sky lit up, Shayne replaced the hand piece. She flushed hot and cold, between a chill and sweat.

For sanity's sake I'll put it down to stress and not oncoming menopause. "Jesus Annu. I cannot believe he did that."
Hyl tortured her via his tongue. "Is this the control you're talking about? I didn't see any collusion between you on that."
Don't freeze him, it's not nice.

Shayne followed a comet's line across the front window to Hyl's position. An epiphany smacked her, her heart fluttered, the pit of her stomach flipped.

The safety she'd derived from the people around her diminished. "You're one of those who wanted to take control aren't you? You fuck arse. How many of you are there? Does anyone believe in us?"

Hyl picked at a hole in his shirt and dropped strands onto the floor. "There's a few of us. Most are prepared to wait and see what happens at the island before taking action."

Shayne jabbed a finger at him, icicles from her fingertips fell onto her lap. "And I thought I had shitty timing. Fucking hell. I've got to worry about you guys turning on us and Shamesh. Fucking brilliant. We are in total control now, even John thinks so. You ask him. Then again even if you did you wouldn't care. Nothing we've done makes a difference."

"You're both not cut out for this, it's clearly too much to handle. If you let us take over all the stress and pressure goes. All you have to do is get the scrolls and you can go back home. We'll take it from here."

The idea lingered in her mind for a moment; Shayne didn't allow it to take hold.

Stay strong. Don't give in.

A chill swept across the base of her neck. "No. Fuck you. One more word out of your mouth and I'll turn your privates into ice and chip them off." Her hand shook. "Ship 2, report now."

Shayne pressed the hand piece against her lips, her teeth clenched. "Annu, I really fucking need to talk to you."

Hyl steered the ship to the left. The island appeared illuminated by the meteor showers, and Annu's mistimed revenge.

Annu's voice broke through the cockpit. "What's your problem? It's all sorted."

Shayne unlocked her harness and belted her head against the console. "I don't even know where to begin?"

"Well what are you screaming at me for then?"

Shayne faced the window and held her hand around the microphone. "Aside from you blowing ships up, we've got a problem, we need to talk about."

"What?"

Shayne raised her voice to a dull roar. "I said, we've got a problem–I fucking need to talk to you about."

"Oh for flark's sake. Now isn't the time to talk about me not kissing you. Will you let it go?"

Her temperature soared, her cheeks burned. "Oh my Gods. I'm not talking about that. Thanks for telling everyone fuck arse."

I'm in a living fucking nightmare. If I do the right thing I'm fucked, I do the wrong thing I'm fucked. Fucked, fucked, fucked, fucked, and fucked. What the fuck am I meant to do. I knew it, the Creator hates me. I'm a pawn in his chess game.

Hyl scoffed–his tone sour. "So you tried to kiss Annu when Irica went missing? What kind of person are you?"

Her blood boiled, her skin cooled. "You don't know the situation so keep out of it."

Annu stuttered through the speaker. "Oh, ah, sorry. I, ah–"

Shayne held down the button and bashed the hand piece on the console. "Yeah too late now, buddy. This isn't over; I'll talk to you when we get there."

Hyl swivelled his seat around and scrutinised her. "Are all people from Earth like you?"

If I jump out the window how long before I hit the water? Hopefully I'll die before I drown. "You mean little and white, or amazing and someone you've made a terrible mistake about and you now deeply regret?"

A smirk flashed across his face. "The first two."

Shayne sank back into the chair.

It kills time.

"Right. No, we are different colours, shapes, sizes, religions and ideals. I haven't seen much of Orion, other than Irica's and the training camp to compare, but it's safe to say we don't have the same technology. We drive cars on asphalt roads and we have planes that fly in the sky, which are nothing like these things." She tapped the console. "Our electricity comes from coal or some shit like that. Actually I don't really know where it comes from, except out of the power point when I plug something in. If I pay the bill."

Shayne imagined the pile stacked under her front door in her absence, she shivered.

His expression suggested she'd said something salacious. "You still use fossil fuels? I've heard of those from ancient times, thousands of years ago. Good Gods, having different religions is simply dangerous and uninformed. I didn't realise how primitive Earth's was or that we'd meet more of your kind. We'll have to rebuild Earth's entire societal and technological systems before your kind are able to understand us at all."

Shane's mind imploded with irritation. "On behalf of Earth, fuck you. We're not bad people—well–some are, and there are wars and what not, but Annu and I will change those things of course."

Concern replaced the smirk. "Do you realise the greater impact all this has and what you're meant to achieve?"

She leapt from the chair and loomed over him in a blue haze. "Of course I do. Look, I don't need this shit right now. Unless you're going to physically stop us, do your job and stay the fuck out of our way, or I swear to the Gods, I'll shove your head up your arse and make an ice sculpture out of you. Got it?"

He pushed back against the wall, his hands in front of his face. "Alright, alright. Take it easy. You better sit down we're about to land on the island."

Shayne's chest heaved, she gulped in oxygen. "Oh fuck. Here we go."

Chapter 41: You Dirty Rats
Enki Island, Orion

Annu dumped the last crate of ammo onto the ground and fiddled with the locket from his neck.

I don't know if I'll ever be ready to say goodbye, but I do care about Shayne even though she messes with my head and drives me insane. Oh and let's not forget tells me the woman who raised me is missing.

A fresh layer of guilt slipped with it into his jacket. "Step it up a notch people, fifteen minutes until we head to the first mound."

On a table next to him, Shayne shoved supplies into a bag while the first base camp went up around them. Operation centres buzzed with activity, armed security stations protected the perimeters. In theory the positions he'd selected, with meticulous precision, provided almost foolproof cover.

Shayne's actual news about the Protectors unhinged the confidence Annu derived in their presence and his logistical skills. Despite the safety measures he'd put in place, they may as well hold up a sign to their location.

The walls closed in on him. Annu squeezed Shayne's hand and nodded. She dropped the bag and followed him behind the main tent to a group of thick trees. Once out of ear shot, he turned their communicators off.

Annu pushed her flat against a wide trunk, his arms splayed either side.

She smells so good.

"This isn't good."

I have a huge problem being close to you.

Shayne scrunched her nose, her breath warmed his neck. "It sucks but it's obvious some or all of them are feeding him information."

Annu's temper flared, flames trickled from his fingers and seared the bark. Burnt wood sullied the fresh air. "It can't be all of them."

Shayne waved smoke away. "Unless we conduct a survey, there's no real way of knowing how many. One's too many. Fuck, more problems. "

Dawn captured her features, Annu wanted to drink her in.

You're beautiful and you've got no idea. When you curse out of that pretty mouth, it drives me crazy. Shit, focus dickhead.

Annu bit his inner cheek. "True." Annu pushed off the tree and clenched his fists. "Ive memorised the map just in case. Hey - why don't we go on our own?"

Shayne placed her hand on his chest, his pulse raced. "Like it or not we need them, at least the ones who are with us. I don't know, this is my first coup. Oh, and Jonn mentioned Irica's supported them."

Annu stumbled a step back, his guts flipped, blood vessel in his brain pulsed. "What? Irica?"

She stared at his chest, her expression blank. "Yep, but he came around eventually. I think. I didn't get the chance to talk to Irica about it. When I went to see her, she--"

Shayne swiped a tear down her cheek, she held her breath.

Annu's mind ran over the last few days. "No. I don't believe it. She would have told me surely? I don't know, I've been consumed by all this, I haven't paid much attention to anything else."

Her hand heated the skin underneath. "Well, she probably did and we didn't listen."

Annu shifted closer, his body acted of its own accord. He held her hand. "We can't trust anyone except each other."

The emotion in Shayne's voice snapped his heart strings. "Oh God, you're right. Dirty rotten bastards. Fuck it." She stroked his belly, his toes curled. "We'll get her back and sort all this out. I know we can do it together."

I'd like to do you together. Over and over. What the hell? Get a grip.

Annu tucked a curl behind her ear, a hand behind her neck, his blood thick through his veins.

'It's not the time. Focus.'

'Now of all the times Mother? Oh come on, please, it's so hard.'

'The time will come, but it's not yet. Be patient.'

'Tell that to my balls.'

'Ah…..'

Annu pulled his hands away, the moisture in his mouth evaporated. The blood rushed from his head and headed deep south.

Shayne's confused expression caused him to second guess his decision.

Banna sliced through the tension and snapped him back to reality. She bounced on her heels. "Excuse me, sir, ma'am."

They answered in unison. "Yes."

Annu stepped away from Shayne and crossed his arms over his chest.

Banna looked between them and cocked an eyebrow. "Base camp is finalised, everyone's in place, and ready to go."

Relief flooded him, he straightened his back. "Good. Make sure the PFD's and camp are moved to the next location directly after we leave here."

"Yes, sir." She lifted her chin; the sun caught dark hairs underneath.

Oh Gods. That's hideous. Must have been to busy looking at her tits to notice before.

His sex drive drove for cover, Banna strode off in the direction of the main tent.

The tree behind Shayne highlighted her diminutiveness. "Even though she's Jonn's daughter we shouldn't trust her either."

Annu swallowed the urge to grab her. "No, just you and me, kid, but we can sort the other shit out along the way."

"Yeah." Shayne scratched a hair free chin. "I'll double check everything before we head off. Pack a few more supplies in case we are delayed or someone forgets something. Like me."

She'd transformed into a strong confident woman in a short time, he'd underestimated her. "Good idea. I'll meet you out front in ten. Shayne?"

Shayne walked around him, paused but didn't turn back. "Yes."

The words poised on his lips, his mouth poised. "I, I, I—" Annu numb tongue stuck to the roof of his mouth.

Another time, but don't leave it too late.

"Never mind."

Shayne thrust her shoulders back and delved into the trees.

Annu smacked his forehead against the trunk and re-calibrated his mind. "I'm flarked, screwed, rooted, messed up. Every time my life spirals out of control, it comes back to Gods' damned women. Always. No, I don't like Shayne. Of course I don't love her. She annoys me and she's all wrong for me. Yeah right, you fucking idiot."

Annu banged his head four more times and caught up with the object of his infection--affection.

Chapter 42: Tricks are for Kids
Enki Island, Orion

A pale pink fog cast an eerie glow and covered their journey across the island. In a daze, Shayne trudged through dense forest behind Annu, the protectors travelled in a wide circle around them.

Daybreak dulled the celestial display, making the untouched environment easier to navigate. The smell of moist grass carried along the breeze and wet the bottom of her pants.

The strange animal noises erupted from the woods at regular intervals and kicked her anxiety up another notch.

I don't even want to imagine what's in there.

A high pitched screech above sent a chill down her spine.

Shayne ran up behind Annu and clutched a section of shirt. He stopped mid step, her face smacked into the backpack he carried.

Her eyes filled with tears, her nose throbbed. "Ouch. Shit. Not again."

Annu blurred before her eyes. "Well I did tell you not to do it for that reason."

Shayne rubbed the bridge of her nose and wriggled it back in place. "I'd rather a sore nose than have my head taken off by whatever is out there. It sounds like someone's being strangled."

She stepped around to stand at his side, the facial injury healed beneath her fingers.

I wish you'd hold me, and protect me.

Annu tapped at his wrist communicator. "They're a kind of monkey. As long as you don't go near or look at them, they won't hurt you. We've got one click to go, in that direction." He pointed toward a group of smaller hills barely visible at her eye level.

Shayne jumped to see above the bushes, and succeeded in tripping forward.

She suppressed a sigh, regained her footing and wriggled the warm chain on her neck. Shayne tingled, her skin buzzed. Since they'd landed, her body starred in its own Twilight Zone episode.

Combined with Annu's ability to switch between kind and cold, she remained in a state of confusion. One minute it appeared he wanted to kiss her, the next he avoided her like a cold sore. Shayne needed to bath in some Zovirax before her entire self esteem disappeared. Stat.

"Hey, did you hear me?"

Shit pay attention.

"What?"

Annu held her by the underarm.

And it doesn't jiggle. Yay.

He waved in her face. "Hello. At the base of the hill over there, we'll dump the stuff. Instead of you climbing up, I'll take you up with me. It gives us another time advantage. The protectors make their way up themselves."

The ability to heal and Shayne's acceptance of the situation didn't change the memory of smelling burnt flesh for days. It reminded her of BBQ, which made her hungry, and well, no one wanted to eat themselves.

Her stomach growled.

Shut up you weirdo.

He grabbed her in a bear hug; Shayne squeezed his middle, her hand moved of its own volition to his belly.

I can't stop myself touching you. I want you.

Annu dipped his head to her level, opened his mouth as if to speak, and closed it. She held her breath, and licked her lips.

Please kiss me, I know you want to.

Branches cracked under footsteps to their right, the past rejections sprung into her mind, and allowed self preservation to override her hormones.

Shayne pulled out of the embrace and adjusted her clothes. Unless Annu flat out told her how he felt, she'd keep her goodies to herself.

Keep it together woman. You're so close, don't fuck up now.

Annu frowned, but signalled the protectors forward with a flick of the wrist. The journey ahead continued in silence, a few yards ahead the scenery changed from green and plush, to rocky and sparse. The first scroll mound came into view between two hills a half hour walk away.

Annu held a long range telescope and pushed buttons on the side. "I can't see anyone else up there yet. We need to move faster, we won't have long before they do."

Shayne swallowed her heart, acid bubbled in her oesophagus. "Oh please don't let them come yet, or at all."

Annu clipped the telescope to his belt and spoke into the wrist communicator. "Quicken your pace."

At some point, she'd touched the wrong button on hers. When she turned it on, boobs and arse filled the screen, and no matter what, it stayed. Shayne pulled her sleeve down over it, no point with Annu right beside her.

Shayne readjusted the sack over her shoulder, stretched her neck from side to side and walked beside Annu.

A group of small furry creatures scuttled from bushes to their right, and ran inches from her feet. She leapt into his arms. "Oh my fucking God."

With a dumbfounded expression, Annu searched the area. "What?"

"Creepy things."

"Oh for Gods' sake woman. Hey--"

Annu flung his arms in the air and dumped her onto the ground.

Shayne rubbed her butt cheeks and kicked his shin. "Ow. What did you do that for?"

Annu looked toward the scroll mound, back at her and at the mound again. He repeated the process a number of times.

Shayne checked his face for signs of a stroke. "Are you alright? Or are you having a stroke?"

Annu tapped his chin and sucked his teeth under his lips. "I've got an idea."

"Does it include picking me up off the ground?"

He walked in a circle. "No, listen. Stay there for a minute, pretend your hurt. They're expecting us to go to the first trap, well, first."

Shayne extended her legs out front and rubbed her ankle. "Ah duh. Because it makes sense."

Annu's smile sent a warm rush through her nether regions. His hot chocolate sans marshmallow tone sealed the deal. "In theory, but we don't have to do them in any order."

Mother Theresa, nuns, dead shit.

"What are you thinking?"

He crouched over and inspected her leg. "Let's do the second one first, they won't expect that. We'll get the jump on them, then go do the first. By the time they catch on, we should have at least two scrolls. And it keeps the protectors on their toes."

The pieces clunked together in her brain, Shayne levered herself off the ground to a hunch, the ring tingled. "Oh my God, that's brilliant."

Annu pushed her back down. "Shh, not so loud. Don't draw attention yet."

"Hey. Not again." Despite a sore butt, a tingle of excitement rippled through her. "We might fucking make it. We could do this shit. Ha ha. Sucked in fuckers."

A smirk turned the corners of his mouth. "We have to change direction a little, instead of heading that way." He jabbed his left hand in front of them and pointed to the east with his right. "We go that way. Then double back."

"What about the others at base camp? They'll be headed where we are meant to go."

"So? They can change direction at the last minute."

Hope twinkled its blue eyes on their horizon. "Let's do it."

A blonde male protector approached them, his gun pointed down. He scanned the area around them. "What's the delay? Why have we stopped moving? Is there a problem?"

Annu winked at her. "She stumbled, fell over and it made me miss a turn."

Shayne rubbed her knee, a faux pained expression on her face. "Yep. Silly me. All good now though. I'll be right to go any minute now."

The man nodded and returned to his position; Shayne's pulse lowered.

Annu placed a hand around her shoulder and brushed the dirt off her pants.

Mmmmmm, while you're down there—Oh crap. I'm on an important mission. Wake up.

Annu helped her off the ground. "We shift direction to three degrees east."

Chapter 43: A Tainted Success
Enki Island, Orion

Annu deposited Shayne before the symbols on the opposite wall. "Great. We're in the right spot."

Shayne stepped ahead of him, a familiar hiss stopped her on the spot, flames projected in bursts from the wall; she raised her arms and froze the trap. "Hah. Not a hair singed."

Annu tapped the communicator. "Shit, it's not working in here. Is yours?"

Shayne adjusted her sleeves. "Um, no."

"You didn't check."

"I did before."

Frustration niggled at him, Annu held his breath. "We're only three rooms away. Do you want to levitate, or I carry you?"

Shayne cocked an eyebrow. "It almost sounds like you want to. Thanks, but I'll levitate over."

When she hit halfway, Annu shot over the other side and walked toward another stone room. He waited for her at the doorway and poked his head through.

Annu placed an arm across Shayne's chest, and brushed her breast. She sucked in air, and trembled.

He lingered for a moment and removed his hand. "Oops, sorry. It's all clear."

Shayne examined the adjacent wall. "Yep all good this way. Damn, I'm sick of being in tight shafts. What were these people on when they built these?"

When this is all over I'll shaft you. Over and over. If we did, what good would it do? You're going back to Earth, and all I've done is push you away.

Annu measured the tunnel; too narrow to fly through and the floor consisted of rotted wooden planks. "This one verges on the ridiculous. I'm going to have to crawl."

He jumped in, and pulled Shayne up behind him. Darkness enveloped them, his butt hole puckered. Annu took the weight off his leg and kneed the floor, the planks creaked.

Torch light marked the way ahead, he crawled into it. The plank beneath his left knee cracked, snapped and fell below.

A cavalcade of arrows whooshed past his face and embedded in the opposite wall. His heart pounded, his chest heaved. "Flark. How can I get across without putting pressure on the stupid plates?"

Annu placed a knee either side of the wooden floor. "You go before me."

Shayne scratched his nerves. "What? Why?"

"If I break this, neither of us gets through and it's the real one. We can't fuck it up."

She pushed his leg to the side. "I won't get past you. We'll have to go out and come back in. Unless—"

Annu adjusted his position to look her in the eye. "What?"

Shayne flattened her palms on the floor; an icy hue crept along its length until it all froze.

She wriggled her eyebrows and smiled. "Hah, fixed."

Annu pushed off the sides and slid along into an opening at the end, Shayne close behind him.

In the middle, stood a wide doorway panelled in gold to another room. "Thank flark, it's in there."

Annu clutched her hand and walked into the room side by side. Dust, moss and vines covered the symbolic walls and floor. At the end stood a stone altar embossed with jewels and illuminated by coloured crystals.

His heart fluttered, the scroll piece hovered above it surrounded in pink light. Annu rubbed a hand over a piece of tablet on the wall closest to him. He blew across the surface, the symbols on the floor lit up with a bright blue light.

Shayne squatted and traced swirls with her finger, the floor exploded in colour. "The incantation's on the floor, like on the walls. We press the right ones; we make it to the other side without getting fucked up."

Side-by-side, they plotted the course.

Annu stepped onto the first plate. It slipped into the floor and lit up the left wall. "One down. Lots more to go."

He lunged to the left, balanced between his feet and stepped onto the next stone.

Shayne jumped onto the first, Annu two ahead. His right foot stumbled and pressed the stone adjacent.

It turned red, the ground roared, a section of roof crumbled onto his head. A blast of fire brushed his back. Shayne ducked down, and covered her head.

Annu wavered back and forth and recalled the stupid meditation classes.

Balance, keep cool. Don't panic.

Annu slipped across to the right stone, it turned blue; the right wall lit up, the roof settled. Shayne followed behind, step for step.

He paused and regained his sense of balance. "One, two, three, one two three. Don't watch my feet, keep it nice and light."

Annu danced over the stones and checked Shayne. On the last one, he launched onto the platform and pulled her onto the edge.

Shayne squeezed his hand at the altar. With their free ones, they grasped and lowered the scroll toward them. The ring heated her chest and wiggled under her shirt.

Sweet satisfaction propelled Annu to grab her. He kissed the top of her head. "We got one."

Shayne wrapped her arms around him, his chest muffled her words. "We fucking did it. I can't believe it."

Shayne ducked under his arm and behind the altar. "Here's the escape hatch lever."

Annu reached around and lifted it, metal creaked, the hatch opened. He slipped his arm around Shayne's shoulders.

Music from the Heaven's filled the room, his energy levels soared. "My plan worked. Everything will be alright."

A beam of white light shot from the altar through the roof, into the sky.

Shayne slumped in his embrace, panic destroyed Annu's enthusiasm. "Oh shit. There's another problem added to the list."

Chapter 44: Smashing Pumpkins
Enki Island, Orion

Shayne shaded her eyes from the beam. "Hey Annu, where are you? I'm a poet and I know it."

Annu popped up behind and tapped her shoulder, she jumped.

He crouched beside her. "I'm sure I heard gunfire over the left side of the hill."

Elation disintegrated, fear ebbed on the shores of her mind. "Shit. They didn't take long. Where's the scroll?"

Annu lifted his shirt to caramel coloured abs, a line of dark curly hair and the scroll next to the map.

Gods damn. When did you get so fucking hot?

He clicked between her eyes, Shayne snapped to attention. "Oh right. Yeah, that's a good spot. Actually it's a great spot." Her face burned; her tongue thick in her mouth. "To put the scroll, I mean."

Annu paused, his mouth half open; a moment of awkward silence between them. The words tumbled out. "Yes, ah, of course."

Shayne clenched her inner thighs.

Oh my God this is impossible. I shouldn't think about him like this now. Fucking hell.

Annu moved closer, and placed a hand on her leg.

Oh God, oh God, Oh God.

"Stay here, I'll see where they are, then come back and get you."

Shayne and Annu became people sized pieces of bacon, about to go from frying pan into the fire.

Sizzle, sizzle, sizzle. Pop.

Shayne hugged the wall and counted. *1, 2, 3, 4…*

Annu re-appeared dishevelled beside her. "About twenty of them over three quarters of the hill side." He scooped her into his arms. "We'll come up behind. You ready?"

Shayne nodded yes, and shook no, but held her breath regardless. Whoosh.

They shot into the air, cold air blasted her lungs. Before she blinked, Annu placed her back onto the ground, her legs wobbled.

The copper of blood and cauterisation burns from laser guns consumed the air. War enlisted the landscape; the flash of lasers, the clang of metal, and the roars of pain confused her senses.

Shit, where do I go first?

Her powers enveloped her, in a blue haze Shayne stepped around Annu in his red one. She turned to a scream on her left, several men hammered Banna. The girl fought back one armed, the other tucked across her stomach. Their lasers sliced across her back, sides, and legs.

Shayne reached for Annu, he'd disappeared amongst a sea of people.

Already? Hell, I'll find him soon.

Fury roared within her, Shayne bounded to Banna and froze her attackers. Protectors pushed her away and sliced their iced bodies. Body part ice blocks exploded onto the ground.

Banna slumped into a heap, a hand to her chest, blood streamed out a deep gash on her torso. Shayne grabbed under her shoulder and froze the flow. "Hang on, lean on me."

A tonne of weight upon her spine knocked her sideways, the attacker along with her. Shayne scrambled backwards into someone's legs, a muddied man barrelled towards her, a weapon aimed at her head.

She raised her hands, he lunged at her. She rolled to the side and kicked. He changed direction. Shayne flipped onto her stomach, crawled between his legs, popped onto her feet and fired with all the energy she could muster.

He smacked into a tree in the distance among a shower of bark and sawdust. She enforced a barrier around herself and searched for Annu. He hovered above several feet away, blasting fire shots at the enemy. The ground detonated around the bodies, dirt billowed in the air.

Thank Gods, he's okay.

To her right, two protectors who fought back to back against a number of Shamesh's men. Shayne levitated beside the Protectors and forced energy at the enemy's heads.

Boom, smash, mush. Blood, bone, and brains painted the vicinity.

Those who'd witnessed the cranial decimation scattered. An equal number replaced them; Shayne swiped the blood and brain from her face.

Laser fire zipped by, she belted ice bombs in their direction. The barrage ceased.

Shayne caught her breath, and the last group of enemy, as they fled through bushes. She flowed in their direction, Annu beat her to it. Aflame, he turned them to ash.

Anger and frustration pulsed through her. With the last of the threat now removed, Shayne rushed to examine their fallen men.

She reached Banna's side, the woman's pulse weakened, her skin pallid. Shayne rubbed her hands together and held them over the deepest cuts. The ends froze together, forming a thin layer of ice over the top.

Shayne stroked Banna's forehead; the girl cold and wet. "Hang in there." She blinked aside tears. "Medic, I need a medic here now."

Annu organised a small number of wounded protectors not far away.

Her mouth dry, her words cracked. "Annu. Get over here quick. She's still alive."

He couched on Banna's other side. "I'll take her to medical at base camp. I'll be back."

Shayne covered Banna in a protective layer. "Where are the medics?"

Annu heaved Banna into his arms. "They're all dead."

He shot into the sky, a red blur amongst the blue.

Shayne found protectors in a huddle, checking each other's injuries. In total, 6 of their group who'd fought remained whole. "Thank Gods you guys are okay. Head back to base camp and get help."

The one with a slash across his chest shook his head. "Not until we take care of our dead men as best we can for now."

Camaraderie overwhelmed her.

I've only watched shit like that on TV.

"I'll help you, then go get help. It's an order."

"No ma'am you must keep going."

"You're right, but I don't want to leave you."

Annu landed to her left, his down expression face tore her heart. "We have to go"

Shayne's heart sank. "I know, I just feel bad."

Annu held an arm around her shoulder. "We can't stay any longer."

Shayne's head pounded, an influx of adrenaline streamed through her blood stream. "Where do we go now? They'll be waiting for us no matter what we do."

He patted where the scroll sat on his belly. "We'll stop at base camp, get a few more men and head to the first trap. We are going to have to fight for the next ones but we've got the upper hand now."

A chill crept down her neck and across her kidneys. "Yeah, but how long will we keep it?"

Chapter 45: Salvation
Enki Island, Orion

From across the yard, Jonn fussed over Banna in the medical unit. While part of him envied their parent-child bond, Annu preferred his position. Worry cast an ugly shadow across Jonn; the gravity of Banna's injuries incapacitated the man's concentration and reliability.

His grief and woe infected base camp and dragged down moral. The upside, it allowed Annu to reconsider their place on the list of potential traitors.

Junior would be around Jonn's age now, and Banna, my grandchild's age. I think I've missed my chance to try again. I'm too old and stuck in my ways.

Shayne restocked supplies into the back pack. For each ration of biscuits she shoved in the bag, one went into her mouth. She licked the crumbs clung to her bottom lip, the movement distracted him.

Annu pushed the thoughts aside before they muddied his concentration. In the middle of the communications centre, he flicked aside the light in his face. The second base camp remained a harried mess in comparison to its predecessor. A quarter of the people rushed around.

He pinched a biscuit before it touched Shayne's lips and ate it in one bite. "I think it's safe to say, those two are probably trustworthy. I can't imagine Jonn would risk his daughter's life and she wouldn't get killed on purpose. Right?"

Shayne arched an eyebrow arched and wiped a crumb off his beard. "Yeah, I agree. Which makes a grand total of two, out of what twenty protectors left to chose from? Treacherous bastards."

Whenever she swore, a thrill rippled through him. He pinched another biscuit and licked crumbs off his fingers. His hands fizzled, a numbness pulled down his arms.

Annu shook them, the feeling grew. "Yep, exactly."

Shayne squinted and cocked her head. "Which trap are we doing this time? First or third trap? We never got the chance to figure out the last one, it's going to fuck us up for sure."

Mmm. Fuck, flark, whatever. Shit, concentrate.

Annu adjusted his pants. "Either way, we've got to go right now. We can't waste anymore time."

Her sigh echoed throughout the tent. "Alright, give me a minute to pack the rest of this stuff. You organise more protectors to go with us, aka lambs to save us from slaughter. Fuck, I hate this shit."

His groin tightened.

Oh, come on. You're killing me woman.

Annu's hands progressed from buzz to throb. He wiped them down his pants, the feeling increased. "Me too, but what else can we do? If we say we're going to the first but go to the third, we'll get another advantage. Maybe. And it might also help us narrow down who's feeding Shamesh the information."

Shayne cracked her neck side to side and tied the bag shut. "Don't you think it's funny how base camp wasn't attacked?"

He clenched and unclenched his fists, his hands a separate entity with their own desires. "It's pretty obvious it's someone, or someone's left behind that are in on it."

Annu flicked them side to side, they hummed in response. "What the heck?"

He rubbed them back and forth across a patch of half dead grass. The grass crackled, greened and sprung back to life.

Annu rubbed his eyes, poking the resurrected grass. "Well I'll be flarked."

He touched another patch, it renewed as quick as the first.

Holy shit. Hey, I can, that means–

Annu leapt to his feet, pushed past Shayne, and bounded into the medical tent. Jonn held Banna's limp hand; he'd aged a decade in an hour. Annu made it to the other side of her bed and clutched Banna's other hand.

A light green glow flowed out his palm and rippled across Banna's skin. It crept up her arm, absorbed into a cut above her shoulder, the one on her side and filled her body.

Banna jolted, and seized, consumed by a green aura. Her cuts, bruises and wounds healed.

Pure love and joy washed over Annu, his heart filled with happiness. He removed his hand; Banna took a massive breath, her eyes popped open.

She probed her torso, head, and shoulder. Banna's tears ran a path through the dirt on her cheeks. "Oh Gods. I'm alive. How?"

Annu found a suitable aphrodisiac replacement. "My new power."

Jonn embraced Annu. "I can't thank you enough."

"It's all good."

Jonn returned to Banna, and sobbed beside his daughter.

In the next bed a young red headed male lay, death loomed over him.

Annu pushed the doctor aside, placed his hands on the boy's chest, and repeated the process.

Bed by bed he worked the room, each person Annu repaired, healed something broken within himself and reinstalled hope.

Annu exited the tent more complete than when he entered, with an end to this nightmare in sight.

Shayne waited for him outside the entrance, her expression exuded awe. "That was incredible, amazing. I've never seen anything like it. I didn't know you could."

Annu hugged her tight, she squealed.

Maybe I can change and you can save me.

"Me either."

A brilliant idea rolled across his mind. He led Shayne around medical, and behind the main tent. "We'll go, you and me, and not tell them first."

Shayne pinched his side. "We're starting to make a habit of sneaking behind trees. It feels naughty. What do you mean not tell them?"

I'll show you naughty woman.

"We go without any protectors. You and me fly off now to the first trap. Come back with the other scroll, check in and do the same again with the third."

Shayne pursed her lips together, concern marked her face. "What about Shamesh's men? The whole reason the protectors are with us?"

Annu stroked her cheek. "We are strong enough to fight his goons without getting anymore good people hurt. Your head exploding act proved that."

She dipped her head and snuggled into his side. "Oh, I didn't know you saw. You annihilated quite few of your own though."

"Hey, I didn't say it was a bad thing. The opposite in fact."

Shayne dragged her fingers up his back. "Whose going to protect them without us here?"

Ah fuck it, I give up. I might die soon anyway. I'm not fighting it anymore.

Annu kissed her finger tips. "We can't be everywhere at once, Shay. Are you ready?"

She pushed off his side. "Wait, let me grab the bag first, just in case."

Annu's eye twitched. "Can't you live for ten minutes without food?"

"No, I'm pretty sure I can't.

He held a breath and gritted his teeth. "Fine. Grab it and let's go."

Shayne returned with the bag over her shoulder. Annu clutched her to him, and shot into the air toward the first trap, his heart in his throat.

Gods be on our side. Keep us safe, and those bastards out of our way.

Chapter 46: Stone Cold Son of a Bitch
Enki Island, Orion

The absence of enemy outside the entrance tripled Shayne's anxiety. "This is too easy. It's not going to end well. I just know it."

The musty stank of the shaft dulled her sense of smell, but heightened the others. Shayne became aware of everything around her; every sound a bellow, each object huge, the taste of potential failure streaked across her tongue. Dirt embedded under her nails, suffocation loomed with each inch forward.

Shayne wriggled towards a sliver of light ahead, Annu slipped into a room below. She dangled her legs over the edge.

Annu held his arms out. "Jump."

Heart in throat, Shayne dropped; Annu didn't shift under her weight. He rotated in a half circle and lowered her to the ground.

Her pulse sped, the pit of snaky despair waited in the next room; the one time Annu may lose his shit.

The sensation of being watched wriggled up her spine and clawed at her neck. A scrape and crunch from the room ahead, put them both on edge.

Annu grabbed her by the arm and held her close. Adrenaline combined with panic into a slurry of fear in her gut.

Side by side, they hugged the wall and edged towards the next doorway. Annu peeked around the door and scooted back.

Shayne's heart skipped. "Who is it? I think I'm going to throw up."

Annu opened his mouth and closed it. Three armed men burst through the door and into the room, their guns aimed at her head height. A pitted skinned man strolled between them and stood in front, his arms crossed.

The contents of her mind disintegrated, she swallowed a chunk of vomit. "Oh shit."

Annu raised ignited hands in their direction; a smile broke out on pit man's face. His voice reminded her of an oil slick. "Don't bother. If you harm me, I kill your friend."

He motioned with his hand to someone outside of the room.

A huge bitch dragged in a dirty old woman by the shoulder. Hair covered her face, a gun to her temple.

The woman grunted at pokes and jabs, turned and spat in the Amazon's face. She open handed smacked the woman across the jaw.

Hair flew from her features, Shayne exploded with hope and hate. "Oh my God, Irica. Let her go you fucking bitch."

Shayne bolted forward, Annu grabbed her. "Shayne, no. Wait."

The man ripped Irica by the arm to his side. "One more step, she's dead."

Annu's cold tone frightened her. "What do you want?"

Pit Face sneered, a sight worthy of nausea. "You know what we want. You two are going in there to get the scroll. Then the next one, and of course you'll give me the one you already have."

Annu spat out the words. "No. We won't do it."

The man removed a knife from his jacket pocket, tapped the button on the side, and sliced it across Irica's face. She screamed, blood streamed between her fingers, and pooled on the ground.

Shayne's stomach rolled, her heart tore to pieces, it took all her strength to stay put.

Pit Face slipped the knife back into his pocket and replaced it with a gun. "I admit I'm surprised by your reluctance. You've both made it more difficult for us than we anticipated. However, we can't allow this to continue, what with the impending deadline and all. Shamesh is a demanding man."

He stroked a scar down his face with the gun barrel.

Shayne stepped back and hit the front of Annu. He held her to his chest, his heart pounded against the back of her head.

Pit Face waved the gun at them. "You two in there. Now."

Shayne shuffled with Annu backwards towards the adjacent room, his arm firmly in place. She mumbled through the side of her mouth. "What are we going to do? We're fucked. Proper fucked. I can't see how we can get her."

He whispered into her hair. "Keep moving, do what they say for now until I, I mean we, figure something out."

Annu jolted forward, she stumbled over her feet and smacked into the wall.

Pit Face kicked the back of her leg. "No talking. Move."

Ah Dad, Ann, now's a great time to pop in and help out.

They stopped at the edge of the pit, hisses and slithers erupted beneath. Annu bristled, she squeezed his hand.

Anytime now, feel free.

Pit Face jabbed the gun barrel into Shayne's ribs. "However you two get over it, do it now. Get the scroll and come straight back here."

Irica squealed, Shayne whipped around, and kicked Pit Face in the shins. He cracked Shayne across the jaw, her brain jiggled.

Annu lunged at him and thrust his hands around Pit Face's neck.

Shayne tumbled sideways and fell; her dangled legs over the chasm.

Her mind too scrambled to levitate, Shayne grasped at the edge, stones and dirt slipped within her hands.

The hisses increased, she slipped lower. "Oh Gods."

Shayne attempted to calm her mind; it filled with images of her broken body slumped over the stones covered by snakes.

Annu grabbed her hands, pulled her back over the edge and into his arms.

Shayne's heart thudded an uneven rhythm, her body fought between panic and elation. "You saved me."

He kissed her head. "You've really got to stop doing that."

Whack. Annu thrust sideways out of her arms, and onto the ground.

Red welts formed around Pit Face's neck. "Now you've got that little episode out of the way, get the hell over there before I shoot you both."

Pit Face aimed the gun at Irica's foot and tapped the button. Irica's foot disintegrated in a mess of blood, bone and torn flesh. Irica's screams tore layers off the walls and pieces from Shayne's heart.

Irica melted into a puddle, and vomited onto the floor.

Shayne clutched grabbed Annu's arm. It trembled, his colour drained.

Pit Face aimed above Irica's other foot, and glared at them.

A blood vessel in Shayne's brain exploded. "No. Stop. No more. We'll do it."

Shayne crouched by Annu, held his face between her hands and forced him to look at her. "Stay with me. I need you. We do this, they pay and you fix her. Okay?"

Transfixed by Irica, Annu wavered, his eyes welled with tears.

Shayne pinched his upper arm. "You with me, big guy?"

Annu licked his lips, and nodded. His eyes glazed.

Stay calm. Don't panic yet.

"You kill the ice traps and we go over together. Ready?"

His lips didn't move. "Yes."

"Okay, let's go." Shayne stuck a hand over the middle of the pit, the walls grumbled, icy water projected across the room.

Blank faced, Annu disabled the trap. Shayne sat cross legged on the precipice and waited for him to fly over to the other side.

Instead, he scooped her into his arms, flew over the pit and into the altar room. Once he'd placed her on the opposite side, Annu blasted the door and crumbled the room. A wall of rubble blocked them in and Pit Face out.

Chapter 47: A Twist of Fate
Enki Island, Orion

Shamesh's men banged, blasted at rocks and shouted threats from the other side. The latest and second scroll piece buzzed in his hand, the band glowed. Annu's sanity joined the lump in his stomach.

A bright red light shot from the middle of the altar, pierced an exit through the roof, and continued its journey as a beacon into the sky.

The outer exit door sprung open with a crash behind the table, daylight streamed into the room. Annu's heart fluttered; his pulse irregular.

Shayne clasped his hand, her skin icy. "I can't believe you did that. Holy shit. She's dead, we're dead. We've got to get out of here."

He trembled, his mind a quagmire. "I just reacted, it's the first thing I thought to do. Oh flarking hell. It's too late to change it now."

Annu slid the scroll under his shirt, alongside the other one. The instant they touched an invisible seam formed between them.

Shayne shook his arm. "Why don't we go through the trap door and come up behind them."

Confusion clouded his thoughts. "Huh?"

Her determination captured his attention. "We shoot out the door, fly around the front and come back in behind them, right before the pit. If we do it quickly, they won't know we've gone out yet. And they can't see the light outside."

Annu's mind raced. "It's a good plan. We might save her yet. "

Shayne shrugged her shoulders. "Let's not get carried away. He still needs her to bargain with."

A thud drummed against his skull. "Yes, you're right."

"We can't give pit face the scrolls and they can't get them without us."

Annu paced in front of the altar. "Alright, when the last one is in our possession, we use them to bargain for her."

Shayne slapped her hands on her thighs. "No, that doesn't work either, because Shamesh will ascend and goodbye universe. Everyone died for nothing. We didn't come this far to screw up."

Nausea pummeled his guts.

Is it too late to run?

"You're right."

"Jesus. If I could work the communicator, I'd record this monumental event."

"Make your gloating quick it won't be long and they'll bust through the wall."

Shayne did 360's on the spot. "Fuck it. Shit. Wait, I'll freeze them all."

"Do you know how to not freeze Irica in the process? She'll be right at his side."

She halted mid spin. "If I do hit her by accident, then you defrost her."

Annu smacked his hand against his forehead. "She's not a steak. We don't know it will work, it might kill her too."

Shayne plonked back onto her heels. "We're fucking right back where we started. Two dumb arses with half a clue and no more biscuits."

Slabs of stone tumbled into the room and created an opening. A man burst through, his weapon raised.

Shayne leapt into Annu, and the man ran across the room. "Get in there to Syrl. Move."

Shayne shook against Annu. "So Pit Face's name is Syrl. What's yours Martha, or the uglier one?"

The man snarled and whipped her in the back of the head with the gun.

Annu's temper soared ignited, he grabbed the man's neck and squeezed, and his skin seared, sizzled, and bubbled.

Screeches invaded the room, Annu tightened his grip, the head caved and melted. The body slumped to the ground.

Shayne tapped her foot. "Ah. Oops."

Annu wiped smoosh off his hands. "Okay, new plan. We're doing what you suggested first."

Shayne nodded, her pony tail flicked across her face. "Let's give them hell and get Irica the fuck out of here."

Annu walked around the altar to the exit door. "I'll go first."

Shayne's heart flip-flopped. "Okay. Here we go."

Annu inhaled, held the breath and ducked into the open air, Shayne nipped at his heels.

He grabbed Shayne and pulled her back against the rock wall.

They inched along the side towards the front entrance, his heart raced, adrenaline pumped through him.

Oh Gods, shit, crap, flark.

With Shayne attached to his hip, Annu darted around the side and into Syrl's gun.

Annu threw Shayne behind him and stepped towards Syrl.

Sryl's gun followed his hand gestures. "Gutsy move. You'll pay for it."

Annu held onto Shayne. "Where's Irica?"

"Give me the scrolls, now. And don't do anything stupid again."

Gods, she's already dead. It's my fault.

Shayne covered herself in a blue film.

Annu straightened and ignited. "Let me see her or I'll tear you to pieces."

Sryl tapped a button on his wrist. Annu and Shayne's powers diminished. "An effective, albeit temporary, solution. You don't seem to understand, you're way out of your league here. Last chance, give them to me."

Stay in control. Don't show him fear.

"No and you can't get the last one without us."

Sryl's smile belonged among the most horrific sights seen by human eyes. "Well it seems we're at an impasse, you have something I want and I have something you want. Don't forget, the thing I have bleeds and screams. Does yours?"

Annu's body temperature plummeted to sub zero, his hands shook.

Shit.

Sryl whistled, two men dragged Irica around the corner and dropped her at his feet. He pointed the gun at her foot. "The scroll is in my hand now."

She's still alive. Shit, I can't think of a way around this without a huge sacrifice. I don't want to lose another person I care about.

"No."

Why doesn't he want the map?

Syrl tapped the trigger, Irica's other foot disintegrated, her screams ripped shreds from his soul.

Annu lunged at Sryl, his blood boiled. "You prick, I'll–"

Sryl raised the gun to Irica's head and held out the opposite hand to Annu. "Now you're getting the idea. Hand them to me."

His guts churned, inner turmoil consumed him. "How do I know you'll keep us alive if I give them to you?"

The smile increased, the pits on Syrl's cheeks became craters. "You don't, but I can assure you, if you do not give them to me, you'll watch them her raped, pillaged and plundered before I kill her."

Irica lay in a pool of blood, her eyes fixed and dilated.

I can't risk us too. Think.

Annu raised his shirt; Shayne slapped a hand over his. "No. You can't."

He brushed her off and removed the scrolls. Annu tucked Shayne under his arm, gripped his side and reached towards Sryl.

Sryl grabbed the other end, a satisfied twinkle in his eye.

With no idea where they'd go, he bulleted into the sky; Shayne and a torn scroll part in tow.

Chapter 48: Crunch Time
Enki Island, Orion

Shayne touched the ground a few metres from the main tent. She hunched over, and heaved in cool air. "While I really appreciate saving me from dying, we've really got to stop doing that. It's not even four-fifths of being fucking funny, let alone smart anymore."

Irica's body on the ground haunted her, what Pit Face might do to her next tormented Shayne. Her equilibrium jiggled, her surroundings wavered.

Slumped against a tree trunk, Annu's grief stricken expression obliterated her last reserves.

Shayne thumped her fists on the dirt, tears streamed, her heart a leaden weight in her chest. "Ahh. We need to stop and think for a minute. Shit's gotten way out of hand, it's fucking mental. Oh hell, Irica."

Annu banged his head against the base. "She's dead, he killed her. It's my fault."

"We don't know for sure she's dead. As to being your fault, no matter what we do, someone's gonna get hurt."

Annu pushed off the tree, hands akimbo. "I, I can't lose–you mean so much to me, and I inadvertently chose Irica. After all she's done for me, you still blur my focus. My first instinct is to protect you. The only chance we have is together. It's messed up."

Shayne's heart flipped, her intestines twisted into a knot. "Jesus Christ on a cracker. Of all the times to start telling me how you feel. I fucking need a joint. A big fat one, that takes me an hour to smoke and three days to recover from."

Annu stroked her cheek. "When this is over, you can get smashed as you call it and I'll get stonking drunk."

Shayne kicked sots of dirt, a Grenberry bush a foot away. Her determination wobbled.

No, no, no. Don't be stupid. Keep your head clear. You're fucking up enough without it.

Shayne perched on her hands and knees. "We're dead in the water when they use the power disruption thing."

Determination stampeded across Shayne's brain, no fucker ruined her chance at love and having a mother.

Shayne leapt up, and clutched a handful of Annu's shirt. "We are not giving in. Let's kick bad guys' arses. Are you still with me?"

Annu thrust out his chest. "Yes I fucking am."

Shayne released him and brushed his shirt down. "That's the fuck face I know and lo…"

Too soon idiot.

"And tolerate."

Banna bounded from the side of the tent, her arm movements frantic. "Where have you been? You aren't meant to go anywhere without us."

Shayne swallowed a modicum of guilt. "We had ah, had business to attend to."

The young woman continued her search for clarification. "You weren't here when another light went off; we assumed they'd taken you too."

Shayne extracted herself from Annu and turned towards Banna. "No, well yes, nearly, but no. They have Irica and a scroll part."

Banna's expression dropped. "Oh Gods. Is she hurt? Is she alive?"

Annu's voice crackled with emotion, her heart plunged. "Is Hyl here?"

Banna screwed up her face. "Yes why?"

Ugh. That's horrid. Yeah, he's never around when there's trouble.

Annu's steadiness calmed her heightened anxiety. "Curious. Did anyone get hurt while we were gone?"

"No, so far so good."

Annu glanced down at Shayne. "Okay. Get everyone together in the open area, we're going to the last trap in five minutes."

"Yes sir." Banna spun on her heel and strode through the trees.

Shayne slumped onto Annu. "Do we have to take them with us?"

He wrapped an arm around her back. "Yes, it doesn't seem to work without them, and any on our side should help. I hope."

The muscles across her shoulders tightened, Shayne shrugged and circled them around. "Me too. You look like you have a plan of attack brewing. What is it?"

Annu kissed her head and lead her behind the tree. "Attack. That's the plan. No subterfuge, just head right at them. Grab Irica when we can, if… either way we get her."

Shayne adjusted her torn clothes and power walked to the main area. "That's a heck of an idea. We better pull it off."

Annu embraced her; she soaked in his musky man smell. He stroked her back. Her skin tingled, her pulse raced.

I know it's the wrong time, but please kiss me.

Annu mumbled into her hair. "I'll fly overhead with the protectors around you. I want to fly as close to possible to the third site without being spotted, so I can see where they are located. After, I'll come back and fill you in."

Or not. Back to reality I guess.

"Okay, makes sense. I, ah, I wish you were beside me though."

"Me too." He tightened his hold. "In a few hours you might go home."

Where is home for me now? Does he want me to go?

A moment passed in silence, Annu walked by her side into the open area to down cast faces, and troubled expressions. The losses never more evident.

Shayne hollered above the murmurs. "We're all going together this time. The camp, all this shit," she swept an arm across the yard, "Stays. Anything precious to you, should be attached to you because we're not coming back. This is the big one. Get your shit together, arm yourselves and get in line."

She scrutinised expressions for hints of disloyalty, a taint of guilt for the loss of their fellow ma, and outright hatred. "For those of you who are true and loyal, after this is over, you remain with us. However," Shayne jabbed a finger to the group, "To the mother fuckers who ratted us out, got people killed, we know who you are. You're fucked."

I even believe me.

Icicles spread over her arms; she flicked them on the ground.

Annu grabbed her around the waist. "I'll survey from above, cover Shayne at all times. Ensure your communicators are on. You've got five minutes. Get to it."

He tapped the communicator screen on his wrist and showed Shayne. "There's plenty of woods and stony structures around. Enough places to hide behind before we ambush them."

Shayne swigged a bottle of water, her eyes full of grit and heavy.

When did I sleep or eat anything other than biscuits last?

A downward breeze brushed past her, body odour wafted up her nose.

Okay, or showered. No wonder we haven't kissed yet. Damn, I'm a stinky bitch. But, it's going to wait.

Chapter 49: By the Grace of Gods Go I - I Mean We
Enki Island, Orion

The group scattered, Annu ducked behind bushes. He lifted his shirt and removed the scroll from his pants. One hand either side, he pressed it against the skin of his abdomen, and pressed on the paper's edges.

Intense heat seared the scroll to his skin, Annu flinched. He exhaled the pain, cleared his mind and healed the edges. He burned the map beside it.

Shayne bounced around the tree beside him, the bag over her shoulder. "Why are you back here by yourself?"

Annu flashed open his shirt, her mouth dropped. "It's the best place I thought of to keep them, where it wouldn't get loose anyway."

Her breath brushed across his belly, he tingled. "Well, I, I, it works, but you shouldn't have hurt yourself for it."

A vice gripped his chest. "That's why I did it when you weren't here."

Shayne touched the edges; a shiver ran along his spine. "Everyone's ready."

Annu pulled his top down, the moment passed. He followed her back to the main area, dread weighted his legs.

'Mother if you hear me, whatever you can do to protect and help us, please do it.'

Shayne and Annu approached, conversation between the protectors ended. Tension crackled the air; distrust tainted his perception of those around him. Every twitch, frown and side glance represented betrayal.

Why's he checking his wrist? Is he waiting for a message? No, he's got an itch. Shit. The woman to his left looks shady; she's always at the back somewhere. And never speaks up. What's she hiding?

Without confidence to provide a motivational speech, Annu winged it. "May the Gods be on our side. Let's move."

I flarking hope they are, though maybe they like to watch us screw things up.

Armed, the group encircled Shayne.

This way anyone making odd calls gets noticed.

Cement coated his tongue and slid down his throat. He caught an up draft and hovered feet above. "We've got to pull this off in a short amount of time."

Shayne's pushed up sleeves revealed a bare wrist; fear squeezed his heart in a vice.

Annu thudded in front of her, everyone stopped. "Where the hell is your communicator?"

Face flushed, she examined her arm and shrugged. "I must have lost it in the Pit Face debacle."

Annu smacked himself in the forehead and bit his tongue. "Shit woman. Grab one from a protector, now."

Shayne jogged to the closest one, a young man. He trembled, unclasped the communicator off his wrist and handed it to her.

She smiled, secured the strap and jogged back with her arm held out. His blood pressure lowered, the vein in his forehead constricted.

Annu pushed through a side draft, his mind a muddle of post battle stress and anxiety.

The group trudged ahead in a tight circle, Shayne, a dot in the midst of people twice her size. The queen of his chess board, an integral piece of the puzzle he wanted on his side, forever.

I don't want her to go back to Earth, not even for a moment. What if she changed her mind about coming back? And Shit, I'd miss her. Ha if we get that far. Who'd have thought? Not flarking me.

The higher Annu soared; everything below shrank into specks across the landscape. Tension slipped from his shoulders, he embraced synchronicity with nature.

I've got to stay alert. They could get the drop on us any time. Is it too much to ask for Shamesh to die before he got here and his men to give up?

The group worked their way through heavy woods, Shayne disappeared. He tapped the communicator. "Shayne, you there?"

Her response crackled amongst static. "Huh? I can't hear you. What's the rushing noise in the background?"

Annu held it under his jacket. "Probably wind."

"Wh……at?"

Annu cupped the microphone. "I'm checking out further ahead."

"Wh…."

Annu right eye twitched. Re-assured of Shayne's safety, he disconnected the call.

In his current position, the third mound waited a few clicks ahead. He scoped across the tree tops to end of the wooded terrain, where it changed to rocky and open.

A few hills prior to the mound provided sufficient cover for the group to launch their ambush from. The stone temple in his sight, anxiety pummelled him, he patted the scroll. "Well, one way or the other, an end to this mess is coming."

Shadows scattered across the mountain, too far in the distance for definition. Annu circled around for a bird's eye view, without revelation of his presence.

At the top of three hundred plus foot Hyperion tree, Annu crouched down and shifted aside sticks and leaves.

His butt hole puckered; at least a hundred men covered the top of the mound, another bunch trickled down the front and either side. "Of course they're flarking there already. Shit."

Perched on a thick branch, Annu leant against the trunk. The branch groaned under his weight. Cold air fought against the warmth of his lungs, anticipation painted a second skin across his flesh.

Annu launched off the tree and found the group behind the last ridge line.

Breath held, the air cold in his face, he plunged towards Shayne.

Chapter 50: Me, Myself, and I
Enki Island, Orion

Rocks poked through the soles of her boots, shrubs and bushes scratched her arms. Shayne dredged up recollections of the few war movies she'd seen and combined it with the brief attempt at battle before she'd gotten creamed. So far she'd achieved a sore brain, failure, and wasted time.

Annu boomed across her wrist. "One click left and there's places we can hide and ambush from."

"Alright, it got too late to ask, but now it's bugging the shit out of me. What the fuck's a click? If it's not to do with my fingers, why should I care?"

Annu circled overhead, his laugh vibrated along her skin. "I can't believe you waited so long to say something. It's another way of saying a kilometre. The last one's only one kilometres away."

Shayne rubbed her temples, a storm brewed in her head, thunder roared. "Oh well that's just stupid. It's already got a name, why complicate it?"

Lightning cracked her thoughts; a discombobulated sensation filtered down her limbs and displaced her awareness. The weapons slipped from her hands, she dropped to her knees.

A vice gripped her chest, Shayne's mind lightened, bees buzzed in her ears. An unseen force separated her spiritual and physical selves. Fear, the only tangible substance in the vicinity wriggled between her fingers and crept up her arms. Shayne's heart wanted out of her chest, her guts wrenched.

The rocky terrain, the protectors and Annu disappeared. Black space replaced Shayne's surroundings, disjointed awareness plagued her being. "How–what–oh God. Where the hell is the rest of me? Where am I?"

The dark transformed into a white walled room, with a rugged floor. Shelves of books lined either side of where a see-through version of herself hunched, and spied through a gap at a figure behind a wooden desk.

What am I doing there? Whose am I looking at?

The other her shifted closer; an old man raised his voice to a desk communicator. He reeked of power and arrogance. The man turned towards the shelves, a rage filled expression.

Surely he can't see me, us, whatever? Just in case other me, get down and hide.

Physical Shayne slipped down to a lower shelf.

She does what I think, kind of like a ghost golem. Weird, fucking creepy.

A vein bulged across the man's forehead and pumped emphasise into each word. "What? You allowed them escape?"

Holy shit balls. He's fucking Sham-man. The one and only. I'm in his place. Oh, I thought he'd be taller.

Shayne screamed at herself, no sound emitted from her.

Shit. Stay hidden dickhead.

How do I get back to the real world? Well, it would help if I figured out how the fuck I got here first.

Shamesh swiped an arm across the desk; the contents tumbled onto the floor. "Don't give me excuses you pathetic piece of human vermin. Stay close to them, but do not reveal yourself yet."

He's talking to the rat bastard.

Golem Shayne released the shelf, inched closer and cocked her head. She smacked her invisible head on a book.

So she's a dumb arse too. Great.

"Lower your voice, someone will hear you. I'm leaving in twenty minutes. If I arrive and you don't have the pieces when I get there, I don't need to remind you what will happen."

He kicked the mess at his feet across the floor and thumped a fist on the desk. "I told you, those two are nothing for you to worry about. Just keep them alive until I get there. Imbecile."

Shamesh ripped the communicator from the desk and hurled it at the opposite wall. His roar bellowed around the room bounced off the walls and rang in her mind.

Shayne's other self vibrated, wavered and flickered.

No wait, not yet. I need to know who the rat bastard is.

The office melted away; replaced by a dimly lit stone room in the midst of the third trap. "Fucking hell. We never figured this one out."

Terror crippled her mind, the endless chasm lurked in the middle of the chamber. Horrific screams erupted from its depths and crept around the edges of her sanity.

In the opposite corner, a body lay crumpled on the stone floor, her panic level shot into overdrive.

An arm tucked under his robe, Sham-man kicked it several times.

It groaned, the head lolled sideways and Shayne's mind snapped. "Irica? How?"

He limped across the room to another body face down on the ground, the mop of black hair–familiar. "I told you like I told your mother, I always win."

Unable to rush to either person she loved, her screams tortured only herself. Shayne remained helpless, trapped in an invisible box.

Another her, in a physical form, entered the stone room, her hair matted, face streaked with blood, an empty look on her face.

How many of these fuckers are there?

She came up behind Sham-man and leapt onto his back.

He flung at her and shoved her off one armed.

Shayne landed on the ground, bounced off, and grabbed at his robes.

She clung on, dragging him with her to the pit's edge. With a cruel smile, the other Shayne jumped in, Sham-man in tow.

Shayne plunged behind them, her mind exploded; darkness consumed her. Bony hands clawed and scraped across her reality.

At the bottom of the pit, she thudded into her physical self. Cold from the damp grass soaked into her bones.

Shayne's body shook side to side, Annu yelled in her ear. "Shayne, Shay? Are you there? Come on. Don't do this to me."

She kept her eyes closed. "Am I in hell? Are you here too?"

Relief oozed seeped from his words. "Oh thank the Gods. I, I thought I'd lost you."

Shayne cracked open one eye, bright light forced it closed again. She probed Annu's face with her fingers. "Am I really back? Is that you?"

Annu pushed her hand away. "Hey that's my eye. What the flark happened? One of the protectors saw you walk out of yourself and drop to the ground. You just fell back in again. You freaked us all out. Please don't do it again."

Her butt ached, her head pounded. Shayne rested on her elbows. "Holy shit. That was not fun."

Annu rubbed his face. "Where did you go? Are you alright?"

"Either I had a flashback LSD trip from college or," Shayne's mind cleared, the storm gone. "I, I, I'm not sure, but I think I have to kill myself to stop Shamesh."

Chapter 51: This Is the End My Friend, It Never Ends
Enki Island, Orion

The protectors huddled around Annu and Shayne, his concentration spread over a thousand places. Shayne's declaration remained at the forefront of his thoughts, pain shot through his heart.

I can't let it happen. I've got to change things and save both her and Irica. Even if it means I die doing it.

The meteors slowed overhead, the ground rumbled, grey murk covered the sky. Their time ran short; it took all his strength to focus on the next step.

A cold draft billowed between their legs and whipped along the ground. Annu grabbed Shayne's hand, swallowed apprehension and spoke above the wind's roar. "The three groups you're separated into will attack in waves. If anyone sees Irica at any time, get her somewhere safe until I can fix her. Group one,"

Annu tightened his fingers around Shayne's, "You're first up, annihilate the men up the hill side and any others who come your way."

Oh please let this work.

His heart palpitated. "Group two, your directive is to go around Group one, and remove the men from around the tomb's entrance. Keep it clear as best you can."

Annu rubbed the base of his spine.

I'm too old for this shit.

"Group three; locate Syrl—"

Shayne grunted. "Aka pit face."

Way to flarking old.

"Right. Anyway, he has Irica and one scroll. We aren't sure if she's alive. Don't kill him without either of those, or I'll kill you." Thunder grumbled, his guts gurgled. "We all know what this means, so go with the Gods and thank you. Resume formation."

The men and women shifted into place, the three groups before him and Shayne. To save his sanity, he refused to think about their low numbers and odds of success.

This is it, be strong.

Annu bellowed into the communicator. "Group one…..attack."

The atmosphere electric, the first group stormed the hillside. Adrenaline coursed through his veins, he jogged beside Shayne to the end of group two, who poised ready for direction.

Halfway up the mountain, Shayne squeezed his arm. "Now?"

Heat poured from his head to his feet, he ignited. "Yep."

The temple mound in sight, she engulfed in blue and tapped her wrist. "Group two go."

They charged forward into a flurry of gun fire, crackle of laser sticks and roar of battle.

Annu grabbed hold of Shayne. "Holy shit, don't lose concentration."

He trudged ahead–she dangled at his side–his guts in his throat. The faces of the people around them changed.

A rip tide of people flushed them back to the bottom of the mound. Annu pulled at Shayne, she slipped through his fingers, two men in her stead. "Shayne––"

Smack. He plunged onto his hands and knees. "How the hell?"

Annu flipped onto his feet, arm out, he whirled around and coat hangered a guy behind. He dropped his weapon.

It looks different.

He scrambled for it; a mammoth force pushed him sideways. The air shot out his lungs, his chest on fire. The fiery aura around him diminished, his power waned.

Flark, they've got it on their weapons too.

Annu grabbed a gun in each hand and swiped at the communicator. "Shayne? Stay where you are and wait for me. Their weapons disrupt us."

Static answered him. "Shayne?"

A blow to the torso thrust Annu into the air and projected him backwards.

Someone reefed him to his feet; Jonn helped Annu up and shot people around them.

Zaps from his gun interspersed Jonn's words. "What happened to your powers?"

Annu grabbed a gun from a passing protector. "They've got technology which disrupts them temporarily."

Zing, splat. "Hell. We'll have to work around it."

He ducked down and fired in a line around them. "Have you seen Shayne?"

Jonn glanced at him. "No. I've been looking for both of you. Did you call her?"

His intestines clenched, his pulse disrupted. "Flark it. Yes, no answer. I've got to find her. We're so off course."

A sense of dread he set aside for rectal exams and funerals muddied his thoughts.

Jonn nudged his shoulder. "Don't worry. Stick with me, we'll find her. I'll get you into the damned entrance if it kills me."

For each enemy he shot, several more replaced them. Annu ducked and weaved around missiles exploding across the ground. "Cover me."

"Got it."

Annu leapt over a pile of bodies, grabbed the top one and used it as a shield. Each non Shayne person he encountered angered him to the point of destruction. Faces blended into a blur.

Half way up the hillside, gunfire erupted in front of them. Jonn dropped; a dark red patch grew on his side. Annu slid an arm underneath him and dragged him behind a shattered monument.

Jonn groaned, colour drained from his face. "This might be it for me."

Annu healed the gravest wounds. The constant barrage of enemy fire screwed the peace his power derived from fixing Jonn. "You're not going anywhere yet. Come on."

Jonn heaved and pushed himself to sit up. "Give me a hand up and I'm good to go."

Annu dragged him to his feet, grabbed an extra gun from a set of dead hands, and held it to his chest. "Alright, on the count of three, let's go."

I'm going to die. "1."

Please don't let me die. "2."

Shit, shit, shit. "3."

He and Jonn burst from either side of the rock in unison, Annu kept his finger on the trigger, pure bravado propelled him forwards.

Whack. Pain exploded across his skull, he dropped to the ground face first. Thud. Another strike to the back of the head and stars circled behind his eyes.

Chapter 52: Lost
Enki Island, Orion

I wish I'd never come here, never moved into that fucking house, and never lost my unit.

If wishes turned to shit, Shayne waded neck high in it. "Annu?"

The weapons flung from Shayne's hands, she strengthened her energy field and blasted the enemy around her.

Laser fire skipped past her ear, Shayne's powers faltered. "Fucking hell. They've got it too."

Dirt exploded at her feet, a grass clod landed upside down on her head. She swiped it off and somersaulted out of the way.

Shayne landed on an older security guy's feet, he pulled her up. "Are you alright?"

I won't ever be alright again after all this.

A lack of familiar faces troubled her, the amount of those wanting her dead increased in kind.

Shayne functioned on automatic, the events around her a nightmare scarred into her brain.

Sanity poured through her fingers and stained her skin. "Where's Annu?"

The man's laser swords sliced through a large woman, body parts sloshed to the ground.

Oh this is fucked up. I won't sleep again.

He stepped over the upper half. "I don't know, haven't seen him. Call him."

Shayne ran beside him towards a mass of shattered stone statues

Boom, boom, boom. Heavy artillery decimated a monument ahead, her ears rang.

Shayne dove behind the stone remains of a long lost family member, the man on her right.

She gripped the handle of a free gun on the ground and fired at enemy running between structures. Zing, zing, zing. "Got ya fuckers."

Sweat swam down her back, Shayne gulped air. "The other communicator came undone and someone stomped on it. Can you call him?"

He thrust out a bare arm. "The same happened to me and almost everyone else I've come across. They're making a point of it."

Shayne reinstated her aura, and poked around the statutes legs. Whoosh. Enemy fire removed it. "Fuck it. They're leaving us with nothing to work with."

Shayne fired blind shots ahead.

Please don't hit any of ours.

"Can you cover me while I get to the end of the statues? I've got to make it back up the hill."

The protector nodded and blasted the area around them. Shayne covered her head and run amongst fallen debris.

Like a week or so ago, I worried about Sam and Rosie being pissy at me. Now I'm worried some mother fucker will shoot me in the head. Quite the turn around. Annu, you big lug, I'm coming to find you.

Shayne jogged around a massive pile of rocks to the bottom of the hill.

Pain erupted across her left side. She dropped the gun and twirled on one foot. Agony tore along her lower half, and blinded her senses. Shayne bit her lip and froze the assailant.

Another man barrelled through his iced companion, laser stick colours whirled.

A sword held by a decapitated hand lay at Shayne's feet. "Are you fucking kidding me?"

Stomach in her throat, Shayne freed it from its predecessor, the hilt warm in her hand.

Vomit swallowed, she sliced across the man's middle. The top half slid left, the bottom stayed in place.

1, 2, 3, 4, drop. I'm never going to watch a horror movie again…. Maybe.

With her wound healed and the pain dissipated, Shayne jumped to her feet, and ditched the sword in favour of two laser guns not otherwise attached.

Shayne arced the guns to and fro. On the next rotation, someone grabbed her shoulder and pulled her behind a rock.

Her heart skipped. "Annu. Finally I've been—-"

Shayne palpated disappointment; a line of blood teemed down Banna's face and covered the sword she held.

Banna wiped it on her pants. "Shayne. Thank the Gods I found you."

Frustration, dashed with relief, washed over her; a constant barrage of shots fired at them from every direction.

Guns raised, Shayne blasted back. "Have you seen Annu?"

Banna's grave expression filled her with dread. "Yes. I'll take you to him, he's near the entrance."

Doom impeded her thoughts. "Is he okay? What about Irica?"

Banna eliminated two men with one shot. "He's hurt, Shayne, we can't waste any more time. I'm not sure about Irica yet." She grabbed Shayne's arm. "I need you to come with me—now."

Shayne's heart flipped; her imagination rampant with possibilities. The thought of Annu injured her guts turned to lava.

Please let him be okay.

A realisation stalled her movement, a blast skimmed overhead. "Wait, why hasn't he healed himself yet?"

Banna manoeuvred her way across the side of the hill with Shayne in her grasp, the entrance in eyesight. A stab here, a slice there, dead bodies paved a way from the main battle. "The weapons disrupted his powers. Look, he'll explain it to you, just keep moving."

The entrance in the distance taunted her, as if to say, 'you should be here now, you're failing.'

Shayne's heart pitter pattered, a thousand centipedes travelled along her brain.

As long as we stop Sham-man from succeeding, dead or not, we've won.

No matter how many times Shayne repeated the words it soured the contents of her stomach.

Goosebumps covered her skin; they shifted away from the entrance. "Aren't we meeting him over there?"

Banna whirled around, her face scrunched up. "Gods dammit, we don't have time for this shit. Move it."

The abruptness of Banna's manner and her indignant tone set Shayne's teeth on edge.

Tension snapped across her shoulders, she resisted kicking her in the shins. "Where's your dad?"

"What?"

Distrust wriggled in Shayne's brain, she grabbed hold of it. "Your father, Jonn. Where is he?"

Banna gritted her teeth. "I haven't seen him. Why?"

They reached a rocky patch on the east hill side, the level of fray diminished, yet the amount of bodies on the ground rose. The stench of death drenched the air, the ground shimmied; she stumbled over a crevice.

Shayne steadied herself, her heart pounded against her chest, her pulse sprinted. "Curious that's all."

They turned behind a bunch of stone slabs, Shayne froze, panic invaded her every sense. "Oh shit."

The person who stood before her was the exact opposite of who she expected to see.

Her mind disjointed, Shayne's blood iced in her veins.

She spun to her right, hands aimed at Banna. "What the fuck is going on? You said you were taking me to Annu."

Chapter 53: Abandon All Hope Ye Who Enter Here
Enki Island, Orion

Annu spat out a wad of dirt, his head transformed into a cloud of pain, and thundered with the sky. He probed the back of his skull, semi-dried blood stuck to his fingers. His attacker remained behind him; he reached around, grabbed her, and shot into the air.

Several metres above Annu dropped the woman. Her body eliminated half a dozen other enemies, and formed a crater under the impact site.

His heart hammered against his chest, hatred poured through his veins. Lasers skimmed his protective field. Annu's dropped a foot at a time and landed knees first on the ground.

Jonn rushed to his side and helped him stand. "You okay."

Two guns appeared under Annu's nose; he wrapped his fingers around the grips and started shooting. "Flarking hell. We can't catch a break."

"You're going to slum it with us mortal's, friend, unless we find a way around it."

Annu blasted a group to his left. "Well--" Ping, ping, ping. "We've made a dent in their side."

Boom. Boom. Boom.

The ground beside him exploded, chunks of stone rained down. A large piece dropped on his back and pushed him down. Annu stumbled over dead legs and grabbed hold of a broken monument.

His ears rung, his head roared. "Jonn? Shit. Shit. Shit."

Annu poked above the monument's edge, Jonn limped in his direction. "Come on, you're nearly there."

Gun fire hit the top of the stone and blinded him with dust. He ducked down flush with the ground, stuck his guns out and glanced after them.

Another series of explosions erupted between his position and Jonn's. The man froze mid step, thrust forward and fell to the ground. Blood covered the back of his shirt.

A bitter taste filled his mouth, blood cold in his veins. "Oh Gods no. Jonn—-"

Annu ignited; the red glow dull, only his finger tips lit. He struggled between his two choices; heal Jonn and himself.

Damn it. Wait for me Shayne, I'll get there.

On his belly, Annu crawled to Jonn, gun fire discharged around him. Pain shredded his thigh; a river of blood warmed his skin.

Annu sucked his lip, grabbed Jonn and dragged backwards.

A shot grazed his shoulder, heat seared the wound. "Fuck. Shit."

Annu's guts churned, a blast hollowed his right foot, agony infiltrated his thoughts. Annu's chest constricted, his breath caught in his lungs.

Despite the gravity of his own wounds Annu held his hand over Jonn's back. The healing sapped his energy; Annu slumped against the stone and heaved in air.

Jonn roused and crawled towards the safety of nearby stone structure. Annu dragged along behind him, pain dulled his senses, each movement ripped another layer off his ability to cope. Annu's world unravelled around his ears, hopelessness created a cavernous wasteland in his soul.

Jonn pulled him around the corner and leant him against a wall.

Annu hunched over and plunged his head between his knees. "Flark the scrolls and shit, I need to get Shayne out of here. I don't think we're going to stop anyone."

Jonn wobbled before him. "Stop talking crazy. You are not giving up now. Catch your breath, you'll be okay."

Despair a blanket upon his legs, the cold reality of defeat his pillow. "I, I, don't know if I've got it in me."

Jonn slapped him across the face; his brain hit the back of his skull. "Wake up to yourself. It's no time to quit."

The shock forced negativity from his mind, Annu shook himself and blinked. "Flark. Alright. Take it easy."

A small green glow emitted from his hands, Annu stemmed the blood flow and sealed the edges of the main injuries.

Come on mother flarker get up and get her. Be the man and God they need.

Jonn fired around the corner. "Are you ready yet? I can't hold them off by myself much longer."

Annu alleviated weight off his right side and tipped onto his hands and knees. "I hope so, I'm getting there."

Jonn dodged errant gun fire. "Great, have at it. What's the plan?"

He climbed the wall to stand, his brain swam. "Find Shayne, kill Shamesh."

"And the ascension?"

Annu removed his hands from the stone, the movement tortured him. "I, I think that ship's sailed. No way we'll make it in time. Sorry, looks like no one's getting the big prize."

He dismissed the regret John's sigh elicited. "It doesn't matter as long as Shamesh doesn't. We've only got to hold them off until he arrives and kill him." Boom, boom, boom. Jonn brushed dust and rocks from his head. "If we make it out of here."

Annu struggled to find a handy weapon. "Let's run to the other side while we've got the chance."

Kaboom. The other end of the wall exploded and tumbled around them.

A barrage of weaponry blasted the structure, large holes blew out the middle, and blocked off their exit.

The impact shook the ground and pushed Annu onto his side. The wounds screamed and tore reminders into his flesh. Jonn lay on his stomach, his arms covered his head.

'Son?'

'Mother, help me.'

'You have to help yourself. You can do it. Now get up--'

'This is messed up.'

'Go.'

Annu bit back pain and grabbed a laser stick from the ground. "What are our odds of getting out from behind here at all?"

Jonn peeked around the corner, a shot skimmed his knee. "About 10 to 2. Give or take a couple." He emptied the gun's cartridge in return. "Make it 8 to 2."

Annu propped himself up, gathered things to throw and held his breath. "Let's do this. Go hard and go home."

'Mother, Gods, I don't care what happens to me but keep Shayne alive.'

Chapter 54: Only Good Bitch is a Dead Bitch
Enki Island, Orion

Shayne blinked at the barrel of Pit Face's gun, fear trickled down her leg and pooled in her sock. She discharged her aura, icicles dripped from her fingers. Shayne's hands throat height, she lunged at Banna.

Another gun appeared between her eyes, alongside a sneer on Banna's face.

Banna pressed the tip to Shayne's nose and tapped a button. Shayne's protection and energy fizzled.

Oh God, I'm fucked. Double fucked. What the hell am I going to do?

Shayne's heart skipped a beat, panic destroyed her semi-calm facade. "What the fuck's going on?"

Banna's sneer grew. "I think it's perfectly clear what's going on, but you aren't the brightest person are you, Shayne?"

What can I do without my powers? All the training I did must have taught me something. Right? Hurry up, think woman. Shit, I suck at being under pressure.

The contents of Shayne's stomach solidified, a chunk of concrete plonked to the bottom. "How could you do this? You're part of our team, Annu saved your life. What about your father, is he in this too?"

"Of course not. Since my youth, he's rattled on about the old ways, how I'll follow in his footsteps to be a great Protector for the

Gods. After a while I did my own searching, and discovered a whole other perspective. I wanted my own power and worth."

"You mean an evil one point of view? How is that better? Sham-man's evil, you know what he's capable of."

Hatred cast an ugly shadow across Banna's face. "It's flarking Shamsesh you idiot. Don't be so naive. I'm meant for more than babysitting a pathetic Earthling and her lug head boyfriend while they traipse around the countryside. The other planets will be under our control, he's promised me my own. Your primitive people will be mine."

Shayne jumped on Banna and wrapped her hands around her neck. "You crazy bitch. I'm trying to see things from your point of view, but I'm having a hard time getting my head far enough up my own arse. Trust me, bad guys never––"

Shayne tumbled backwards onto her butt, pain shot across her arse.

Pit Face loomed over her, with two guns aimed at her head. "This is all enlightening but a total waste of time."

The tip of Pit Face's boot dug into her ribs. "Get up."

Shayne scrambled to her feet, Banna grabbed her side.

Pit face stood behind Shayne.

Fuck, fuck, fuck. And another fuck.

He shoved the gun into her spine. "Move."

Shayne's pulse competed in a race with her heart. The sky cracked, the ground grumbled, and vibrated.

She hyperventilated, her brain buzzed. "Where are we going?"

The edge in Pit Face's tone shivered down her spine, her butthole shrank. "The mound, move."

A boot to the shin forced Shayne forward, she plodded ahead.

Gods help me, no Creator help me. I need the big guy.

"Where's Annu and Irica?"

Banna tightened her grip. "You'll see her soon enough."

"I didn't ask you, bitch. I asked Pit Face."

Pain exploded across her skull, Shayne dropped to her knees. Blood trickled down her cheek into her mouth. She spat, wiped her mouth and shook herself.

Shayne levered off the ground, her legs wobbled. She paused halfway, took a few deep breaths and stood.

Syrl's acrid breath wafted up her nose. "Keep your mouth shut. Walk."

Birds chirped, bees swarmed in hives. "You could really use a breath mint."

Shayne's head whipped left, her brain jiggled against her skull.

Now would be a great time to shut up, but fuck it and fuck them.

One foot in front of the other, Shayne ambled. The ground vibrated, she used the opportunity to stumble onto the ground.

An arm reefed her upwards, her shoulder screamed for its former location. A foreign thought popped into Shayne's head.

'Slow down, bide your time.'

'Dad?'

'Yes.'

'You're in my head now? When I see you again next, we're going to have a big talk about boundaries and stuff.'

'You must. I can't--'

'Yeah, yeah, you can't stay long. If I slow down they'll beat me up more.'

'It's important.'

'Fine. Whatever. If they kill me, I won't be happy.'

'Dad?'

"Oh for fuck's sake. Of all the times--"

"Who are you talking to?"

Shayne stuck up her middle finger. "Noneya, bitch face."

"What?"

"None of your business, bitch. Now off you fuck."

Whack. Shayne's skull went one way, her brain the other.

'Happy now?'

Shayne shook herself and waited for the world to steady. "Well thank you. I needed that."

Syrl shoved her forwards, the tombs entrance swayed ahead.

The whir of a PFD close by deafened all other sounds, a large ship landed a few feet from their destination.

Shayne's intestines cramped, bile burnt the back of her throat.

I'm in shit so deep I require scuba gear.

The gun dug into her back, the trio stopped and watched the ship land.

An explosion of colour detonated across the sky, a robed man exited, her blood froze.

Oh crap. It's Sham-man. We're fucking done for now.

Sham-man straightened his robes, pushed his shoulders back and strode towards them.

The hair on the back of Shayne's neck rose.

Ground please swallow me whole.

Sham-man reached them in seconds, Shayne shrank into herself; his presence consumed her personal space.

Sham-man reached towards her face, Shayne flinched away from him.

Her rebuke brought a smile to Sham-man's face; the sight sickened Shayne. "It's hard to believe you're the one who's created so much bother."

Sham-man glared at Banna, a snarl replaced the smile, both sights equally horrific. "I told you to have them both in the trap by the time I got here. You've wasted precious time."

Banna shuddered and pushed her chest out. "I did the best I could. It wasn't--"

A weapon flashed past Shayne's face, she leapt into Syrl's front. The gun flattened against her back.

Zap. The blast destroyed Banna's head; bone, brain and mush teemed upon them. The rest of her body slumped on the dirt.

Shayne removed the mess from her face with her sleeve and double middle fingered the bitch's remains. "Ha. Sucked in. Only good bitch is a dead bitch."

Sham-man shifted to her side and outstretched a hand to Pit Face. "The scroll, if you please."

Pit Face's Adam's apple jiggled up and down. He pulled the paper from his pants and gave it to Sham-man.

Sham-man examined it, a smile returned. He slipped it under his robes, Shayne's heart dropped.

How the fuck am I going to get it from there?

Defeat clouded her thoughts.

It doesn't matter, it's too late anyway.

Sham-man dipped his head down to her level and offered her his arm. "Now, where is the other scroll?" The moisture evaporated from Shayne's mouth. Sham-man searched her face and raised an eyebrow. "Ah, the other Demi God has it. I'm sure he'll be here presently. Shall we wait?"

Shayne plastered her arms to her side and shook her head. Sham-man licked his lips, pinched her arm and stuck a gun to her temple.

I'm so fucking dead. He'll plaster me across the countryside too.

Sham-man faced Pit Face. "Is the old woman alive?"

Syrl's voice cracked, his fear palpable. "Yes, as you instructed."

Sham-man whispered in her ear, Shayne's innards churned. "If you want to see her and the other Demi God again, you'll do exactly as I say. Do you understand?"

Shayne nodded, the barrel of the gun moved with her. He re-linked her arm between his, and dragged her to the temple.

Annu stay away, don't come here.

From behind a set of rocks, Annu appeared out of nowhere with a gun raised at Sham-man.

In a flash, Sham-man raised his own gun and depressed the trigger; Annu dropped to the ground. Shayne's mind exploded, her screams drowned out her other thoughts.

Chapter 55: For Jaid
Enki Island, Orion

Four heavily armed enemy and a tonne of debris, stood between Annu, Jonn and the top of the mound. For its short distance away, it may as well be located on Earth. The island environmental countdown procedure tormented him further.

A recent burst of energy enabled him to heal enough to continue and returned his determination.

Jonn hunched over to his right, Annu motioned towards the entrance. "I'm sorry man, I need what I've got left to finish this or I'd fix you completely. It's not far to go. Will you make it?"

His arm over his torso, his clothes bloody and torn, Jonn straightened. "You're more important. Go, I'll cover you. I'll get there."

Filled with gratitude, Annu patted Jonn's shoulder. "You've got guts man. Thanks for sticking with me. After all this is over—-"

The four men directed their focus away from Jonn and Annu. "What the flark?"

A PFD floated above and landed a few feet from the entrance. A robed man strode out, and glanced in their direction.

Annu bolted down, his bowel's clenched, his heart at the back of his throat. "Shit, shit, shit. Already?"

Jonn grabbed his torso, a fresh hit poured through his fingers. "What?"

Breath, I knew he was coming.

"It's Shamesh."

Jonn paled. "Damnation."

Annu peeked, three familiar figures approached Shamesh. "Shit. They've got Shayne and Banna's with them. I flarking knew it."

Jonn pushed up on his elbows and around the stone. "I've got to stop him."

Annu stopped him with an arm across the chest. "Wait, get down. We'll get them both killed."

Jonn's chest heaved, he clutched Annu's hand. "He better not lay a finger on her."

Annu's blood boiled, fury pulsed in his veins.

Please, please, please be okay.

He crawled around the side; Shamesh pointed a gun at Banna, bang.

Her head exploded, Annu's sanity fractured. "Oh Gods. No."

Caught up in the horror, he missed Jonn's escape; he staggered towards Shamesh, a gun wavered in his hand.

Annu stumbled after him, pain ripped throughout his body. "Jonn. No. Stop."

Jonn continued, his armed hand drooped with each shot, missing their target.

Shamesh whipped the gun around, tapped the trigger and hit Jonn in the chest. The impact thrust Jonn close to Annu's side.

He reached down and ripped the gun from Jonn's hand. "I'm so sorry."

A shot skimmed past his head, Annu found no place for protection. Blast after blast barraged the area, the dirt around him erupted.

Save Shayne, give it all you've got.

Annu jumped onto his feet, gun forward and ran at Shamesh. Shayne's screamed ricocheted across his ear drums.

Liquid heat pierced his chest and tore his heart. Agony magnified along his torso, and consumed his body. Force flung him into the air, Annu spluttered vomit into his mouth, hot blood gurgled up his throat and out his mouth.

He thudded to the ground, the air shot from his lungs.

Shallow jagged breaths stabbed Annu's ribs and stole his strength to fight. He tasted death, sweet with a bitter aftertaste.

I'm sorry, Shayne, I'm not going to make it this time.

Each breath grew further apart, an anvil on his chest dropped lower and sunk into his middle. Annu tried to roll on his side, the pain too unbearable, the light too intense.

It hurt down to his core; Annu closed his eyes and allowed darkness to envelope him. The pain eased, calm washed over him; the confusion, stress, worry and fear ebbed away.

White light sparkled around the edges, warmth blanketed him. Bells tolled, beautiful music played from somewhere in the background. Every note resonated absolute love and peace, it welcomed him home.

The light increased, in the distance a shape appeared. They stepped forwards and walked towards him, his heart burst with joy.

Tears welled in Annu's eyes, Jaid as beautiful as their wedding day.

He wept, grabbed Jaid and embraced her. The smell of honey and cinnamon filled the space around them. "I'm never leaving your side again. Nothing else matters anymore. Not now. I've missed you so much. I'm sorry about the accident. I should have been there."

Jaid stroked his hair, he nuzzled into her hand. She cupped his chin under her palms and kissed his lips.

Her honeyed voice allowed a new level of happiness to grow inside him. "My darling, it wasn't your fault. You couldn't have prevented it. You can't stay here. It's not time."

The first hint of emotion ruptured perfection. "No. I don't want to go. Please don't make me leave. I've waited so long." Annu tightened his hold. "There's so much time to make up for. I've missed so much. And aren't I dead?"

Jaid's smile washed his cares away. "You're healing right now. You still have a job to finish, with Shayne. This is only the beginning. One day my love, we'll see each other again, but you're heart will be lighter. You have to let me go. It's time to get the last scroll and find Shayne."

Shit, Shayne, the mound. Shamesh. I'd forgotten for a moment.

The memories flooded back; the smell of moist dirt invaded his nose, the sweet aroma's diminished.

Annu body tingled, everything around him flickered. He shook his head, and embraced Jaid tighter. "Not yet, don't go."

Jaid whispered in his ear. "Your future is with Shayne now. Get up and go to her, stop Shamesh."

Either choice meant losing someone or one's he loved, not again, even for a short time.

A decision lumped to the front of his thoughts. "I'm too badly hurt to move, there's nothing more I can do."

"That's where your wrong my love, there's always something you can do." Jaid placed a hand on his chest, he jolted.

Pain slammed back, the air chilled, noise returned.

Jaid placed her other hand on top, Annu seized again. She disappeared.

He gasped in air, a mixture of relief and anguish twisted within him.

A terrible thought struck, his hands rushed to his torso. Scars replaced where the scroll once laid and again the map remained. "Oh fuck it."

Ire propelled him to roll over, onto his hands and knees, the entrance within walking distance. Alone on the hill top, Annu crawled towards the entrance until strong enough to stand onto his feet.

Annu limped past Jonn's body, and avoided Banna's remains. Annu mustered his strength for the fight ahead.

A foot from the entryway, he gathered a few weapons. "Here I come."

Chapter 56: Tormented
Enki Island, Orion

Shayne's soul ripped into a million pieces, her screams bounced across the ground. Rocks smashed, structures ruptured, the sky bled upon the earth. Oblivious to her surroundings, the world around her imploded.

Sham-man released her arm; she fell to the ground, her heart torn.

He turned the gun at Syrl. "You buffoon."

Zap. Pit Face became no face, his body fell backwards.

Sham-man reefed her by the arm and dragged her to Annu.

Shayne fell to her knees at his side and sobbed. She stroked his hair and wiped his face clean.

Sham-man rifled through his clothes. "Where is it?"

Annu can't really be dead, it's not real.

|She pounded her fists on his chest. "No. No. No. It can't be."

Sham-man screeched in her ear. "Where is it?"

He tore at Annu's shirt, Shayne slapped his hands away.

Sham-man grabbed them in his and squeezed. Her joints crunched, her tendons tore, pain ran down her arms. She bit a chunk off his hand; the other whacked her across the forehead.

Shayne fell over Annu's legs and held on. "Please wake up, come back to me. Don't leave me here. I can't do this without you."

Sham-man pushed her aside and ripped open Annu's shirt, the scroll apparent on his torso.

With a satisfied smile, and no apparent interested in the map, Sham-man ran a finger nail along the edges, the skin sizzled, the scroll unsealed.

Sham-man removed it from Annu's flesh, Shayne hurled onto the ground. Stomach empty, she leapt at Sham-man, clawed at his arms and kicked his shins.

He held her at bay one armed and stomped a boot upon hers. "Ahhhh."

Shayne struggled against him, he elbowed her in the ribs; she chomped on her tongue.

Sham-man held the two pieces of the scroll together; thunder roared across the mountain side, a golden light sealed them together.

He slipped them under his robes and pulled her forward.

She dragged along beside him, numb, vacant, devoid of hope and courage. "Why haven't you taken the map?"

Sham-man squeezed her arm harder, she squealed. "I already know where the scrolls are. I'm the one who put the half map into the underground market in a last ditch attempt at flushing the Demi-Gods. It worked better than expected. Especially considering how far away you came. Now, walk properly and it won't hurt."

You bastard. What about the other half I had.

Shayne quickened her pace, he relieved the pressure. Her heart lay slain next to the one man she'd loved.

He lead her inside the entrance, natural light disappeared. A chill settled in her bones, and seeped into her marrow.

Sham-man fiddled around with something on his side and pulled out a torch. He shone it around the stone room; illuminating one figure lumped into the corner, another on the ground next to it. Shayne's pulse shifted gears, from erratic to cataclysmic.

Hyl walked through a doorway into the light, his face covered in scratch marks.

Ire and hatred pulsed in her veins; she fought against Sham-man's hold. "I knew you were in on it too. You fucking bastard—-"

Shayne kicked his legs, as if she didn't exist, Sham-man moved closer. "Has anyone of you done what I demanded? It's a complete mess around here."

Shayne's temperature plummeted, icicles formed.

Sham-man pinched a chunk on skin on her forearm, her powers disappeared. "Please, not now. I'm a little busy here. They'll be plenty of time right before you die to be silly."

Oh God. What am I going to do? I can't give in, but nothing I do makes an impact.

In silence, he dragged Shayne inches from Hyl, the gun raised.

Boom.

Hyl mush covered the tomb and her in pink goop. Shayne brushed it off her and swallowed vomit.

I've seen way too much of people's insides for one day.

Sham-man chuckled, the tone reminiscent of a dentist's drill, and left the same effect upon her. "You better pray you can get the last scroll by yourself, or you'll end up the same way."

Sham-man shifted towards the lump against the wall, he kicked it, the body grunted.

A flash of white hair fell away from her face, Shayne jolted at Irica. "Thank Gods. You're alive."

Pain detonated through her shoulder, the muscle tore from the joint. "No you don't. You've got important business to take care of first. Move it."

Sham-man aimed the gun at Irica, Shayne went for his eyes. "No. Don't. If you do, I won't help you. Please, no more. She's suffered enough."

He cocked his head to the side, as if to consider her request.

Sham-man paused at the doorway, looked back to Irica and shot her.

Shayne fell to the ground and tore at his legs. Hot tears and snot streamed down her face. "Why. Why did you have to do that? She didn't hurt anyone. I'm doing what you want me to do."

An emotionless expression coveted his face, brain matter stuck to his robes, blood covered his cheeks. "I can't risk the chance she'll come after me."

Sham-man dragged Shayne by a chunk of hair into the next room. Regret, failure, and defeat weighted her legs.

The one time her memory didn't let her down, the way to the chasm flooded into her mind.

This is why I had the vision, we failed. It's all fucking over. No, I can't let him have it.

Please Gods, tell my kids somehow I didn't leave them, and I'm not a failure. I died doing the right thing. I'm sorry. I'm so fucking sorry for everything I messed up. The cursing, the wasting time, feeling sorry for myself. For being so damned selfish for so long.

Shayne's mind tingled; her father's voice broke her thoughts. *'Stay strong. Not much longer now.'*

'Are you kidding? You never have pleasant suggestions.'

'It's not important, stay strong. It's almost time.'

'Until I die and the world ends? I can't do this alone. I lost Annu, Irica, everyone.'

'Have faith and trust. Be smart; use your talents, your sass.'

'Right, finally permission for it and I'll die doing it.'

Shayne's jaw whipped across her face, her brain jiggled. One more blow to the head, she'd travel back in time.

Sham-man hissed at her. "Snap out of it and pay attention."

She wriggled her jaw side to side. "Gods' dammit. I haven't been smacked around like that since the week I left my ex husband. How do you feel about a trial separation?"

Sham-man stumbled back a step, a stunned expression over his face. Quick as she blinked, the moment passed.

Sham-man backhanded her on the opposite side, Shayne's legs wobbled, she remembered her fourth birthday.

'Stay strong, you can do this.'

'Yeah, yeah. We'll see.'

"I totally forgot about the My Little Pony I got as a present." Smack, her jaw realigned. "Compared to my ex husband, I'd consider you a pussy, but you don't have the depth and warmth to live up to it."

I can't believe I said that.

Sham-man yanked a chunk of hair near the top of her head, Shayne squealed. "Which way?"

It will grow back right?

"Dead people to the left of me, musty guy to the right, here I am, stuck in the middle of poo, what the hell am I gonna do?"

He kicked the back of her knees, she fell onto her hands. "What the hell is that noise?"

Shayne brushed her hands on her pants. "I'm singing."

Sham-man stomped on her foot, and twisted. "Don't. It's terrible. Shut up and show me the way."

Oh fuck.

Shayne rubbed her foot, it throbbed but healed. "Alright, left, turn left."

They turned into the next room, and hit a dead end. He grabbed her with both hands, and threw her at the wall. She splattered like a bug, her brain jiggled.

In seconds, Sham-man clasped two of Shayne's fingers in his hand, removed a knife from his robes and poised it under her middle finger.

Her heart two stepped across her chest.

Sham-man sliced the underside of her hand, the pain instant. "You'll take me the right way, or for each wrong turn you lose a digit. Understand?"

Shayne nodded; her mouth dry. "Yes, yes, yes."

Sham-man released her hand; Shayne wrapped the end of her shirt around it.

'Stay strong.'

'You know what; you're really starting to piss me off. Can I get some real help here?'

Sham-man thrust his arm out; she linked the uninjured one into his.

They reached the main hallway without Shayne's feet touching the floor. She ignored the symbols on the outer door and guided him the opposite way.

A few more incorrect rooms, a couple of wrong turns, no ascension for him, and a whole lot less body parts for me.

Left, right, right, left, they hit another dead end. The ambient temperature soared; the knife appeared from his pocket.

Before Shayne blinked, he'd lopped her middle finger off. Plop, it hit the floor.

Fuck the wrong person's getting dismembered here.

A fresh level of pain pummelled her, she heaved oxygen and collected it. "I might need you later."

Chapter 57: Death Becomes Him
Enki Island, Orion

His experience with Jaid in the centre of his mind, Annu dragged himself into the tomb. The stench of shit, copper and death wafted into the entry. He followed a trail of blood into the next section, his heart fluttered.

Against a wall slumped the remains of a man, to his right, plastered across the floor lay a small body.

The face unrecognisable, the long white hair brought instant despair. "Oh no, no, no. You were alive and I failed you anyway."

Annu paused over Irica's body and suppressed a roar.

Vengeance sullied his thoughts, fear invaded his bravery.

'Go to her, stop him.'

'Give me a minute.'

Annu extricated himself from her side and bolted through the doorway. Not a shred of light aided him, Annu ignited a hand. The dim glow lit his way.

He turned left and headed down a narrow tunnel. Identical rooms complicated his ability to pinpoint Shayne's direction.

Annu's memory of the way to the pit laid buried under he and Shayne's fight, and the horrific day. "Flark, flark, flark."

Rats spewed from a hole in the wall and raced along the wall's edge. A shiver tickled his neck. Once they passed, he headed down the tunnel's length in a daze.

An echo of Shayne's voice broke his daze and drove him towards the sound.

Annu placed his ear to the wall, followed its course through two rooms, and into a third.

At the end of the fourth, the noise dulled. "Shit. Come on, help me out here."

Annu backtracked, retraced his steps in reverse and turned right instead of left; he heard Shayne again. "Finally. Thank you."

His heart thudded, hope surged through him. Annu crept ahead, the ceiling lowered the deeper he delved, but Shayne and Shamesh's voices loudened.

He scrambled his brain; *two lefts and a right? Or right, left, right? Didn't we go through a long tunnel? Flark.*

Annu took two lefts and turned into a moss covered wall. A blast of ice screamed past his back, the splash wet his hands and dampened his source of light.

Black flush against the wall, he waited for it to pass, and dried his hands on his pants.

'If you get lost, look for the symbols.'

Annu banged his head against the wall, he'd forgotten those too.

The blast stopped, Annu recollected his second idea, with symbols attached.

Three feet ahead, the air thickened, the temperature plummeted. He relit his hand, the flame flickered.

Room by room, section after section, Annu recovered sounds at the end of yet another hallway.

His pulse quickened, Shayne's groan turned his blood to molten magma.

By the symbols above the doorway to his left, only two rooms and they reached the pit. He gathered his wits and fastened his pace, his right leg lagged behind.

The ground trembled, Annu held onto the wall. A burst of flames erupted from a room ahead of him.

The flames ceased, the doorway's edges froze.

Shayne.

Shamesh's bellow vibrated through the floor. "You're still getting us lost on purpose."

Crack.

His guts curdled, heat overflowed, his body ignited.

Annu hovered behind the doorway, his ear to the wall.

'Be patient. Don't rush.'

'I don't want her hurt anymore.'

'Wait until they are near the pit.'

'Her vision, I can't let it happen.'

Shayne's words crackled. "I've only been through here once. So, I messed up. But I remember it now. We've got to go through there and two rooms after."

She sounded broken, tormented, at the end of her strength and determination.

I can't wait any longer.

"Get up and get in there. If you make one more mistake, you'll lose something bigger than a finger."

Oh Gods, no. You fucking bastard. I'll tear you to pieces.

Annu shoved away from the wall, an unseen force plastered him back.

'Not yet.'

'No, I can't let her suffer. It's cruel.'

'She will be okay. Have faith.'

'How can I have faith when he's killed everything I care about?'

'The true test of faith is having it when times are difficult.'

Shayne groaned, Annu's heart leapt into his throat.

'If you let me down, I'll make you pay and I'm coming for you all next.'

'We won't.'

Annu listened for Shayne to drag herself up and into the next room.

Her spunk inspired him, her determination kept him focused. "Your face looks like it was on fire and someone put it out with a wet brick."

Burnt tears stung his face.

She hasn't given up, I can't let her down.

Annu slipped into the room they'd exited from, a puddle of blood in the middle of the floor nauseated him.

He crunched over ice deposits and around a rubbled doorway.

She'd said two more rooms to go.

Annu followed Shayne's red footsteps and blood splatters.

She's hurt bad, I can fix her.

He loomed flush beside the outer doorway, Shayne shifted in his periphery. She glimpsed at the doorway, confusion flashed across her face.

Shayne moved away from Shamesh's front, and revealed the joined scrolls in Shamesh's right hand, and pointed to the pit. "I told you already, the last one's in there."

Shayne stepped backwards, stumbled and fell to the ground. Shamesh flung at her, and blocked his view.

Annu barrelled through the doorway and flashed past Shayne. "Oh my God, you're alive. I can't believe it."

Shamesh spun around; Annu collected him around the middle and slammed into the opposite wall.

Rubble spilled around them, Shamash's touch disrupted his powers. He pushed Annu back, Annu fought against him; they hurtled in the opposite direction.

Chapter 57: Unholy Crap
Enki Island, Orion

Shayne's butt stuck to the floor, her mouth open, a real life action film took place before her eyes.

Annu, in a ball of flame, mashed with Sham-man and blew past like an unholy force of nature.

Smash.

They catapulted into the side wall, shattered stone and destroyed a section of roof.

Shayne scrambled out of the way of falling debris; her left-half hand stuck under her jumper.

Annu's powers faded, the Sham-man/Annu tornado whizzed by in the other direction.

Crash.

Another wall decimated, the force threw her back onto her arse.

Shayne failed to reconcile recent events; seconds ago she'd resigned herself to death by Sham-man, now, she reconsidered her options.

Thank you Gods, he's alive. Now please get us out of this.

Shayne hightailed it out of the way.

Annu and Sham-man wrestled on the floor, in the corner. Annu flipped Sham-man over, and body slammed him.

Shayne slapped her thigh. "Ouch. Get that fucker."

The air whooshed from Sham-man, Annu bounced to his feet. He reignited, grabbed Sham-man, pelted him out the door, and went after him.

Surrounded by her blue aura, Shayne levitated to the door and followed their fight into the next room.

Shayne blasted Sham-man's back; Sham-man flew off Annu, and down the hall.

Annu scrambled around on the floor, Shayne continued to blast Sham-man. "I can't believe you're alive."

"Me either. I'll tell you about it later—-"

Sham-man barrelled through the doorway at Shayne, she heightened her protection.

Please stay up this time.

Sham-man caught her across the middle, her guts smashed into her spine, Shayne slammed into something hard, pain ricocheted throughout her torso; breathing pain free now a luxury.

Sham-man smacked into her and raised a hand above her head, electricity zapped between his fingers.

Whoosh, the weight disappeared, he hurtled backwards.

Annu cast him through a wall, into the pit room where Shayne died in her vision.

Agony a blanket around her, Shayne shoved aside the urge to vomit and shuffled after them. "Oh this is so fucked up."

Sham-man dodged Annu's fire balls and rubbed his hands together, the electricity between them increased.

Annu held an arm out, grabbed the knife from Sham-man's waist and sliced through the limb.

It smacked to the floor, rolled and fell into the pit.

The chasm hissed, screamed, and wailed. A haze covered the hole's surface.

Sham-man's shrieks irritated Shayne's ear drums; he clutched the bloody stump to his chest. His painful shriek almost extracted a gram of pity from within her, almost.

Shayne wobbled over to Annu's side, her hands frozen. "I told you pickle dick. You have to do better than that."

Sham-man flipped his attention between her and Annu, the surprise changed to detestation. The atmosphere intensified, the air evaporated from the room.

Shayne and Annu stepped back, the edge of the pit only a foot away. The sounds frenzied, their pleas crawled like a cold worm up her legs.

Sham-man shivered at the noises, red energy pulsed from him. He blasted Annu through two rooms. Annu's journey ended in a crash, thud and drop.

Shayne lunged at Sham-man, and groped at his neck.

He grabbed her by the back of her scalp and ripped. "Will you get the last scroll for me?"

"No and fuck no." Shayne edged closer to the chasm, heat licked her skin.

Sham-man rattled her side-to-side, her teeth vibrated, her jaw cracked.

I jumped into the pit to stop him, it's the only way. The only useful thing I've ever done kills me. Better than death by chocolate I suppose. Crap, they better have chocolate and weed in heaven.

The intensity of his energy flushed her face; Shayne clutched a handful of his robes and back stepped over the edge.

Shayne fell with acceptance of her fate, completion spread through her. *I'll see Nana and Pa. And… I'm pretty sure I won't go to hell now after this.*

Crack, crack, crack.

Sham-man's skull smashed into large and sharp rocks along the walls, the left side of his head caved in, blood splashed onto stone.

But, you're definitely going there.

Horror and satisfaction muddied her mind. Shayne drifted atop disconnected arms and bony fingers.

Inert, Sham-man tumbled in a different direction amidst torrid screeches, and whines.

Shayne drifted further away from the cold into a white space, her mind calmed.

Love cuddled her, warmth spread along her body. She sank in a pillow of marshmallow.

The blood from her injuries slowed, her pain released.

Ding. The trap's twisted puzzle's solution stumbled into her brain. "Ah duh."

I'm precious alone; to myself, to the Gods, to the creator and to Annu. We had to give ourselves to faith. Oh the irony.

Shayne floated down like a feather, soft light bathed her. Her body tipped forward, she stepped, onto the altar of the last scroll, the floor vibrated.

Shayne rotated in a circle and scratched her head. "Huh? How? What?"

Sham-man's severed arm lay to the right of the altar, his maimed body twisted around a corner, his tongue protruded, his gaze fixed.

Shayne shifted the robe aside and removed the scroll. "I should kick you in the nuts a few times and the head, but I don't have time."

The stone room hummed, Shayne turned around, the scroll–the last scroll, vibrated above the altar.

'You can get it, and finish this.'

'Ah no I can't. I don't have Annu.'

'Think. You must try.'

Shayne's heart fluttered, she grabbed the end of the scroll and tugged. "Shit. See, I told you. What now?"

The answer hit with a thud, she eyed Sham-man's dead arm. "Oh you're fucking kidding me. You guys have the shittiest sense of humour."

Shayne tip toed over to it, and shoved it with her foot. Satisfied it remained dead and not able to crawl around the room, she picked it up with by the sleeve.

Dead juice dripped onto the floor and trailed her back to the altar.

Shayne inhaled, tipped the hand up, and touched touch the scroll beside hers. It released its bonds and fell into her hands.

She hurtled the dead limb across the room and wiped her hand clean.

Bright yellow light burst from the altar, shot out and impaled the roof. The room lit up, glorious sounds erupted above, joy exploded in her heart.

Colours danced upon her skin. Hinges squeaked behind the altar, the escape hatch clunked open. Shayne burst towards it and crawled her way out the side of the mound.

She ran, dragged, and limped her way to the top, the entrance a beacon of hope. The sky a cavalcade of nature's brightest colours.

Please Gods, let him still be alive, again.

Shayne screeched her way through the entry, room after room, her heart raced. "Annu. I did it, he's dead. I'm coming. I think we can make it."

Chapter 58: Redemption
Enki Island, Orion

Annu bolted up right. He fought against pain and stumbled back to the pit room. "Oh Gods Shayne, what did you do?"

A lead weight dumped upon his chest, he bypassed doorways and entered through the holes where walls once stood.

Annu retrieved them, his back creaked, his heart leaden. "You troublesome pieces of shit. What a complete mess this ended up. You've completely flarked up my life, and for what?"

The scar on his belly itched; he relieved it with his sleeve.

Annu removed the map and raised it in front of him. He ignited a hand and flickered the flame at the bottom. It lingered along the edges and caught on the corner.

Yellow light exploded from the pit, blinded him and forced its way through the roof. Annu stumbled back, vibration rippled through the floor, his pulse fluttered.

He dropped the scrolls and stomped the flames out. "Shit, shit, shit. Shayne. Shit. You did it. You flarking did it."

Annu waved the paper around, it stopped smoking. He shoved it in his jacket and leant over the edge. "Shayne. Can you hear me?"

Where would the trap's exit take her out?

The lead weight lifted, his heart rate lowered, hope soared in his veins. "Come on, man."

We don't have much time, I've got to find her.

Annu ran out the smashed doorway and paused, smacking himself in the forehead. "I've got no idea which way to go. I only came in here to kill Shamesh. Damn it."

Okay Gods, I didn't mean it about coming after you. I apologise profusely. Can you help me get out of here to Shayne please? We're so close.

"Or not."

Annu followed a reverse path, climbed over broken rocks and around chunks of stone. "Shayne--"

Every so often he stopped, cocked his head and waited for her voice.

The further he went, the higher his frustration. Annu entered the room he'd come up behind them in, the ground shimmied.

Energy pulsed and surged within him; his cuts and bruises healed.

At the end of the room, into the next hallway, Annu cupped his hands and yelled. "Shayne."

A sound rose above the shaking structure, faint at first, louder as he jogged ahead. Annu repeated her name at ten second intervals.

He whipped left and right, Shayne shouted his name in response. He shoved away a pile of rocks and scrambled into a tunnel.

Annu burst out the other side and searched the room. Close, not there yet. "Shayne. Where the fuck are you."

"Oh--God--Annu."

Annu belted out the door to the left, she ran at him. Joy overwhelmed him, Shayne leapt into his arms and squeezed around his neck.

Something scratched him; Shayne held the three pieces side by side, in her hand. "Look what I got."

The three joined as one, the mound trembled, the roof crumbled its way along the tunnel he'd exited. A plume of stone dust blasted into the room.

Annu plastered a kiss on her lips and shoved the partly burnt map into his pocket. "You're awesome."

Shayne frowned, and cocked her head. "Ah, what happened there?"

"Never mind. It doesn't matter now. Let's see what happens now."

"Well it doesn't matter anyway. Sham-man was behind it to start off with. He used it to find you. As for my half, I haven't found out yet."

Shayne stuck the scroll into his waistband. Annu carried her, as per her directions, back out the entrance.

The intense light of the sky invaded his eyes. He blinked, no time for them to adjust. "Shit, we've got fuck all time to reach the ascension room before it ends."

While inside the mound, the pink fog thickened and now obscured the view at ground level.

Annu placed Shayne's feet on the ground, she bounced, excitement exuded from her pores. "It's not too late. We can make it. We are going to do this."

He clutched her to him. "Let's go."

Annu readied to fly and stopped. He squeezed her hand, his words stuttered.

He removed the locket from around his neck and slipped it into his pocket. "I'm sorry for all the terrible shit I said, and did. You didn't deserve any of it, I'm an arsehole."

Shayne flashed a smile. "Oh my God. You took it off for me? I'm sorry too. I'm the reigning queen of bitchiness at the best of times. I really need to work on it."

Admiration filled him, each moment with her surreal and unexpected. "I don't hate you at all."

Annu thrust into the sky with her hugged to him.

Shayne wriggled in closer. "I know, and I feel the same way. Actually, fuck it, I love you."

Annu's heart turned warm and gooey and melted into a puddle in his chest. "Well, I--" He exhaled the words. "I love you too. When this is finished, you and I are so on. You won't be able to move for a week."

Shayne's mouth and legs moved, but no words came out, her colour matched the red sky.

Oh shit, I screwed up already.

"Sorry I didn't mean to freak you out. I guess you'll go home soon? Will you come back?"

Hundreds of years drifted away, memories of his awkward teenage self tumbled back. *Idiot.*

She raised an eyebrow at him. "Maybe a little, I--ah--it's been a while for me. I'm not sure it still works down there. Bats may fly out. And dip shit, we finally said I love you to each other, and you think I am not coming back here? I'll go home in a few days to sort some things out with the but afterwards, I'll come back. Okay?"

Annu's heart swelled. "Yes, things are extremely okay."

They flew across the sky towards the cave. Hope, love and faith renewed.

Chapter 59: Digitaless
Enki Island, Orion

Shayne and Annu strode into the entrance side by side.

Suck shit mother fuckers, Annu loves me. Someone not blood related fucking loves me. On purpose and shit.

Not even detached fingers disrupted the parade of happy thoughts raced through her mind.

Yeah, but, he wants to have sex with me. Sex, sex. Which means, no clothes, and he'd see me naked. Oh. Oh crap. I'm not sure I remember how to have sex. What if he freaks out once he sees me or my stretch marks and shit? At least I've got abs now. Argh.

Oh shut the fuck up. We're about to do something galactic changing. Concentrate fucktard. It's probably too late to get a bikini wax, or get a landscaping crew in.

Three quarters of the tunnel, Annu stroked her cheek, anticipation plastered over his face. "We're so close."

What's going to happen when we get in there? Everything will change, here, home, everywhere. Can we really do this?

Shayne's heart skipped, she filled her lungs and willed herself calm. "Okay."

Annu glanced at the hand under her jacket, pulled it out and examined it. His concern warmed her heart. "It's not bleeding anymore. I'll heal it as soon as I can. I'm sorry, but I don't think whatever I do makes them grow back."

The sight of the stumps sickened her. The sound and smells of Shamesh cutting them off will forever be burnt into her brain. "I live in hope. I don't want the nickname stumpy."

His eyebrows joined in the middle, a smirk swept across his face. "Right. You say the strangest things sometimes."

"Ha, I just realised your stuck with me and my weirdness."

Annu kissed her forehead. "Yes, I do. Not sure what that says about me though."

Shayne grabbed his hand. "I've got to tell you, me either."

Coloured lights from rooms ahead highlighted the gold edged tablets and gems down its length.

Annu fixed his attention on the way ahead. "I, I ah saw Jaid when I kind of, died. She brought me back to life."

Shayne flushed, Jaid's name stabbed her heart.

I'll never compete with a dead woman and she'll always be in the background. I bet she cooked and cleaned too.

Panic chilled her thoughts and curried her brain. "Oh. You must have loved seeing her again. I understand if you need time to--"

Annu turned her head to look at him. "I didn't mean what I said about you not comparing to her. Well, in many ways you don't, but in good ways not bad. I'm not sure how we'll make it work, but I'm willing to figure it out along the way. If, it's what you want too. It's time to take the locket off."

Shayne kissed his chin and nuzzled into his neck. Her fear scattered. "For me? I am worthy. God, I'm like a damned teenager again. All this is new to me."

Annu smiled. "Trust me; I haven't had a relationship for a long time either. I've waited for the right one."

"Aw, that's so fucking sweet."

She'd forgotten how far the tunnel went. "Over rocks over trails, over rocky mountain trails and the good guys keep —"

Annu placed a finger on her lips. "I love you but let's not push it." Annu turned and softened his tone. "You did see him dead right?"

Damn. No one likes my singing.

Shayne kept moving. "Well I didn't exactly check his pulse if that's what you mean. Given his mangled position around a wall, and his head twisted backwards with a vacant stare, he looked pretty fucking dead to me."

"Sorry. You're right. It doesn't matter which one of us killed him, he's dead and out of the way."

The planets above aligned, a beam emitted from the middle one directly into the ascension room.

A hum buzzed down the tunnel, calm washed over her. Shayne stumbled over a rock, and tripped forward. The chain around her neck broke; the ring fell onto the dirt before her.

Shayne retrieved it, and shoved both in her pocket. "Of all the times."

Annu shimmied around the last corner; light from the ascension room a foot ahead illuminated them.

Shayne kept pace with Annu, a familiar figure formed in the door way.

Her heart exploded with joy. "Irica, we fucking did it."
She shimmered in the light, divine peace across her features.

Shayne gasped, a hand over her mouth, her excitement overflowed. The closer they got, the clearer Irica became.

Death restored the former glory of her youth, Irica's appearance injected confidence and calm into his soul.

Shayne's awe emanated from her pours, tears rolled down her cheeks.

Annu turned his face away and wiped a hand across his chin. "Irica, I'm sorry I didn't get to you in time. I'm sorry for not listening to you, I'm sorry for--"

Irica's spirit placed two fingers on his lips. "Ssh. It's alright, everything is okay. My time came, there's nothing either of you could do to prevent it. You succeeded, you stopped Shamesh. I'm so proud of you; I knew you both could do it."

Shayne's voice faltered, a smile tainted with sadness marked her face. "Are you sure you always thought so?"

Irica's expression erupted with kindness, she stroked Shayne's cheek. "Mostly, and now it's finally time for the pay off so hurry up."

Shayne ran beside Annu and stepped onto the circles. The toll of bell's resonated across the floor, the circles spun in opposite directions. Their revolutions increased, light from the sky infiltrated every available corner and surface, and filled him with energy.

A figure materialised beside Annu, he faced them. "Mother."

Ki formed at Ann's side; Shayne shrieked and jumped. "Ghost Dad. I mean dad, Ki, or, father."

Ki pointed to the scrolls they'd forgotten in the excitement. "The incantation, quickly."

Shayne tugged Annu's jacket. "Oh yeah, the whole reason we went through all this shit, get it out."

Annu pulled it from his waist band and held it before them. The paper shimmered, the incantation formed across the page.

He squeezed her hand, her skin glowed. His heart fluttered. "Stay strong, I love you."

Shayne clung to his side, she held his forearm. "I will, I promise. I love you too."

"Ready? We'll say it together."

Shayne nodded—her heart full, her mind in a flurry.

The words rolled off Annu's tongue. "Eheieh, eheieh, eheieh."

The concentric circles on the floor rotated faster and faster, a rainbow of coloured lights emitted from each circle's edge.

They repeated the next sequence. "Yahweh, Eloah, Va, Daath. Bring Down the light from Above."

The scroll flew out of his hands and delved amidst the main light beam.

Annu lifted into the air, Shayne hovered beside him. The life force of the above planets enveloped them, energy pulsated through Shayne. She hummed in time with the bells, her mind imploded with ancient knowledge and awareness.

Shayne's consciousness hurtled backwards to the Annunaki Gods' time on Orion, and Earth, the rebellion flashed past scene-by-scene. A young Shamesh, Irica, his mother, the other Gods. Fast forward hundreds of years, and the rebellion played its sordid mess through his mind. It ended with millions of people killed and the planets shut off from each other, one travesty after another.

Shayne experienced the defeat of previous failures and the deaths of past ascender's, too much to comprehend at once. Their pain and sorrow became his, their fear surged through him.

She delved further back, and witnessed the planets before human kind; the beauty of the creator's intervention overwhelmed him. At once, Shayne understood her minuscule, yet monumental, importance to the galaxy.

The images faded, he returned to the altar room, glorious music surrounded her.

Ki drifted to Shayne's side, his honeyed tone exemplified the calm he exuded. "I placed the map and ring in your pantry hundreds of years ago, ready for this moment. Now my daughter, you shall receive the Gods, and universal power from the Creator. Don't be afraid. Once the process is complete, we'll speak again."

The marriage between her physical self and mind wobbled. They scraped against each other like nails on a chalk board; the unseen bond ruptured, fractured, and tore. A dramatic shift, followed by complete separation between them, disconcerted Shayne. She no longer felt the weight of her body, nor able to touch something tangible.

Vulnerable, she lay bare and exposed at the most basic level. Every molecule, fibre, and cell of Shayne's being transformed into particles of light; for a half second, she ceased to exist as a whole entity.

On the brink of insanity and unconfident in his broken mortal coil, Shayne's atoms re-configured. Smashed, blended, twisted and twirled, he landed butt down on a cloud, complete love filled him.

Humility cloaked her shoulders, repentance combined with grace unburdened her sins, and removed her worries.

A massive golden hand broke through white haze and approached him. Overwhelmed by omnipotence, Shayne sunk onto her knees, hands to her chest.

A timbered voice plucked the right chords across the strings of her soul. "Shayne, are you ready?"

"Yes my Creator."

Power, energy and enthusiasm blasted Shayne's molecules. Amongst pink hue, she wriggled a fresh set of fingers. Shayne smoothed over the skin on her stomach and pinched it. Scar free, the skin sprung back.

Chapter 60: Huh?
Enki Island, Orion

On a strip of space junk in the middle of the galaxy, Annu dangled his legs over the edge, his mother on his left. Stars exploded in the distance, planets rotated around their suns. Lights flickered across their surfaces and day turned to night.

His minuscule place in the universe solidified, awe filled him. "What are those wriggly things between them?"

"Wormholes which interconnect the planets to each other. Though at present they don't have access to them."

Annu swung his legs. "Are all occupied by human life?"

"Yes in its distinct forms. All unique and in need of guidance from you and Shayne."

Annu's mind boggled. "How do we reach them and how will they find us?"

Ann swept an arm across the sky, the pathways twinkled. "Some through visions, others drawn to you or you'll learn about them. I'll be here to guide you. Sadly, Shamesh won't be the end of the threats against you and us. They'll come in many forms. From those who don't believe, despite evidence to the contrary, those who believe yet reject it nonetheless, and those dedicated to the other side. The change won't be easy for all."

Annu sighed, he'd not considered other threats. "I hope they're not in any rush. We'll have to rebuild structures, find and train more protectors."

Ann held his hand. "Now it's important you and Shayne keep your band and ring on until thirty days after ascension. The powers are unpredictable until then and it helps control them. There's a group long dedicated to the God's, The Brotherhood of Orion. They'll come and assist you in the news few days. They've waited a long time for this too.

Annu's personal space diminished. "Yeah, I've heard about them. I thought they were crazy. This place is going to get inundated with people soon."

Ann stroked the nape of his neck. "Beyond the ascension room is the God's Garden, designed for the Gods obviously. It contains ancient books from our time, including the Lexicon of the Gods and their powers. Reference them to learn more about your past and how things work. The garden also provides privacy, making it an ideal place for you and Shayne to live, and set up base close to the recourses you'll need."

The pile of information shoved into his brain in a short time frame, smashed into each other. A thought poked its way through the quagmire. "What about my father, who is he?"

Ann grabbed Annu's face within in her hands. "I'm sorry, I'm forbidden from divulging any information about him at this point. I ask you to trust me when I say; you not knowing doesn't impact your destiny. But--"

The air crackled with electricity. Once, not long ago, after such a statement he'd lose his temper and demand an explanation. "Knowing does. I understand."

Ann smiled and kissed his forehead. "Exactly, my wise son. Our time's over for now. I love you. Be strong and brave."

"Mother?"

In a blur the galaxy and rock they sat upon disappeared. He returned to the ascension room, his mind reeled, his thoughts muddled.

Annu adjusted to the light with a hand over his eyes. "Shayne?"

She launched at him from the side and flung into his arms. "Annu."

Love pulsed through him, his heart whole again. "There you are."

He picked her up, his heart fluttered, all previous worries evaporated.

Shayne pushed her face off his torso. "Not so hard, boof head. You're squishing me."

Annu loosened his embrace. Somehow, perhaps because of Shayne's loud voice, he often forgot her tiny stature. "Sorry, but I'm not waiting any longer. I'm going to squeeze, hug, kiss, and you know."

Her skin shimmered; she wriggled a new finger in place of the stump. "Well there you go. No more stumpy."

Annu wriggled his eyebrows up and down.

Shayne batted at him and poked his ribs. "You idiot. Well you're stuck with me for a month before I go home."

Annu's groin stirred, he grabbed her face in his hands and kissed her over and over. "It's the best news I've heard since, well, maybe ever."

He dipped his head down, blood seared through his veins. Annu inhaled the smell of coconut; she leant on her toes and kissed him back.

Annu ran his hands over her body and pulled her shirt out of her pants, she gasped.

He searched for a soft place to lay her, she pulled away from him.

"What's wrong?" He kissed a line down her neck, she shivered.

"I realised, we've got no real idea about what happens next. Apart from the book, and occasional parental visits, we're winging it. What do we do now?"

Annu kissed her along her cleavage; the copper of blood didn't deter him. "I thought we were working on it at the moment."

Shayne cupped under his chin and shifted his focus up. "So you want the first time we do it to be in the middle of the stone floor? No bed, not even a cushion or foot rub? Ah a little foreplay and romance first would be nice."

Annu's rational side agreed with her valid point, his groin wanted to chase it with a carving knife. "Alright let's go back to my place."

Shayne continued her erection killer conversation. "Where do we go, what do we do? There's a lot of stuff to work out, the sooner we start, the better."

Her butt in one hand, he squeezed a boob with the other. "Fine, in between sessions. Let's go."

She wriggled into him. "Mmmm, but all those bodies lying around. We can't just leave them there, remember those and Irica? They're going to stink up the place soon and deserve to be buried."

A chill settled at the base of his neck, he put her at arm's length for safety's sake. "You're right, again. Flark. Don't make a habit of it. After we've taken care of those, we'll go home and check out the garden tomorrow."

Shayne's smile gave him hope for their future. "Sounds good. We'll need food first though." She rubbed her stomach. "Speaking of which, I'm starving."

Barter coins disappeared in his mind. "How? Where do you put it all?"

Shayne leapt into the air. "Oh, my God."

He joined her side and checked the room. "What? What's wrong?"

"I can bring chocolate back from Earth when I go and you'll finally understand why I love it so much."

The ground vibrated, the air electrified, Shayne's hair stood on end.

Annu wiped a hand over his head. "Oh good God's Shayne. Yes okay."

"Oh Earth. Once so far away. You'll love it and my dog and my kids. I can't believe I'm even going back to Earth."

The room rumbled, the stones beneath his feet rotated. "What the hell?"

A speck of light fractured beside Shayne, she stared at it. "What th…"

An explosion of coloured erupted and thrust forward, dread poured from his forehead.

In seconds it collected her and ripped her out of his grasp. Shayne grabbed at him and fumbled with her pocket, her expression crazed.

He dug his boots into stone. "No, no, no, no. Not now, stop--"

As fast as she'd arrived on Orion, Shayne departed leaving Annu in the middle of the room, hormones stalled and mind baffled. "How the hell do I get her back?"

Chapter 61: WTF?
Enki Island, Orion

Shayne zoomed along the wormhole in what she now considered the wrong direction. She tried to face the other way and clawed backwards.

Panic shredded her. Without effort, she'd fucked up again. "Dad? God? Please, help me?"

Hopelessness weighed Shayne. "What am I going to do?"

The blender tumbled by headed somewhere, her heart sank.

Shayne thought of Annu in the ascension room, and hurtled forward at the same pace.

Exhaustion overwhelmed her, her power and energy waned. The stone wall of her pantry replaced the galactic view, disappointment smashed her. "No, no, no."

Shayne burst through the wall, and flew upside down across the other side of the room. She hit the middle shelf, and dropped back first to the ground.

Bathed in sweat, Shayne's ears rung, her equilibrium wobbled.

The internal mayhem settled; she dug in her pocket for the ring; its absence drove her manic.

Shayne pulled the light cord, and combed her fingers through the dirt. "Where are you, I need you?"

Her head swam, the stiffness in her joints returned, her back ached.

She beat her fists on the ground, dirt plumed into the air. "No. No. No."

The front door slammed, Shayne searched for salvation. "Please, please, please be here."

Footsteps thudded down the hall, and into the kitchen. "Mum? Where are you?"

Ryan popped into the pantry, rushed to her side, and grabbed her arm. "What are you doing in here? Why are you covered in dirt and blood? Mum, are you okay?"

Shayne pushed him away, her thoughts jumbled. "Help me look for the Jade ring."

"What? Why are you covered in blood? And you've lost weight, you look--different."

She riffled through the dirt around him.

He held her hand. "Mum, just stop for a minute and talk to me."

Shayne slipped hers out.

She crawled behind him and checked under his feet. "I didn't mean to go there, but I did, and I'm okay. You don't need to worry but I've got to get back there now."

Ryan held her still by the shoulders. "Back where? You're not making any sense. Did you take something you shouldn't?"

"To Orion and Annu. He's frantic."

"Where? Who are these people? I haven't heard from you in three days, you usually message me every day, so I came to check on you. Fuck, I'm glad I did. You're a mess."

Shayne delved under the shelves, her brain wobbled. "It's been weeks, not days. Help me."

"Mum, I have a text message from you three days ago. We spoke that night, look I'll show you."

Ryan dug into his pocket, pulled out his phone, and stuck it under her nose.

Shayne swiped it out of the way. "Not now, I told you I have to get back."

"Who are Annu and Orion? How did you get there and back? You don't have a car."

Shayne's thoughts jumbled. "Annu, the man I love, the other Demi God. Orion is the planet he's from, well me too. Look I don't have time to explain."

"Mum you're talking crazy, how exactly did you get to this other planet?"

His voiced buzzed like a swarm of bees. "Through the wall."

Ryan disappeared; he returned seconds later with a glass of water and a wet dishcloth.

He wiped it around her mouth, examining the patches of blood on her clothes, and underneath. "It doesn't seem to be yours."

Shayne's head pounded, the hem of her sanity frayed, and unthreaded in strands. "Some was, but most of it is other people's, and they deserved to die."

Ryan probed her cheeks. "Does the left side of your face feel heavy? Is your arm or chest tingling? Do you have a headache? Have you had a fall?"

"Only if you count the space travel." Shayne rose to her knees, Ryan held her down. "Let me go, Ryan. I'll prove what I'm saying as soon as I find the ring."

Ryan swayed on the floor beside her. "I need an ambulance to 3 Bailor Street, Rendelshem please?"

Shayne reached for one of the phones. "Ryan, hang up. Listen to me, please."

Ryan shifted away from her.

"Oh whatever, it won't matter soon." Shayne crawled along to the rear wall, pulled up, and banged her fists. "Annu, if you can hear me, I'll be back soon. I promise I didn't do it on purpose."

"No, not me, it's for my mum. Yes, she's conscious. No, I don't think she's fallen or hurt herself but I can't be sure."

Shayne dove under the bottom shelf, sifted through dirt, and found piles of mouse poo beside a full mouse trap.

"She's talking about being on another planets and stuff. She's not right. Please, can you send someone soon?"

She threw the mousetrap across the room, and tried the next shelf.

"I'm not sure if she's dangerous to others but she's covered in blood, and it's not hers."

Ryan grew distant. "No, don't call the Police. I'll take care of it. How long until they get here?"

Shayne checked along the base of the rear wall.

"Okay, we're in the kitchen, well, she's in the pantry and the front doors open."

*****

The day after Shayne's session with Doctor Unders, she groaned and placed the pillow over her face. "Fuck off, morning. You suck."

Lisa bounced around the room, one more question, and she'd sacrifice UV cover to smother her. "I'm so excited for visitors. Are you excited? You should be excited; you can share some of mine if you like?"

She removed the pillow; the glare shoved aside her homicidal urges. Shayne rolled over and stared at the wall. "Lisa, is there any coffee left in the kitchen or did you drink it all?"

"What? I don't know; you'd know if you got up for breakfast. You should get up and face the beautiful day, the birds are singing, the sky is cloud free."

Shayne tightened her grip, her words muffled. "Do realise we are in a mental hospital, and not a hotel?"

"It doesn't mean we can't make the most of it."

It must be her blue pill day; surely nobody could be this happy on purpose.

"I think it actually does."

The room door creaked open, Shayne didn't turn over.

"Oh goodie. Good morning, Nurse Bell."

"Good morning, Lisa. Shayne, get up, it's medication time."

Shayne whipped around her upper torso. "Are you telling me she hasn't had her meds yet?"

Nurse Bell's tone grated across her nerves. "Come on, Shayne, get up."

Shayne rolled halfway and stopped. "What's the point? Do I have a pressing appointment to attend? Has someone who allegedly cares about me, bothered to come and visit? I'll answer for you, none, no, and no."

"Well, actually the answer to the last one is yes. You do have a visitor."

She rolled all the way over and perched on the edge of the bed. Excitement, a rare gift these days tickled her ribs. "Why? Who? I didn't think I was allowed any visitors, even if someone did come."

A wry smile softened the nurse's prune like features. "Well, Doctor Unders thought it might put you in a better frame of mind. Once she's processed I'll send her down here."

Lisa jumped from foot to foot. "Ooh, Shayne's got a visitor."

Nurse Bell placed a hand on Lisa's shoulder. "Your mum and dad are in the Visitor's Lounge when you're ready, Lisa."

"I'm ready." Lisa bounded out behind the nurse and closed the door after them.

Shayne's heart thudded, she rushed over to the mirror and tidied up. "Who on Earth came to see me?"

She pulled on fresh hospital scrubs and sprayed deodorant with abandon. Toothpaste fixed her bad breath, but nothing short of a lawn mower saved her legs.

Shayne waited on the end of her bed, and twiddled her thumbs.

The door opened inward, Nurse Bell walked in and held the door open. "I didn't realise how much your daughter looks like you Shayne. You'd pass for sisters."

Erin stepped into the room, a disgusted expression on her face.

Shayne swallowed bile and rushed to her daughter.

Do I hug her or not? What if she pushes me away?

"Ah, I, Erin. After your text message I didn't expect to see you."

Erin patted Shayne on the back. "Yeah, well I thought maybe if I visited it might, I don't know."

Shayne smoothed her top down, shame waved over her.

She examined her surroundings with fresh eyes. "Ah, there's a plastic chair to sit on, or at the end of my bed, if you, ah, want to?"

Don't sound desperate, relax. She came.

Erin shrugged; devoid of emotion, she selected the chair opposite the bed and sat with a bottle of water between her legs.

Shayne sank into the mattress, her heart beat loud in her ears.

Just try, it can't hurt.

She reached toward Erin. "It's so good to see you, love, it's been a while."

Her daughter pushed back on the chair, out of reach. Erin ripped her heart out of her chest, and kicked it across the floor.

Erin stared at the opposite wall. "It's not easy seeing you in here. Nathaniel's parents don't understand it either."

Shayne watched the pool of blood around her heart grow, the hollow in her chest ached. "It's not easy being in here, but what does it have to do with Nathaniel's parents."

Erin shifted her focus to the roof. "It doesn't look good; the mother of the woman who's marrying their son is in a nut house."

She wanted the bed to consume her, drag her somewhere else. "Wait, what? You're getting married, why didn't you tell me?"

Erin fiddled with the water bottle. "I was waiting until you got out, but it hasn't happened yet."

Shayne's cheeks flushed. "I'm sorry, I, I'm happy for you both. We'll plan an engagement party when I get out soon."

"And when will soon be, Mum? We all thought you'd be better by now."

Shayne's skin crawled, spikes poked through the mattress. "I am better, there's nothing to fix."

"Oh good, so we can move past all this crazy talk?"

Shayne's thermostat rose, anger invaded her despair. "It happened Erin, all of it."

Erin screwed up her face. "Oh, for God's sake. Are you doing this for attention?"

Shayne pulled the collar from around her neck. "Oh yeah, this is a great thing to do for attention. Look, it's all true; my father told me you'd believe me. Hah."

Erin dumped the bottle on the desk, and pushed off the chair. "Oh my God. You really are crazy. I didn't quite believe it until I saw it myself."

The hair on the back of her neck rose. "I'm not, fucking, crazy. It all happened."

"This is unbelievable. I can't believe you're doing this to me." Erin paced the room. "Where's the toilet?"

"What?"

"The toilet, Mum, I need to pee. I drank too much water on the way here after stressing out. We'll continue this discussion when I get back."

Shayne jabbed a finger out the door. "Oh, will we? It's on the first left, there's a sign."

How's it possible I raised a daughter more selfish than me?

Erin flounced out the door, Shayne eyed the water bottle on the desk, a quarter of it remained.

She stumbled upon a not so nice, yet necessary idea, her pulse raced.

Shayne removed two sleeping pills from the night before, went over to the desk and opened the lid of the bottle. Her hand shook; Shayne dumped the pills into the bottle, swished it around and plopped back on the bed.

She waited for guilt to arrive, Erin got there first.

Good genes ensured Shayne and her daughter shared the approximate size, and if Shayne tucked her hair under Lisa's baseball cap, she'd pass.

Erin plonked onto the chair and downed the rest of the water.

Shayne held her breath, a mental battle ensued.

It won't hurt Erin to get a few good hours sleep. She needs it; maybe that's why she's cranky all the time. Wait, oh my God. What kind of mother drugs her daughter to escape from the mental home?

Erin yawned in succession and rubbed her eyes. "I might have to sit down for a bit. I feel whoozy."

Well, me I guess.

Shayne waved at the nurse's station, and waited for the buzz of the front door. Erin's car keys jingled in her pocket.

Come on, hurry up, let me out of here.

A voice trailed down the hall. "Didn't the visit go well?"

Shayne's stomach leapt into her throat, she didn't turn around. "She fell asleep."

Please don't follow me or ask me more questions. Please God give me a break.

"See you next time?"

The door opened, Shayne ignored her hips, bolted out into free air and fumbled down the steps. She slipped on the bottom one and grabbed the rail.

Shayne's bowels cramped; only a few metres to the car park from the front path.

Hang in there, keep it together.

She shallow breathed all the way to Erin's car and pressed the unlock button. Three beeps later, she reached another step closer to home.

Shayne slid into the driver's seat and started the car. "I'm sorry baby. I'll make it up to you, I promise."

******

Back in her former hell hole, Shayne finished in the bedroom, and headed to the bathroom. "No time to waste."

The hot water and solitude tempted her to stay in–yet not enough.

I've got a date with my hot chocolate hulk.

Shayne dragged herself out, and dressed walking to the kitchen. "Speaking of chocolate."

With the fridge door shut, she closed her eyes. "Oh please great Creator of all things and really awesome dude. I mean guy. Please can I have chocolate in here?"

Shayne opened the door, and half an eye. On the top shelf shone three blocks of chocolate and a post-it note from Sam, 'This is for when you come back. I'm sorry I got mad at you. Love ya.'

Tears welled in her eyes. "Oh fuck yeah. Thank you, thank you, thank you."

Shayne stopped herself ripping the packet open, shoved them into the back pack, and threw it over her shoulder.

The pantry loomed in the corner; innocent, no hint of its universal capabilities. "Okay, let's do this shit."

Shayne took a utensil out of a drawer and walked over.

She dumped the backpack next to the wall and on her hands and knees, scooped under the shelves; the second pass yielded the chain and ring. "Oh thank fuck."

The front door slammed open, footsteps stomped down the hallway towards the kitchen, deja-vu overwhelmed her.

Shayne clasped the ring in her hand, and slid across to the kitchen door.

Chapter 62: Crap on a Cracker; Part Two
Enki Island, Orion

Annu surveyed the Protectors' camp ground, the new buildings fitted together without obstruction to the landscape. Despite his concerns, the end result satisfied him. Sufficient distance existed between the compound, and the God's mountain ensured privacy and protection.

A fresh batch of protectors scattered over the field, the children of children; young, green and unprepared for what may come. "Now all I need is Shayne to come back."

What if she doesn't want to leave now she's home?

Anxiety coveted his thoughts, in the weeks since Shayne's disappearance; Annu tried everything to open a wormhole aside total devastation to the planet. He'd re-read the Lexicon but considered it better served as a door stop.

He glanced over the list of potential trainers provided by the appointed head protector Rolf. Annu prepared himself for another busy day alone.

I miss you so much, Shayne, please come back to me.

Brother Jacob strode in his direction, a communicator tablet in his hand. Annu suppressed a groan.

Great, just who I need to annoy me this morning.

A metre from his feet Jacob dropped to his knees and bowed. "Your Grace, the temple is almost completed. They've made adjustments as per your latest requests."

Annu rubbed his eyes to remove a layer grit and irritation. "Jacob, get up, and it's Annu. Why do you insist on calling it a temple? How many times do I have to say, I want a meeting place."

He remained knelt. "Your Grace, a place where mortals meet and worship their Gods is called temples or chapels."

His head pounded, he gritted his teeth. "I get it. You've explained it to me a dozen times. Surely, given I'm the God in question, I call it whatever the hell I like?"

As if Annu struck him, Jacob flinched.

Guilt disrupted his building irritation. "I'm sorry. I won't say the 'h' word again. I didn't realise when Irica told me about you guys, you'd be quite so–involved."

Jacob sat back on his feet. "You can't make light of such a place, your Grace, and this is our, my purpose."

He tapped his foot. "Aha, okay, but, can you call me Annu, please?"

A patient smile crossed Jacob's face. "Ah, no, your Grace."

Annu's left eye twitched. "Any luck with the wormhole problem?"

"It appears clear to me, her Graceness must open her side of the wormhole, at the same time you do."

Oh she's going to love being called her Graceness. They'll be no living with her then. What if she knows or doesn't know already?

Annu's heart palpitated, he held his chest. "Alright. I'll keep trying. What else can I do?"

Jacob tapped the tablet's screen. "Might I suggest you focus on your new powers? You've mastered the truth aspect, which enabled us to field any threats from the new protectors. Your speed abilities helped immensely with many aspects of production. However the other powers should be strengthened."

Annu shivered. "I haven't found a pleasant application for inter-dimensional travel, and I'm not going to try again soon. The transmutation's fun, but not useful, yet. The other stuff will get there."

"Perhaps, your Grace, we can take care of things down here for while, and you could attempt to contact her Graceness again?"

The protectors went from building to building, their arms laden with supplies. Annu averted his attention from them to the mountain top.

How much more disappointment can I take? I'm tired of being alone without her.

Any longer and the house he'd built for them would turn into a shrine.

Annu faced Jacob, weighed down by mental exhaustion. "Sounds like a good idea, I might even get some rest. You know where I am."

Chapter 63: The Truth Is in Here
Enki Island, Orion

Shayne leant against the kitchen door and pushed with her legs. "Oh, no way. Not this close. No fucking no. Just no. No."

Someone knocked on the other side of the door, she shoved her arse back.

"Mum? It's Ryan, let me in."

Guilt persuaded Shayne from the door; her current dilemma cemented her in place. "No, I'm sorry son, I can't."

He banged on the door. "Erin called me from the hospital, she's hysterical. She said you drugged her, Mum. The hospital's called the police. Don't do this again, please."

I've messed up with both kids in one day. So much for mending fences, I bulldozed over them, and set those fuckers on fire.

Ryan shouldered the door; Shayne put a leg on the wall and pushed. "She'll be okay. A long sleep will do her the world of good. I'm not crazy, Ryan."

He eased off; Shayne put all her weight onto it. "Mum, let me in so we can talk about things before this goes too far. Please?"

Shayne's determination wavered. "Only if you promise you'll let me show you the truth. And, you'll video tape it and show Erin, Rosie, and Sam, and sort shit out with the hospital while I'm gone. Okay?"

Ryan's sigh vibrated against her spine. "Yes, if it means we finish this saga once and for all."

Her legs ached, her hips twinged. "Swear to God."

"Yes Mum. I swear."

She swapped sides. "No, you have to say it."

"Fuck me, okay. I swear to God."

Shayne backed off the door and skipped to the pantry. "Okay, well remember no matter what happens, you promised. Give me a second then you can come in. But only if keep your promise. Okay?"

"Fine. Okay, I promise to keep my promise."

At the entry, her heart beat kept time with the kitchen clock. "You can come in now."

The door creaked open; Ryan thudded across the kitchen and appeared before her, dishevelled, his clothes creased. "Holy fuck, Mum. You've caused a big shit storm. If you think Erin was pissed before, you're in for a real--"

Shayne stood on her toes and placed a finger on his lips. "Ryan sssh. Please listen to me for once, look at my face. I'm not crazy. Watch this."

Shayne stepped back, picked up the back pack and slipped the ring onto her finger. Her body tingled, her fatigue lifted, relief flooded her.

The floor vibrated, Ryan grabbed the door frame. "What the fuck?"

Shayne smoothed down her hair and checked her breath. "Don't freak out with what happens next. Okay?"

Bells tolled through the house, the walls shook, the colour washed out of Ryan's face. "Oh shit. We were all wrong."

Please let this work. I don't want to beg but I fucking will.

Shayne turned and concentrated only on the ascension room, a pinpoint of light pierced the middle of the wall. The ground trembled, her legs wobbled, Ryan grabbed hold of the door frame.

The light grew larger each second. She yelled behind her. "Get out your phone, and start taping right now."

Ryan mouth flopped open. "Ah, okay."

Open mouthed, Ryan pulled the phone from his pocket and held it out.

Fuelled by a fresh wave of confidence, she stroked his cheek. "Hold it up, love; remember you promised to show Erin and the others."

The wormhole covered three quarters of the wall, a liquid tunnel formed in the middle.

Ryan shook himself. "Oh I will, believe me."

Shayne held his hands in hers. "I love you. I'll be fine, trust me."

Ryan blinked away tears. "Fuck, Mum. I'm so sorry I didn't believe you. It seemed so crazy, but, shit."

"Yeah I know. Thank you, Son. When I come back I'll explain everything, there's a lot to tell."

"When will you be back?"

Her heart raced, it took all her strength not to leap through. "A few days, a week maybe. I've got lots of stuff to sort out–I disappeared in the middle of some really, ah, important shit."

Her whooha tingled, her stomach fluttered.

I hope you've missed me and haven't changed your mind after so long.

Shayne kissed his forehead and walked backwards to the wall. "See you later."

She fell into the wormhole, consumed by light; Annu remained at the forefront of her thoughts. "I'm finally fucking free."

Chapter 64: Bad Songs and Blue Balls
Enki Island, Orion

Annu scattered chunks of gold and gems onto the work bench. "What matches well with pale skin?"

He selected a ruby and held it to the light. Annu focused and reshaped the gem into an oval between his fingers. The communicator in his pocket buzzed, Leah's face flashed across the screen.

If Shayne doesn't show up soon, I won't be able to ignore the woman much longer.

Annu's groin tightened, he adjusted his crotch; he sucked at distractions. "Roses are red, my sex life's dead, my girlfriend's gone away. My dick is sad, it drives me mad, why am I punished me this way? Until she returns, I shall yearn, Gods help us all today."

I'm lonely.

His temperature rose, he dropped the ruby, grabbed a hammer and smashed the communicator. "Flarking hell. How much more can a man take?"

Annu slammed his fist on the bench, the ruby shattered, pieces sprayed over the bench. He grabbed a chisel and pelted it at the wall; it bounced off and hit his nose. Pain exploded across Annu's face, he spat tears, snot and blood onto the dirt.

He bifurcated the bench with his boot, everything on it scattered. "Sonofabitch, cock sucker, dick licker, crap heap, shit fest, twat waffle."

The workshop door opened. "Ah um. Are you alright, my Grace?"

Annu flung around, Brother Jacob jumped back. "Not flarking really. Give me a damned minute."

He closed his eyes, second by second the pain lessened, his nose rejoined. When only the disjointed memory remained, he swiped the blood from his mouth. "What do you want Jacob? Now isn't a good time."

"I apologise, your Grace.

Tension shifted from Annu's nether regions to his head. "Jacob, did you come here to frustrate me, or for another reason? Which is basically a distinction without a difference."

A smile consumed Jacob's face. "You recall it's the best time to contact her Graceness is right now."

How could I forget?

Annu's heart thudded, his chest tightened.

Please let it be today, I promise I'll think about sex less.

He edged past Jacob, paused and patted him on the back. "Thanks."

Annu stomped out of the work shed into the main house and cleaned up. "Please I bet you, let it be tonight.'

He weaved around the garden, and into the ascension room, his heart heavy, he dared not hope.

A beam shot from moon's centre, and lit the room.

Power surged through Annu, he thought of Earth and Shayne, the ground danced; in a flash of bright light, a wormhole formed a metre before him. "Flark yes."

A burst of white light exploded from the crux, a bundle of arms and legs spilled out onto the floor at his feet. Annu bent down, and pulled the figure into his arms. His heart palpitated, the person jolted alert.

Annu imploded with joy, he squeezed her tight. "Oh my Gods, Shayne. You're finally back. I thought I'd never see you again."

At arm's length, he soaked in the sight of her.

Shayne launched at him, circled her arms around his neck and leapt onto his waist.

She kissed a line across his face, her words mumbled. "It's you. It's really you. I'm really fucking here. You're not going to believe what happened to me. It was crazy, and I mean crazy."

Light returned to his life, Annu's hope in faith and the Gods restored in a single moment.

He cupped her face in his palms, tears burnt his eyes. "It doesn't matter now. Nothing does. I love you so much. Don't leave me ever again."

"I won't. I promise."

Chapter 65: Thank Fuck and All Things Holy
Enki Island, Orion

Power surged and exploded within her, the ring hummed around her neck. All her desperation, frustration, panic and fear disappeared within Annu's presence. For the first time in her life, the world, her world made sense. The back pack at her feet, Shayne snuggled as far as possible into his arms, without slipping into his skin.

Shayne buried her head in his shirt, his scent calmed her. "I can't believe it's really you, and I'm really here. I did it."

I can be happy, it's possible.

Annu tightened the embrace. "Either I weld the ring to your finger or I adjust it for you."

"I prefer adjust it, so done deal."

Hot drops plonked on the top of her head. "I missed you so much. If you didn't come back today, I don't know what I, I--"

"Like you said, it doesn't matter now, we're back together. And I bought chocolate."

Annu kissed her over and over. "Oh Gods woman, you drive me nuts."

Shayne melted into his arms, long forgotten hormones surged through her. "No one's ever made me feel like you do."

She lost herself in the moment, ran her hands up his shirt and over his hot skin.

The crunch of boots on rocks pricked their happy bubble, Annu groaned. "Not now, Jacob. Go away."

Shayne stuck her head under the crook of Annu's arm; a white haired robed man filled the doorway.

He waddled over and bowed. "Ah, your Grace. I saw the light and realised you'd succeeded."

Confusion dampened her desire. "Annu, whose he and why is he in here with us?"

Annu slumped his head to his chest and placed her feet on the ground. "This is Brother Jacob, from the Brotherhood of Orion, aka the pimple on my arse. A lot's changed since you've been gone." He winked and wiggled his eyebrows. "You've got some catching up to do."

Jacob rose, pushed between them and resumed a bow. "Ah, so it is you, your Graceness. It is my honour to finally meet you. I am at your service."

Sorry, what now?

Annu wrapped his arms across his chest, and loomed over Jacob. "Seriously, come on, you're killing me."

Her promotion from mental patient to royalty in one day blew her mind. "What did you call me?"

Jacob raised his voice and smiled. "Your Graceness."

A shiver tickled Shayne's spine. "Well, isn't that some exalted shit."

"It's my pleasure, your Graceness."

Annu lead her out of the room. "Catch you later."

He headed down the tunnel and turned left instead of right.

"Holy shit, it's all cleaned up."

The beauty of their surroundings appeared to elude Annu, he dragging her through its midst.

Shayne inhaled crisp air. "It's fucking amazing."

Annu walked down a worn dirt path. "Aha. Yep it is."

They passed an orchard filled with fruit. "Oh yummy."

"Yep. Later."

Heat flushed into Shayne nether regions.

Thank the Gods I tidied up down there. I hope it still works.

They approached a house in the middle of the garden, constructed with stone edged in gold, with wall length windows and a glass roof.

Shayne leant against a tree before it. "It's incredible, whose is it?"

Annu pulled her into his arms, her pulse soared. "It's yours, well, ours. Our home."

A barrage of emotions filtered into her thoughts. "What? It's really ours? But it's a whole house, no missing parts, and it doesn't look like crap."

He walked her over to the front entry and a doorway edged in shiny wood. "Um, yes it is."

Annu gathered her into his arms and one handed pushed the button. Their front door whooshed open; he carried her over the threshold.

Joy and happiness formed a barrier around her heart. "I finally feel like the Goddess I am."

Moon light bounced off his black eyes, his head drooped. The tension between them crackled, the air heated. "Wait until we get into the bedroom."

Her whooha tingled, her chest tightened. *Fuck, maybe I should have dusted down there too.*

*****

It's just like the first time, what if he doesn't like it, or me after? What if I've forgotten how to do it? He might change his mind about everything if—oh, screw it. Here goes.

Shayne shimmied her butt into the middle of the bed, anxiety churned her guts.

She shifted her hips and poked Annu's belly. "Well? Was it ah–okay?"

Annu mumbled into her left breast, she ran her fingers through his hair. "Oh my fucking God, oh my Gods. It was amazing. Give me more. Please."

Jesus, I'm not sure how this is going to work long term.

"Really? I don't know if I want you liking it this much. It's like the third time. You'll kill my reserves, and I won't have any for later."

Hi slips vibrated across her neck. "Yes, I'm positive. Sssh, relax."

I don't want to but I'll do it for love.

Shayne held her breath and stuck her finger in his mouth.

Each suck elicited moans. "Mmmmm, oh yeah baby. Come on give it to me. Shayne, this is the best thing I've ever experienced."

Shayne snatched the rest of the goodness out of his reach. "You're making all the right noises for all the wrong reason my love. And I can't have it."

He kept eye contact with the chocolate. "Ah, come on now. You wanted me to try it, and I totally get why you raved about it all this time. It's kind of your fault. Actually, all your fault."

Shayne counted the remaining chunks.

Two for me, no wait three for me and one for him.

"Are you sure you'd rather more chocolate than sex again?"

Annu's smirk sent shivers across her belly, he pushed the block under a pillow. "Not a hundred percent. Want to convince me?"

"Yep."

And that makes another piece for me later.

Chapter 66: Happy, Happy, Joy, Joy
Enki Island, Orion

Annu wriggled his butt back into the cough and removed the ring from his pocket. Shayne snuggled into his side.

What if I ask her and she says no? Flark, what if she says yes? I'll be a step father. Shit, they might hate me. Maybe it's too soon. Ah screw it.

His pulse escalated, butterflies nested in his stomach, a vice gripped his chest.

Why didn't I have a drink first?

God's damned I love you, like I've never loved before.

Annu retrieved the ring from his pocket and under Shayne's nose.

She squinted at it. "It's gorgeous; did you get it for me?"

He kissed her cheek. "I made it for you."

Shayne took it, and placed it above her middle finger. "I love you so much. It's beautiful, I'll always wear it, I promise."

Annu removed the ring, and positioned it above her left ring finger. "I want you to wear it on this finger; I want you to marry me."

Her hands trembled. "What? What did you say?"

"I want to marry you. I want to spend the rest of eternity with you as my wife and companion."

Shayne's eyes dilated the size of dinner plates. "Did you ask me to marry you?"

"Yes I did."

She slapped his chest. "Oh my Gods, say it again."

Annu cleared his throat; the confidence he'd lacked earlier, arrived in spades. "Will you, Shayne Adelaide James, marry me, Annu of Yebu?"

Shayne threw her arms around his neck, and kissed his cheeks. "Yes, yes, yes. A million times yes."

Annu slipped the ring onto her finger, it fitted. "Now this one shouldn't slip off.

"I can't believe you want to marry me. Me. I'm getting married, we're getting married. Crazy little me, and you. Who would have thought when I tumbled through the wormhole it would end like this?"

Annu nuzzled into her neck. "I can't believe it sometimes either, but here it is. Whatever happens we're in it together, and together we can accomplish anything."

"Hell, yes."

Annu held his breath. "I have one more question for you."

Shayne's wrinkled her face in confusion. "Huh? Whatever it is can't be more exciting than your last question."

"For me it is, for you I'm not so sure? How do you feel about having kids?"

Her mouth moved, no words came out.

"It's okay; you don't have to decide right now. But at some point, I want kids–with you. And now we pretty much live forever, there's no reason not to."

"I, I, I, I, I."

The front door bell tolled, and killed the mood.

Shayne groaned and rolled her eyes. "Who the fuck is here?"

He followed her off the couch to the lounge room doorway and placed an arm around her shoulders. "I bet it's Jacob."

"You already told him not to come back tonight."

Annu tapped his fingers on her collar bone. "Well, however it is, hurry up so we can finish what we started."

Shayne pushed off his leg, and strode through the entryway. "You always make me answer the door."

"You're good at it."

For the first time, Annu revelled in levels of happiness, he didn't realise exited.

Shayne poked around the doorway, her face paled. "Ah - um - ah - you better come here."

Annu's hackles rose, his chest tightened.

He pounced off the couch and met Shayne in the doorway. "Are you okay? What's wrong? Who is it?

"I, ah, don't know yet. This has more to do with you than me. Just come and look."

Annu swallowed apprehension and entered the hallway. At the front door, a young man leaned against a porch beam, hands in his pant's pocket.

Something familiar about his features disturbed Annu. In short strides he reached the doorway. "Hi, can I help you?"

The boy crossed his arms against his chest. "Yeah I'm looking for my father. Someone told me he's here."

Hurry up and tell me what you want. I've got plans with my woman.

"Sorry, but what does that have to do with us?"

Shayne's confused expression revealed nothing. "Just wait. Come on kid. Spit it out."

Annu widened the door. "Yes, please do."

"I'm Zeke, and if you're Annu, you're the one I'm looking for, you're my father."

Annu's knees folded, he slumped against one side of the door frame. "Huh, I, I, I."

Shayne leant against the other side. "And there it is."

Zeke reached behind the beam he leant against, and slipped a bag over his shoulder. "My mother told me you're the one, and to look you up before she died. She's sick. I'm moving in for a while."

He pushed between them, and marched dirty foot prints into the entry.

Annu's leg's wobbled. "Who's your mother?"

Zeke stomped towards the kitchen. "Her name's Eli, saw you on the interweb."

Shayne grabbed Annu before he hit the floor. "It's not possible."

Shayne handed him a flask, rolled a joint, and sucked it down.

"Well this will be interesting. By the way–I'm not sharing."

The end.

Stay tuned for Shayne and Annu's next adventures in: A Goddess's Guide to Interplanetary Parenting.

Bio

R.L Andrew is a former Legal Executive, chronically ill Australian writer and Movie Reviewer. Along with many short stories published in International Anthologies R.L. is also a regular, long term contributor to the CrypticRock.com Website based in New York.

Her second book, 'A Demigoddess's Guide to Intergalactic Parenting' is currently in revision stage.

Social Media links:

Amazon Author Page - includes short stories in anthologies http://www.amazon.com/-/e/B00R0OY14A

Facebook Page: https://www.facebook.com/robyn.andrew.9

Blog: rlandrewauthor.wordpress.com

Twitter: https://twitter.com/RAndrewAuthor

Good Reads:
https://www.goodreads.com/user/show/46603326-robyn-andrew

Articles & Reviews: CrypticRock.com